MW01034414

Praise for Carrying Independence

Incredibly well-researched historical details that deepen the narrative and the characters—historical and fictionalized—transporting the reader to walk with them. The author dismantles facts both well-known and rarely taught about the American Revolution, and breaks down the language of the Declaration into experiences, thereby making the time period truly accessible. The author allows us to temporarily live and breathe 1776 so deeply that we feel we have been the ones Carrying Independence for us all.

— Kathleen Grissom New York Times bestselling author
of *The Kitchen House* and *Glory Over Everything*

⟶

Karen A. Chase's fast-paced and panoramic narrative captures the drama of declaring and fighting for—and against—American independence. Her sharply-observed scenes bring abstract principles to vivid life, reminding readers of the human dimensions of making a nation at a time of radical change and revolutionary uncertainty.

— Peter Onuf. University of Virginia (Emeritus), co-author (with Annette Gordon-Reed)
of *"Most Blessed of the Patriarchs": Thomas Jefferson and the Empire of the Imagination*

⟶

Sometimes you can learn more about a war from a good novel than you can from a history book. That's what Karen A. Chase does… She vividly evokes what it was like to be in the trenches of the Revolutionary War in a way that few—if any—historians have done.

— Marc Leepson, author of *What So Proudly We Hailed*,
and *Lafayette: Idealist General*

⟶

Historical fiction at its finest…It was so refreshing to read of the personal sacrifices and high principles that were behind this necessary American Revolution. In the end, the book is inspirational in terms of seeing the bigger picture of what American life can mean if the rights of all people are taken into consideration and proper compromises can be made. Ms. Chase's book gets my highest possible recommendation.

— West Coast Don, Men Reading Books Review
MenReadingBooks.Blogspot.com

KAREN A. CHASE

224PAGES
RICHMOND, VIRGINIA

224Pages
P.O. Box 23259
Richmond, VA 23223
224Pages.com

⌒⌒⌒

Cover Design: 224Pages
Book Design: 224Pages & Leslie Saunderlin

BOOK INTERIOR IMAGES
Cover: Declaration of Independence, William Stone facsimile c1823.

Background Images for Part I, II, II & IV
An east prospect of the city of Philadelphia; taken by George Heap from the Jersey shore, under the direction of Nicholas Scull surveyor general of the Province of Pennsylvania.
LC-DIG-pga-01698

Public Domain Images (Insets) from Library of Congress Collections
Part I: *Harmony weeps for the present situation of American affairs*; LC-USZ62-45533
Part II: *Title Page of Pennsylvania Magazine, Jan. 1775, illus. with allegorical scene of Liberty seated with liberty-cap and shield with Penn arms...*; LC-USZ62-50342
Part III: *Liberty triumphs over Tyranny*, Taylor, Isaac, 1730-1807; LC-USZ62-45534
Part IV: *Frontispiece-when fell debate & civil wars shall cease...* 1775; LC-USZ62-45499

Reader Insights: *Signing of Declaration of Independence* by Armand-Dumaresq, c1873 Public domain image. Original at The White House Historical Association.

⌒⌒⌒

CARRYING INDEPENDENCE ~ First Edition
ISBN 978-1-7337528-0-0
ISBN 978-1-7337528-1-7 (ebook)

To Ted
You're the best adventure of all.
(It's time for a bigger boat.)

&

For Margaret, Cecil, Bruce, and Telva.
Chasing histories began with you.

&

To Nathan Chase and Jacob G. Klock, and all my
patriot ancestors who supported the Cause of Independence.
Without you, I would not be a
Daughter of the American Revolution.

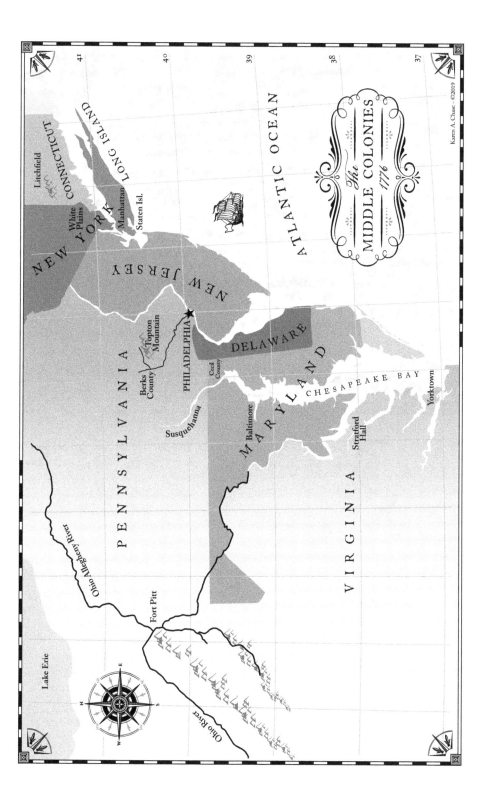

The
MIDDLE COLONIES
1776

Karen A. Chase · ©2019

ATLANTIC OCEAN

CONNECTICUT
Litchfield

LONG ISLAND

NEW YORK
White Plains
Manhattan
Staten Isl.

NEW JERSEY

PENNSYLVANIA
Berks County
Topton Mountain
PHILADELPHIA
Susquehanna

DELAWARE
Cecil County

MARYLAND
Baltimore
CHESAPEAKE BAY

Stratford Hall
Yorktown

VIRGINIA

Ohio Allegheny River
Fort Pitt
Lake Erie
Ohio River

N E S W

Berks County, Pennsylvania
January 22, 1777

THE CONDITIONS HAD CHANGED, and not for transient causes.

Nathaniel clasped the Declaration of Independence by the edges. In his shaking, raging hands, the engrossed names on the parchment merged into a tumultuous blur.

He stood alone, in his own moccasins, his familiar buckskin jacket once again across his taut shoulders. Alone, before the dresser in the room he'd shared with his brother, in the stone house his grandfather had built, on the Marten family farm he'd always called home. Now he, the barren land, and the shattered house groaned with a crackling cold brought on by both winter and grief. None of this felt like home. All because of the fifty-five signatures expecting one more.

Collecting them was supposed to have been simple enough.

You have nothing to lose, Franklin had told him six months ago. Franklin had lied.

It is not a declaration of war, Jefferson had said. Jefferson was a fool.

It was a declaration of freedom, they'd insisted, and yet for Nathaniel it invoked a sentence no one he knew was willing or able to pay. It was irony on parchment, that's what it was, and the consequences of carrying it were not his fault—no more than they were Franklin's or Jefferson's. No, the blame for all the losses, his losses, lay with just one.

"This damn document!" Nathaniel cursed the signatures before him, and folded it one last time. *Snap. Snap. Snap.* He shoved it deep inside the dresser drawer along with the scope, the cursed bag of silver, and other instruments he'd carried all these months on that impossible, catastrophic task. He grasped the drawer with both hands and shoved it shut, pushing with all the force of his six-foot-three frame. The dresser rocked back and cracked against the stone wall.

It was buried and there it could stay. Undeclared. Unfinished.

He was finished.

He drew in a ragged breath. It still didn't feel like enough to bury it here, in a wooden dresser. After all, he'd had to bury her in the ground. He'd been the one to dig the hole—him, not them—so that the dirt and her blood were still lodged beneath his nails. Her English blood that would forever run in him.

He curled his calloused hands into fists and whispered, "I will be burdened no longer."

There was only one way to end the suffering, to bring true freedom. The document needed to be destroyed so it, and he, could never be found. He turned on his heel and headed outside, to the woodpile.

Nathaniel strode across the vacant yard between the stone house and his father's gun shop, not weighed down by the axe in his hand but driven by the conviction that this choice was the right one.

Nathaniel squared a log upright. He grasped the axe with both hands, and swung it high. His already aching muscles screamed as he brought the blade down hard, slamming it through the wood as the sun dragged any hint of warmth below the wintery horizon. Again and again, a burst of hot air puffing from his lungs with each thrust, his long hair breaking free from the leather tie, Nathaniel begged the metal to cut out the memories that still came unbidden.

The memory of mosquitoes sniping at his face, he and his horse tethered to a traitor, as he descended Virginia. *Crack.* The city of New York overrun with soldiers and the hills of Harlem moaning with miles of ragged men. Starving men. Dying men. *Crack.* His family, his friends—all of them—so accusing. *Crack.* All of them walking away or taken from him. *Crack.*

At last, the log broke. Separated.

A section spun into the cold earth, thumping into a nearby drift. In the plume of violet snow, the memory of her tear-ravaged face swirled before him. Nathaniel looked away, the axe hanging, forgotten, from his weakened limb. He searched the darkening eastern horizon, as if it held the answer to all he had lost, but the gaping field was barren, bereft. Or was it?

At the edge of the meadow, far across the drifted snowbanks, a shadow moved. Nathaniel narrowed his eyes, straining for a clearer view. The last vestiges of twilight reflected off a figure moving in and out of the trees toward him. An elk? No.

A horse. A man. A redcoat.

Nathaniel's heart pounded out a warning. He flung down the axe and ran for his rifle, sprinting the few dozen feet to the stone house and back within seconds. The loaded weapon in hand, he ran for the oak tree at the edge of the yard. He scrambled up the trunk, his heart thrumming with vengeance, his fists tearing frozen bark from the limbs. He stretched out long on a strong branch and aimed his rifle at the lone rider. Six hundred yards.

He drew his broad shoulders up tight as the figure flew across the land. He swallowed thickly and kept his gaze focused on his target, his weapon steady in his hands. Five hundred yards. The last time he had fired at another, the enemy had fallen. He was only a boy. Four hundred yards.

But that was war. This was now, and the conditions had changed.

This was survival.

Three hundred yards. Nathaniel steadied his finger on the trigger, and trained the barrel on the invader's chest. Once again, just as he had been seven months ago, Nathaniel was eager for the hunt.

★

PART I
preamble

*Three things prompt men to a regular
discharge of their duty in time of action:
natural bravery, hope of reward
and fear of punishment.*

– George Washington

CHAPTER ONE
July 10, 1776

THE TEMPERATURE IN THE Marten family gun shop climbed higher with the sun. Nathaniel kept his head down and pushed the file across the rifle barrel clamped in the vise. Late morning rays stretched through the east-facing window, glinting off shards of metal that fell to the workbench like shattered glass.

With each long, swift stroke, Nathaniel felt the file bite at the rough metal of the octagonal shaft. He pushed. He scraped. He pulled. Nathaniel's only pause in the motion was to lift a hand to wipe at the sweat on his brow, or to push away a strand of hair refusing to stay restrained at the nape of his neck. His movements had become rote, as ordinary as the acrid smell of hot metal and burning wood from the hearth filling his nostrils. His tasks were as repetitive as the hammering, heaving, and shuffling of the five other men—his father, brother, and three blacksmiths. As they each tended to their tasks, just as he had for nearly seven years, Nathaniel bent to his. He pulled, he scraped, and he pulled. Until his rhythm was interrupted by the caw of a crow outside.

Nathaniel raised his head just as the lone black bird swooped across their Berks County farm. It floated upward with abandon on a circle of warm air, its shadow cast across their fields of green corn. Nathaniel kept watch, the file momentarily forgotten, aching to feel such freedom beneath his own limbs. Then the bird turned and, with a single sweep of its wings, it sailed east toward Topton Mountain.

Next to him, at their shared worktable, Joseph Marten groaned. Nathaniel dragged his attention from the distant Pennsylvania hillside and returned to his filing again, trying to ignore the strain in his father's voice.

"This wood… Tiger Maple is stronger. More beautiful." Joseph cursed beneath his breath in German, his clipped accent thick and rippling with disdain as he applied a final coat of stain to an oak rifle butt. His hand rubbed at the wood harder than usual with a scrap of linen.

Skipping strokes of the file, Nathaniel lifted his eyes toward his older brother, who was hunched over his worktable-turned-desk next to the door.

"It is not about that now, Father." Peter's dark hair hid his eyes so he did not see what Nathaniel did—wary glances exchanged by the three hired blacksmiths shaping flintlock pieces at the hearth. Peter folded a letter he'd been examining and slid it back into an envelope, then rubbed at a groove that had been deepening in his brow with each passing week. "The oak is cheaper."

"But look at the grain." Their father held his finished rifle up to the sun, turning it back and forth, cradling the weapon in his thick hands like a newborn, but his mouth was downturned. "It is dull. Flat."

His father's rifles were not well known for being either. Joseph had taken up the craft of a gunsmith under the guidance of his own father. Years of honing his artistry had made his rifles—etched with a scrolling, floral design and his own initials, *J~M*—prized possessions among the hunters of Pennsylvania. They were a contrast to Joseph Marten; his business dealings were as straightforward as the plain, gray breeches hugging his aging, rounded frame.

Nathaniel stiffened when his brother rose and came to his father's side. Ignoring the newly finished rifle, Peter dropped an account book on the workbench, tapping at it with the envelope still in his hand.

"We lost two more of your old customers last month. One joined the militia. The other died," Peter said, lowering his voice as Joseph lowered the rifle. "We had to borrow to keep them on."

Peter tilted his head toward the three blacksmiths who hammered their silver into flintlock pieces, their eyes averted beneath concerned brows. The men had been working in the Marten gun shop since Nathaniel and Peter were first apprenticed to their father.

Back then, the shop had been a place of wonder to both brothers. Nathaniel had been just ten and Peter twelve. Tools that previously hung out of reach on soot-stained walls were finally in their grasp, and they had thrown their boyish energy into hammering heated metal into barrels and bending it into scopes and casings. They had raced each other to fit the puzzle of metal and wooden parts together. Tiger maple had come alive in their hands, stained with linseed oil and heated to magically reveal the striped grain, until their father proudly etched the *J~M* into each finished piece.

As months turned into years, the brothers divided. While Nathaniel continued to bend over the workbench alongside his father, Peter took to studying the accounts and ordering supplies. One brother pounded the silver. The other pounded the books. One rugged and fair. One dark and refined. Now, the one place where Nathaniel thought they might find harmony was only an increasing source of grievance.

Nathaniel rubbed his fingers together, feeling the shards of flint lodged in them, and wondering at the tension pulling Peter's shoulders taught. Lately, long after their family evening meals in their stone house just across the yard, Nathaniel could see Peter's wavering candlelight spilling from the gun shop. Before breakfast these last few mornings, when Nathaniel carried the first load of wood into the shop, he'd been surprised to find Peter already engrossed in his ledgers and correspondence. The same ledger that his father now pushed aside.

"Engraving might improve the piece." Joseph picked up a chisel.

"It takes too much time." Peter took the tool from their father's fist and sat it upon the bench, and his voice grew tighter. "You can add your initials but I am telling you, we must simplify." He punctuated his last words by waving the letter he held, the Philadelphia postmark visible.

Nathaniel had seen that handwriting before. It sent a coldness up his back. Whoever had been writing to his brother from the city these last few months, they'd been exacerbating the problems between his father and brother. Each time those letters arrived, their discussions grew in fervor.

Through tightened teeth, his father said, "You cannot deprive me of my tools—"

"We must. The Pennsylvania militia is expanding. Muskets. Bayonets. Rifles. We are to produce more."

Like Nathaniel, his brother who was more than six feet tall towered over their stocky father by nearly a foot, but the older man stood firm and took back the tool.

"You speak of production. You know our rifles are more than that." Joseph waved a hand beneath Peter's nose with the chisel as if swatting away an irritant fly, then waved it toward Nathaniel. "Isn't that right, son?"

Peter's black gaze dismissed him from the discussion. Nathaniel dropped his chin and stared at the barrel pinched in the metal clamps. Nathaniel was wont to agree, yet he did not. Could not. Primogeniture ensured it. The law granted all rights and property to his brother as the oldest son. Farm. Home. Gun shop.

Peter had held this unearned position over Nathaniel since he was a toddler, delighting in making even insignificant decisions for him, like which book to select before bedtime. When Nathaniel finally learned to read, he found it was better to be alone with a book than be chided by Peter for choosing the wrong one.

Now, as his brother and father verbally battled over how to manage the new orders, Nathaniel bent to his work again, pushing the file flat across the iron barrel, trying to smooth out the rough patches and drown out the grating exchange. As their voices grew more strident, he shoved the blade forward and dragged it back harder. Push. Pull. Scrape. The sound shuddered up his spine, making him shiver, for one thing was certain. Although Peter's changes would make the work a grind for his father, for himself it would make the gun shop nearly intolerable.

Nathaniel knew he was not the gunsmith, the true craftsman, his father was. Nathaniel's shoulders and back were sore from the fatigue of labor, his fingers always chapped and blackened with iron flint, and his body daily drenched in sweat from stoking the fires, even during the frigid winters. As Nathaniel finished each piece, his father would hold it aloft, warmly patting his son's shoulder with pride at the artistry, while Nathaniel's gut simply sank over the next weapon waiting to be conceived. Now, he wondered how long he would be disposed to suffer.

As if in answer, Peter said, "We all must adjust until we're told otherwise.

You included, Father." His brother once more grabbed the chisel from their father and threw it to the back of the worktable. It fell with an echoing clang among other discarded tools. "Quantity is what matters. You can return to being a craftsman again after the war."

He said the last word casually. Too casually. Nathaniel looked to the letter again, wondering what word his brother had received. Had war been officially declared? By whom?

But Peter turned on his heel and went back to his desk. He dropped the latest envelope into his black leather account portfolio and snapped it shut. The finality of the click echoed in Nathaniel's ears, as his brother said, "The order is due in Philadelphia by the end of the month. The colony demands we produce more, so we—"

"What does the colony want us to produce?" Nathaniel's mother came through the open door carrying a tray laden with slices of chicken pie. The savory scent was as warm and welcoming as Jane Marten herself.

Nathaniel abandoned his station to dust a pile of wood shavings from the workbench. Taking the burden from his mother's hands, he placed it upon the bench while his father tossed Peter a look that said the argument was done, but not over.

Jane Marten caught the look between the two fuming men, one eyebrow marching toward her hairline. Joseph met her gaze, but his mouth remained pinched. Peter stared at his own reflection in his polished shoes. She asked again, but when neither man would answer her, Jane pushed a strand of graying hair from her forehead with the back of her hand and turned to Nathaniel.

He could no more lie to her than his own reflection, for she had the same high brow, and in her youth the same blond locks hung over matching oval, green eyes. Even now, their square jaws were both set with determination, a contrast to their pale, English skin.

Nathaniel's shoulders sank. "More weapons. Rifles. Muskets. Bayonets. The militia is expanding."

With each word, the strength in his mother's sturdy yet slender bearing slipped. She grasped the workbench, a hand clasped at her heart. Jane Marten had come to Pennsylvania from London as a small child with her father. Her mother had died in childbirth, and her father, longing for a new life far from reminders of his wife, bought them passage on a ship bound for the colonies with only a few trunks of possessions, mostly consisting of family storybooks and his botanical journals. They had left extended family behind, though rarely out of touch. Even all these years later, Jane Marten would devour their regular missives like a starving stray before tucking them inside her family cookbook. Lately, the subject of the letters was often of separation. At dinner, over their potatoes and stew, she read their letters aloud to the family, followed by a prayer to keep the window of reconciliation open.

As if heeding that hopeful thought, his mother now stood strong again, dusting off her hands. Wood chips fell to the floor. Shards clung to her skirts. "Preparation does not a war make."

Her voice rose slightly at the end, making her statement more like a question. And there was that word again. *War.* Were he and his mother the last ones to accept it had really begun the year before, during the battles at Lexington and Concord? Could it be marching toward Pennsylvania?

His mother took a deep, steadying breath.

"We must hold out hope for peace for all our kin." With her optimism, and the hearth's dwindling fire, the air in the gun shop cooled, and she waved them over to the lunch tray. "Hope needs nourishment. Come. Eat."

Nathaniel and the workers circled the chicken pie, ignoring the strained faces of his father and brother. The tightness in Nathaniel's stomach turned to rumbling hunger as he lifted the pie to his lips, but the sourness of the argument tainted the food. Warm gravy slipped down his chin and he wiped it away with an already stained sleeve.

His brother, however, turned away from the lunch to straighten up his desk. As Nathaniel savored his last bite, he watched Peter rub a hand at his neck and shoulder. Antiquated inheritance laws didn't just provide benefits, they also inflicted burdens. Was Peter strong enough to carry them all?

His brother caught him staring, and Peter's hand fell. "Don't let your fire go out, Nathaniel. Ever. Go get more wood."

Nathaniel swallowed the rest of the pie, and he brushed past Peter, giving him a sharp elbow on the way out the door.

Alone at the woodpile, the axe felt heavy in Nathaniel's hands. As always, he knew the large movement would be a welcomed release. He raised the handle high over his head and brought the blade down into the chunk of wood.

Crack. Was he to live out his days bound to the gun shop? *Crack.* Would Peter's demands increase, as each manufactured weapon reduced his father to a mere minion in his own business? *Crack.* Would the rifles they were to make, be aimed at his mother's family? *Crack.* Not just her family. His family. *Crack.* He threw his sense of helplessness into each wide swing until, through his own ragged breath, he heard his name being called.

"Nathaniel!"

He looked eastward, the axe hanging by his side, and shielded his eyes from the sun. The incoming rider, just beyond the rows of young corn and moving swiftly toward the farm, waved a brown leather hat high over his head.

"We found them!" The rumpled figure of his friend Arthur Bowman came into focus. "Elk!"

Nathaniel's heart leapt. He flung down the axe and ran for his horse corralled in the paddock attached to the gun shop. As Nathaniel saddled Bayard, named for his deep reddish-brown coat, Arthur raced into the yard between the house and gun shop, his own horse skidding to a prancing halt. Arthur's freckled, Irish face was flushed as crimson as his hair.

With his chaotic arrival, Joseph and Jane ambled through the door to wave hello, followed by the blacksmiths still feasting on their pie. Peter remained behind, rigid on the threshold.

"I can see by your face, there is good news, Arthur." Joseph's voice was warm toward Nathaniel's lifetime friend.

"Kalawi sent me… he just kept saying *wapiti,*" Arthur spoke through ragged breaths, the last word—Shawnee for elk—tumbling out with an exhale. Kalawi was part of a small Shawnee Mekocke Clan—a faction known for peace and healing—that lived on Saucony Creek between Arthur's and Nathaniel's farms. The clan had mostly kept to themselves until Nathaniel, Arthur, and Kalawi met on the mountain a dozen years ago. "Kalawi waits for us at the mammoth oak, at the base of Topton Mountain."

Nathaniel's mind raced ahead to the lush forest as he strapped in his rifle, a tiger maple barrel he'd built with his own hands. The elk were once plentiful in these eastern Pennsylvania mountains, but as farms expanded and people headed west, settlers took more of the land, careless hunters grew more abundant than the elk, and now it had been over a month since one had been seen. Already Nathaniel could envision their Shawnee friend, Kalawi, dancing impatiently at the trail head. Two good-sized elk were much needed to feed his neighboring Shawnee clan and give them materials to fashion for trade. Nathaniel warmed at the thought of the clan's celebration when the three boys brought in the elk.

Even Bayard tossed his black mane and tail, eager to ride free from his pen. But as Nathaniel swung into the saddle, his brother pushed through everyone, strode over, and grabbed the reins.

"You have orders to fulfill and we have all the food we need." Peter waved an arm in the direction of the sheep and cattle roaming over the hill behind their stone house. When Nathaniel did not dismount, his brother tossed his chin eastward toward the Shawnee town. "Forget them."

The two words coiled in Nathaniel's stomach. Behind his brother, his father was waving him away, and his mother was silently mouthing, "Go."

Nathaniel's back lengthened and he snapped the leather strap from Peter's hand, leaving a red welt across his brother's soft knuckles. "Fulfill the order with your own hands this time, Peter. I know you know how." He kicked his heels into Bayard, and drove him from the yard. As he and Arthur thundered across the fields to meet Kalawi, Nathaniel's heart pounded wildly. On the wind, he could hear Peter raining curses at him.

CHAPTER TWO

ON TOPTON MOUNTAIN, NATHANIEL ran his finger down the scars on the beech sapling at the edge of the game trail. The green core still oozed—a gash made by elk scraping velvet from their antlers. Nathaniel rubbed the sticky sap between his fingers, and inhaled deeply through his nose. In the heat of the forest, the dampness of trampled ferns mixed with the heady musk of bull elks, and Nathaniel headed up the mountain in the direction of the scent.

Over the last year, aside from a few hunting excursions like this, Nathaniel's only means of escape from the shop was delivering missives for The Post. He had volunteered, thankfully with his father's blessing, to run Express letters for Berks County. It was during those excursions, as it was for him now, that the pressure from the gun shop eased with each step, and he found his real footing.

Here, in the forest, he knew by the depth of the sound how big a creek was before he reached its bank. The trees showed him where the sun rose and set by which side held the moss. He knew if there was dew on the ferns after darkness, a rain would douse them by morning. He no longer needed the first map he had drawn of Topton Mountain years ago, for he knew the little dip in this game trail preceded a steep climb that ran more than three hundred yards.

Here, he knew what was coming.

Now, just a few steps up the familiar embankment, Nathaniel found Arthur and Kalawi whispering together, shoulder-to-shoulder.

Kalawi dragged his moccasin along hoof marks scraped through the under-brush, ending at a pile of warm scat. A relief-filled smile rippled across the Shawnee's long face, half-framed by jet-black hair grown long on one side.

"*Me-ci?*" Nathaniel asked. A great many?

"*Niiswi.*" Two. Kalawi scratched the shaved side of his head, then stretched out his arm, pointing up the trail to a trampled patch where a pair of elk had clearly bed down. "And they smell worse than Arthur."

Arthur leaned over and sniffed Kalawi's exposed armpit. "That's you."

With a low chuckle, Nathaniel nodded to Kalawi, "Go."

Kalawi padded up the mountain, to circle above the elk and push them back down the trail. He was one of a few grown men from his Shawnee town able to hunt, each of them often sent in different directions. Now, he eagerly disappeared into the forest, swiftly becoming another of the silent shadows, while Nathaniel and Arthur ran to take cover and ready their rifles.

Pine needles and stones skidded and tumbled ahead of Nathaniel's feet, as Arthur ran on ahead of him. Nathaniel leapt lightly from the trail to hide behind a fallen oak. The languid heat of the forest wrapped around him like a coat. Sweat trickled down his back and into his breeches as Nathaniel searched down the mountain trail for the hiding spot of his friend.

Lichen-covered boulders lined one side of the path, dotted with clusters of mountain laurel and ancient oaks. Jutting out from among a clus-ter of rhododendrons, he found Arthur's brown leather hat with the crudely stitched brim. The rip had been a result of Arthur diving heedlessly into a pile of Shawnee during a game of handball. Kalawi had given him bright yellow moccasin leather to sew it back together, and the stitching always made Arthur easy to spot.

Nathaniel stood to his full six-foot-three height, and butted his long rifle in the ground. He drew the humid air deep into his lungs and held it as he readied his rifle, instinctually moving through the steps. Gunpowder from the horn. Cloth and ball. Tamp the contents. Replace the rod. Prime the piston. Close the frizzen. Pull the hammer to full-cock with the back trigger. Nathaniel swung the rifle back to his shoulder. He let the breath out slowly between his lips, and grinned with pleasure at his own swiftness. He heard a click from down the path as Arthur finished loading his own rifle.

The midday sun had just begun to slither down the western side of the pines. Nathaniel turned to search the upward slope for signs of Kalawi and the elk. The trick, he reminded himself, was not to look for the elk but to look for anything that was not a tree. Within seconds a silhouette moved, far up the hillside. Then came the thump and snap of hooves and branches. Soon the familiar murmur of Kalawi's voice reached Nathaniel.

Kalawi was born into his Wolf Clan with the name *Wetakke*, meaning "he approaches." When he began to speak as a child it was in full sentences that never seemed to cease. So, his clan nicknamed him Kalawi, "the talker," and he had lived up to the endearment. Now, as the elk wound in and out of the trees, into the light and back into shadow, their hooves moved in rhythm with the soothing cadence of Kalawi's voice.

"With one tentative tug, he pulled the glistening sword from the stone—" Kalawi ceased the story when the elk stopped. A hush fell over the mountain. When the elk tentatively thumped forward again, Kalawi continued. "Could this naïve, young boy be the one in whom everyone had put their hopes?"

Nathaniel smiled. *The Knights of the Roundtable.* As boys, Nathaniel's mother had read the stories to the three of them from her father's books. Kalawi had been grateful when she offered him the book as part of his efforts to learn English, and in turn he had used the tales to help Arthur and Nathaniel learn Shawnee.

"Is the boy strong? *Mata.*" No. Humor sparkled in Kalawi's voice. "But maybe he is man enough to take two elks."

Nathaniel tried to ignore the barb, and steadied his barrel upon the bark of the fallen oak trunk just as the first bull elk stepped fully into view. Four hundred yards.

The animal was robust, the tips of his rack easily towering two feet over Nathaniel as they snagged at branches at the path's edge. A second, younger elk stepped into view. He was just as solid and impressive, only a hand or two smaller. Nathaniel's nose filled with their odor, like soured molasses. It was to his advantage to be downwind. Two hundred yards.

He aimed at the younger elk knowing his shot would drive the first elk down to Arthur. He felt the tension in the trigger and was about to pull when gunfire came from Arthur's direction. *Pow-pow.* The elks reared up. *Pow-pow-pow.* Another three shots echoed through the forest.

Snorting and kicking, both elk swung around to run back up the mountain. Nathaniel leapt from his hiding place and knelt on the trail to take aim, but Kalawi was running down. When the Shawnee saw the elk charging toward him, he slid to a skidding halt.

"Damnit!" Nathaniel cursed at him. "Move!"

Instead, Kalawi attempted to pull an arrow from his quiver. The elks charged. Too fast. Too close. At the last moment, as Kalawi leapt from the path, an antler tip clipped the arrow from his hand and sent it spinning down trail.

The bulls ran back up the path, pushing through brush, snapping limbs, the oaks and pines closing behind their retreating white hindquarters.

As their crashing sounds faded, Kalawi climbed back onto the game trail. He let out a stream of curses as he picked leaves and twigs from his hair.

"Did they hurt you?" Nathaniel ran to his friend.

"*Mata.*" Kalawi snatched up the fallen arrow and jammed it over his shoulder into the birch bark quiver. He scowled at Arthur's rifle in disbelief. "Was that you who fired?"

Arthur uncocked his rifle with a jerk of his arm, and pointed northward. "The shots came from the direction of the church. At the edge of Bieber's farm."

"Arthur's rifle is also higher pitched," Nathaniel said, his ears trained to know the difference between firearms. The gun shop often repaired long rifles, muskets, and pistols, testing each one to ensure they fired correctly. "That is musket fire from a Brown Bess. Several of them." Five more shots crackled from the fields, followed by the sounds of men shouting in the distance.

Nathaniel uncocked his rifle with a snap of his wrist, and his fist tightened on the barrel. "Come, let us gather our horses and see who has cost us our food."

CHAPTER THREE

NATHANIEL UNWOUND THE REINS from a low limb, Bayard champing at the bit, and the three boys rode from beneath the mammoth oak tree. A landmark in the county, the oak's branches stretched out nearly thirty feet in each direction so a dozen men could stand side-by-side under one limb. It was where Bieber's farm fanned out from the base of Topton Mountain, his cornfields flanking the southern boundaries of Nathaniel's property, the Shawnee town, and Arthur's farm. In the tree's gloaming shadows is where the three boys always tethered their horses before the hunt.

Once astride his horse and riding toward the small stone church across a fallow field, Nathaniel could easily see a group of men gathered near the graveyard, firearms in hand. A hundred yards from the church, five wooden boards leaned against trees, charred black, a large "X" cut into the soot.

"Target practice?" Arthur looked to Nathaniel. "Here?" Nathaniel and Arthur occasionally gathered with other men for this skills challenge, but usually they met up in Kutztown, northwest beyond Maxatawny Township.

"And with wooden boards." Kalawi, who had never been to the competition, scoffed. "Try elk. Aim always improves with hunger."

Arthur laughed, but concern tightened Nathaniel's shoulders. The last time he'd seen armed men gathered outside this church was a year ago, in May. The second Continental Congress in Philadelphia had called for able bodied men between sixteen and sixty to volunteer should more militia be required.

"Maybe Congress passed the resolution to go to war?" Arthur's voice was high. Boyish. Just as it had been back then. His grandfather had fought in King George's War in the 1740s, repeatedly regaling his brood of grandchildren with his tales of triumph. In the last few years, the old man had grown offended by the King who had turned his back on his greatest warriors. Arthur's flame to support his birth land first was ignited, tempered only by his mother's urging to joining the Express Post with Nathaniel. The empty rum bottle she found beneath her father's bed most mornings was proof enough about the effects of war.

"War," Kalawi sniffed, and began a tirade with, "Will these men expect the British to have an X on their uniforms, too…"

Several of the men with whom Bieber chatted—nearby farmers, and other Express riders from the county—turned upon hearing the boys approach, and among them were four men Nathaniel had never seen before. When the strangers' concerned gazes fell on the boys, Kalawi pulled up on the reins and Nathaniel and Arthur slowed to stay with him. Neighbors in their Maxatawny Township had long been at ease about the boys' friendship, the people of Berks County having lived peaceably among neighboring Indians for many years—with the Lenapes who originally settled the land, the Munsee Delaware, and for the last three generations with Kalawi's small Shawnee Wolf Clan.

"Bieber knows you well." Nathaniel waved toward the group, and stocky Mr. Bieber swiftly waved an arm over his head.

"Still, ignorance can eclipse truth." Kalawi pulled back more, his sun-darkened legs tightening around his horse. Had these newcomers heard about the skirmish between a Shawnee faction and Lord Dunmore's troops at Point Pleasant, where seventy-five Virginians had been killed? That had been a warring faction, and Kalawi's was a peaceable clan. "Fear can overshadow fact."

"Would Sir Gawain of the Round Table ask for the courtesy of trust without first giving it?" Nathaniel knew the knight-errant's romantic tale had everything Kalawi loved: quests, seductive women, and an honorable ending. "Remember the oath we made together as boys?"

Kalawi glanced sideways at Nathaniel, his chin rising slightly. After only a brief moment, he nodded them forward, but as the three dropped from their horses—a gentlemen's courtesy when a rider approaches others on foot—the newcomers stood stiffly, their mouths aghast. Through the strangers' eyes, Nathaniel realized, he and his friends looked as wild as the elk they had been hunting.

They towered over the group of stocky German farmers and townsfolk dressed in their fine linen suits, knee socks and buckled shoes. The men were a contrast to Nathaniel and Arthur's pale buckskin leggings and sweat-stained linen hunting shirts gaping open at the neck. Their shoulder-length hair hung loose around their tanned faces—although for Arthur, it was as if all his freckles had simply joined together. Nathaniel and Arthur both wore beaded leather moccasins (gifts from the clan) their chests crisscrossed with rifle, powder horn and knife straps. Kalawi wore no shirt at all, and carried five visible weapons—two knives, a tomahawk, his bow and arrow, and a rifle Nathaniel's father had given him. The simple loincloth covering Kalawi's buttocks and genitals garnered an awkward inspection. To outsiders, they were two frontiersmen and a savage.

"Morning, Mr. Bieber." Nathaniel warmly shook the hand of his neighbor, a stout man of German stock whose brown linen suits were usually rumpled, but who was always quick to smile. Arthur and Kalawi nodded their hellos to the other men who were gathered on one side of a makeshift table—two barrels topped with planks of oak—set up outside the church. On the other side of the table, with his back to the church's exterior stone wall, his jacket cast aside and the pits of his fine linen shirt ringed with sweat, a rather rotund man had his head down, sorting through papers. Mr. Bieber quickly introduced the boys to him.

"My neighbors… Mr. Anderson."

Mr. Anderson raised his head from his work, his face ruddy but creased with good humor. However, the smile faded when his gaze landed on Kalawi. Anderson's thumbs immediately tucked into his belt, to which a pistol was strapped, as he took in the Shawnee's half-shaven head, and bare torso and legs. Kalawi turned his eyes to the ground and Arthur cleared his throat to end the awkward examination.

"Is Mr. Jameson organizing this practice?" Nathaniel asked. Jameson was their Postmaster, the only Express rider missing from the small group, and often the one to encourage the competitions up in Kutztown.

"Jameson left the Express," Mr. Anderson said, turning on the smile again. "Joined a battalion."

Nathaniel and Arthur looked to each other, and Arthur shrugged. The riders gathered together weekly, and Jameson had never said a word about joining the militia, or even wanting to. Nathaniel wondered why the man would leave his position now.

"Guess you've not heard the good news." Anderson set out a quill and inkwell, then hooked his thumbs back into the belt. Thumbs on pudgy hands, soft from lack of labor, and with ink staining the nails of his right hand. "The colonies have at last declared independence from Britain."

Nathaniel faltered, the image of his mother sagging onto the workbench returning. "When?"

"Voted in favor of it July second. They read the Declaration aloud in Philadelphia on the eighth, two days ago. They're sending copies 'round to the colonies so you can read it yourself when it arrives."

Now Nathaniel understood the force behind Peter this morning. That letter. What a coward Peter was; he had stood silent in the gun shop, letting them cling to a false hope of reconciliation, letting his own mother think she might still stand on British soil.

"All men are to sign an oath promising loyalty to the colonies. Denounce the King and loyalist causes. Come fight the enemy." Mr. Anderson smiled as he said the last word. He stabbed a stack of documents on the table with an inky finger. *Oath of Allegiance* was typeset across the top sheet.

Nathaniel shivered and a sour taste filled his mouth. Over the last year or so the three boys had debated this exact situation, even as recently as last week while they were hiking through the forest after a hard summer rain.

"If we have to fight, which side would you choose, Kalawi?" Arthur had asked as he'd scrambled over a fallen tree trunk, his moccasins blotched with mud. "You are American, as are we."

Kalawi followed Arthur over the log. "I would join up with whichever British soldier married your sister."

Nathaniel climbed over it last, laughing. "The soldier would be better off marrying awkward Arthur."

"The King himself would be better off marrying me." Arthur bowed, rolling a hand forward. "We would break bread together every night."

"You would break wind." Nathaniel had given Arthur a stiff elbow in the ribs, and their play had descended into a slippery chase up the muddy mountain trail.

That was then. Now, it was serious. War had arrived.

CHAPTER FOUR

NATHANIEL'S DESIRE TO DELAY signing an oath—by any one of them—was overwhelming, his heart pounding so hard he was certain everyone around him could hear it. While Kalawi's mouth tightened as he stared at the oath, and he took a step backward, Arthur leaned forward as if leaning toward battle. Toward glory.

"We are Express riders. That's as good as an oath, I think," Nathaniel said.

Bieber shook his head. "Heard rumblings up in Kutztown… they fear spies are riding in and out of Philadelphia. Volunteer Express riders might come under the army. Or be let go."

Nathaniel felt Arthur stiffen. When the county had called for additional Express riders last summer—given that Berks County still lacked its own post office—Arthur took the paid work not only to appease his mother. And not just to help provide for his siblings. Like Peter, Arthur's older brother would inherit his father's land and the sheep upon it. Unlike Nathaniel, Arthur had not been skilled in a trade. If it wasn't the Express, the militia was his only option, and one his fist had been aching to grasp.

Nathaniel stared at the papers with distaste. He did not want Arthur to go soldiering alone, yet he had no intention of picking up a rifle for the militia. Who would he be aiming at exactly?

"We'll take all the bodies we can get," Mr. Anderson said, then he added, "but a better rank awaits those who actually hit the targets."

Nathaniel studied the planks of wood leaning against the trees, a dozen yards from the church. Hardly a hole had been shot through them, despite all the gunfire they'd heard. He looked back over the farmers, tanners, and riders clustered around Bieber near the table. These men were going to fight a trained British Army?

Mr. Anderson put his hands in his pockets and gestured with his belly toward Nathaniel's rifle.

"'Course with them cumbersome things, you might be assigned to muckin' out the privy."

The men around them laughed, but Arthur took a step toward the table.

"I'm a better shot with this here long rifle than anyone with an ol' Brown Bess." Arthur re-cocked his rifle. He tugged down on his hat.

Nathaniel and Kalawi groaned at the familiar gesture. Even Arthur's torn hat was the result of his inability to refuse a challenge. Before the fateful handball game, he'd tugged on that brim after Kalawi claimed Irish boys were given flaming hair because they had no fire in their loins.

"Where is the marked line?" Arthur now asked, his chin high.

"Scraped in the ground, 'bout a hundred yards yonder." Anderson pointed east. "Five targets. Three shots each."

Arthur immediately turned and walked toward the line, saying over his shoulder, "Come on. A little target shooting is not an enlistment."

Nathaniel hesitated. When Arthur kept walking, Nathaniel gave in and waved to Kalawi to come with them.

"Not the barbarian." Mr. Anderson's smile was still in place. Nathaniel stepped toward the man, but Kalawi grabbed his linen sleeve, softly nodding toward their neighbor who had taken a step away from the table. Though the other men stared at their own boots, Bieber's worried gaze darted between Nathaniel and Anderson with uncertainty.

"You go. I will take the horses back over to the oak." Kalawi turned away and grabbed the reins of Bayard and Arthur's horse. As he mounted his own horse, Kalawi flipped up his loincloth to give everyone a clear view of his bare backside. As he rode away, in Shawnee he muttered, "*Moneto.*"

The Shawnee word meant snake but also devil. Nathaniel's anger subsided into a half-concealed grin, and he turned and ran to catch up with Arthur.

"I won't do anything rash today," Arthur said, when Nathaniel fell in step. Arthur tugged on his brim again. "Except for maybe showing that bastard how to shoot."

Nathaniel laughed and tucked away his fears about oaths with each step they took together. When they found the line the others had used, they winked at each other, and with knees high, they stepped over the deep scrape in the ground and kept walking. They could hear Mr. Anderson and some of the men laughing.

"You'll take the targets from left to right." Arthur's voice was cock-sure. He counted off their paces. They had done this plenty of times up in Kutztown. They stopped and turned. The original line was almost half-way between them and the targets. Diagonally across the field, watching from under the Massive Oak, Kalawi waved from atop his mount.

"And you'll take right to left." Nathaniel cocked his weapon, and together they shouldered their rifles. "Nice wind on our backs."

"Yep." Arthur exhaled. "Ready?"

"Yep."

"Fire!"

Ka–crack. Arthur's rifle fired, followed directly by Nathaniel's.

Almost immediately the bullets could be heard hitting the white pine targets and they grounded their rifles and reloaded together. Powder. Ram. Tamp. Their limbs lowered and rose in unison like a coordinated dance. Resheath. Full-cock. Fire! *Ka–crack. Ka–crack.* Powder. Ram. Tamp. Resheath. Full-cock. Nathaniel pulled the trigger for the third time a split second after Arthur. *Ka–crack.*

Gun smoke drifted across the field toward the church. They slung their rifles over their backs and walked back to the men who had gathered to examine the boards.

"We heard three shots each." Mr. Anderson pointed to the boards, the stains of sweat having widened under his outstretched arm. "Each board was shot through the center. Nice enough, but only five holes. One of you missed." The other men grumbled their agreement.

Nathaniel strode to the middle board, and tapped the center with a strong, tanned finger. "That hole is bigger than the others."

"We both hit it." Arthur's cheeks rose high as the men gathered around the board.

Mr. Anderson looked out to the field, disbelief and ire rising on his face. "But that was over a hundred and fifty yards."

The other men careened their necks, and several claimed it was farther. Mr. Bieber, who often joined them for target competitions in Kutztown, kept his chin tucked down in his jacket, his shoulders shaking with amusement.

"Definitely closer to one-seventy, right, Arthur?" Nathaniel asked.

"But it probably wasn't our best reloading time. Remember that time we were reloading on the run—"

A high whooshing sound cut him off, and far above the targets, into a nearby tree, cracked Kalawi's iron arrowhead. All eyes flew to the turkey-feather fletching wavering back and forth from the trunk over their heads. Out under the mammoth oak, Kalawi raised his bow in the air and hollered, his warrior call echoing throughout the valley.

Mr. Anderson's face deepened to purple. His hand reached for his pistol, but Arthur grabbed the man's wrist while instinctively pulling out his own hunting knife. Nathaniel stepped between them, his palms up.

"Not necessary. We will go and let you men get back to your trials." Nathaniel turned slightly to Arthur and whispered, "Please. Let's leave."

Arthur held his gaze, but he let go, and backed away. Nathaniel turned and spoke to the group, but his words were for Arthur. "It might be wise to serve with the Express until we see how this war turns out. This could all be over in a few months."

"You can help ensure it is." Mr. Anderson's face was stern, his tone severe, clipped. "Sign an *Oath of Allegiance.* Join Colonel Andrew Kachlein to push Howe's army out of New York. Six months' pay could get you a hundred and fifty acres around here. You might even be posted at home to suppress the natives who side with the loyalists. You know the kind." His eyes darted toward Kalawi beneath the tree.

Arthur's mouth twisted as if he had eaten something rotten, and he faced the man squarely. "I'll sort this out with my uncle in Philadelphia, Colonel Bowman."

Now, as always, the mere mention of Arthur's uncle made Nathaniel's heart thump erratically, his mind filling with cobwebs at the image of the man's sweet daughter, Susannah. Nathaniel shook off her visage, and nodded to Arthur. "He will write with advice."

"A letter will only delay the inevitable." Anderson stood taller, as if he alone knew the direction of the war.

"Then don't write," Nathaniel said to Arthur. "Ask him in person. Come with Peter and me. We've a shipment to deliver to Philadelphia the end of the month."

"Ah, that reminds me, Nathaniel. Will you deliver this?" Bieber took a letter from his coat pocket. "Jameson asked me to send a request for a new postmaster for the county until they figure all this out."

Nathaniel took the letter and glanced at the addressee. A small gasp escaped his lips. It was a name as well-known as the moon.

Benjamin Franklin Esquire
Member of the Continental Congress
Philadelphia – Chestnut Street

Franklin's flip-flopping politics had made him both famous and infamous. He had been a major supporter of the British Parliament and Stamp Act, turning pro-American only in the last few years. Nathaniel also knew Franklin was the Postmaster General, and the Express riders came under his command.

Nathaniel looked up from the envelope to find Arthur studying him carefully. Nathaniel tucked the letter into the satchel at his hip, a carrier never divulging the name of a recipient, and assured Mr. Bieber of delivery. As he strapped the satchel shut, and turned to say his goodbyes, he found Mr. Anderson eyeing him.

"Might be the last letter you deliver."

Nathaniel ignored the warning, and turned to leave with Arthur by his side. As they made their way across the field, Mr. Anderson shouted after them, "If your uncle is a wise man, he'll have you sign an oath! You will suffer the consequences if you end up on the wrong side."

His strident voice faded as they moved toward the horses and rejoined Kalawi. Nathaniel loathed self-righteous men who encouraged action with fear, but still he wondered, would a time come when they'd be forced to pick a side?

That now pressing concern, clearly hung between the three friends as they made their way toward the Shawnee town, evident in the unnatural, uneasy silence lingering between them. The joy of their hunt, lost.

CHAPTER FIVE

NAKOMTHA WAS WAITING. Kalawi's mother was steadfastly surveying the thicket of white oaks through which they came, her slight figure as stately as a statue carved at the edge of the village. The afternoon sun alighted the handful of gray just beginning to show at her crown as she shielded her eyes with a strong hand. As always, Nathaniel felt a sense of calm settle deep into his bones at seeing her, and returning to the village.

The land east of Nathaniel's farm was an abundant haven for the Shawnee clan. The Wolf Clan came each spring when the star magnolias bloomed, rebuilding the circle of nearly thirty *wegiwa*, longhouses covered in bark and skins, facing a central council house. They would reclaim the fallow field that ran between the corn and creek to use for their dances and games. The clansmen would hunt alongside Nathaniel and Arthur until after the Green Corn Celebration—when the gold of fall had blown from the trees, and the harvest complete—moving to higher grounds in the mountains. Nathaniel would wait through long, silent winters for their laughter to return along with the trilling chatter of the first yellow warblers.

Now, as the three boys rode into camp, a small group of older men playing handball in the gaming field ran to greet them. The children flew like geese from Saucony Creek to gather around the skirts of the women who abandoned their beadwork and tanning. The fifty or so welcoming smiles of the clan quickly fell at the sight of the men returning without quarry.

"M'sikkanwi—the wind—it has shifted," Kalawi said, as they dismounted.

"Lamatahpee." Nakomtha told the clan members to sit, waving a hand

CARRYING INDEPENDENCE ★ 31

toward a fire pit outside the council house, a crease deepening in her otherwise smooth brow. She helped to settle Wapishi, the clan's eldest male, in the innermost circle. The shock of white hair he'd had since birth gave him the name, and though he was once a robust warrior, he now folded himself onto bony limbs.

With Arthur and Nathaniel seated close by, Kalawi took his rightful place next to his mother. As he relayed the morning's events, murmurs of worry and sadness rose and fell. Kalawi ended with Anderson's final warning, then looked to his mother for guidance.

They called her Nakomtha, or grandmother, after the Great Spirit, *Waashaa Monetoo*. Shortly after Kalawi was born, her husband and nearly two dozen of the elder clansmen had been killed in a battle against the Chero- kee—a battle which she as their Civil Chief, or *hokima*, advised them to not fight. With their numbers severely reduced, the clan had migrated north to Berks County to join another small faction of the Wolf Clan. Over the years, Wapishi had pressed his tongue into the space where his front teeth used to be, encouraging Nakomtha to speak for the clan.

"This Mr. Anderson," Nakomtha said, her voice pensive, "this man who spoke of the English family's quarrel…"

Kalawi opened his mouth to speak, but Nakomtha placed a hand gently on his knee.

"I know you want to share what you think. It is more important to tell us what you did not hear."

Nathaniel waited with the clan. Kalawi would turn eighteen in October. As the son of Nakomtha and the clan's past chief, he would soon be ex- pected to assume leadership. Though he had to publicly suffer these teaching moments, Kalawi's inheritance also came with an enviable benefit. He was free to choose a wife this year, and she would become the new *hokima*, her voice nearly equal to his own. Nathaniel had encouraged Kalawi to choose wisely, and now he waited with the whole of the clan to learn what concerned his friend most.

"He did call us barbarians, but…" Kalawi blinked several times, clearly working hard to be the man they needed him to be, "he did not call us peace- keepers, despite our Mekocke division striving to keep peaceful relations with English settlers."

Nathaniel had long ago learned the Shawnee were governed by five divisions. The Kispokotha counseled on matters of war. The Thawegila and Chalagawtha were leaders in times of peace, and the Pekowitha were the helpers. The Mekocke division—to which Kalawi's Wolf Clan belonged—governed medicine, and had been among those who had negotiated treaties, even in nearby Philadelphia.

"Perhaps Mr. Anderson sees what I saw a year ago in Chillicothe." Nakomtha turned her oval face south, her dark eyes searching the light as if retracing her journey to the tribe's annual meeting grounds of division delegates. "The Shawnee were splitting into two factions. Some of the Chalagawtha and Pekowitha members were involved in raiding white settlements in western Pennsylvania, Kentucky, and Virginia."

"Are these factions aligned behind different leaders?" Kalawi asked

"A-ha, niiswi." Yes, two. Nakomtha smiled, clearly pleased with his question. "Hokoleswka from the Ohio—the whites call him Cornstalk—urges conciliation. But Blue Jacket of the South… Two years ago, he clashed against the British Governor Dunmore in Virginia, but then at Chillicothe he suggested we align with the British. He has an unpredictable heat."

Kalawi contemplated Nakomtha's words, then swept an arm toward the clan's cornfields, stalks shoulder-high, and just beginning to turn green. "Anderson also said nothing about the land they will fight upon."

"Fight for," Nathaniel spoke, knowing he was free to contribute. "My father says British and colonists both want ownership of American lands. On the Ohio and in Kentucky. Even here along Saucony Creek." Although most Shawnee had migrated further west into the Ohio Valley in the 1760s, the land upon Saucony Creek had stayed a protected refuge for the Wolf Clan. For how much longer, Nathaniel now wondered. "Both sides believe the land has a price."

Kalawi sniffed. "That we believe the land is free to everyone is what frightens them most."

"*Mata.*" No. Arthur held up a single finger. "It is that you believe one man cannot rule another. Between tribes and within your people. If a few Shawnee are on the war path, they assume all Indian nations run wild together."

"White men and our people…" Wapishi let out a low moan, dusty with age. "We suffer the same ignorant opinion of one another; we are each barbarians."

"And your land?" Nakomtha turned to Arthur and Nathaniel. "Do you consider it British or American?"

"The soil is British Pennsylvania—land granted to our grandfathers. But our estate is also our rifling business." Nathaniel was certain even Peter would agree. "Though, even that is changing." He told them of Peter's command to increase production for the militia.

"And this spring, as Congress requested, we waited to slaughter our sheep until after May," Arthur added, "to shear more wool for uniforms and blankets for the Continental Army."

"Your flocks graze upon British grasses, and grow wool for Continental soldiers?" Nakomtha raised an eyebrow.

Wapishi clicked his tongue. "So even the sheep are uncertain who to follow."

Arthur picked at the grass at his feet. "Some of us are not so uncertain."

"One of us, you mean," Kalawi said.

"My family once fought for Great Britain." Arthur squared his shoulders. "Now the King sends his Royal troops to kill their American grandsons. Shouldn't which nation to fight for be obvious?"

"Maybe to you who were never British." Nathaniel bristled. "Which nation would I fight for exactly, Arthur?"

"Yes, which nation?" Kalawi's dark glare snapped between them.

Breaking through the heat in the circle, came Nakomtha's low chuckle.

"How is this funny, Mother?" Kalawi turned his gaze on her.

"I knew this day would come. Three boys from three families." She pointed to each of them, the smile unwavering. "You began life swaddled in three different blankets, until Topton Mountain stitched them together."

"How did a mountain do that?" A young Shawnee girl nearest Nakomtha asked.

"You've not yet heard the tale of their meeting?" Nakomtha asked. The little girl shook her head, her short braids swinging. "It is Kalawi's favorite story! It would serve you well to recall it now."

Kalawi crossed his arms and looked away, but Nakomtha took a long breath. "Very well, I will start it for you. Autumn's Corn Goddess had already painted the leaves on Topton Mountain when eight-year-old Kalawi ventured into the forest. Alone."

When the little girl gasped, eyes wide, and before Nakomtha could encourage him again, Kalawi took up where she left off. He couldn't help himself.

"I was seven, the time of each Shawnee's Vision Quest. I left the village as the sun came up, to search for my spirit. My purpose." He tapped his own chest with a fist, and the clan's few teenage girls giggled. "Day turned to night. Night to day. As the moon climbed high the second night, I began to grow weary. Was I to find the spirit or was she to find me? In the darkness I found a large flat rock in a clearing. I climbed upon it and I waited for her silently—"

"A difficult task for our young Kalawi," Arthur said. A ripple of laughter moved through the clan but Kalawi waved away Arthur's comment.

"I *did* stay silent. But then I heard a song pulled from me, calling out to my spirit, bringing her toward me. With her came the mist. It swirled through the trees and enveloped the mountain, swept into the clearing, and my spirit settled on the ground before me."

"You saw her?" The littlest girl's eyes were wide.

"Yes, but I was not the only one." At last, Kalawi smiled at Arthur and Nathaniel.

"Arthur and I were lost in the haze." Nathaniel felt his chest warm with the memory. "We'd passed the same hollow tree three times before coming into the clearing. That's when we saw her."

"M'wah!" Kalawi breathed. A wolf. When the little girl covered her mouth, Kalawi leaned toward her. "Black eyes set deep in snowy white fur. More than twice my size, yet she was gentle, like a soft wind."

"Mysterious as the fog," Nathaniel said, lost in the memory.

"Like the moon." Arthur stared up at the sky, though the late afternoon sun still shone.

"Like the moon," Kalawi nodded. "But then the wolf swiftly stood. I feared she might come toward me, but instead she looked back over her shoulder, to the edge of the clearing. There were Arthur and Nathaniel. When the wolf padded away, she took the fog with her, and left the moon shining down upon the three of us."

"It was not long after, we created the brave knight's oath," Arthur said.

One at a time, taking turns, line by line, the three recited it.

Push with prowess through the world
Not by another's will, but for a nobler goal
Protect the meek
Secure a fair maiden
Honor the past with humility
Step gently into the future
And so on this journey we each our own way go…
Wela ket nee ko ge.

"We are one." Nathaniel translated the last line.

"*Wela ket nee ko ge.* The wolf, she had called together your spirits." Nakomtha smiled warmly at the three friends, and her melodic voice softened further as she turned to the little girl. "Arthur and Nathaniel were welcomed into our Wolf Clan. So now they help carry our *messawmi,* a sacred message for the Shawnee tribe. All of us carry it, as one, but each Shawnee also has a *pawaka:* a sacred bundle, deep in their hearts, to guide themselves."

Nakomtha interlaced her own fingers and showed the girl her hands. "The *messawmi* and everyone's *pawaka* are woven together, inseparable. The question we each must answer is how our sacred bundle will become part of the tribe's fabric. Your *pawaka,* your sacred bundle, will present itself to you when you are ready to carry it." She looked to each of the three boys separately, her gaze landing last, and fully, upon Nathaniel. Her next words made his heart pound. "You must be prepared to receive it, to choose how you will contribute. If you do not choose, a choice will always be made for you."

Nathaniel looked to his two friends, their attentions cast inward as they each contemplated her words. Nathaniel wondered how their three different views could possibly unite in a single vision for the tribe. How could he, an ordinary second son of a gunsmith, do anything of significance for a whole people?

"Nathaniel!"

The shout came from the edge of the town, startling the pensive clan. They all turned in unison toward the thicket not two dozen yards away, where Peter sat stiffly astride a grey mare, both hands clasping the reins.

"Mother calls you home for dinner. And we have work to do." Peter's dark eyes briefly fell on Nathaniel's horse, devoid of elk, before turning into the woods for home. Nathaniel's face grew hot, and he scowled at his brother's retreating back. As the clan members rose from the circle and began to disperse, Nakomtha came to Nathaniel, and put a hand on his arm.

"Leaves upon the same tree do not all receive the same amount of sunshine; those that thrive in the damp shadows and those that reach for the light are both required for the tree to survive."

Nathaniel nodded, but Peter's presence reminded him of the journey ahead. He told Nakomtha of their trip to Philadelphia, adding, "Perhaps we can discover what this separation might mean for the tribe."

"We will learn more at my Uncle Bowman's." Arthur dusted off his breeches, and fetched their horses.

Once again Nathaniel's thoughts flew to the colonel's home. To Susannah. Nathaniel saw her curtseying as she had after their first dance—her golden hair framing her face, peering up at him through lowered lashes.

"You both usually return from a visit with this cousin of yours far more civilized." Kalawi winked at Nathaniel as he embraced Arthur goodbye, giving his friend's armpit a good sniff. "Less like those elk."

Arthur punched him as Kalawi turned to Nathaniel, holding him at arm's length. "Go, knowing I go with you. We are one, my brothers."

"Wela ket nee ko ge," Nathaniel replied as they embraced.

They mounted their horses, and Arthur led them from the Shawnee town. He rode off, bouncing and waving his hat over his head, his thoughts already turned toward the luxury of his uncle's refined house, a fair change from his rural home bursting with the noise of all his siblings.

Nathaniel, slower to follow, kept his eye upon Nakomtha and Kalawi until he reached the thicket. He drew in a deep breath to hold onto them, missing their counsel and friendship already. When the trees closed behind him, he turned forward in his saddle. He braced himself for the task that would await him when he arrived home. He knew he had to do what Peter would not. He had to say the four words that would make his mother cry.

CHAPTER SIX

THE WOODS EDGING NATHANIEL'S family property seemed disagreeable. Normally, they were his last sweet taste of wilderness before returning to the gun shop. However, as he crossed Saucony Creek, the babbling brook cried as he knew his mother would, and he decided to wait until morning to tell her about the Declaration. Riding through the looming shadows of white oaks lining the road to their farm, he turned cold at the thought of hiding it from her. So, when the fields of green corn bowed down in the wind, he hung his head with resignation. Then the four-room stone house came into view. Smoke curled from the chimney, bringing with it the smell of his mother's pork and beer stew. Perhaps it could wait until after dinner.

At the sound of Bayard's hooves coming up the drive, his father and Peter left the crates they had been loading near the gun shop to meet him in the yard. His father stopped short when he saw what Peter had already seen: no quarry. When his mother came out of the house to wave from the porch, the towering Eastern Hemlock her father had planted at the corner of their home cast its long shadow across her. She took one look at Nathaniel's face and her hand fell to her throat.

Nathaniel dropped from Bayard and summoned the words, "Congress has declared independence."

"Dear God. We are separated." Jane Marten sank onto the top step, a fist clinging to her empire waist. Joseph rushed to sit with her, and only once in his embrace was Jane able to speak through her tears. "I still feel... I am

English. Where does this leave me? Us?"

Nathaniel told them about the call for more men to enlist, and the oaths they were expected to sign.

His mother shivered. "Did you—"

Nathaniel shook his head. "Against you?"

Jane closed her eyes and sagged into the curve of Joseph's embrace, bereaving with her for the loss of distant in-laws he had never met. Looking at their despondent faces, Nathaniel wished it had been a message from the Express he'd delivered. Not knowing the contents of a letter or its recipient, meant not being responsible for whatever it contained. And yet, in this moment, wasn't it better that her own son, and not some stranger, had broken such news?

It was then Nathaniel realized that Peter, during these last few moments, had kept his hands stuffed in his pockets and his bottom lip clamped between his teeth. Nathaniel groaned. He had seen that look many times before. Once, he and Peter had come home from school splattered in mud, their knuckles bleeding from an altercation with the Thomson triplets. Peter had claimed the three boys had bullied Nathaniel, then his teeth gnawed on that bottom lip. When their father eventually heard that Peter and his thuggish friends—a gang he had fallen into when he turned thirteen—had begun it, Peter received a lashing for the lie, and Nathaniel was given one for going along with it.

As his brother now stared at the dirt, Nathaniel kicked a rock toward him. "You already knew."

Peter caught the rock beneath the toe of his shoe. "Of course." His voice was even, as if relaying the weather.

"What's this?" Joseph said, looking between the two boys.

Jane raised her head, confused.

"When? How did you hear about the Declaration?" Nathaniel asked.

Peter waved a dismissive hand toward the crates stacked outside the gun shop. "I received word that a ship is waiting in Philadelphia to carry our firearms and a Pennsylvania battalion to New York. Just after the vote."

"That was a week ago. Who wrote you?" Nathaniel asked, but the only sound came from the blacksmiths near the gun shop hammering one of the crates shut. The banging rang out across their land. Like gunfire itself.

"An old acquaintance now in Philadelphia." Peter picked up the pebble, and rolled it in his fingers.

"What else does he want?" Nathaniel's jaw tightened, hating that he had to draw out the details. When silence filled the yard again, his father stomped a foot.

"Your brother asked you a direct question, and by God you'll answer it. For all of us."

"He wants to discuss a different offer, about more supplies. For the army. I've agreed to meet him." He flung the insignificant stone across the yard. "War brings with it opportunity. I have to grasp it. You may no longer be British, Mother, but this American gun shop can turn a nice profit from it."

Nathaniel winced, but his mother moved from weeping to standing.

"War or no war this business is here because of your father and grand-father." Jane Marten demanded to have Peter's eye as she spoke. "I happily married a fine artisan, not a military supplier."

Nathaniel knew it to be true. At nineteen, his mother had met Joseph Marten selling his rifles in the Philadelphia market square. She said he described each piece, "like a painter describes a woman," making the man she was betrothed to seem "as dry as old bricks." She had not pleaded with her father to end the other engagement. She had told him it was over. Even now, with her sharp words directed at Peter, one hand rested tenderly on Joseph's shoulder, and his hand was united with hers.

"I won't see you gamble our legacy on the idea of profit alone," Joseph added. Although he was still seated, he spoke from a position of authority. "Do not accept short-term gains at a long-term cost greater than we are able to pay."

Nathaniel's father's words were wisdom gained by experience. His younger, rebellious brother had died during the first year of the French and Indian War. The gun shop was further strained when the battles spilled into Pennsylvania, and Joseph struggled alongside his aging father. With each day of those seven lean years he helped them survive, Joseph's reluctance to enlist was reinforced as a wise decision.

"Be mindful of with whom you align in Philadelphia," Joseph said to Peter. His eyes tracked to Nathaniel. "That goes for you, too."

Their mother wiped at her cheeks and tightened her apron strings. "You can plan your journey after dinner, and I will write a letter to my family for you to post."

Later, with all of them seated before serving their stew, they joined hands as the last vestiges of the setting sun cast crimson upon them through the kitchen window. The candles on the table flickered in their pewter holders, illuminating the gouges in the wood and the creases of worry on Nathaniel's parents' faces. Peter stared at his empty plate avoiding everyone's gaze. Nathaniel sat across from him, finding it appropriate that he and his brother were connected only by way of both parents.

"May God grant the King mercy on his children." Jane led the prayer. "May we be brethren living in freedom and joy, no longer enemies in this war—"

When her voice faltered, Nathaniel squeezed her hand. His mother managed a warm smile, returned his gesture. And then she let go.

CHAPTER SEVEN

NATHANIEL, ARTHUR, AND PETER drew their horses up to the western bank of the Schuylkill to await the ferryman at Gray's Landing. Philadelphia stretched up out of the valley between the Schuylkill and Delaware rivers, as if it were trying to touch heaven itself. The sparkling city shimmered from across the waters, the late-day sun casting a fiery glow over the church spires and the State House tower.

Bayard stamped, attempting to pull back from the shore. Nathaniel had learned of his horse's fear of water on their first trip to Philadelphia when Bayard had kicked a barrel of rum, and almost the ferryman with it, into the Schuylkill River. This time, though Bayard was still anxious, Nathaniel's bones ached with the relief of having at last arrived after five harrowing days of travel.

The morning of their departure from Berks County, nearly bursting from his mother's breakfast of poached pears and biscuits, Nathaniel and Peter had said their goodbyes. The wagon driver pulled ahead, his lorry filled with a dozen crates of firearms, and their rations. Nathaniel, the last to head down the drive between the oaks, turned to take in one more view home. His parents stood arm-in-arm with forced smiles, his mother waving her linen handkerchief, damp with tears. Nathaniel raised a hand before the dusty road dipped, obscuring their hopeful faces. Turning forward, Nathaniel found his brother rigid in the saddle, staring ahead. That was Peter; he never paused to look back upon who or what he is leaving behind.

Within hours of meeting and continuing on with Arthur, severe storms had swept over them, washing out roads, overflowing creek banks, and reducing their travel to fewer than ten miles per day. Two of the four nights they'd pulled the wagon to a spot of high ground and slept beneath it, lined up like water-soaked logs.

Now, Nathaniel held fast to Bayard, the sun warm on his back, as they rode across to Philadelphia, the largest city in the colonies, comprised of an energetic mass of 30,000 people, and nicknamed the "Athens of America." As their group disembarked and joined the clatter of horses, carriages, and carts heading over cobblestones toward the Delaware River docks, Nathaniel was amused by the continual thrum of the port city, just as he had been during his few previous visits.

This time, however, within mere moments, Nathaniel felt a prickling concern. The streets of the city felt altered. They rode past familiar shops, but some had closed since their last visit, and the businessmen striding past who used to welcome them with friendly grins, now cast avoidant glances.

The group turned onto Market Street, two blocks north of the State House. Twice weekly, the street transformed into a bustling market. Seventy-five vendors usually shouted gaily from beneath covered stalls, hawking goods ranging from muskets to pewter bowls. Today, however, the blacksmiths and gunsmiths were absent. A few dozen merchants and farmers haggled desperately with hesitant customers over unripe apples and day-old bread. A few of the sellers who usually added the smell of their imported spices and teas were not in their stalls. Nathaniel could only smell the briny air of the fishmongers.

Per usual, Arthur's head swung from side-to-side taking in the multitude of girls in their fine floral frocks. However, as a group of girls approached nearer the docks, this time when Arthur winked and smiled, their heads dropped and they abruptly turned down a side street, glancing back at him as they quickened their pace.

Arthur's brow furrowed. "Do I look so formidable after our journ—"

"Yes," Nathaniel said in jest, and yet he was unable to shake the feeling as if he were in a different town.

Across the square from him, men hammered dark shutters over the windows of a modest home. Out front, a man strapped numerous belongings and bags onto a black carriage. A small girl clung tightly to the skirts of her mother until they all bundled into the carriage. As they pulled away, a man bolted from the house next door, swinging a fist overhead. "Good riddance, you damn Tories!" When the family passed Nathaniel, the mother's face peered out from the carriage. Her face, streaked with tears, looked high above the crowd. Nathaniel followed her gaze to a flag waving atop a nearby building. It was not the British Union Jack that normally flew over the city, but a red-and-white striped banner.

It was then Nathaniel found the label for his own prickling feeling. It was the fear of uncertainty that comes from immense change. A fear that had surely instilled doubt in a populace if they were not all of the same mind.

"Nathaniel." Peter drew next to him and jabbed him in the arm. "I have to get the shipment to the dock, before the rain." He waved an arm westward, toward low, gray clouds tumbling out of the sunset. "Afterward I'm expected at City Tavern; we will stay there the next two nights. Meet me there."

"I'd trade a sister for an ale. I'll meet you both after I've checked in with my uncle." Arthur nodded toward Nathaniel's satchel. "You have just that letter to deliver, yes?"

Nathaniel pulled the letter from his satchel, anxious to at last meet this Ben Franklin. As a boy, Nathaniel's father had given him old issues of Franklin's *Poor Richard's Almanack,* their pages brimming with science, proverbs, weather, and astrology—a reward for a job well-done in the gun shop.

"Just the one letter, yes. And then…" He turned to confirm the arrangement with his brother, but Peter was already riding away, leading the wagon to the docks.

CHAPTER EIGHT

NATHANIEL TOOK THE THREE steps of the State House in a single bound, and pulled open the door. He had attempted to deliver the message to Franklin's residence, but was informed the delegate had not returned from the assembly hall. With Bayard tied up outside, as the door clicked shut behind him, he found a discernible silence inside the expansive central hall of the State House.

Only a dozen fluted pilasters stood guard; sentinels of the gray vast space tucked into paneled walls. At the far end beyond a soaring arch, a stairwell dignified with a blue balustrade rose to the upper floor and bell tower above. Nathaniel was certain his own stone house could fit inside the entry hall.

He poked his head into a room on his right, flanked by sturdy columns and strewn with vacated chairs facing a raised bench, whispering, "Anyone here?"

Nathaniel's call echoed back to him, and he made his way to a doorway on the opposite side of the hall, hearing only the soft shuffle of his moccasins padding across the herringbone bricks. Above the door, set into a graceful arch, a carved plaster face of a woman wearing a crown smiled invitingly upon Nathaniel with blank, unseeing eyes.

Muffled voices drifted from within the chamber, and Nathaniel inched toward the open door, straining to hear. Strident male voices spoke over one another. Two… no, three different men. Nathaniel waited for a good moment to interrupt, but none came. Eavesdropping was a far graver offense, he knew, so he stepped inside.

Three men stood together amid tables covered in green cloth with empty chairs scattered about. An inkwell and stacks of letters were on the nearest table.

"Our time to select a rider is running out." A wigless, balding man with his back to the door thumped the floor with a gold-handled walking stick, and flung his arm toward the entrance. "It's not as if he is going to walk through that door!"

All three men were silenced to find Nathaniel upon the threshold. The older man examined Nathaniel over the round spectacles perched at the end of his nose.

"Who the devil are you?"

Nathaniel was the perfect picture of a wild frontiersman; his fringe jacket, breeches and moccasins had grown more weathered and muddy through five days of storms. His rifle and powder horns were slung over his shoulders.

"Excuse me, sirs," Nathaniel said, flushing under their scrutiny, each one studying him as if he were a strange animal as he moved toward them. "I am in search of Mr. Franklin."

"I am *Doctor* Franklin," the man with the glasses corrected him.

Nathaniel stopped mid-step. He knew Franklin to be nearing seventy, but he had not seen an illustration or painting of the man other than those in the almanacs. Nathaniel had envisioned he would be more thoughtfully put together, rather than this rumpled man who leaned awkwardly on his stick to favor a lame foot.

"I have an Express message for you, sir," Nathaniel said. When Franklin held out a hand, Nathaniel moved forward again and opened his satchel, streaked with rain and mud. Since he first began riding with the satchel a few years earlier, the thick leather had curved to his hip and hardened from wear. It kept the interior and the letters completely dry.

"You are an Express rider?" Franklin asked, eyeing the weathered bag.

When Nathaniel nodded, Franklin took the message from him and dropped it on the table without opening it. The bright, inquisitive eyes beneath the bushy brows resembled the younger Franklin from the publications.

"Who are you? Where are you from?"

"Mr. Nathaniel Marten, sir. I ride from Berks County, Maxatawny

Township." Nathaniel stood uneasily, his hands hanging by his sides. He was not used to being asked questions while delivering messages, least of all conversing with Benjamin Franklin.

But Franklin only raised an eyebrow at the other two men. One was nearing mid-life and the other in his late thirties. Both nodded toward the elder statesmen, answering some unasked question. Franklin waved an age-spotted hand to introduce the other two men.

"This is Brigadier General John Dickinson of Pennsylvania." The older of the two men bowed slightly, and Franklin nodded to the other. "And this is Mr. Thomas Jefferson of Virginia. Now, tell us about your county's best Express riders. What makes them the best?"

Nathaniel nodded his hellos, but his attention was drawn to the Virginian, immaculately dressed in a pale linen jacket cut in the Quaker fashion, with a single row of polished metal buttons. Word had reached Nathaniel during his journey to the city, that it was Thomas Jefferson who had drafted the Declaration. Though he'd yet to see the document, Nathaniel was surprised to find the writer nearer his own age and height than Franklin's.

Franklin thumped his walking stick. "Well, tell us. What makes your riders the best? Start with a measurable characteristic, such as how fast they ride."

"Surely speed is not our primary concern," Dickinson said, his posture matching the rigidity of his speech. He crossed his arms over a handsomely tailored waistcoat, but Nathaniel noticed the man's fingers were thick and strong, like those of the farmers back home.

"Let us start with speed," Franklin said, his gravelly voice reverberating in the assembly hall. "Well? Who is the best and why?"

Nathaniel quickly sifted through the Express riders he knew well. After himself and Arthur, the next best were two brothers from Kutztown.

"We few are swift to be sure. In fair weather, we will ride a solid twenty miles per day, depending upon terrain and to maintain the health of the horse. Our knowledge of the post roads is essential; we know to look for the axe hatches upon the trees that mark its route. By necessity we can find game trails when the roads are impassable."

"Did you say 'we'?" Jefferson's slender face, framed by reddish-blond hair, grew pensive, skeptical.

"I am one of the best riders. Best shot in the county, too. Though my friends, Arthur and Kalawi might disagree." Nathaniel felt his face flush hot when Jefferson was the only one who smirked. "I… I must protect the letters and myself, and secure food along the way."

The three men exchanged glances Nathaniel did not comprehend. Franklin limped toward Nathaniel, pushing his glasses higher on his nose, coming near enough that Nathaniel could smell onions and liquor on his breath.

"Fast, self-sufficient, and a good rifleman. Is that it?"

"Well, no," Nathaniel said, then he recalled a favorite proverb. "'There are lazy minds as well as lazy bodies,' as you have said, sir." The delegate chuckled heartily then exchanged another private look with his compatriots.

"A good rider has sharp wits." Nathaniel wondered at the reasoning behind Franklin's questions. "We must be observant. I carry maps—some old, some that I've made—so I can plan for what is ahead. Although it used to be that weather and unfriendly tribes were our greatest challenges." Nathaniel told them of a messenger from Berks County who had recently taken a letter to Philadelphia. When the courier did not return, Jameson had broken the news: a British courier had intercepted the message and swapped it with a letter containing incorrect information.

"We struggle with spies even within our own Congress." Franklin patted a pile of communications on the table where he had thrown the letter.

"Since your war began," Nathaniel nodded, "we riders have to be even more cautious."

"Our war?" Dickinson cocked his head and examined Nathaniel. "Are you not with us in the Cause, Mr. Marten?"

Nathaniel winced. It was one thing to share his position among his family and friends, but to voice it to the very congressmen who had declared separation was an insult to be sure. In the silence, a light rain began to click at the windows of the assembly hall.

"I… I am neither for or against."

"Why?" Jefferson's soft voice drew attention as he lit a few nearby candles to replace remnants of sunset snuffed out by the storm. Blowing out the match he added, "Please, Mr. Marten. We would like to know." His compassionate expression in the candlelight seemed to indicate that

Nathaniel could answer honestly.

"I... I have signed no oath for either side, but I was born in the Pennsylvania colony to a German gunsmith. My mother was born in England—is English. My boyhood friends are a third-generation Irish American and a Shawnee. The Wolf Clan is my second family," Nathaniel paused, searching the faces of the three men. "How can I support a Cause that asks me to choose which of them I love the most?"

Rain slid down the darkened panes. Thunder rumbled. Nathaniel's shoulders fell. If these three men could not provide the answer to that question, who would?

Eventually Dickinson turned to Franklin and Jefferson. "Should not our man have unquestioning faith in the Cause? In what he carries?"

Franklin sniffed. "So asks you, a Quaker who could not in good conscience vote for separation. Yet you are about to be our Brigadier General in New York."

Dickinson looked to the floor while Franklin turned back to Nathaniel and leaned forward upon his walking stick with both hands. "Do you always agree with the messages you deliver, Mr. Marten?"

"I am rarely privy to the contents. They are sealed before I receive them, and remain so until the recipient cracks them open." He nodded toward the letter he had given Franklin, the red wax seal intact, as proof. "It is not the message but my duty that compels me to deliver it."

"And was duty the reason you became a rider, Mr. Marten?" Jefferson asked.

Nathaniel hesitated to answer.

"That he has accepted the responsibility matters most," Franklin said, but Jefferson shook his head.

"The motives that propel a man to choose, to act, speak more to his consciousness than the act itself." Jefferson's long fingers added emphasis where his soft, even voice did not. "Slaying Goliath was not David's heroic act; David's reasoning behind picking up the sling... that is what made him a man."

"Even Michelangelo carved his statue to illustrate that moment when David left boyhood behind," Dickinson added. "He looks back, beyond the burden carried over his shoulder, and yet he is stepping forward."

"A fine point," Franklin conceded.

Dickinson turned back to Nathaniel.

"Mr. Marten, character is developed when a man can admit his motives to himself and others. Good or bad. I can appreciate your confusion over supporting the Cause, but why did you volunteer to be an Express rider? Was it simply to avoid becoming a soldier?"

Nathaniel's heart thumped. The walls, chairs and tables all seemed to be waiting for his answer along with the three men. Nathaniel took a deep breath and shook his head.

"I am a second-born son. My father apprenticed me in his own gun shop. It's not that I am ungrateful… but being a gunsmith is an assigned life." He rubbed his fingers to his thumb and felt the chafe of the metal shards still residing in his fingertips. He dropped his gaze to his moccasins. Listening to the rain slow, he recalled the feeling of riding under a pristine sky after such a storm. His shoulders dropped at the thought of charting the meandering post roads in his journal, of having hours and hours to himself to ride beyond Berks County. To explore his own thoughts. Bayard, his only companion.

"It's difficult to explain." Nathaniel kept his eyes cast to the floor. "Riding for the Express, my time isn't taken. It's given. I pursue my own path. I suppose, being a courier provides me with—"

"Freedom?" Jefferson asked.

"Yes!" Nathaniel's head snapped up. "Is it wrong to feel I have a right to such a thing?"

Jefferson smiled. "I see our man standing before us."

"Your man?" Nathaniel looked to each one.

"What if we ask, and he refuses?" Dickinson said.

Franklin rubbed his brow as though his head pounded like the retreating thunder. "We have two days left, General Dickinson. So far, our search has yielded a lieutenant with the brains of a buffalo who couldn't find the State House, and an Aide-de-camp who quite rightly took a position with General Washington. Neither one was as well-versed in the post roads as Mr. Marten. Nor as plainly honest."

Dickinson picked up the quill and a blank sheet from among Franklin's papers on the table. "I shall draw up an agreement. With the Post possibly coming under the army, he'll no longer be an Express rider…"

Nathaniel gasped. So, it was true.

But Dickinson continued. "I can see to it that he is enlisted in the army—"

"No!" Franklin stepped up and took the quill from Dickinson's hand, and shoved it back in the silver holder. "We cannot enlist him in the Continental Army for two reasons. We run the risk of his identity being discovered by spies and, given Mr. Marten's feelings about the war, he will refuse."

"We cannot command it of him," Jefferson said. "In the spirit of the document, he must willingly choose to carry it for us."

"Sirs?" Nathaniel raised his voice, tired of being spoken of as if he were not in the room. "Please, what message are you asking me to carry?"

Franklin hobbled back to Nathaniel and placed a fatherly hand upon his shoulder. Although his face was filled with portent, the statesman's eyes were twinkling. "Mr. Marten, we are asking you to carry the Declaration of Independence."

CHAPTER NINE

"THE DECLARATION?" NATHANIEL STEPPED away from Franklin's hand. "That's impossible."

"Nothing is impossible until it's disproven. Even then it's wise to be skeptical." Franklin limped back to the table and dropped into a chair, his leg clearly giving him pains.

"But I was told a copy was being sent to the colonies—"

"A copy, yes," Franklin stacked his hands on his walking stick. "One of two hundred public notices printed by John Dunlap, distributed after we voted to approve Mr. Jefferson's rough draft on July fourth. One went to the King of course."

Jefferson added, "The intent was to show the people what we had approved."

Nathaniel shook his head. "If the agreement is already approved…"

"It was passed verbally, and the copies contained only names of the president of Congress, John Hancock, and the secretary, Charles Thomson." Franklin pointed to the inkwell. "Signatures are more binding than words. More than half our congressmen are lawyers, and many are businessmen or merchants. They understand this.

"We must prove to the King that his colonies have not only declared independence," Franklin wove his fingers together as Nakomtha had, "but that we have become one nation of separate but equal states. Without it we are susceptible to British influence—each colony and each man could be pitted against the other to remain loyal to the Crown."

"The few men who voted against separation, like me," Dickinson said without a hint of apology, "will resign from Congress. Even I will admit unanimity is the strongest defense when we are already at war."

War. There it was, Nathaniel conceded.

"Consequently, two weeks ago, a resolution was passed to draft a formal parchment to be signed by a unanimous Congress. Here, on August second." Franklin held up his index finger. "One document. One set of signatures. A unanimous Declaration of these united states."

"Where do I come into all this?" Nathaniel asked.

Franklin knocked his walking stick against the leg of an empty chair. "Six men are unable to come—scattered from Virginia to Connecticut. A few of them are occupied by war efforts. Two are kept away by illness. One of them has not been heard from in weeks. August second is two days hence."

"Until we… *you*… gather the remaining signatures," Jefferson inhaled a breath, "neither the fifty-five men, nor the thirteen states are bound to one another. We are not one without you."

Nathaniel didn't know what to say. He knew the rebellion was about leaving the Empire, but he hadn't thought beyond that, as to what bound the colonies, the people, together in the fight. He looked away from the three men's expectant faces toward a large map of the colonies hanging on the wall near the assembly room door. Why would they choose just one man to cross all that land? Why him?

Nathaniel asked as much, knowing Franklin had personally inspected over sixteen hundred miles of America's post roads—copies of a few of Franklin's maps had helped him chart his own postal routes. Of all the men in Congress, surely Franklin knew the safest routes for such a document to take. "I would have thought it natural for you to use the Post for such a task."

"Switching horses and riders every ten or fifteen miles?" Franklin scoffed. "Each time the Declaration is handed off it will increase the likelihood of errors. Interceptions. The damn horses might begin to talk. The British might suspect, or even know, who we are, but our signatures are absolute proof of our treason."

"If the British find the Declaration first," Dickinson's face was grave, "they will prevent us from uniting the best way they know how. They will hang the signers… and those associated with carrying it."

Nathaniel turned cold.

Franklin raised a reassuring hand. "Only the three of us will know what you do. Congress has agreed that we are the sole members of a secret Carrying Committee."

"In a week's time, I leave to join the troops in New York," Dickinson said. "I will report on our whereabouts. We cannot have the Declaration riding through the middle of a battlefield."

"Myself and Mr. Jefferson will remain in Congress to communicate with you. So, there you have it." Franklin thumped his stick once more. "The job is yours, if you choose to accept it."

The three men faced Nathaniel, their shoulders set and their minds clearly made up. Nathaniel drew in a long breath. Then a word of Franklin's stood out starkly from the rest. He let out his breath in one swift burst and asked, "Job? Will I be paid?"

"Yes, handsomely," Franklin said. He blinked only once then said, "Thirty thousand pounds."

Nathaniel's breath caught in his throat.

"Doctor Franklin!" Dickinson pushed away from the table so hard it slid back several inches.

Jefferson gasped audibly and then he laughed. "Congress has not agreed to this—"

"Fifty-five lives will rest in his hands! That's five hundred pounds per man!" Franklin's face flushed as he stood again. "Less if you include all the men already fighting for the Cause. We three alone could pay the entire amount if Congress refuses."

"We have already agreed to commit our fortunes," Jefferson said.

"We agreed to commit our fortunes because we have them. He has none!" Franklin turned to Nathaniel. "Great rewards are given for great risk, Mr. Marten. We'll pay a portion to begin—funds enough to complete the task. The rest upon delivery. I will pay you myself if Congress cannot be persuaded. However, this reward does mean one thing: you must be willing to risk everything for it."

"Everything?" Nathaniel whispered, but he knew Franklin was right. He had nothing. No wealth. No property other than Bayard and the rifle over his shoulder, and no prospects beyond the gun shop. What did he have to risk, beyond his own life?

"There are only two things in this world for which we should risk every-thing, Mr. Marten. This is one of them," Jefferson said. If the Declaration was one, what was the other, Nathaniel wondered, but the question slipped from his mind when Franklin spoke again.

"If you have nothing to risk and everything to gain, you have nothing to lose." Franklin snapped his chin down like an exclamation mark at the end of one of his maxims.

Everything to gain. The words sank into Nathaniel and he thought back on the arguments between his father and Peter about the gun shop. The mon-ey Franklin was offering would be enough to prevent his father from having to produce weapons for the militia. The three blacksmiths could stay no mat-ter how many clients died or joined the war. But was carrying this document just another short-term gain his father had warned them against?

Nathaniel rubbed a hand at the tension building in the back of his neck. "I… Even I am not certain I am the right man to carry a declaration of war."

"It is not a declaration of war. This is both a divorce decree and a bind-ing marriage contract," Jefferson corrected him, and then he held fast to Nathaniel's gaze. "Moreover, it is an assertion of our commitment to uphold basic human rights. Including your freedom from tyranny. Surely you can appreciate that, Mr. Marten."

The tick-tock of a distant clock filled the air between them.

Nathaniel shifted uncomfortably. A simple delivery. To six men. Thirty-thousand pounds. If he could avoid a noose. He could hear his father's voice in his head whispering that only a fool would take such risks. The image of his mother's tears mingled with the yearnings of Kalawi's Wolf Clan. What of his own desire to remain neutral?

If he said yes, he would know the price of his convictions. If he said no, he would learn what they were worth. Nathaniel felt as though it was not just the three men in the room awaiting his answer, but all his loved ones and the whole of the colonies.

Franklin stood, breaking the silence. "It is wise for you to think this over, Mr. Marten. Congress had no fewer than fifty conversations to reach our agreement." He asked where Nathaniel would be staying and exacted a promise of confidentiality. When the information was given, Franklin added,

"We will be right here in these chambers the morning of August second, awaiting your answer. At the very least, we trust you will find us. Or we will come looking for you."

"Yes, sirs." Nathaniel swallowed thickly. "Understood." He bid the men goodnight and walked stiffly toward the door, feeling as though he were dragging a massive weight from the room. He crossed the threshold into the quiet hall, pausing just outside the assembly room door. He turned to look once more at the carved face of the woman. Though she still gazed upon him with vacant eyes, now her high brow seemed afflicted with an uncertainty equal to his own. Nathaniel's doubt doubled when he heard Jefferson's words fall into the hall.

"I hope we have selected wisely, gentlemen. If he says yes, Nathaniel Marten will be the one carrying independence for us all."

CHAPTER TEN

TUCKED IN A CORNER BOOTH in the bar at City Tavern, Silas Hastings waited, nursing a simple pint of cider. Silas glanced at two men dining nearest him—merchants, by the looks of their finer, imported clothes. The smell of their rabbit and carrot stew made the saliva pool in his mouth.

From the moment City Tavern was built two years earlier, its Walnut Street location, in close proximity to the docks, attracted ship captains, travelers, Germans, Irish, and English alike. It had a designated coffee room, a ballroom on the second floor, and finely appointed rooms to let on the third. One of Philadelphia's finest meals could be had in the first-floor, white-and-green dining room, or in the adjacent and cozier wood-paneled bar. And yet it gnawed at Silas that the citizens haggled in the market for bread, while businessmen and delegates ate lavishly at the tavern. Even now, his own stomach churned with hunger. City Tavern fare was beyond his reach, too. Not for much longer.

Silas fished a watch from his faded waistcoat pocket, and stroked a thumb across the casing—a beloved scene of a mother and her son cast forever in gold. It was his only possession of value. Using hard-earned savings from his first clerkship, he had bought the gold piece as a gift for his father. An olive branch, really. Last winter, the watch returned to him, bound in the very box in which it had been given. Inherited. Unwound. Unloved.

Silas clicked the catch, and the case sprung open. The delicate hands on the white face showed exactly eight forty-five, the gears ticking faithfully in his hand. He frowned and closed the case. *Snap.* He waited. His thumb habitually worked at the catch. *Click. Snap.*

Across the candlelit room, the longcase clock began to toll. Silas counted. *Gong. Gong.* Eight. Nine. It was running fast. *Click.* At last Peter Marten slipped into the booth. He was running late. *Snap.*

Silas slipped the watch into his pocket, and held out a hand.

"Sorry for the delay." Peter raked a hand through his rain-soaked hair before reaching out the same damp palm to Silas. "Things were a frightful mess at the dock, but the delivery is done."

Silas took out a handkerchief and dried his hand as Peter expounded on his horrible trip from Berks County. This past December was the first time he had seen Peter since they were boys at school in the county. The physical differences in how they had grown into young men were as Silas had expected. Peter was tall and much like Silas' own brother Sebastian had been. A square jaw defining a face destined to be handsome. Agreeable. A hatch of jet black hair as dark as Silas', which was thinner in every way. "Frail from the first breath," his father had often said. Frail, and yet Silas' coming into the world had been strong enough to drain all life from his mother.

"But enough about me." Peter smacked a palm against the table, snapping Silas back to the present. "Tell me about this offer."

Silas shook off the aching memories and took three documents from his portfolio. "When I first contacted you, I had finally secured a private secretarial job within Congress. A congressman knew about my—"

"Your father? His practice truly flourished after moving from Berks County." Peter smiled, then his head tilted briefly to one side. "I was sorry to hear of his passing. No doubt his fine reputation preceded you."

Silas pushed his shoulders back against the booth, stunned once more by how others mistakenly viewed his father—even old acquaintances like Peter who knew him from Berks County. Silas was ten, Sebastian fifteen, when his father determined to establish them in a finer Philadelphia society. Over the years, the man's incisive council had turned many of the colony's early merchants into respected gentry, but not always does a man bring home to his family the benevolence he shares with strangers.

"Alas, no. My employer heard about my education at Middle Temple in London, also his alma mater," Silas clarified. "My impeccable service these last eight months has resulted in a promotion of sorts."

"How so?" Peter snagged the sleeve of a passing bar wench, and demanded their best glass of port. He turned back to Silas, oblivious of the woman's rueful sneer as she went off to fetch the drink.

"The man I work for is to command a unit in New York. I will be his Aide-de-camp." Silas tried not to smile at how the pronouncement had left Peter's mouth gaping, his gaze reappraising. "Among other duties, I'll be delivering communications between the army, the Congress in Philadelphia, and the supply Quartermaster, Stephen Moylan. I will be ordering supplies and munitions, and we need everything." Silas ticked the list off his fingers, "Muskets, spoons, blankets, buckles, kettles... So much is required, but each need reveals more problems."

"Such as..."

"Gunpowder. Now that we are no longer British, how do we acquire enough when the colonies have just one manufacturer? These colonies have not been built on manufacturing, which means we must establish trade agreements. But how do you fashion trade as a nation when thirteen colonies issue their own currency? How do you establish a single currency when your Congress is busy cobbling together war departments against an army already on your shores?"

Through the explanation, the frown on Peter's face became a smile that indicated he could see what Silas already knew; where chaos exists, so does opportunity. "Tell me what you need."

Silas slid the first document across the table to Peter.

Peter read the list, his brow creasing with each line. "All this? But... It is more than three times our last order for the militia—"

"That's for the Continental Army."

Peter's head snapped up. "Congress wants us to supply the Army?"

"Not directly." Although the two merchants had finished their meal and were engrossed in a game of draughts, Silas kept his voice low. Even new taverns have well-tuned ears in wartime. "Congress will establish suppliers, who will be contracting manufacturers. I am one of the supply agents."

"How did—" The barmaid returned with the port. Peter snatched it from her and swiftly waved her off. He took a substantial drink. "How did you manage that?"

"I was in a position to secure the contract." Silas did not add the word "easily." Continental supply chains were ridiculously inept with no logistics systems, no means to properly vet supply agents, and no means to enforce what few regulations Moylan established. When Silas was asked to issue and monitor supply contracts, he'd eagerly agreed. And then simply issued one to himself. "My little business will fulfill the munitions requests, but what I cannot do is manufacture the supplies."

"How can our family gunsmith–"

"In the event of a lasting war, Peter, the colonists don't need gunsmiths. We need armories."

"Armories!" The two merchants looked their way. Peter took another drink, gulping the port like it was cheap cider, then lowered his voice, leaning in. "Are you asking me to turn my father's—"

"We need you to do more. *For* more of course." Silas handed the second sheet containing the payment schedule to Peter, pleased with the gasp that escaped Peter's lips. Silas let him sit with his future income in hand a moment longer before setting out the details.

"Four payments of Continental Currency per year until the war ends. To build shops and a kitchen. To staff your armory with gunsmiths and blacksmiths. Buy new equipment. A dozen or so workers sent by me from Philadelphia to help you build it."

"All this?" Peter's eyes were still filled with disbelief. Or was it distrust? "We've done only a little business together. Why me?"

As a boy, Silas had fought his way into Peter's group of strong-armed boys with one purpose. Joining them meant no longer being their target. For Silas, his fear of Peter then was as strong as the glue of envy felt now. Peter had three advantages: an affectionate father, who was intent on leaving him a thriving rifle business, which he would legally inherit. A week ago, Silas would have settled for any one-third of that scenario, but now, perhaps *with* Peter, he could do far more. Not with. Through.

"I must do business with people I know. People I can lean on." Silas allowed a flattering smile, even though he knew from a few well-placed questions that the Marten gun shop had lately been feeling a strain. "The Marten gun shop... *your* shop... is one of the finest in Berks County."

Silas watched Peter inhale the false compliment, his chest filling with the drive to choose his own path. His desire for it was as obvious as his want of clean, crisp cuffs, like the ones that framed his unsoiled hands.

"There is one other detail," Silas added, pulling his jacket down one by one over his own fraying sleeves. Then he handed Peter the third document. "Congress has insisted anyone building an armory must sign an Oath of Allegiance."

Peter dropped the sheet as if the paper were on fire. "Fulfilling an order is one thing, but my father…" Peter shook his head. "I cannot choose sides."

"I thought you would understand the benefits that war might provide." Silas shrugged as Peter's gaze returned again and again to the payment figures on the table. Silas eyed Peter, wondering if inheriting the gun shop had left him soft; an easy life could turn a man lazy in his own ambition. Perhaps he needed a bit of a shove. "I imagine nearby gunsmiths like Angstadt and Dickert might be eager to provide, to contribute."

Peter scowled at the sheet, and drained his glass, but before he could speak again, Silas put a finger on the paper containing the offer and pulled it away. With the utmost calm, Silas said, "I suppose it is only right for you to continue managing the business the ol' Joseph Marten way."

"No," Peter said, his face crimson. He cut at the air with a flat hand. "He does not grasp these changing times as I do."

"I know you want to make him proud, as I did my own father. But if you want to ensure your family's business survives the war…" Silas tilted his head and let concern soften his voice, "What is an oath compared to guaranteeing that, my friend?"

Peter hesitated no more. With a slight nod, he conceded. "Tell me how we arrange the contracts."

A few moments later, as Peter scratched his name across the sheet, Silas pulled out his watch. *Click.* Now it was the ninth hour.

"I'm glad I can count on you," Silas whispered. *Snap.*

CHAPTER ELEVEN

THE WALK TO CITY TAVERN was too short. Nathaniel stood in the doorway searching the lamplit pub for his brother over the heads of patrons. Their forks clinked too brightly against chinaware, the levity of their chatter, too light compared to the gravity weighing Nathaniel down. He pushed his way to the back where he found his brother hunched over his work in the corner.

City Tavern had become his brother's preferred inn the moment it had been built; Peter held a deep appreciation for both the new guest beds upstairs and the seasoned statesmen downstairs in the pub.

Nathaniel dropped into the booth, but Peter kept bent to his ledger. Nathaniel waited as sumptuous scents wafted over him—savory meat pies, hearty thick stews, fresh breads, and roasted welsh hares mingled with smoked trout. His stomach rumbled and he flagged a barmaid carrying a steaming chicken pie.

"Might I get an ale, ma'am, and one of those pies if you please?" Nathaniel smiled, for the woman's rosy cheeks reminded him of how his mother flushed as she cooked. The barmaid returned the smile but tossed a hostile glare at his brother. Nathaniel examined Peter's black head. "Made friends here already have you?"

Peter shrugged and kept at his work, but truthfully Nathaniel welcomed the silence. He let his head drop back against the booth and closed his eyes, his mind aching from the shards of his conversation at the State House. *Fifty-five lives in his hands. Everything to gain.* The funds would be a help to the gun shop, true, but what help would he be to his father—to anyone—if he didn't survive?

"Why the grave face?" he heard Peter say. When Nathaniel opened one eye, Peter was studying him through narrowed lids. "You look terrible."

"Just hungry," Nathaniel rubbed a palm over his eyes. "It's been a long day."

The barmaid delivered the ale, and Nathaniel tried to ignore the gooey sweet smell that lingered on her from the tavern's kitchen—baked pastries and cakes seasoned with nutmeg, cinnamon, and cardamom. Nathaniel drained a quarter of the pint and wiped the foam from his mouth with his sleeve.

"All you did was deliver a letter." Peter pushed a linen napkin at him.

"Sure. Just a delivery." Nathaniel left the napkin between them. He wanted to add, "and then I had a long conversation with Thomas Jefferson and Doctor Benjamin Franklin about working for Congress." That would wipe away the look of reproach growing on Peter's face. Instead, Nathaniel nodded toward the ledger. "What happened with your meeting?"

Peter's gaze fell away. He stacked his papers. "We have a new request."

Knowing Franklin's offer was more than they could fetch for ten thousand rifles, each one crafted with Joseph Marten's scrollwork, Nathaniel asked, "How many rifles this time?"

"It's not just for rifles."

"What then?"

"Buckles. Knives. Kettles."

"But we are a small gun shop—"

"Not anymore." The two words tolled a warning, which reverberated in Nathaniel's chest when Peter added, "We've been asked to build an armory."

"I don't understand."

"Of course not." Peter's sharp response drew the attention of several nearby diners.

Nathaniel's face grew hot and he pushed his beer out of the way as the patrons returned to their meals. Nathaniel leaned forward. "What is going on, Peter?"

"Go see for yourself." His brother pointed toward the docks, his voice dropping to a harsh whisper. "Ships loaded with soldiers are leaving for New York. Rifles alone are not enough when we are at war."

"We? Is mother included in that?"

Peter waved him off. "If the Continental Army is to win, we need munitions. We need to build armories."

"Father will not agree to this." Nathaniel looked about the booth as if a different solution lay between them. He searched Peter's determined face across the table. "We can find another way. In fact, I might have another—"

"No." Peter sat back, arms crossed. He stared at the table, but his teeth bit at the bottom lip.

Nathaniel's shoulders dropped. "You've already said yes. And the terms?"

Peter's eyes flit to the pages on the table, three words typeset across the top sheet. *Oath of Allegiance.*

Nathaniel sank back against the booth, the flicker of hope at being able to help, extinguished by the stroke of Peter's pen. Nathaniel groaned as Franklin's words rang in his ears. *Which carries more permanence? A voice, or a signature?*

"Father specifically told you not to—"

"I did what was best for all of us." Peter gathered the pages and shoved them inside the leather portfolio. "With this we will have more than new orders. We'll have stability. Expansion. Even funds for new buildings."

"Leaving me and our father as what?" Nathaniel asked. "Gunsmiths or bricklayers?"

"I don't care what you do, Nathaniel." His brother's voice was cold. "Building the armory begins in September. With or without you."

Nathaniel opened his mouth to protest when Arthur appeared, stuffing himself into the booth, and crushing Nathaniel against the wall.

"They are throwing a ball," Arthur said between gulps of air. "My aunt and uncle. Tomorrow night."

"What on earth for?" Nathaniel shoved him off.

"Some big announcement." Arthur elbowed him back and waved to the barmaid serving a nearby table. Failing to get the woman's attention, Arthur grabbed Nathaniel's remaining beer and took a swig. "You know my aunt... any opportunity to extravagantly display her position."

"By position, do you mean socially or in support of the Cause?" Nathaniel glared at Peter, who stared at the table.

Arthur held the nearly empty glass aloft, looking between the brothers. "Nathaniel, the fact is—"

"The fact is clear." Peter slid from the booth and stood over them. "It is easy to be righteous when you have absolutely no responsibilities."

Nathaniel watched his brother push through the crowd toward the stairs to their shared room.

"It's just a ball!" Arthur shouted after him, and drained the rest of the ale. He then slid from the booth, mug in hand. "I think we could both use some more. Did you get your letter delivered?" Arthur threw the question over his shoulder, but Nathaniel's "yes" was lost amid the din of chatter, plates, and knives.

Alone at the table, Nathaniel wallowed. *Causes. Documents. Signatures. Oaths.* Peter's words tumbled with Franklin's. To them, Nathaniel was nothing but a tool from the gun shop. Useful, but only in their hands. This wasn't the freedom Jefferson encouraged him to find. This was being both hemmed in and squeezed out. Nathaniel committed to telling both Peter and Franklin to go to hell.

Arthur fell back into the booth across from Nathaniel with two full glasses, tilting his head with compassion when he took in Nathaniel's face. "Forget Peter. No matter what you think of him, he'll always think more of himself." He took a drink, then said, through a mischievous smirk, "Now about that ball. My uncle quite easily agreed for you to attend. Perhaps he is beginning to see you differently."

"Meaning?" Nathaniel took a long drink.

"Perhaps he sees you as I do." Arthur's grin deepened. "A possible suitor to my cousin, Susannah."

The barmaid at last delivered the savory chicken pie, but Nathaniel was afraid to eat, to swallow, for his heart was thumping wildly in his throat. The thought of holding Susannah not just again, but for all his life, extinguished the last of his anger, and warmed him from head to toe. If what Arthur said was true... Franklin's offer be damned for certain.

Arthur, smiling along with Nathaniel, lifted his glass and toasted with his favorite Irish proverb. "May you kiss whom you please, and please whom you kiss."

Nathaniel raised his glass to Arthur's and let the liquid drown out all thoughts of revolution.

CHAPTER TWELVE

IT WAS MORE THAN a year ago, in May of 1775, when Nathaniel was first permitted by the Bowmans to accompany Arthur to an intimate dance at their home. That night, as they'd dressed together at the tavern, Arthur had insisted Nathaniel reserve a dance for his cousin whom he claimed was the sweetest lass upon the earth. Nathaniel's mother had taught him and Peter the minuet, cotillion, and contradance figures, but he had never danced among those born and bred to it. Would this cousin see the country boy within?

Nathaniel had tried to downplay his concerns. "Does she look like you?"

"Not really." Arthur stood with his gangly arms akimbo, in his dress shirt and stockings. His hair was not yet combed, and it stuck about in every direction over his freckled face. "Why, do you fancy me?"

"Not any more than my horse. Heaven help me," Nathaniel stopped with one arm in a green frock coat he had borrowed from Arthur, and choked, "Does she look like Bayard?"

That night, the grandeur of the brick Georgian house on Walnut and Fourth wiped all mockery from Nathaniel's face. Though Arthur was accustomed to their society, having often visited throughout his childhood, Nathaniel felt pinned to the ground, scrutinized by the house itself—by the two long rows of windows, each taller than a man—looking down upon him in the street.

And then Susannah appeared on the top step. She flew through the door to greet Arthur, waving to them below, the light spilling from the open door matched only by the gaiety radiating from her porcelain face. When Arthur introduced her to Nathaniel, the scent of spring's honeysuckle swirled around them. Her smile shifted and a flush spread from her yellow bodice up to her golden hair. And yet, she met his gaze, holding a hand out to him.

Throughout that first evening in the second-floor ballroom, his eyes had followed her as she politely danced with numerous guests in the glittering light of what seemed to Nathaniel like a thousand candles. When at last, it was his turn to guide her to the floor, he'd prayed his feet would not fail him.

He stood to one side with the men, bowing to Susannah in the line of women. As the music began, they stepped toward the middle together. He grasped her gloved hand. Again and again they met and retreated, falling in step together. Violins hummed. Flutes whispered. Then, as the music shifted, they switched partners down the line.

As required, Nathaniel moved his body to dance with the next person, but to Susannah, his eyes strayed. To the rustle of her skirts, his ears were attuned. Yet when she stepped before him again, his tongue nearly failed him.

"I wish… uh… Too bad the minuet is not in fashion."

"Do you not like the six-eight time of the English contradance?" she whispered as they met shoulder-to-shoulder in the center. Her arm brushed his sleeve as she stepped back into her line. The warm streak on his arm, even through the heavy brocade, emboldened him to speak when she came toward him again.

"The minuet is danced by one couple at a time. I… I would not be required to share you."

Susannah flushed as she moved on to the next man stepping in to spin her, maintaining eye-contact with the new partner, as protocol dictated. Nathaniel struggled to do the same with his own partner.

When they met again, Susannah was smiling. "Do you know why the French minuet was replaced by the contradance, Mr. Marten?"

"So more couples could dance together?" He stepped around her, should-to-shoulder again. "Not an advantage from my position."

"You flatter me… but 'tis not the only reason." She turned away and dropped back into the line. As they both came forward once more and joined hands, walking to the top of the formation together, she was so near, he could smell the sweet scent of lemon lingering upon her.

"Does it matter the reason as long as we are dancing?" Nathaniel asked.

"The contradance is more democratic."

"Democratic?" He was perplexed and intrigued by her all at once.

"The minuet was reserved for couples of the same social standing." She looked to their clasped hands, and squeezed his fingers. "It is the contradance, and not the minuet, that permits you to hold my hand, Mr. Marten."

When she met his gaze, an eyebrow raised, Nathaniel's ability to respond died on his lips. Then she let go of his hand and they each cast off to move down the line. Back in their rightful positions, they turned to face each other again. When it came time to meet in the middle for the central spin, Nathaniel grasped her gloved fingers and pulled her closer.

"I pray then democracy will sweep the colonies forevermore," he whispered.

She met his gaze and they began to turn. Susannah's teasing expression softened. Time slowed. Suspended. Reflected in the room's mirrors, they spun together far into the distance. Nathaniel's chest rose and fell in time with hers. When the steps changed, they retreated to their separate lines. Nathaniel bowed to Susannah, both of them out of breath, and unable to look anywhere but to one another as the waltzing tune came to an end.

* * *

Now, on this first night of August, a year later, the gilded-framed mirrors surrounding the dance floor were once again deceiving Nathaniel. From his solitary position on the marble balcony outside of the Bowman's commanding ballroom, beneath a full moon, Nathaniel watched the guests repeatedly twirling, reflected in an infinite hall. Nathaniel swirled the Madeira in the crystal goblet, grateful for the quiet spot on the terrace, away from all those preening peacocks—men and women clucking and gossiping, their heels snapping at the pine floors.

He had been to the Bowman home half a dozen times with Arthur in the last year or so. Each time it was as dizzying as it was now. Their meals of many courses. The conversations bounding from one topic to the next, each one of less substance than the one before. To Nathaniel, it was all just like the reflection; an illusion. With one exception.

Susannah. Only she seemed real. He let the contents of his glass resettle and resumed his search for her through the large glass doors. He found her near a white marble hearth, and his whole being softened.

She was being presented by her mother to one of the numerous officers attending the ball. She curtsied, but when she lowered her head, the polite smile slipped from her face. When she stood, her cheer returned, and in one fluid gesture she let go of her indigo blue petticoats and stretched out a white gloved hand to the man. Nathaniel marveled. How does awkward Arthur have such a gracious cousin?

Over the last year, as Nathaniel had returned with Arthur and the Express, Arthur had invited him to the Bowman home where they'd tell her tales of the frontier. At first, she'd merely nodded, dutifully stitching her needlepoint. Eventually, her needle was forgotten, and she confessed to wanting the feeling of riding so free across wide open land, no longer pinned down. And as the months passed, Nathaniel thrilled that each time Susannah extended a hand to him it lingered within his a little longer. Soon, letters passed between their palms, until the infatuation first found upon the dance floor was drawn into an unbreakable, silken thread that tied Nathaniel's heart to hers.

Now, as Nathaniel watched Susannah graciously endure the latest of her mother's introductions, he determined to choose her over all else. Franklin be damned. Nathaniel lifted the glass to his lips, drained the last of the wine, and took a step toward the doors. Inside, a large man in a black jacket stepped in front of the glass, blocking his view. Instead, Nathaniel saw his own reflection.

His blond hair was held captive with a black ribbon. His broad shoulders, stuffed into another of Arthur's embroidered black coats. His neck, wrapped in a white stock. Nathaniel stepped back into the shadows, away from the image of a man he did not recognize. A man in borrowed shoes pinching his feet. A man with no means to provide for Colonel Bowman's only daughter.

Risk everything... Franklin's words suddenly offered hope. And heavy burdens. Carrying the Declaration for money, just to get what he wanted, would make him just like Peter. No, Nathaniel tried to justify Peter's motives. His brother was driven by greed, and this… This was love. Wasn't it? Nathaniel sat his glass on the balcony railing, looked to the moon, and whispered, "Please, Great Spirit, *Waasha Monetoo.* I need a sign."

He heard the click of the balcony door and spun toward it, his heart pounding.

Susannah shut the door and leaned against it, her eyes closed. When at last she opened her eyes, it was to Nathaniel she looked.

CHAPTER THIRTEEN

ALL PREVIOUS CONCERNS FLEW from Nathaniel's mind and he crossed the few paces to take Susannah's hands in both his own. He bent to lay a kiss upon her fingers, wishing for the removal and permanent destruction of the glove.

"I have not yet danced with you tonight, Miss Bowman."

"Mr. Marten, I cannot. My mother…"

When Nathaniel stood again to his full height, he followed Susannah's gaze, over her shoulder, toward the ballroom. Her mother was near a table bearing the weight of pastries, nuts, and fruits. Alice Bowman had one bejeweled hand clamped upon the arm of a lieutenant, the other gesturing extravagantly with a Shrewsbury cookie, evidence to the fact she lacked the grace she had miraculously instilled in Susannah.

"Fear not, she is far away." Nathaniel said. During his frequent visits, and despite genuine attempts to present himself well to Susannah's mother, his efforts drew only a polite but frigid breeze. He hoped in time, even Alice Bowman might warm to him.

"Mr. Marten…" Susannah's voice pulled his attention back to her. Her eyes searched his. "Our encounters this last year, our letters… I have felt immeasurable joy—"

"As have I." He ran a thumb across the ridges of her knuckles, pleased to feel her shiver at his caress. It emboldened him. "You must see by now, I no longer want one dance with you. I want them all. Susannah, I want to ask your father for your—"

"No!" She pulled her hand from him. Her face crumpled and she lowered her gaze behind lashes suddenly flooded with tears. "I… I cannot."

His heart weakened. Had he been mistaken in reading her? He quickly dismissed the notion for even her last letter was signed, "with sweet affection, yours." Could it be his doubts about his worth were shared by her? He stepped closer to her, standing taller.

"I know I am not what your parents expect, but they cannot deny that I love—"

She raised a hand, then pulled away, shutting her eyes again. "I cannot look at you as I say this… I am not free."

Nathaniel began to ask her meaning but the door swung wide, knocking them into one another. Nathaniel righted them both, but Susannah slipped from his hands, turning away to wipe her cheeks and smooth her skirts. Music spilled onto the balcony along with Arthur and Susannah's father, Colonel Bowman.

"Here he is!" Arthur said as Susannah ducked back through the door. As she departed, she cast a tear-stained glance over her shoulder at Nathaniel. He watched her go, weaving through the crowd to exit the far end of the ballroom, the mirrors revealing her profound expression of grief a thousand times over.

Nathaniel felt Arthur's elbow jabbing his arm, as his friend said, "Remember what we heard about the rebellion and the Express? Tell him what you told me, Uncle."

Nathaniel tried to shift his attention back to Colonel Bowman. The man's red cheeks under a dome of whitening hair made him appear more like Arthur's grandfather than his uncle. An empty sleeve was pinned to the pocket of his waistcoat with a gold-headed pin. During the French and Indian War, a fallen horse had crushed both Colonel Bowman's military designs and left side. Having lost the arm valiantly alongside a young George Washington, Bowman had returned to Philadelphia with a reputation that secured him an equally well-connected woman. At Alice Bowman's insistence, his aspirations and connections grew, enabling him to be at the forefront of politics, and now the Cause.

"It is far more than a rebellion now." The colonel's warm baritone voice rumbled from his belly, rounded by comfort and authority. "General Howe and his brother, the admiral, have been moving British troops and ships into New York."

"Thirty thousand troops are estimated to be on those ships." The fire in Arthur's eyes was thick with fury and fear. "As many men as the population of Philadelphia. The situation is not just worsening; it is dire."

Colonel Bowman nodded. "Unfortunately, in June, Congress shortened volunteer periods to six months. The brief enlistment keeps each man strong, but it weakens our army when troops constantly rotate in and out. We need men who will stay."

"What's more, is Bieber was right," Arthur said. "Congress is bringing the Express riders under the Continental Post and the army. We'll have to sign an oath, or lose our positions." Arthur swallowed, then let the rest tumble out quickly. "If we volunteer for one year of service, Uncle Bowman has agreed to arrange our commissions as Second Lieutenants."

"Commissions?" Nathaniel stared, words about all they'd said lodged in his throat.

"I had originally intended a position for Arthur alone, but at his request I will submit my referral tomorrow morning for you as well." Colonel Bowman nodded as if it were already done. "There is no time for you to go home first. I am pleased to arrange for your essentials from here. You will join the third battalion of the Pennsylvania militia; Colonel Kachlein's regiment moves to New York at week's end."

Nathaniel looked between the two men. "But… what about Susannah? Who is going to—"

Her father puffed. "Her fiancée is already a captain."

"Fiancée?" Nathaniel felt his world tilt, sliding out from under him, as his conversation with her replayed in his head. *No*, she had begged. *I cannot. Not free.* Nathaniel's legs grew weak. His mouth went dry.

"Susannah's engaged?" Arthur surveyed his Uncle, his brow creased. "To whom?"

"Captain Pemberley of Philadelphia." The colonel gestured across the ballroom, toward the man still humoring his wife. The man's blond head was held high above Alice Bowman's shoulders. He routinely nodded in her direction, a smile briefly falling from his lips between sips of Madeira when she laughed too loudly. Mostly, his expression remained as flat as the wall behind him. Nathaniel's stomach turned—for Susannah and for himself—as the colonel added, "Long established family with a grand estate in Maryland near our hemp farm. Susannah's mother arranged the match. Tonight, we are to announce the engagement."

How long had Susannah known, Nathaniel now wondered. Had she been writing to this captain all these months, too? Doubt tumbled through every shared memory and Nathaniel pinched the bridge of his nose, trying to cease the flow. He felt Arthur's hand on his shoulder.

"Nathaniel, I am sorry. I didn't know. And here I was encouraging you to be a suitor."

The colonel began to chuckle. Nathaniel uncovered his anguished face, and the man's mirth died away.

"Sir, with due respect. Our encounters… She and I…" Nathaniel glanced at the far door of the ballroom through which Susannah had fled, then raised his chin and held on to one last shred of hope for winning the Colonel's favor. Honesty. "I know I am not of her station… your station… but I give my word that my affection for your daughter is deep. Our affection, I know it to be mutual."

Colonel Bowman glanced into the ballroom. His gaze landed upon his wife who was twittering on through a long story, spitting an occasional crumb. He sighed. "Without that, my boy, marriage can be both long and tedious." The colonel looked to his own arm, and added, "And I am proof that it is possible to marry up."

Silence fell over them, and Nathaniel clung to the pause as the colonel surveyed him, head to foot.

"Pemberley is gallant in his own right, without merely depending on his family's station. Can you prove to be worthy like that?" The shrill sound of Mrs. Bowman calling her husband shattered through the cracked door, causing the colonel to add, "The wedding has been set for September twenty-eighth. With no other options, I'll support the choice."

"Choice?" Nathaniel was beginning to loathe the word. "Susannah's? Or your wife's?"

Compassion evaporated from Colonel Bowman's face. "An arrangement in the militia is all I will make for you—as a favor to Arthur." The colonel tugged on his waistcoat and yanked open the door. Sounds of another contradance fell onto the balcony. "I will have your orders in the morning. Goodnight." He stepped back into the ballroom, pulling the door firmly shut.

"Orders!" Nathaniel glowered at the closed doors and then spun on Arthur. "How could you?"

"I did what was best." Arthur, to Nathaniel's surprise, did not shrink. "He will secure our future."

"He has secured our fates! Yours. Mine. Even Susannah's. We are all pawns in a game where others control the board. Do you not see it?"

"Over thirty thousand British troops are landing on America's shores! Control the board…" Arthur blew air through his pursed lips. "It's enough to hope the colonies will survive."

"If that is how badly we are outnumbered, we won't. Why risk so much?" Nathaniel took a step back, retreating into a corner. He closed his eyes and rubbed a hand across his stiffening neck. Was it just a week ago they were enjoying a morning hunt with Kalawi? Now, they were to march off to war with no time to go home again?

"This isn't about risk, Nathaniel." His friend's voice was strong. Forceful. "This is about duty."

Nathaniel opened his eyes, stunned by how Arthur's presence filled the balcony. Candlelight from the ballroom glowed all around Arthur as he leveled a firm gaze on Nathaniel.

"I am through with waiting," Arthur began. "I will stand alongside the men of these colonies. I want to stand alongside you, too, but I am going. With or without you."

Nathaniel wished he could feel the fire of glory burn within him, but there were so many voices—those of his mother, father, Kalawi, Nakomtha, and even Peter—clamoring inside his head and they always blew out the flame.

"I do not have another option." Arthur shrugged one shoulder. "Do you?"

Nathaniel looked away from his friend, feeling the distance growing between them. He watched the gentry glide around the beguiling ballroom, waltzing through a life beyond his reach. Now, with the added sting of heartache churning in him, it was clear to him what he had. Nothing.

Susannah was betrothed to another. Peter had agreed to build the armory, and in the end both it and the land beneath it would belong to him. Even Kalawi would become the leader of his own clan. Nathaniel turned away and searched the darkness beyond the balcony. Jefferson's words came back to him.

If you have nothing to risk, you have nothing to lose. Nothing.

Nothing to risk, Franklin had said.

From the ballroom, a violin drew out a long low note. A new tune began and Nathaniel's mind clung to three of Franklin's words. *Everything to gain.*

Peter said construction wouldn't begin on the armory for another month. *I am our only hope,* Peter had said.

September twenty-eighth Susannah was due to marry. *Can you prove to be worthy?* the colonel had asked.

One task to complete. No Oath of Allegiance to sign. No war to fight. A lone rider. Six signatures. Not beholden to the contents of the Declaration he would carry. Thirty thousand pounds. His father freed from an armory to carry on the craft of an artisan by his second son's own hands.

"Do you?" Arthur's voice was sharp behind Nathaniel. "Do you have anything else?"

Nathaniel's heart slowed, his back straightened. A calm settled into his bones—a deep feeling of sureness and relief that comes with finding a way out of the darkness. He faced Arthur, the light from inside shining upon him. Without blinking Nathaniel softly nodded. "Yes, Arthur. Yes, I do."

★

PART II

*statement of
beliefs*

*The opinions and belief of men
depend not on their own will,
but follow involuntarily the evidence
proposed to their minds.*

– Thomas Jefferson

CHAPTER FOURTEEN

IT WAS AUGUST SECOND when Nathaniel returned to the State House as promised. The formal signing was over, but the chairs of the assembly hall were still occupied by congressmen and their aides, the din of their collective conversations creating a wall Nathaniel hesitated to penetrate. With his feet once again rooted to the threshold, he scanned the room.

Doctor Franklin, at a far table, worked alongside Jefferson. Brigadier General Dickinson stood by, a uniform now clothing his lean frame. Behind them, a pen hovering over an inkwell, a wiry man stared at Nathaniel. Finally, he leaned forward and tapped Dickinson.

When the men looked to the door, Nathaniel answered the question on their faces with a simple nod. The three men smiled, just as his parents had the first time Nathaniel returned from an overnight hunt with quarry—with relief and pride. A few moments later, Franklin ushered Dickinson, Jefferson, and Nathaniel into a small chamber beneath the back stairwell. The private room housed only a small table and a map of the thirteen colonies.

Franklin set out a stack of papers, an inkwell, a leather-bound journal, and a roll of parchment. "We hope you've easily sorted out your affairs." A velvet bag jangled as he dropped it on the table.

Nathaniel ignored the bag, wishing he could tell Franklin yes, but nothing had been easy about saying goodbye.

"You are really not going with me?" Arthur had said. His friend had come to City Tavern for breakfast, his last before leaving for New York, but Nathaniel could not stomach the idea of trying to make it through a meal full of questions. He'd met Arthur at the tavern door with a letter for Susannah. When Arthur pressed him, Nathaniel's evasiveness left a sour taste of betrayal in his mouth. He only embraced his friend and said, "Remember our brave knights' oath, Arthur—the one we made as boys. Heed it over the one for the colonies. And keep your head down."

Arthur had smiled briefly, but when he opened his mouth to ask more, Nathaniel turned to go. When he looked back once more, his friend stood alone in the doorway with sagging shoulders, the letter dangling from his hand.

Just this morning, Nathaniel had told Peter, giving him several letters to take back from both himself and Arthur. Guilt churning in his gut, he was about to offer apologies when Peter said, "What could you possibly need to do that is so damned important?"

"I thought you didn't care what I did?"

Peter seemed as if he might say something else, but in the end, he'd remained silent, and Nathaniel was the one to watch him leave for home without a backward glance. Now, standing with the statesmen, Nathaniel was thankful his task would soon move him forward again, taking him from a city rife with stinging memories.

He nodded toward the items Franklin had set on the table. "What's all this?"

Franklin unfolded a one-page document. "First, signatures matter more to Congress than verbal promises. Yours is required, too. It's not an oath—you made your feelings quite clear about that."

Nathaniel scanned the document, a contract for "importation of goods" by a merchant named Mr. Mirtle.

"But my surname is not—"

"How could we ask Congress for currency and provisions in your name," Jefferson said, "when no one is to know about you or what you carry?"

Franklin flipped open the journal to a marked page. "This is today's entry in Congress' journal—"

"The *Secret* Journal," Dickinson clarified. "When our Continental Congress first gathered two years ago, we were required to send minutes from meetings to Britain. We sent one set for the King to see. This was kept for those decisions that would not be viewed so… well, favorably."

"You call it the *Secret* Journal?" Nathaniel chuckled.

Jefferson smirked. "An obvious name, to be sure. It now contains notes from our meeting this morning, and this new veiled request."

The Declaration of Independence being engrossed,
and compared at the table, was signed by the members.
Resolved, That the secret committee be empowered to contract with
Mr. Mirtle for the importation of goods to the amount of thirty thousand
pounds sterling, at his risk, and fifteen thousand pounds sterling
at the risk of the United States of America, for the publick service.
That the marine committee be empowered to purchase a swift sailing vessel
to be employed by the secret committee in importing said goods.

"We felt it wise to imply all the members were present, rather than the Declaration incomplete and in transit," Jefferson added.

Nathaniel traced his finger over the rest of the entry. "This Mr. Mirtle… it is me?"

"Yes," Franklin said. "Marten is a name of Roman origin, from the god of war and fertility, *Mars.* An Old English form of it is *Mirtle.* Although Marten is a common name, your brother's agreement to build an armory links you too closely to the Congress."

Nathaniel felt foolish. Of course, these men would know of any contract for their own armory. Still, he cringed at the mention of it as Franklin continued. "As for the funds, sterling allows us to bypass traceable paper notes that risk being devalued. Congress approved it unwittingly." Franklin nudged the heavy purse of silver. "A portion as promised to cover your expenses. The bulk of it delivered upon completion."

Franklin held out the pen.

Nathaniel paused only briefly. He grasped the quill, and dipped it in the ink. He affixed the signature of his pseudonym, becoming Nathaniel Mirtle. Despite his confidence in taking on the task, the worry that he might have just sealed his fate nagged at him like an itch he couldn't reach. He ignored it and focused on another line within the journal.

"What about this fifteen thousand for public risk, and this vessel?"

"A payment to a very cooperative captain. His ship is headed to Yorktown to meet you—"

"A ship? Yorktown?"

"We're getting ahead of ourselves." Franklin handed Nathaniel a short list. "First, you must know the names of the men you seek. Thomas McKean. Richard Henry Lee. George Wythe. Lewis Morris. Elbridge Gerry. Oliver Wolcott."

"Your first signer is here," Dickinson moved to the map on the wall, and traced his finger along a post route from Philadelphia to Delaware. "Dover. The home of my friend McKean, at Third and Pine Streets. He is there drafting the state's constitution, and I've written to him to await your arrival. Your next stop is here," he traced the roads into Virginia, "at Stratford Hall on the southern bank of the Potomac. Mr. Richard Henry Lee last wrote us from there. He is expecting you near the end of the month."

"From there, you will go south again to George Wythe in *Devilsburg*," Jefferson said.

Dickinson clicked his tongue at Jefferson. "He means Williamsburg."

"With the exception of that town," Jefferson raised his hands to the heavens, "if God created the earth, he made Virginia on an improved plan."

Franklin puffed at them both and filled in the rest of the details. "Wythe will accompany you to the ship we've commissioned; it will arrive in Yorktown by the beginning of September. The *Frontier* and Captain Hugo Blythe will take you and your horse to New York." Nathaniel shivered at the thought of Bayard in a ship, but Franklin added, "It is far safer to go by sea given the reports of British troops up north."

"The last three delegates are in New York," Dickinson said, circling the area around Manhattan and Long Island. "I leave on the morrow for headquarters there, and shall instruct Lewis Morris, Elbridge Gerry, and Oliver Wolcott to remain."

"You are to return the Declaration here to Charles Thomson, our secretary," Franklin said. He confirmed that Nathaniel had memorized the names, then took back the list, ripping it into small bits. "We are estimating six signatures in as many weeks if all goes as planned. Above all, finishing the task is more important than how swiftly."

Franklin's word 'if' stood out from the rest, so Nathaniel asked, "And should something change? Who will let me know?"

"I will be of little use," Jefferson offered, sorrow passing over his face. "My wife has taken ill so I return to my home, Monticello."

"It is me then," Franklin said with a nod. "Safer for you to communicate with just one person anyway."

"That brings us to this." Jefferson unrolled the parchment, pinning opposite corners with the journal and inkwell.

The Unanimous Declaration of the thirteen united States of America.

Nathaniel had been unsure of what to expect, but as he looked upon the document, hand-styled in perfectly elegant lines, with a smattering of signatures clustered in uneven groups in the bottom fifth, he could only think of one thing. This was the document that officially separated his mother from her family and made her American. And soon it would be within his hands to complete. He swallowed back the gravity of it, the guilt of it, and focused on Jefferson's next instructions.

"The signatures are organized by state from south to north—they begin in the top left with Georgia, and end at bottom right with Connecticut. Have each man sign with their fellow delegates if possible. Have faith in the six men to verify the trustworthiness of whoever is in the room with them."

The idea that more than six people would see the document as he carried it led Nathaniel to another concern. "This is, well… so big—"

"It is momentous," Dickinson said.

"No, I mean it is large." Nathaniel held his satchel next to the parchment. The document was almost two feet wide, and nearly thirty inches in length. "How am I to move about without it being seen?"

Without hesitation, Jefferson stepped up. He folded it twice by thirds, the supple animal skin crinkling with each bend. "Try not to open it too often," he said as he held out the document.

Nathaniel reached for it, and the Declaration of Independence left the author's fingers, coming into his own. He slipped it into the satchel, and dropped the strap over his shoulder.

Franklin handed Nathaniel the pouch of silver, patting him on the shoulder and remarking, "Spend it wisely, but remember the use of money is all the advantage there is in having it."

"Although the other item you carry has a much higher value." Jefferson extended a strong hand, his sure eyes locking with Nathaniel's as he added, "Take good care of it. And yourself. Enjoy Virginia."

Nathaniel shook Jefferson's hand, though he felt unworthy to hold the statesman's confident gaze for too long.

"And I shall see you in New York soon, Mr. Mirtle," Dickinson said, affection warming his voice as he emphasized Nathaniel's new surname. "May God carry you and our document safely to headquarters."

Nathaniel nodded to them all, and with that, Franklin opened the door.

* * *

In the hallway, Silas Hastings tucked into a corner, away from the opening door to which his ear had been pressed. His heart thumped too loudly. From the darkness, he watched the backs of four men move down the hall. Jefferson. Franklin. One tall stranger. And the man for whom Silas worked, Brigadier General John Dickinson.

Silas was shaking. Overwrought. The general had required endless paperwork for their move to New York, so there'd been little time to find all the men to build Peter's armory. He'd been about to excuse himself from the assembly room when that wild backwoodsman had filled the doorway. Something about him was familiar... That build. That jaw. When the three men had gone to meet with the stranger, Silas had slipped down the hall behind them.

At first, he'd heard only fractured snippets through the heavy oak door. But voices, he knew, always grew louder nearer the end of a conversation. Sure enough, more seeped through.

A name. Mr. Mirtle. One rider. Going to Virginia. Then New York. And carrying a document. But what?

Silas watched the men walk toward the entrance. Clearly Dickinson had not been confiding in Silas about everything as he'd thought. Silas' chest grew tight with the familiar feeling of being excluded. He grasped the watch in his pocket for comfort. *Click. Snap.*

Silas' father and his brother Sebastian, both lawyers and equally handsome, had shared a private language. Five years ago, when Sebastian traveled to meet a client in Saint Dominique, Silas hoped his father would finally turn to him in the void. That dream was killed, along with Sebastian, by a mosquito carrying yellow fever, and Silas became nothing to his father but a reminder of two loves lost. First wife, now son. He became a pane of glass for his father to stare through. To walk around.

Now, Silas refocused his gaze down the hall. He had to know what Dickinson was having delivered. He cursed having to leave for New York in the morning.

"Someone must go with you," he whispered.

Someone hungry enough. A particular spy had already given Silas valuable information about the supply Quartermaster's drinking habits. For a few nearly-spoiled apples, Silas now knew when to submit requests to Moylan, who was too embarrassed to question them when he was sober. Perhaps for the promise of more, that same spy might go farther.

The door of the State House opened and sun flooded into the hall. Silas stared at the dark silhouette of the rider framed in the doorway. He made another promise.

Whoever you are, Mr. Mirtle, I will find out where you go. And what it is you carry that is so damned important.

CHAPTER FIFTEEN

KALAWI PUSHED HIS WAY downriver, finding toeholds between the rocks in Saucony Creek. Water gurgled around his upper thighs as he moved in unison with a line of men, their long spears raised and ready. The water, sparkling white with the early morning sun, was broken by dark patches just below the surface—sturgeon corralled toward wicker baskets, sunk and waiting.

"O-Metcheay!" A great many, Kalawi whispered to Wapishi. "They will add to our celebration."

The Green Corn Festival would soon begin, and this year Kalawi would have the honor of revealing the first pearl-white kernels from the harvest. He, not Nakomtha, would place the corn in the central kettle, beginning celebrations.

He glanced toward the thicket. "I hope Nathaniel and Arthur return in time. They always bring pie."

"Shush your howling, Kalawi Wolf." Wapishi pointed his spear at the fish, putting a boney finger to his lips.

Kalawi returned his eyes to the water just as the sturgeon pushed into the baskets, thrashing the water as they fought for survival. The men descended, spears rising and thrusting between the wicker strands. Rising. Thrashing. Thrusting. Until the water ran clear and smooth again.

Kalawi hoisted one of the largest traps out of the creek. Water ran down his back from between the sticks as he looped the leather strap over his shoulder and turned to help two other men don their baskets.

"You are strong. We need more like you," Wapishi said as he scrabbled up the bank using his spear to dig in. He turned back, stretching out a palm to yank Kalawi up the embankment.

"You are stronger than you think," Kalawi said, rubbing his shoulder.

Together, they laughed and walked back to the village to join the preparations. Alongside Nakomtha, several women pounded berries with mortar and pestles, while children collected pumpkins at the edge of the corn fields. Some of the clan were already bringing out their sacred spoons, symbols of the ability to feed oneself. Kalawi smiled thinking of his own sacred *Hem kwa*. It was elk horn with the handle carved like an eagle. It had been his father's, and Kalawi had carved similar spoons for Nathaniel and Arthur.

Kalawi looked toward Nathaniel's land again, searching for his friends, but the smile slipped from his face. Joseph and Jane Marten stood together at the edge of the thicket.

Only one other time had Nathaniel's parents crossed the threshold between their lands. Several years ago, Nathaniel had suffered a cough and fever for days that had worsened despite the white doctor's treatments. When Nathaniel had cried out for Nakomtha, they had at last come.

Now, as Jane gave a small wave, Kalawi shrugged off his basket. He tapped Nakomtha's shoulder and pointed toward the thicket. The same memory passed over her eyes, and she set aside her pestle. As Nakomtha and Kalawi walked out and shook hands with the Martens, the clan fell quiet, pausing in their work to watch the meeting. Joseph Marten waved a kind hello to the clan. Jane handed Kalawi two letters.

"We heard from the boys."

"They did not come back?" Kalawi shuffled the two letters, and ran a hand over his friends' familiar handwriting.

"Just Peter," Joseph said.

Nakomtha nudged Kalawi, and he agreed to translate for her.

"Nathaniel wrote us, too, but only saying he would return in a month or so." Jane eyed the letters in Kalawi's hand. "Perhaps he has told you why."

Kalawi broke the wax, and read it aloud.

Kalawi,

I wanted to return with news of the rebellion, but I cannot. Not yet. I can say no more without unraveling the promise I have made. Instead just know I am seeking my pawaka. Arthur has gone a soldiering, seeking his, too, I suppose.

I am sorry to miss the Green Corn Festival, especially knowing it is to be your honor. I hope to return long before the Bread Dance in October. Until then, please protect my parents, for I know not what Peter's decision brings in my absence.

Remember our brave knight's oath we made as boys:

> *Push with prowess through the world*
> *Not by another's will, but for a nobler goal*
> *Protect the meek*
> *Secure a fair maiden*
> *Honor the past with humility*
> *Step gently into the future*
> *And so on this journey we each our own way go...*

Wela ket nee ko ge.
We are one.
- Nathaniel

Arthur's brief letter confirmed his enlistment, conveying his own apologies, and repeating the knight's oath. Kalawi's heart plummeted at their not returning, and he clung to the memory of the summer they'd first created the pledge. They had stood on rocks at the creek, wearing golden leaves as armor, raising sticks as swords to salute the rising sun and against imaginary dragons. Now, Kalawi feared real demons were afoot.

Kalawi tapped Nathaniel's letter. "What was Peter's decision?"

Joseph's face darkened. "He agreed to a different oath. We are to become an armory for Congress."

"Workers are being sent to expand our buildings." Jane cast a worried glance over her shoulder at their land. "We know not when. Or how many."

Kalawi felt a knot tighten deep in his belly. When he translated for Nakomtha, as Jane had, she turned to survey her own land, and the clan still rooted behind them.

"We will let you be." Joseph returned Nathaniel's letter with a warm nod of goodbye.

"Don't you worry about us," Jane said as she bid them farewell. But before turning to leave, she gave Kalawi's forearm a small squeeze. Kalawi put his hand where hers had been as he watched the Martens weave into the woods.

The first time he had gone to the Marten farm to seek out Nathaniel, he'd gotten as far as the woodpile when Peter had screamed one word. *Indian.* Peter had knocked Kalawi to the ground and reached for an axe. Kalawi had shielded his face. Jane swept between them, grabbing Peter's arm before the blade came down through the bone. Later, when Jane had wrapped the linen bandage around Kalawi's wound, she'd sealed it with a motherly kiss. Now, Kalawi rubbed the spot, as if the wound still ached.

Next to him, Nakomtha nodded to the still visible white scar, and said, "Divided loyalties can be as divisive as disloyalty."

"Nathaniel is of our Wolf Clan, too, Mother."

"And we are lucky the Martens welcome us like kin. But they are not."

As the clan began to return to their task, Kalawi turned away from the thicket. Nakomtha turned with him, toward their village, and said, "If you are to lead the Shawnee, you must understand what is required. There are three needs the nation must meet, that we need in abundance, in order to remain strong." She nodded toward Saucony Creek. "Like the sturgeon, our first need is water. For ourselves, for our crops.

"Our second need is land. The land, the forests, and fields—it is home to more than just us. The wolf, the rabbit, the snakes–"

"The elk." Kalawi looked to Topton Mountain.

"No game means no meat, no skins, no moccasins, no furs, no spoons…" Nakomtha's voice trailed off, both of them knowing that what the land provided was far more than just those items. "Having nothing to trade is an increasing problem when it's difficult to know who to trade with. But there is another, third and far more pressing concern for our people. Do you know it?"

Kalawi scanned their village. The creek, the corn, the forest behind and beyond. He searched for the answer as three girls near his age stacked wood at the fire. One was a cousin of his. Another was Olethi, who had grown to embrace her name, meaning *pretty*. The last was Kisekamuta from the Rabbit Clan, orphaned after the battle in which Kalawi's own father had been killed. Now, under Kalawi's scrutiny, Kisekamuta looked up at him through lips pressed into a smile. Kalawi returned the shy look.

Nakomtha cleared her throat. *"She* is not the answer. Tell me, how big is our Wolf Clan?"

"A few more than fifty," Kalawi said confidently. In their small community, their numbers rising and falling only by deaths or births, the number was known by all.

"Not always were we so small," Nakomtha said. "Disease reduced us. Battles took our warriors. And our clan has not merged with another in many years. To remain Shawnee, to remain strong, what we require most are more Shawnee. Now, how many near marrying age are not related to one another?"

Kalawi surveyed the village again. Besides Kisekamuta, two other girls had been born of a Wolf Clan male and a white settler, captured as a child. There were two other boys nearing their time, and the mixed girls were likely matches for them. After the Green Corn Festival, it was expected that Olethi would marry Hunawe, another boy Kalawi's age, if she would have him. Hunawe's family had recently delivered furs and goods to Olethi's, approving the union. That left Kisekamuta, his cousin, and himself.

"How many?" Nakomtha insisted.

"Not many," Kalawi said, unable to look at his mother.

"Not enough." Nakomtha walked away, leaving him standing at the edge.

* * *

The sun had set on a day that had risen with such promise. And now Kalawi sat at the Green Corn Festival, darkness upon him, his eyes cast to the ground. Before him a ring of women hopped toe-to-heel, spinning clockwise around the raging fire. Their deformed shadows, like ancestral ghosts, danced across the dirt. The hoots of the clan, like the shells tied to the moccasins of the dancers, jangled too loud in his ears. They tangled with worried words spoken that afternoon. *Oaths. How many? Not enough.*

He rolled his sticky fingers together, still gooey from the first sweet cornbread of the summer season. Concern tightened in his neck—worsened by the weight of his new ceremonial headdress of porcupine and red deer hair—over what Nathaniel's words meant in his letter. *In search of my pawaka. Arthur in search of his too.*

To where and to what end?

A burning log popped like gunfire, snapping his attention back to the central ring. Kisekamuta danced by, her arms wide, her smile carefree. Then the pitch of the drumming lowered. A dozen men, Hunawe among them, jumped to their feet and formed a circle, spinning outside the women, in the opposite direction, for several beats. Then both circles slowed. Hunawe stopped behind his betrothed, Olethi. Her expression softened as she reached back with her hand and grasped his palm, the traditional signal that she accepted their union. Their parents, sitting with Nakomtha near the council house, smiled and exchanged approving glances.

Although Kalawi's heart warmed for them, it felt constricted by an uncertain future. He looked away to the full moon. A yellow halo blazed around it in a murky sky. *Ring around the moon, rain soon,* elder Wapishi had taught him. Will it be merely rain?

"How strong will this storm become?" he whispered to the Great Spirit, *Waasha Monetoo.* He looked over his clan rejoicing, carefree together, then turned his eyes west, beyond the thicket to Marten lands. "And how much closer?"

CHAPTER SIXTEEN

IN DOVER, NATHANIEL CLIMBED the steps of Thomas McKean's home, eager to acquire the first signature. Two days of dust and sweat filled his pores, but he did his best to dust off his buckskins. He made to knock, but found a note tacked to the door. Scrawled upon it: *Attention, Mr. Mirtle.* Nathaniel scanned the street, suddenly wary of the rueful glances of neighbors walking by. He tugged it from beneath the nail and cracked the wax seal.

> *Forced to move to New Castle, Delaware*
> *22 The Strand. Find me there. - T.M.*

McKean had not waited as promised? He swallowed his worry that he was off to a bad beginning. With only these instructions in hand, he had no choice but to point Bayard north again to New Castle, to the very town he'd come through on his way to Dover from Philadelphia.

Five hours of driving rain later, Nathaniel stood dripping upon the doorstep of number twenty-two. He knocked. He waited. He knocked again. When no one came, he leaned forward, and cupping his hands aside his eyes, peered through the door's window, devoid of curtains. Not a skiff of furniture graced the entry, and the wallpaper was darkened from soot except where paintings once hung.

"What the Dickens," Nathaniel whispered.

**

"What the Dickens!" Doctor Franklin said upon finding Nathaniel on his doorstep later than night.

"I have been chasing a ghost."

Franklin waved Nathaniel into a parlor where the smell of old musty books and roast beef added to the warmth from a small fire. As Nathaniel sank into one of the offered chairs next to the hearth and explained, Franklin's face scrunched with concern.

"Doctor Franklin, am I to have this much difficulty with each delegate?"

"I would think not…" Doctor Franklin began to sink into the opposite chair, but then he stood, nearly knocking over the small table between them. "What if that note was not from McKean? Or suppose someone else had read it? It could have been a trap."

Nathaniel felt the heat of the nearby flames. "How can we be certain—"

"From now on, instructions come from me only, and only using a cypher," Franklin said, and he was off to fetch a quill and paper.

Nathaniel had heard of letters being conveyed using secretive methods—special inks, secret stashing places called dead drops, and codes or cyphers—especially since the war began. There were many ways to build a cypher, and Franklin returned explaining his method.

"We will write messages by replacing the alphabet and numbers on a bottom line with the corresponding letters of a sentence on the top line. We'll use a phrase I assure you we can both easily recreate."

Nathaniel opened the small sheet Franklin handed him, and laughed.

THERE ARE LAZY MINDS AS WELL AS LAZY BODIES
ABCDE FGH IKLM NOPQR ST UWXY Z1 2345 67890!

"An ideal choice," Nathaniel chuckled. With a few of the letters in the original phrase being duplicated, it might take longer to decode messages, but it was sure to confuse anyone trying to decipher it. In keeping with the alphabet commonly used, the *J* and *V* were omitted because the letters *I* and *U* sufficed.

"You do not move to the next spot until a cyphered letter arrives from me. And you write to no one but me. Understood?"

Nathaniel's thoughts flew to the one letter Susannah had from him, and the one brief response from her before his departure from Philadelphia. Return to me. Would their love sustain through several weeks of silence? Certainly it could not if he never returned.

"Agreed," Nathaniel nodded.

Franklin took back the cypher and tossed it into the fire. "I will work with Dickinson to find Mr. McKean. You must continue on to Virginia to Mr. Lee, but," he tapped his chin with a finger, "I do think you should be armed with more than a cypher."

"I have my rifle."

"Yes, but your mind tells your finger to pull the trigger, so it must be informed," Franklin said as he shuffled from the room, returning moments later with several items in hand. First, he opened and closed a collapsible telescope. "A Spyglass. Expensive, but akin to seeing the future. I expect you to return it." Next, he unfolded a weathered map of the middle colonies upon the little table. "I made this back in the fifties. It is our past I suppose."

The drawings were well styled, but in the creases the ink had faded from wear. Nathaniel pointed them out, saying, "A few of the post roads might have changed, too."

"Then I expect you to mark corrections on it. Now, to help define the present." Franklin handed him a small compass in a wooden case, and also a pair of metal pincers. "This is a divider compass. Use it to measure the scale on any map, and you shall see how far you have to go."

"I am grateful for these," Nathaniel said. He opened his satchel and took out the Declaration to arrange the heavier items beneath it.

"What is this?" Franklin gasped, pointing to the back of the folded parchment. "Did you write on our Declaration?"

"You sent me with two of the Dunlap broadside copies, for posting in Delaware. I had to put that on it," Nathaniel said, nodding to the writing in his own hand. *Original Declaration of Independence dated 4 July, 1776.* "I was worried I would tack up your signatures in a tavern in Dover."

Franklin grumbled that perhaps that was wise. As Nathaniel put the document back in his bag, buckling it closed, Franklin eyed the satchel with interest. "'Tis solid as a saddle. I should like to have some made to replace the

Post's linen haversacks." Franklin turned the pack over in his hands, seeming to memorize the specifications. Then, with the same interest, he scrutinized Nathaniel. "Your satchel is unassuming enough, but perhaps an importer should be dressed less… er, more…"

He pounded Nathaniel on the shoulder. Dirt puffed from his sleeve.

"You mean I need to appear less like a frontiersman having wrestled a bear?"

"Indeed." Franklin laughed and dusted off his hands. "Come, a fat pot roast and a fine wine await. Then we shall do our best to make you a gentleman."

CHAPTER SEVENTEEN

SUSANNAH HID BEHIND HER needlepoint pinned in the wooden loom. She didn't need to see her mother's rouged face opposite her in the parlor to know it was set with a reproachful look. No doubt the lips were downturned while the eyebrows rose into a furrowed forehead framed by curls forced into their rightful position under a tight, white bonnet. Her irrepressible, high voice pushing through the thin fabric and vibrating off the forcible red wallpaper was indication enough that all was not right in Alice Bowman's world. Yet again.

"What am I to do? We cannot sit your father's aunt next to Reverend Ewing at the wedding banquet given her agonizing laments about her late husband, or our poor Pastor will be obliged to pray for her alone at First Presbyterian on Sunday." Her mother reviewed the list of wedding invitees. "God bless him, he is overburdened by the war and this was to be his one happy event of the season. Do you not think?"

Susannah pushed the needle through the next required hole, trapped in the parlor by windows kept shut to keep the warmth out. "Reverend Ewing will be grateful for your thoughtfulness." She had learned over the years to pay close attention to even the most banal of her mother's words, lest she bear a lecture for being insolent as her father or the servants so often suffered.

"Indeed. That is settled then! Reverend Ewing must sit next to someone else, so that leaves... Oh, dear me... Mrs. Esther De Berdt Reed!" Her mother barely breathed before moving on to the next issue—and there was always a next issue. "I am resigned to Mrs. Reed's attendance for she is connected with everyone who is anyone. Do you know, I have heard it said, that the Reeds had dinner with the Washingtons and Dickinsons before Colonel Reed went north with the general? 'Twas shortly after Mr. Dickinson married that much younger woman who some say had a dowry of over thirty thousand pounds, but I suppose that explains Mr. Dickinson giving up his law practice, as, of course, he would be required to manage his newly acquired estate."

Susannah puzzled over the gossip, recalling her father recently saying John Dickinson had given up his business to lead a battalion. Wasn't he Brigadier General now? Had she heard wrong? She bit her tongue as her mother continued.

"Anyway, as I confess, I am resigned to Mrs. Reed's attendance, but..." a deep inhale was followed by a sigh overwrought with pity, "at our last ball her glass of Madeira was refilled so often it never seemed to empty. So, it simply will not do to have the wine flowing too easily, but how am I to manage the serving if another of our footmen joins the Cause by that time. I will share my concerns with our cook and she can adjust accordingly, do you not think?"

"'Tis a complicated matter Lydia will help solve." Susannah knew no detail below stairs ever escaped the watchful eye of Lydia. Just before Susannah was born, the woman had come from Germany as an indentured servant—a skilled cook and the rare artisan skill of making bread—along with her husband, a footman. He had died shortly thereafter of consumption, leaving a very pregnant Lydia alone to pay back both her debt and her husband's. Alone, she raised their son, Joshua, until he was old enough to assume his father's position.

"I must speak with the cook at once." The efficient rustle of her mother's abundant skirts preceded her departure to the kitchen, with a pause at the door to instruct once more. "You stay and attend to Mr. Pemberley's fine wedding gift."

As she listened to her mother's heels snap into the distance across the marble hall of the foyer, Susannah pushed the yellow thread through a center of a daisy, letting go of the needle. *A fine wedding gift...* A fine flower in the center of fine fabric. Fine linen for a fine handkerchief. For a fine husband to carry while fighting a fine cause.

Susannah's head pounded. She took off her white bonnet, tucking slender fingers into her hair to loosen the curls and rub at her scalp as she tried to breathe. The air felt sucked from the stuffy room, from her chest confined in the constricting yellow bodice. She ran to the window and threw it open, gulping in the hot August air, holding fast to the sash. When her heart resumed a genteel pace, she gave a brief glance into the room.

Alone.

She pulled a letter from her pocket. The edges worn. Folds frayed. The ink of Nathaniel's words *My Dearest Susannah* smudged by her constant touch. Her heart pounded as it had the morning after the ball, after her sorrowful conversation on the balcony with Nathaniel, when the letter first arrived.

I seek to fulfill your father's challenge: to prove myself worthy of you. Do what you must to keep going. Know that I am doing what is necessary for you. For us. I will return before the end of September. Wait for me.

She looked back at the needlepoint. Every stitch was a way to keep going. Every false agreement she made about her impending happily-ever-after, was a way to keep going. A way to believe that his signature contained the real ending to her story: *I am yours, Nathaniel.*

She had shown the letter to only one other. Her father, over the next breakfast meal they had alone, her mother typically taking a tray in bed. Her father had long encouraged a sharing of not just his newspaper with Susannah, but also a meaningful discourse about any and all matters, with an unstated promise it would be kept between the two of them.

"Did you tell Mr. Marten to prove himself?" Susannah had asked.

"Yes, I suppose I did," the colonel had said. A youthful smile tugged at his mouth as he read the letter, but then he frowned and handed it back to her. "Be careful of falls from such hopeful heights. Boys do not always become the men their wives envisioned—just ask your mother." Susannah could not repress a sorrowful smile for him as he continued. "Speaking of her, I will not stop her from planning your wedding to Pemberley. That will be yours to handle when… *if* the time comes."

"I will, Father. And it will!" She popped up to kiss him. His hair and brows had grown more flossy and white by the day, softening his usual warm expression even more.

"Not another word of it now, my pup," he said, putting his palm to her cheek. "Your mother will not have you mooning about when practicality must prevail."

Susannah had kept her promise, keeping her joy close, but even now, a wave of guilt now washed over her. When Nathaniel did return, she would have to confront her mother. And let down Matthew Pemberley, if indeed he felt any hint of happiness at their proposed union.

The kiss he'd left upon her glove before leaving for New York, had been tepid. Although faithfully his letters arrived, so far his words relayed daily routines rather than romances. Only one line had once referenced his return in September, and it was more of a postscript than a declaration.

She refolded Nathaniel's letter and slipped it back in her pocket, alongside another letter just as dear. The first one received from Arthur, written after a harrowing sail and a long, exhausting march to New York. His feet worn. His heart torn. His words she'd memorized.

I am confused by Nathaniel's absence. His evasiveness. Yet I am buoyed by the knowledge that I have chosen well. I am determined to fight for our freedom, come what may. Write to me often so I may remember each day that I fight for you, too.

Susannah turned her face to the window, to the morning sun, aching for the warmth of her cousin's smile. For Nathaniel's touch. She closed her eyes, and inhaled the perfume of the Sweet Alyssum wilting in the window box.

"When you come home, it is in one piece, yes?" Lydia's throaty German vowels rose from the street below. Her "when" sounded like "ven." Susannah open her eyes and leaned forward to inform Lydia about her mother needing her, but the scene stole her words.

Lydia had let tears streak her plump cheeks. She grasped her son Joshua's hand. A hat and his father's old travel pack were slung over Joshua's shoulder, the sun shining on his blond hair, and his chin trembling in a tightly-set jaw.

It was the same look Susannah remembered upon Joshua's angelic face the day her own mother forbade her to play with him. She'd scolded Susannah as if Joshua were not there. *He is beneath you.* From that day on Susannah had been molded into an obedient daughter fit for a wife. Joshua, into a footman. Until today.

"Be assured I am choosing to go fight." Joshua tugged a scarf from around his neck and wiped away his mother's tears. "For us. What did you tell me when we read the Declaration together?"

"We should always, all of us, feel this free," Lydia nodded, but fresh tears sprang forth. Susannah tucked behind the curtain to give the normally stoic woman room to cry. When she peeked around the drapery again, Joshua was holding his mother against his chest, kissing the top of her graying hair. Susannah's own arms ached for that depth of affection.

"I will write you so often it will be as if I am here, Mother. I will make you proud."

"I am already. Just come back. This," she said, patting her own chest, "is only home with you in it. Otherwise empty."

But Susannah knew the echo of emptiness was seeping into all their lives. Another footman and a valet had joined the militia along with the butler, and his wife had left her housemaid position to be a camp-follower by his side.

The clap-clop of hooves that usually carried visitors to the Bowman home had also diminished with each day, and the number of empty spaces in the pew next to Susannah grew at church each week. So many people were choosing to go, either for the Cause, or because of it. And now Joshua, too.

Susannah wanted to run to him. To go with him. To move toward something. Anything. But her feet felt fastened to the floor. She sagged against the window frame, clinging tightly to the two letters in her pocket.

"I could not find that Lydia anywhere... Susannah!" Alice Bowman, enveloped in her usual layers of luxurious silks and petticoats, suddenly filled the room and bustled up to the open window. With a huff, she rammed the sash down tight, waving a hand at her own flushing cheeks. "That putrid summer air is not healthy, child."

Without a pause her mother went back to relaying her exhaustive plans, but her twittering words were muffled by the buzzing in Susannah's ears as she watched Joshua walk away. His purposeful shoulders were as square as Arthur's the day he'd left for New York. The day Nathaniel had written to declare he would do what was necessary. For her. For them. While she stayed behind the glass. Trying to breathe. Doing what she must to keep going.

"Susannah, are you quite alright?" Her mother's words broke through.

A moment more and Susannah nodded. She turned back to the room, to the pin stuck in the needlepoint awaiting her hand. "Yes, mother," she forced a smile. "I am just fine."

CHAPTER EIGHTEEN

"BAYARD, YOU WILL BE FINE. We have to cross the Potomac." Nathaniel patted Bayard as he tugged him down the ramp of ballast stone, and into the wooden scow ferry. The two ferrymen looked warily at each other as Bayard snapped his teeth on the bit. With one last tug, Nathaniel pulled him aboard and tied him off.

"Eight pence," the larger of the two men said. "Four for yerself. Four for dat horse."

Nathaniel paid the customary fare, and the two ferrymen pulled up the ramp and set to rowing. They left the shores of Maryland, traversing the narrowest strip of the Potomac toward Hooe's Landing at Barnsfield, Virginia. Nathaniel dropped onto a crate near Bayard's head, wishing for more of the roast beef he'd had with Franklin. He also wished he hadn't agreed to the stockings of a proper importer. In the heat and humidity, they stuck to his legs like tar. He was glad he refused the wooden insert some men tucked into their leggings to accentuate their calves. The unassuming brown suit was comfortable enough, but already his feet longed for the moccasins in the bundle on his saddle.

"'Comin' in," the ferryman said as he flicked a thumb at Bayard. "Steady that animal."

Nathaniel grasped the reins and patted his horse's neck. "Welcome to Virginia, Bayard."

All day he and Bayard pushed eastward, climbing upward from the shore at Hooe's Ferry. The summer air weighed on him like a thick woolen coat. At the crest of the road, Nathaniel stopped to revel in a small breeze and took out Franklin's map. A few of the riverbanks had changed shape, and Nathaniel had come across two new inns, all of which he'd clarify on the map tonight when he rested at Stratford Hall.

This spot was marked *The Clifts*. To his left, long grasses skirted a precipice of faded stone cliffs that dropped one hundred and fifty feet to the Potomac. A brown spot at the edge he'd mistaken for a rock suddenly took flight. An eagle. She unfolded her wings with a whoosh, catching the warm air. Another larger eagle joined her, soaring up from below. The two spun together on a funnel of wind. Each one leading. Each one following. They spun over the Potomac, continuing their own contradance.

The memory of Susannah in his arms returned. It flooded him with purpose, and he pushed onward. To the south rolled an unending cotton field. Each soft white tuft, nearly ready for the September harvest, sparkled like a diamond on the weathered finger of an old crone. According to the map, Stratford Hall was beyond an upcoming grove of poplar and chestnut trees. As Bayard's hooves pulverized the pieces of oyster shell on the pathway, Nathaniel heard another screech from one of the eagles. He spun in the saddle to look back, but saw something else.

A rider. Black horse. Blue coat.

A chill ran over Nathaniel. He spun Bayard around. Searched the distance. Cotton fields. Trees. He pulled Franklin's scope from his pack and swept the field. Bayard pranced. The hot summer air shimmered and danced. But Nathaniel saw nothing. No one.

He lowered the spyglass, overcome by a prickling sensation, just as he had the night he crossed the Susquehanna on the ferry into Maryland. That night, the hair on his arms had bristled, but the only other riders had been a woman gazing softly upon the head of her son, who had fallen asleep on her shoulder, and a lone ferryman who offered genuine indifference. Nathaniel had put the goosebumps down to the cool night air. Now he wondered differently.

He decided to tell Lee of his concerns about being followed, and turned Bayard east again. As the lane curved south and widened, the sounds of people, horses, and equipment broke through the trees. When they exited the shadows of the grove, Nathaniel yanked Bayard to a stop.

"Good heavens."

The shell drive curved past southern slopes of grape vines and orchards of apples and pears. Among the trees men, women, and several children toiled, climbed, and picked. Beyond them, fields of tobacco stretched far out into the distance, their stocks drying in the late August sun. Following the curve to the north was a village-sized collection of sheds and workshops. Buzzing in and around them like bees at the hive were blacksmiths, carpenters, coopers, brewers, and tradesmen. Every last one of them negro. Near the orchard, wiping sweat from his brow, a robust, tall white man in wide straw hat leaned upon a stack of crates.

"This is no mere farm," Nathaniel whispered.

"That you, Mister Mirtle?" Nathaniel startled and turned to find, at his feet, a man taking off his straw hat by the fraying brim. His accent made the word 'mister' sound more like 'mistuh.' The man's deep black skin absorbed the sun, and the crudely cut shock of graying hair was matted with sweat and dust. He tipped his head, exposing a long red welt that ran down behind his right ear and into his sweat-stained shirt collar. Nathaniel frowned at the gash, but smiled when the man looked up at him again.

"Yes, I am Nathaniel Mirtle." He made to get off Bayard, but the man stopped him with a shake of his head.

"Please. I am Elam." Elam quickly put his hat back on and took Bayard's reins, pulling him toward the house. "I was told to wait. They've been expectin' you."

Nathaniel sat rigid in the saddle as they walked on. Out of the corner of his eye, he saw the workers in the orchard turn their heads like folks gathered to watch a parade. Nathaniel flushed hot. With a grunt, Nathaniel hopped down, and shrugged to Elam. "Been in the saddle for days. I'd prefer walking a bit with you."

"If you wish." Elam kept a lowered head.

As they moved toward the house, Nathaniel heard the sound of a whip crack. The slave-master in the field hollered to return to work.

Stratford Hall was a solid brick, H-shaped structure, nearly equal in size to the State House in Philadelphia. It faced the cliff upon the bluff, and more slaves scurried between the home, kitchen house, and outbuildings. Four large chimneys stood guard atop each wing of the house, dwarfing the roofline. At the foot of a wide set of stone stairs rising to a second story front door, Elam stopped.

"Miss Sarah will greet you up there, sir." He pointed to a run of buildings just to the west, twice the length of the Marten's barns back home. "I'll take your horse there, to the livery stables for feedin' and waterin'."

Nathaniel smiled his thanks. When Elam walked away, Nathaniel saw the dark stain on Elam's shirt below the welt. Nathaniel winced as if feeling the whip himself. Questions filled his mind about who would add injury to the shameful insult of being owned. A memory from two years ago crowded his thoughts.

When the news of the clash with the redcoats at Lexington and Concord had reached Berks County, locals had submitted so many new rifle orders to his father, it forced him to hire a few men to help bail the ready hay. Late one evening, Peter studied the ledgers across the table from their father, shaking his head.

"Our expenses are going to be higher than our profits. Next time I'm in Philadelphia, I'll go to the yard next to London Coffee House and buy a few blacks outright." Their father had stood and cleared the contents of the table with one swing of his thick arm. The open ink jar smashed against the far wall, and Joseph had waved a finger at Peter, his hand speckled by some of the gall.

"I would rather owe 'til they put my body in the ground! A man cannot, and more importantly should not, ever be so arrogant as to own another human being. You would do well to learn the value of a man, and not his price." It had been another two months before Peter had been allowed near the ledgers.

"Mister Mirtle?" A girl called from the doorway of the home.

Turning back to the present, Nathaniel climbed the steps to meet her. "Good evening. Miss Sarah?"

She nodded and showed him into an entry foyer, a back door swung open opposite the one he had just entered. As Sarah ran off to announce his arrival, Nathaniel's eyes adjusted to the lower light of the darkly-painted foyer. A few plush pieces of furniture were pushed against the walls. Their insignificant presence made the high-ceilinged space feel barren. Cold. Nathaniel shivered as he compared two large portraits at opposite ends of the parlor. Each man was dressed in colorful clothing, before a rich landscape filled with abundant sunshine.

Nathaniel knew very little about Lee beyond him being the Congressman who had put forth the resolution to separate. That resolution had resulted in drafting the Declaration. Nathaniel studied the paintings trying to determine which was the man he was to meet. Both stern men stared, looking down on him.

He left the emptiness and stepped out the open back door. Sunset cast an orange glow over two large gardens behind the house, edged by rows of cedars. Their late-day shadows stretched across the vegetables, fountains, and topiaries. Several female slaves moved amid the rows picking chard, plump tomatoes, and late summer herbs.

"How many people does it take to run one estate?" he asked aloud.

"More than they might think up north."

Nathaniel turned to see the man he presumed to be Richard Henry Lee standing in the doorway. A high forehead, topped off with a fashionable wig, emphasized a long face with root-like veins stretching out from the long, straight nose. The man could not be further from Ben Franklin in attire, from the crimson silk jacket with gold brocade stitching and matching breeches, down to the red slippers adorning his feet where his pristine white stockings ended.

"Two hundred slaves here." Lee gestured over the property with an ivory cup in his right hand, a heavy ring clunking against it. His left arm was pressed across his stomach, his hand bound in black silk cloth that did not obscure the fact it was deformed. "Another sixty on my own estate, Chantilly, on the southeastern end. My family has been graced with over seven thousand acres."

Nathaniel followed Lee's gaze toward the fields, but he quickly stole another glance at the man. The expression was as flat and uninformative as those of the portraits in the parlor. Lee briefly narrowed his lower lids, as if in pain, and took another drink. He swallowed and nodded back into the house.

"I will sign that document now." He turned on his heel.

Not once had Lee made eye contact with Nathaniel.

Nathaniel followed him to a private study, glowing reddish-purple from the sunset. Two sconces flanked a large, cold fireplace, the candles already lit for the swiftly approaching evening.

Lee waved his cup at another man sitting in the room, upon a purple velvet settee. "My brother, Francis Lightfoot Lee. Frank, this is that rider we were expecting. Where is that letter that came for him?"

The man, also in mid-life, rose with a groan from a chair in the corner. He closed the book he had been reading and nodded to Nathaniel. Francis Lightfoot Lee had a casual presence, but he had in common the receding hairline, elongated face, and closed expression of his brother.

Francis Lee was among the Virginia delegates who had signed the Declaration in Philadelphia on August second. His brother Richard had been too ill, Franklin had said. Seeing the pallor on Richard Lee's cheeks and the way he occasionally gripped his stomach as he took a seat at a large mahogany desk, Nathaniel could see he was still unwell.

"The letter is upon your desk where I put it last night, R.H.," Francis Lee spoke, patience ringing false in his voice. He found it himself, and handed Nathaniel the sealed envelope.

Nathaniel cracked open the wax. Folded inside the outer envelope was a page torn from an old copy of Franklin's *Poor Richard's Almanack*. On one side was the printed weather prediction for the month of September, and on the other was advice on how to become rich through thrift and care. But no note.

What is Franklin up to? Nathaniel wondered.

"Can you read it, boy?" Francis Lee asked.

By the tone, Nathaniel realized he was being asked if he could read at all.

He was about to retort when it occurred to him what Franklin had done. He strode over to the fireplace and held the sheet near one of the illuminated candles. Twenty-two letters appeared.

ELSEEELZZLTYAHWSRAENSA

Invisible ink. The area, where the ink had been written, most likely put down in lemon juice or vinegar, had weakened the paper fibers, so when held to the candle, the words burned darker than the rest of the sheet.

"Brilliant!" Francis Lee whispered over Nathaniel's shoulder. "What does it say?"

"It's a cypher," Nathaniel said as he pulled a small pencil and a notepad from his satchel to write down the agreed-upon code.

"Why?" Francis Lee sniffed.

"There have been issues with spies among messengers." The comment reminded Nathaniel to tell them about his suspicions of being followed. "Speaking of which, I—"

"I don't have time for all this. Bring the Declaration here," Richard Lee waved his good arm at Nathaniel. "I will sign it while you figure that out."

Nathaniel took the Declaration from his satchel and Lee unfolded it with his one good hand. As Lee made to dip his quill in the inkwell, he discovered it nearly empty. He slammed the quill onto the desk under his palm.

"Damn it, how often do I have to tell that stupid girl to keep it filled. Sarah!"

At his command, the girl came running into the room already shrinking. Richard Lee waved the empty bottle at her. She scurried to a side cabinet a few feet from the desk and returned with a full bottle. She replaced the vial, nearly spilling the ink with shaking hands, then she backed out of the room. Richard Lee returned to his task and scanned the bottom of the document, looking for his fellow Virginians' signatures so he could add his name to theirs. Francis Lee, returned to the settee, clearly more interested in his book.

Nathaniel swallowed his desire to defend the girl, and instead bent his head to his own sheet to decipher the message.

THERE ARE LAZY MINDS AS WELL AS LAZY BODIES
ABCDE FGH IKLM NOPQR ST UWXY ZI 2 3 4 5 6 7 8 9 0 !

Twice Nathaniel decoded Franklin's new message, the lines making no sense, until on his third try the message was clear.

ELSEEELZZLTYAHWSRAENSA
WYTHEWILLIAMSBURGSEPT3

Nathaniel nodded, relieved the schedule had not changed. He lit the page with one of the candles, and dropped it into the hearth, watching to ensure the page burned to ash.

"It is done," Richard Henry refolded the document, holding it out for Nathaniel to take. As Nathaniel put the Declaration containing the first of the last of the signatures in his pouch, Richard Henry said, "Elam has been ordered to feed and water your horse. He has a bundle of food for your journey. Safe travels."

The two words fell solidly in the room. Nathaniel blinked. His hope for a warm bed, and a tasty meal turned to ash like the decoded message.

When Francis nodded a curt goodbye, Nathaniel moved toward the door. He turned to bid Lee goodnight, but the cup had replaced the pen in the statesman's hand. Nathaniel knew he was beneath the delegates in stature, but Richard Henry Lee had lowered him further. A mere errand boy.

Nathaniel left the house, his shoes thumping hard across the floor and out the door, as he marveled at the difference between this exchange and those with Doctor Franklin.

At the stable, after passing a carriage house containing three handsome, glossy, black coaches, he found nearly a dozen fine stallions, their tack of the thickest leather, embossed with a solid silver emblem, an elaborate letter 'S' for Stratford Hall.

He found Elam with Bayard near the back. Elam acknowledged Nathaniel with a nod as he buckled Bayard's saddle around a puffed-up belly, full from eating his fill of hay and carrots. Bayard's coat was shining from having been washed and brushed.

Nathaniel smiled. "He looks good, Elam. Clean. Fed. Rested. Thank you."

"Yes, sir." Elam patted Bayard, cooing and waiting the required moment or two for the horse to relax before tightening the belt a notch more. Bayard whinnied and Elam gave the horse a gentle nudge with his shoulder. "A new shoe on that right front hoof, too. The other was near worn out."

Nathaniel bent to lift Bayard's leg, and found a shiny shoe nailed in place. He looked down at his own dusty, scuffed shoe. Bayard had been treated better by the slave than he had been by the two gentlemen.

Although Nathaniel had acquired a signature, he had a strange sense that Richard Henry Lee was more like the very thing they were fighting against than what they were fighting for. Would they all become slaves to men like the Lees? Why separate at all when Congress has such kingly bastards right here in the colonies, Nathaniel reasoned.

Nathaniel clicked his tongue.

Elan came around with his brow crinkled with worry. "That shoe alright, sir?"

"No… Yes, it is fine. Thank you. We have a long journey, so we are both grateful." Nathaniel reached out and patted Elam's back, realizing too late as his hand fell upon the blood-stained welt. Elam winced and turned the shoulder away.

"I am so sorry." Nathaniel held his breath as the man rode out a wave of pain.

Elam waved a hand and bent to retrieve a package from a nearby stool. "It will heal. 'Tis just the skin on the outside." Elam handed Nathaniel the bundle of food that had been prepared, then picked up Bayard's bridle to finish his job. Nathaniel watched Elam leave his own pain behind and place the bit in Bayard's mouth. He soothed the horse with whispered words in his native tongue. Nathaniel wondered more about the man before him.

"Elam? Is that your birth name? Or were you given that when you came here?"

"They told it to me when I was brought here."

Nathaniel chided himself for using the word 'came,' as if the man had traveled to the colonies of his own accord.

"What were you called before?" Nathaniel asked as Elam grabbed the reins. Together they walked Bayard out of the stable. Elam kept his eyes on his feet and Nathaniel watched the man's face as he wandered through his memories. At first, Elam smiled but then his whole round face fell with grief and sadness. He stopped walking and inhaled deeply.

"There is a proverb in West Africa." He squared his shoulders, his whole being calm with wisdom. "It is not what you are called, but what you answer to."

Nathaniel studied the man's inviting expression and asked, "And what do you answer to?"

Elam smiled, raised his chin and met Nathaniel's eyes. "Myself, sir." When Nathaniel returned his smile, his tone softened as he said, "My name is Jawara. It means a lover of peace."

Nathaniel nodded his head, and extended a hand to say goodbye. "Then peace be with you, Jawara."

Long after he had left, Nathaniel still felt the warmth of the man's work-worn palm in his own, their brief conversation lingering long after the road had curved south. Long after the silhouette of the slave standing on the plantation's bluff had receded into the darkness.

A few days later, another silhouette appeared on the horizon. It was then Nathaniel realized he had failed to send word to Franklin about what was now obvious. He was being followed by the man in a blue coat.

CHAPTER NINETEEN

"THE TROOPS HAVE EVEN less than I imagined," Dickinson said.

"What should we request first?" Silas' pen hovered over a page dated the twentieth of August on yet another letter to Congress. Dickinson sorted through the lists that covered the desk between them like a threadbare tablecloth. A multitude of needs for the army.

"And for which troops first? Long Island? Here in Manhattan? Or the quarter of our men bedridden with typhoid?" Dickinson rubbed a hand over his eyes.

Silas splayed his aching fingers. Since they had joined the troops in New York two weeks prior, Silas seemed to do little but pen missives for Dickinson to other statesmen, generals, and Congress. And yet not one word or letter, sent or received, ever hinted about Dickinson's meeting with the man at the State House. Not one letter had arrived from Silas' spy either.

Dickinson reached for a list, shaking his head as he ran a finger down the many lines. "Shoes. So many of them need shoes, let us begin outlining costs there." As Dickinson dictated requests, Silas wondered how much would be fulfilled given Congress' increasing struggles to find funding. Thankfully, the monies for the armory had come through before they'd left Philadelphia.

With the funds, Silas had paid a stipend to a handful of workers—men from Philadelphia desperate to avoid the battlefield—to go to the Marten farm. He couldn't guarantee such half-hearted men would work hard, but once in Berks County, their directives and pay would come from Peter and what Silas sent him. For now, half the remaining funds were stitched into the lining of his bedroll he carried. The other half was squirreled away in a lockbox buried in Philadelphia. Even now, Silas smiled at the thought of the trove waiting beneath the dirt, just beginning to grow, behind his father's headstone.

"I'd give the shirt off my own back but 'tis not enough," Dickinson said.

"Pardon, sir?" Silas blinked at him, his pen stalled.

"Shirts. The men need shirts. Osnaburg if we can still get the fabric imported. It wears longer. Otherwise homespun cotton."

"Perhaps homespun wool," Silas said. When Dickinson made to object, he added, "In case supplies do not come before winter."

"Very thoughtful, Mr. Hastings. There's our Middle Temple practicum in practice." Dickinson patted him on the arm.

Silas gripped the pen, unsettled by praise or touch. After Sebastian had died, Silas was sent to Middle Temple in London—his father's way of increasing an already discernible distance while keeping up appearances—the school being known in the colonies as a "gentlemen's education" for the elite. For Silas, he'd been invigorated by boundless academia, and unburdened by paternal expectations of failure. But during his second year, the reprieve ended. Called home, his father dead from heart failure. The watch his inheritance, along with immense debts the old man had accumulated in trying to prove his worth to everyone else.

As his father's loyal lawyer promised confidentiality. Silas promised himself to not only pay down every cent, but to accumulate, by his own efforts, every shilling of an inheritance he'd been denied. It's why this supply business was so important, he easily admitted. It was also why he let Dickinson assume he had finished his schooling at Middle Temple; fidelity instilled the blind trust Silas needed to advance.

"Shall we make the list of munitions next?" Silas now offered and Dickinson reached for another stack of pages. The list of armaments was costlier than the food, clothing, and medical supplies combined. Although, Silas knew it likely meant the army was to engage soon, and his strongbox would only grow heftier with each battle—providing the Army could survive even one. They had yet to fight.

"Excuse me, sirs." A young rider stepped into the tent, his ragged clothes sodden from a drizzling rain. He looked between the two men. "Mr. Hastings?"

When Silas nodded, the boy shoved a letter at him and swiftly exited. Silas turned the letter over in his hands. The handwriting was smudged, unfamiliar. Only his name was on it. A black wax seal intact.

"'Tis your first letter from home since we arrived!" Dickinson smiled with the same familial warmth he had each time a letter arrived from his wife.

Silas feigned a smile. *Home.* There was no one, and no place, to call that. "Excuse me a moment, sir."

"Of course," Dickinson shooed him away with a warm wave.

Silas retreated to the corner of the tent and broke the seal. The letter contained a time. A well-drawn map. And the words, *come alone.*

Perhaps at last, my little spy finally has returned, Silas thought.

He checked his pocket watch. *Click.* The rendezvous was two hours from now. He tucked the letter into his breast pocket, and returned to the table. *Snap.*

"Shall we finish this one list?" Silas picked up his quill again, but his knee bounced, counting out each passing second. The location was a few miles outside of Fort Washington. He'd have to leave soon.

"Everything quite alright, Mr. Hastings?" Dickinson asked reaching to pat Silas' arm again.

Silas stiffened once more. "Just a note from a friend."

"You look as worn out as I feel." Dickinson stretched his arms overhead. "Let us call it a night, shall we?"

"Yes, sir." Silas gathered up the pages, trying not to show his haste. Soon, and as swift as he could, he was on a horse heading east.

* * *

Silas waited where the road zig-zagged east then south. His horse was tied to the fence post at the edge of a farm, next to a twisted tree. He looked down the crooked road in both directions. Empty. Just as he was thinking he'd come to the wrong spot, a two-horse landau came clattering over the rise in the road, bathed in purple twilight.

"Get in," the coachman said, his face half in shadow as the carriage bumped to a stop.

Since when does my little spy have the means for such luxurious transport? Silas wondered. He sniffed at the driver's curtness and yanked open the door.

"How the hell do you—" Silas' hand froze on the open door.

Inside, two older men sat side-by-side, their faces grim under the dim light of an oil lantern. Both attired in British uniforms.

Recognition swirled through Silas. Several months and miles of ocean had not been enough to dampen his memory of their portraits or the family history he'd learned while in London. His hands grew cold.

"The Howe brothers."

"Get in and shut the door, Mr. Hastings," the older of the two ordered. Admiral Richard Howe had a boyish face with a half-lidded, brooding expression. Commander of the Fleet of the Royal Navy, he was often called "Black Dick" for a face darkened by years at sea, and the somber soul that had grown with it.

Silas felt commanded to do as told.

Silas knew the younger man was General William Howe of the British Army, though the puffy eyes were closer to that of aging drunk. He'd fought alongside colonists in the Seven Years' War. Silas had heard the King had sent the brothers in the hopes that their well-known admiration for the colonists would bring the rebels back in line. At the very least, it was thought they'd uphold the reputation their eldest brother had earned when he died in defense of the colonies during the French-Indian war.

Silas wondered what could they possibly want with him, when the admiral got right to it.

"We know you are helping Congress build at least one armory, and that you slide requests through a drunken Quartermaster. All the while Congress unwittingly pays your supply company."

Silas sank back against the cushions. He'd been so careful to tell no one. Dickinson, in the chaos of preparing for New York, had entrusted Silas to file new supply agents' applications and manage their payments. Coupled with having listed his own supply business under an assumed name, the trail to him should have been cold.

"How did you—"

"Silver acquires anything desired," the general sniffed, his gaze directed out the window toward the descending darkness. Silas was unsurprised by his aloof, pompous airs. Born into a privilege to which they'd become accustomed, the Howes' mother had spent her life in the King's Court.

"What do you intend to do about—"

"At first, we thought to eliminate those supplying arms to the rebels," the admiral's words hung in the air. Silas prayed for the word "but" to follow. Seconds ticked by.

"But I'm not fond of bloodshed," the general conceded, his brow furrowed.

Relief thrummed in Silas' ears, though he knew the statement to be true. The general, insistent on fighting with European tactics upon unfamiliar American terrain, had incurred great losses at the Battle of Bunker Hill in 1775. Although he'd succeeded in taking the hill and Boston, that winter Howe refused to fight. Some said it was to console his pride over the two thousand men he'd lost in the city he'd won.

"Yes, well," the admiral said, "we also figure a man whose actions are undetected to both his employer and Congress might be more valuable alive. In exchange for two things."

"Which are?" Silas asked, his relief replaced with a foreboding curiosity.

"We become silent partners in your supply business," the admiral said.

"And you inform me of the whereabouts of the rebel army," his brother added.

Although his life might depend on saying yes, Silas hesitated. "Partners? Why?"

"The Continentals are not the only army in need of supplies." The admiral waved a hand dismissively, his gold ring catching the light from the oil lantern. "Buying munitions in the colonies, means less time waiting for shipments from overseas."

"So like me, you profit from the business your government funds," Silas said. The two men nodded, but still Silas puzzled. Being part of the business seemed at odds with their second request, so he asked, "But why have me spy for you? Profit is reliant on war. If I tell you where the army is, you could swiftly end this."

"Or not," the general said. His heavy lids didn't blink.

Silas fully realized their end game: Agree to suppress a rebellion far from home, then use that distance as a veil to amass a fortune with the very funds the King provides to achieve a goal you've never fully committed to. Perhaps this was some twisted retribution by the Howes against the Crown. Although their mother had been at court, the rumors in London indicated their grandmother was merely the mistress of King George the first. Regardless of their reasons, one thing was clear. Although the King believed he sent his greatest advocates, he had failed to see their love of fortune was greater than fidelity to anyone but themselves.

"More time means more money," was all Admiral Howe said.

Silas could hear the watch ticking in his pocket. *Tick tock*. How much more time? he wondered. How long before it would be enough? When would he at last be free?

"We are giving you options," General Howe said.

"You can promise to fill the holes in our pockets," this time the admiral held Silas' eye, "or we'll promise you one six feet deep and find someone else."

Silas thought back on the oath he'd made Peter sign. The same oath he'd signed in front of Dickinson upon becoming his secretary. A promise to support the colonies. Only the colonies. Then he recalled learning the philosophy of Machiavelli: 'The promise given was a necessity of the past; the word broken is a necessity of the present.'

Silas looked out the coach window, his breath ragged. The last few minutes had drawn night fully down, obscuring his vision. He couldn't see the horizon that stretched beyond the crooked stile where his horse was hitched. He thought about running toward the small stash of money buried at the grave. Was it enough to disappear? To begin again as someone else? If he made it past the coachman…

Tick. What choice do I have? *Tock.* None. And what of my promise to myself? Isn't *my* end game never having to rely on, or be beholden to, anyone again?

Silas squared his shoulders. "I will need a signed pass if I am to bring information inside British lines. Now that we agree your goal is to keep me alive."

CHAPTER TWENTY

ARTHUR SHIVERED. AN EARLY fall chill cut through his skin in the trenches along Bedford Road. He repositioned his feet in the muck, his boots sucking at the mud. He'd dozed off again, upright with his forehead against the butt of his rifle. He rubbed his damp sleeve across his runny nose, smelling the watermelon upon his cuff.

Last night, along with a light infantry, including four other boys from Berks County, he'd been roused and sent to guard the junction of the Gowanus Road and the Martense Lane Pass, two roads that met at the Red Lion Inn. Jimmy Sanders from two farms over had come carrying the Brown Bess his father had used in the Seven Years' War. Matthew, Harold, and Jonathan Thomson—the miller's triplets from Kutztown—sported a random collection of fowling pieces and blunderbusses they all hoped still fired. Not once in the four weeks since leaving Philadelphia had they been tested. The Third Battalion had only marched and dug trenches and marched and felled trees and marched some more.

Last evening, their reconnaissance mission had been a break from the monotony of camping on Brooklyn Heights for several days. For the five of them sent toward the inn, it had yielded a field of luscious watermelon. Arthur had gorged himself until distant rifle fire interrupted their feast. They had quickly retreated beyond a line of oaks. Jimmy hid by his side, still smacking his lips. The three Thomson brothers were tucked behind a nearby boulder as if they were one, as always. Just before midnight, Jimmy pointed down the lane. A long column snaked over a mile toward the shore, coming up the road from Denyse's Ferry. Cannons and horses amid nearly five thousand men in blood-red woolen jackets.

The boys had run back inside the fortifications, and relayed their report to General Putnam. It had been two in the morning when Arthur and his friends climbed back into the trenches at the Heights.

Night had drifted into morning, and now Arthur drifted in and out remembering the sweetness of the pink, juicy fruit rolling down his parched throat.

Then the first bang startled Arthur awake.

He looked to the sky, filling with fleeing birds.

Please don't be a storm like six days ago, he pleaded. The memory of that thrashing made him shiver. Black, booming clouds had swirled over New York for no fewer than three hours, leaving Arthur to fear he'd never hear again. Sheets of rain and wind washed away their tents and campfires. The morning after the storm, the battalion stood in thick puddles of mud collected in the trenches, up to Arthur's waist in some sections, as reports of the devastation in Manhattan trickled into the lines. Three soldiers had been killed in the city by lightening, coins melted in their very pockets.

But today, the day was dawning clear. Blue. Arthur rubbed his eyes. He readjusted his canteen over his shoulder with his possibles bag.

A second blast rang out. Cannon.

Arthur's blood thrummed in time with a distant drum. Beating. Beating in the distance. Coming closer. Colonel Atlee and General Stirling were yelling orders. Closer still. Finally, Arthur thought, I am to fight.

Gone was the ache in his back. He felt his rifle, light in his hands, and not the blisters on his palms. He could no longer feel the wetness of his socks, but only the tension twitching in his legs.

They came out of the woods down in the valley. Red coats, shoulder-to-shoulder. Dressed so alike they had become one. As dense as a swarm of wasps. A thousand yards away. A front line of soldiers three men deep, filled the entire width of the open field. Eight hundred yards away. Behind the line, column after column of men. Thousands of black shoes in step, trampling the grasses, in time to the *rat-a-tat-tat* of the drum. Five hundred yards. Muskets held taut over their left shoulders. Bayonets pointed straight at the sky. Flags held high. An order was given to halt. Three hundred yards. The wave of men rippled to a standstill. Cannon rolled and bumped to a stop.

For a long, full minute, the fields were silent. Birds chirped. Grass grains floated like angels between the armies. The wind moaned. It pulled at the amber stalks waving in the morning sun.

Arthur could see their faces. Hear his own breath.

He glanced sideways to view his own line. Next to him, Jimmy shouldered his Brown Bess. Beyond him, men and boys. All in a row. Their own clothes and faces the color of dirt. The color of rocks upon which they lay. Arthur's stomach lurched. He swallowed back the taste of tin in his mouth. He tugged down his hat, pulling tightly on the leather stitching.

"The day is ours!" A man in the rebel line cried out.

Arthur cheered with the other four thousand rebels lining the high ground.

The redcoats in the first row kneeled.

"Ready!"

Arthur heard Stirling's command coming from behind, raised his loaded rifle to his shoulder. He aimed at the enemy line. A wind blew lightly across the back of his neck.

"Fire!"

Arthur pulled the trigger. *Ka–crack.*

The crack and pop of thousands of weapons firing at once shattered in Arthur's ears. Cannon fire blasted. Drumbeats thumped out orders. Kneel! Aim! Fire! *Ka–crack.* Rebel cannons thundered over his head. The trench wall rained earth down on him with each blast. Powder. Ram. Tamp. Resheath. Full-cock. Fire! *Ka–crack.* Redcoats dropped. Living bodies moved up, filling the holes of the fallen. Advancing. Firing. Falling. Advancing. British bullets and shells tore into the rebel trenches. Ten yards to Arthur's right, a cannonball ripped through the flimsy fortification like threadbare fabric. Arthur threw himself over Jimmy as the blast sent bodies up to heaven and straight down to hell. Dirt, rocks, and branches spiraled out in all directions plowing through the men.

As the last clumps of dust fell around them, coating their faces, Arthur and Jimmy pulled apart. Jimmy threw him a quick "Thanks" and they reloaded together. As Arthur bent his head to reach for his gunpowder horn at his waist, he heard a whistle and smack. Jimmy dropped into the mud, his eyes staring lifeless up at Arthur. Part of Jimmy's head and ear were missing. Arthur stared. His mouth suddenly dry.

"Fire!"

The order drew Arthur's attention back to his rifle. Arthur reloaded as Jimmy's blood swirled in the mud at his feet, but his hands shook as he poured gunpowder from the horn. He licked his lips, tasting dust. And gunpowder. And Jimmy's splattered blood. Ram. Tamp. Ready. Time both sped up and slowed down as he swung his loaded rifle back to his shoulder. Aim!

But where?

The field was awash in gun smoke. Gunfire seemed to come from every direction. Drums. Screams. Orders. It was more blinding and deafening than the thunderous storm. One loud reverberating hum. Arthur had no choice but to simply aim south. Shoot and reload. Powder. Ram. Tamp. Fire. *Ka–crack.* Powder. Ram. Tamp. Fire. *Ka–crack…*

For three more hours.

Arthur's limbs ached. He could see redcoats coming closer through the choking air. There were gaps in their ranks. Weakened. But too close. Arthur struggled to get his footing in the mud. In the blood and debris. Fatigue and panic shook in him. He fought the urge to run. Then he heard Colonel Atlee yelling through the confusion.

"Move out! Retreat! Retreat!"

Arthur obeyed. He turned to climb out of the trench but twisted bodies lay between himself and the back of the trench. He had to get over them. He had to crawl over them. He tried to ignore their faces but they swam up toward him. Jimmy. Davis. Middleton. Peyton. Peyton? He was only twelve years old. A drummer. Arthur shook him, convinced the boy was calling to him. Impossible. Cannon fire had severed him.

Arthur's lips curled tightly. Rage poured into him like water. His mind emptied. His body coursed with the full rush of adrenaline. He turned to fire south again. *Ka–crack.* Reload… But Atlee was at his elbow.

"Move, move, move!" He shoved Arthur up the wall. Arthur climbed the trench reaching back to pull Atlee with him. From the high ground, Arthur had mere seconds to see it all. Cold fear coursed through him.

The four thousand British soldiers they'd been fighting all morning had merely been pinning the Continental Army in their trenches, keeping their naïve heads turned south while General Howe had brought British and Hessians from the north and the east around the unguarded Jamaica Pass.

Ten thousand of them.

Now, all the enemy's forces converged on the rebellion. Swarms of British breached the rebel trenches. Firing. Running men through with their bayonets. Arthur heard Atlee shout again.

"Retreat, Bowman! Retreat!"

Arthur dropped his canteen and ran. He ran northwest with the others toward Gowanus Creek. All his power focused on pushing his own legs forward. Moving in the only direction he knew to go. Away from all thoughts of pride and glory. To life.

Time evaporated. All his senses ceased. Men and trees blurred past him in all directions. Sound left the world as he ran. Dodged. Ducked. Silent shells flew past his closed ears taking down men around him. Smoke and haze clouded the air. But Arthur's eyes were only focused on the creek ahead. On the marsh. On himself.

If he could just reach it… Cross it…

Fifty feet. Twenty feet. Five feet. He threw himself at the water. The surface around him burst with bullet fire. Arthur grabbed his hat from his head, held his breath and dove under. *Swim! Swim like Kalawi taught you.* His aching arms pulled at the murky, muddy water. Hat in one hand. Rifle in the other. Down below then breaking the surface. Gasping for air. Down again. And up again. He felt a limb under his feet. Another. And another. At last he pulled himself up the bank on the other side.

Heaving. Dripping. Covered in filth and leaves and mud. He turned back and looked across the marsh, five hundred yards away. A long, thick, red, bloody line of Redcoats moved in. They fell on the rebels submerged in the muddy banks. Redcoats shot. Redcoats dove. Redcoats shoved. Pushing men down with their shoes.

"Swim!" Arthur heard himself yell. But the rebels weren't. Couldn't. They were sinking. Drowning. While the British gathered like cheerful spectators at a fair, watching them go down.

Arthur dropped to his knees. The scene muddied by his own tears.

"Arthur? Help us."

Arthur blinked. Harold and Matthew Thomson were struggling up the bank. They carried their brother Jonathan between them, his head rolled back on his shoulders. Matthew's right arm was gone from his shoulder, the fabric of his sleeve hanging in wet shards. His whitened face was contorted with pain. Arthur scrambled toward them, and helped them onto the grass.

"We must keep moving," Arthur heard his own voice return. "Get back to the Heights."

He stepped between Matthew's good arm and Jonathan's limp frame. Matthew leaned hard against him and the four moved together. Two carrying two. They dragged themselves back inside Fort Putnam. The cries of those still fighting and lying and dying in the fields echoed across the smoke-filled valley.

* * *

Jonathan Thomson died within half an hour of returning to camp. Triplets, now twins. Arthur was helping his brothers lay him in one of the many rows of the dead when an aide strode up to him.

"Colonel Atlee and General Stirling have not returned, nor has his aide."

Arthur faltered. He could have sworn Atlee had been next to him when they'd retreated. Had he not?

"You have been promoted. First Lieutenant," the man said as he handed over a letter. "See this message gets to General Washington at Cobble Hill Fort immediately."

Arthur nodded. He pulled together what little energy he had left and forced himself onto the nearest horse, pushing the animal at full gallop for the mile and a half ride. On the hill, he found General Washington searching the battlefields through a scope, a few staff members also looking on. Arthur hesitated, unsure of what to say to his commander, to the man who had seriously underestimated the battle still raging below.

"An urgent message, sir," was all he could muster.

Washington pulled his gaze from the scope, his face tired and drawn, his blue-gray eyes even with Arthur's. The general's hands shook as he opened and read the note. Wind tugged at strands of his reddish hair that had come loose from its tie.

"Please wait for a response," Washington asked, his voice thin. He returned his eye to his scope.

"Yes, sir." Arthur stepped aside.

From the high vantage, Arthur could see the trenches and the marsh where he had just been, and the nearby old stone house. The farm was a defense point where Howe's army from the north, the Hessians from the east and Grant's and Cornwallis' troops from the south were about to collide. Moving west away from it, Major Mordecai Gist and his colonial Maryland soldiers were in retreat. But then, he suddenly turned them back. Another wave of rebels was trying to escape across the Gowanus Marsh and Gist was clearly intent on giving them time to do so.

"But the Marylanders have never yet fought," Washington whispered, his knuckles white on his spyglass. "They'll be slaughtered."

Arthur forced himself to watch. The four hundred Marylanders threw themselves into the fray. They rallied together. Once… Twice… Five times they pushed against the British army five times their size until battle smoke surrounded the small stone house.

Arthur searched through the waning light and thickening haze, the cries from below rising, falling, diminishing. Until a frightening, sad silence with the echo of death in it rose up from the valley. Washington let the lens drop by his side and closed his eyes. "Good God, what brave fellows I must this day lose."

* * *

The next morning, Arthur documented the losses, part of his duties as First Lieutenant. But his hand was unsteady, the letters ill-formed.

Began 27 August as an army of 11,000 upon Long Island.
4000 engaged in the Battle of Brooklyn. Killed: 1000. Captured: 1000
Mordecai Gist and his men returned to camp just after sunrise 28 August.
There were eight.
391 Marylanders have perished. Overnight.

Arthur hated his words. They were cold. A final score in a horrific game. He added another line. A more telling truth.

The army, along with General Washington, lined the road to greet the survivors, our hats in hand and not one dry eye among us.

Arthur felt dread in his bones over what was still to come. The remaining nine thousand men of the Colonial Army were now trapped at Fort Putnam. Behind them was the East River. Their own spies told them this morning that nearly fifteen thousand British troops were digging trenches toward them. The redcoats were awaiting an order from General Howe to breach the lines and end the war.

Was there nothing to do but wait? Arthur wondered.

Arthur waited all day. Not eating. All night. Not sleeping. And the next day he was asked to join a small number of aides and officers at Washington's request. As a wind bit at their cheeks, Arthur, along with the others, promised secrecy.

"Praise be to God," Washington whispered to them as he pointed across to Manhattan. "We must transport everyone and everything—men and munitions—over the East River. We will retreat into New York. Tonight. Try to do so without being heard." His eyes were filled with sadness and, what worried Arthur more, doubt.

That night, Arthur helped lift men into the boats, but his muscles trembled and throbbed. The last rock-hard biscuit he had eaten—he could not recall when—had left him with only a broken front tooth.

As he turned to help the next man he faltered. It was Joshua, Lydia's boy from the Bowman house, his blond hair and angelic face smeared with mud and his body leaning heavily to take the weight off a battered leg. Arthur reached for Joshua's hand—two men once of different stations, now suffering for the same cause—and helped him into the boat.

Joshua mustered a barely audible, "Thanks, Arthur," but little else.

Arthur looked back toward the fort they were leaving. Tents, food, and supplies scattered the beaches. The line of men stretched a quarter of a mile from shore. With their packs, horses, and munitions, thousands of men huddled together. Yet, like Joshua, barely a sound did they utter.

To be quiet is easy, Arthur thought. We are far too tired, hungry, worried, grieving, or injured. And now there was a fog moving in. It surrounded them, collected on him. It turned the dust and blood and filth still stuck to his clothes and hat and skin to mud. But it wasn't enough to wash away the images he still carried, or the emptiness for all the men who would not be coming with them.

Jimmy. Peyton. Jonathan.

Arthur pushed the choking memories aside, comforted by one distant, soulful, yet familiar sound. The long cry of a wolf. He reached for the hand of the next man waiting to board the boat.

"Praise be to God," the man whispered, "let this fog be a miracle for our crossing."

CHAPTER TWENTY-ONE

NATHANIEL WAS FINALLY DRYING out. The sky had opened up within an hour of leaving Stratford Hall, preventing him from reaching Leed's Ferry at the Rappahannock before the last crossing at nightfall. High waters kept away the ferrymen for another few days. As he waited, he'd reviewed Franklin's maps and made adjustments for where landmarks or post roads had changed, in a few cases making new illustrations altogether. He pressed into his journal a few of the plants, new to him, from along the banks.

When he was underway again, Nathaniel applauded Jefferson. Virginia was a wondrous landscape that seemed not only to have been touched by the hand of God, but formed in the very shape of it. Streams and rivers from distant Western Blue Ridge mountains meandered across farm lands like veins on the back of a flattened, youthful hand. Four abundant rivers—the Potomac, the Rappahannock, the York, and the James—each dotted with burgeoning farms and plantations, flowed eastward with the tides toward the Chesapeake Bay. The beauty of the rolling land, free of the sharp rock outcroppings and thick forests of Pennsylvania, registered deeply with Nathaniel, a feeling he could only describe as coming home.

Home.

As he now pushed Bayard forward in the dark, he realized construction was due to begin back home in a few days, on September first. And soon his father would begin mass-producing weapons for an army fighting against his mother's own people.

I cannot stop any of it from beginning, Nathaniel thought, but I hope to end it.

Hope.

That word was too tenuous without action behind it. Nathaniel rubbed his face to ward off sleep, determined to ride on despite the late hour. But as Bayard sauntered, a summer night symphony weighed Nathaniel down. Cicada bugs rattled hollow songs. The crickets sung back a softer echo. Bayard's hooves scuffed the gravel of the barren post road. And Nathaniel's eyes closed of their own accord. He began to slip sideways from the saddle, but caught himself.

It was too late to find a tavern, so to Bayard he said, "Come on, I bet you are tired, too."

He dismounted and Bayard dutifully followed him off the curving trail into a clearing surrounded by chestnut trees, the undergrowth a patchwork quilt of shadowy leaves and moonlight. From this hollow, the trees sheltered him from the road, but Nathaniel could still see it stretching eastward toward the next ferry landing. He tied off Bayard and stretched out on a bed roll, his satchel and rifle at his side. He pulled a handkerchief over his face to keep the irritating mosquitoes at bay that had been sniping and trying to feast on him all day. With the warm, late August wind as his blanket, Nathaniel blew out a full breath through puffed cheeks. The tip of the scarf flipped up. He was asleep before the scarf fell back to his chin.

* * *

First, the warm breeze ceased to blow. The temperature in the chestnut grove fell. In came the fog. Licking the ground. It enveloped the brush. The roots. The trunks of trees. Nathaniel stirred under its cool caress. Then, ringing sharply through the silence... *Snap.* A branch cracked.

Nathaniel sat up and strained to look through the haze. Leaves rustled. Another branch snapped. The haze took shape, like one of the tree roots brought to life. First one long leg, then another. Gray. No. White, like the fog.

His wolf. Their wolf.

Nathaniel relaxed his hand that had instinctively gripped his rifle.

He felt all his fears subside, and stretched out his arm, palm open. She stepped forward, her deep-set eyes holding his. Warm breath puffed from her black nose. When her head was even with his hand, she leaned into his hand. Her dense, soft fur spilled from between his fingers. Then, with a blink and a nod, she turned back toward the trees. As she moved away, Nathaniel trailed his hand down her back to the tip of her tail. At the edge of the clearing, she pushed her head up high. She let out a guttural howl ending with a whistling cry that wrapped all around him. Then she abruptly turned and ran toward the approaching sunrise, gathering the fog and taking it with her.

And Nathaniel awoke.

The air in the grove was as sticky as it had been the night before. He scrambled to his feet and searched the forest. He looked down the road toward the ferry. A lone figure on horseback was moving toward the river. A short man on a black horse. Blue coat. The man turned in his saddle to look back. Nathaniel ducked behind a tree, his heart loud in his ears. When he peered at the road again, the distant figure was moving toward the ferry.

Thank you, wolf, Nathaniel thought, now I am the one to follow.

Nathaniel unhitched Bayard, and pulled him onto a game trail edging the road. Slowly and deftly, out of the range of sound, Nathaniel picked his way on foot. At a turn in the road, just before the ferry, Nathaniel pulled out his own scope. He raised it to his eye, just as the rider turned back to search the road again.

"What's this?" Nathaniel whispered.

The blue coat ballooned around a small frame. That angelic face with long lashes. It was the boy from the ferry into Maryland, not more than eleven or twelve years old. Why would such a young boy be following him? Nathaniel briefly considered what to do as the boy boarded the ferry. With little more thought, he swiftly mounted Bayard. He dropped down out of the trees onto the dusty road. With dirt kicking up behind them, he let Bayard run out hard, flat.

"Hold the ferry!" he yelled.

One of the ferryman waved in agreement.

The kid stood wide-eyed as Nathaniel rode straight onto the ferry, Bayard stomping and frantic. A ferryman stepped in and tied off Bayard as Nathaniel dismounted. The chaos trapped the boy at the back of the boat.

"Shove off," Nathaniel told the ferryman as he slid from the saddle, and grabbed a small rope looped on his pack. "The horse will calm as you row."

The instant the ramp was up and they had pulled from shore, Nathaniel pounced on the boy. He grabbed the collar of the child's coat and flipped him face-first onto a crate. He bound the boy's hands like the legs of the sheep on Arthur's farm in sheering season.

"Who are you?" Nathaniel said, as the boy scuffled and squirmed. Bayard swung under his ties. The boat rocked from side-to-side.

"What the devil!" a ferryman attempted to hold Bayard as his boat mate tried to steady the raft.

"I won't say nothin'," the boy growled through his upright cheek. He clamped his mouth tight, squeezing his whole face toward the tip of his nose.

"He's a spy," Nathaniel said. He sat the boy upright, holding him tight as he squirmed against the ties. The comment gave the ferrymen pause, and neither man dared asked for which side. "Get us quickly to the other side, gentlemen."

As the ferrymen rowed, Nathaniel ran through what to do. There was no way to confirm if farms or towns on his way to Williamsburg were loyalist or rebel, so he could not turn the kid in just anywhere, especially if the boy knew what he carried. Nathaniel groaned. He had no choice but to take the boy to Wythe's home, still a three-day ride. When the ferry pulled to the far shore, Nathaniel paid the wary ferrymen and carried the boy onto land. He weighed less than his saddle. Nathaniel strapped the boy to the black horse, which he tethered to Bayard, and began to move them all south and east.

The whole of the day, Nathaniel tried to coax a confession. Kindness, promises, anger. No matter his tactic, the boy refused to speak. That first night, Nathaniel offered half the squirrel he caught and roasted. The boy looked away, but the tip of his tongue belied his hunger as it darted out between parched lips. Nathaniel gave up and soon turned in. The satchel at his own waist. The boy's hands and feet bound.

But in the middle of the night he heard the buckle of his pack jangle. He grabbed at his bag. Open. He looked up and saw the boy disappear into the trees, the Declaration clasped in his hand.

A quarter hour later, Nathaniel dragged the limp boy back to camp. "You don't eat, so you are weak, and you leave more tracks than an injured elk."

He could not risk him running off again, and clearly the boy had wriggled out of ties like that before. He tethered the boy to Bayard and to himself, the ropes taut between all three. "Each time you move, we all move."

None of them slept more than a few minutes at a time. By the third night, Nathaniel's fatigue caused him to miss what would have normally been an easy shot at a rabbit.

"Now we're both going to bed hungry," he said as he tied the rope end to his own waist. The boy turned away, yanking hard. Nathaniel yanked it back. Bayard protested. When at last they all settled, Nathaniel took in a deep breath and blew it toward the sky.

He had slept beneath that sparkling blanket of stars so often with Kalawi and Arthur during their long hunting treks. He winced over a past that now seemed painfully simple; three young heads together, sharing stories until their full bellies dragged them to sleep.

He looked over at the boy. The blue, tattered coat over thin frame and an empty stomach. Bound to a desperate life, disposed to suffer. Were these to be the boy's childhood memories? Nathaniel wondered. Or did this boy also pray every night for his life to alter, for his own independence? And this document Nathaniel carried, could it affect change for someone so less endowed than a man like Richard Henry Lee?

"One document for all?" Nathaniel whispered. He wondered if Wythe, whom Franklin said was a professor of law, might have an answer to that question. More important, he hoped Wythe would still be in Williamsburg when he and the boy arrived.

CHAPTER TWENTY-TWO

"WHAT DO YOU MEAN GONE?" General Clinton's face was bright red. Under his thick fist, the pens on the table jumped, but the two brothers across from him in the tent at British Headquarters remained calm.

"The rebels have retreated to Manhattan." Admiral Howe lounged in a chair, his legs outstretched and crossed at the ankles.

General Howe stood by, gripping a cup of warm milk.

"But they were here on Long Island last night, bringing in the dead." Clinton stabbed his finger at a report on the table. "Are you telling me they moved nine thousand soldiers, and no one saw or heard a goddamn thing?" Spit flew from his mouth onto the table, and his body seemed wont to burst from a uniform too tight for his rounded frame.

"You waited." Clinton shook a finger at General Howe's face, five inches above his own. "We had them trapped inside Fort Putnam with the East River gushing up their backsides! We had them from three sides. Squeezed. My plan could have ended this!"

"I lost sixty-one men on Brooklyn Heights. Over two hundred were wounded and I will not risk…," the general rubbed his forehead. "No, that's enough losses for one week."

"And the river was so swift, we could not move the fleet up." The admiral puzzled over his own boots. "When that fog of provenance rolled in to mask their movements… well, it seems the rebels received a miracle."

"This is a war, gentlemen, not a Sunday picnic ruined by unfortunate weather." Clinton pounded the table again. "We have ten thousand troops sitting here doing nothing!"

"So, you must go devise a new plan," General Howe tilted his head toward the report papers on the table.

Clinton's mouth fell open. "Would you like me to include where you can deviate from this one?"

"*You* are required to make plans," General Howe growled. "*We* are not required to follow them."

Clinton's face turned solid purple. He snatched up the pile of papers and stormed out, taking most of the tension with him.

After a few moments of silence, the general inhaled a ragged breath and turned his attention to the darkened corner of the tent. "Please join us." He extended a hand toward the table. "We are grateful for you having told us of the retreat."

Silas Hastings stepped to the middle of the tent. After watching the Howes treat their own general with such disdain, Silas was relieved to hear words of gratitude come his way.

"I trust no one knows you are here?" Admiral Howe asked.

"My superiors believe I have gone straight to Philadelphia with their munitions request." Silas patted his breast pocket. A part of him had cringed when he'd lied to Dickinson, who seemed able to sustain loyalty despite Washington's abhorrent failings at Long Island, but the idea of the Howes putting Silas into an early grave, made it easier to ride east after promising to head south.

General Howe took a sheet of paper from a lockbox and pushed it across the table. Silas reviewed the list of bayonets, musket balls, and an extraordinary number of firearms.

"This is far more than I expected." With the increased needs, Silas applauded his own wherewithal to have contracted with two other armories already in production. And yet, if orders of this magnitude kept coming, construction in Berks County would have to accelerate, or at the least, Peter would need to supply whatever firearms the Marten gun shop had finished.

"By not taking Fort Putnam last night, there is more fighting ahead," the general said. "About eighteen thousand hired German mercenaries and

Hessians are en route to join us. When they do we'll cross over and take—"

"Manhattan," Silas whispered. He shivered, relieved he might be south of whatever might be unleashed upon the island. "Why take the city?"

"The King, like Clinton, thinks the colonists need to be punished like insolent children. Lord Germain, who is over us, wants to convert them back to Loyalists. Either way I need to push on, because more rebels join the damn fight by the day." The general rubbed at his brow again, pinching it with fingers and thumb. "I came here believing this rebellion was a small uprising, but it's a rising epidemic. No wonder I've this bloody headache."

"That hangover is not from fighting," the admiral scoffed at his own brother, then turned to Silas. "Until our command can agree on a strategy, we will continue to keep things moving at our pace. And for our supply business."

"And in silver only," the general said as he bent, and lifted a chest from the floor. He slid it across the table. "Paper Continentals are guaranteed to soon devalue—a few of our men have stolen a printing press."

Silas' thoughts raced to the bills he'd hidden. If the British printed more Continental currency, then every dollar he had in that grave would be as worthless to him as the man buried with it. He stared at the chest of silver and slipped the munitions list into the same coat pocket with the rebel's request.

"One more request," Admiral Howe unfolded from the chair. "We decided we want a man of ours overseeing the armory you're building."

"You doubt my ability to deliver?"

"Not after the last bit of news you relayed," the admiral chortled, and he handed Silas a sheet of paper with a man's name and location scrawled on it. "But you can't be everywhere. We simply want this Mr. Dawes ensuring progress, that the weapons are divided appropriately."

"And the funds for him?" Silas asked.

The general produced another bag of silver. He slid it toward Silas, but with his hand still on the pouch he added, "Now tell me where I'm to find Washington's army on Manhattan."

CHAPTER TWENTY-THREE

RELIEF FLOODED NATHANIEL. WILLIAMSBURG. September third. Thankfully, the boy had remained silent when a lone man near the edge of town pointed them toward the Wythe house.

The charm of the still sleeping capital city turned even the boy's head. Duke of Gloucester Street was lined with homes and taverns not yet open. Shop windows begged for pressed noses. Shoes were hung by the tongues at the cobbler's. The millinery displayed straw brims with ribbons that gaily beckoned despite gray skies.

Nathaniel turned onto Palace Green. The small, white fences surrounding the houses on either side had been built to keep the livestock out of yards, rather than in. Goats, sheep, and cattle grazed on a central carpet of emerald grass running several hundred yards up to a palatial home. Guarded by a curved brick wall, the estate faced down the palace lawn like a crown atop the head of town.

To his right, Nathaniel heard the familiar *tink-tink* of iron on iron—the hammering of a rifle barrel. It came from a small shed, over which a sign swung in the breeze. *Gunsmith.* Guilt sagged his shoulders over not having stood next to his father these last weeks, but he turned away with the recognition that not once had he missed a single moment of the work.

He tied the two horses to the metal ring on the white hitching post outside a two-story red brick residence. With the sullen boy tethered to him and lagging behind, Nathaniel climbed the steps to the double front door. He was about to knock when the door swung open.

"Oh, dear me!" a pale woman dropped a Bible and it thumped to the wide-planked floor. As Nathaniel retrieved the book and handed it to her, a man came into the house at the opposite end of the hall. He wore a thick green robe and slippers. He came down the hall, whistling and toweling at the wet, white hair encircling a balding head.

"May we help you?" The woman warmly nodded her thanks to Nathaniel. Her smile faded as she saw the rope trailing to the boy's bound wrists.

"Mrs. Wythe?" Nathaniel asked. When she nodded, he said, "I am Nathaniel Mirtle. I believe your husband is expecting me."

At the mention of the name, the man in the robe scurried to the front door. "'Tis me! We have been anxiously awaiting your arrival." He ushered them inside, closed the door, and nodded to the boy. "And what is this?"

"There's a story there, but perhaps…" Nathaniel nodded to the man's remaining hair, quite wild around his head.

"Forgive me!" Wythe attempted to pat down his hair and then clenched at the open flaps of his robe. "You have caught me after my morning shower. I shall make myself presentable. Mrs. Wythe, please show them to my study."

Nathaniel tied the boy to a chair in the modest room at the back of the house that overlooked an English-style, symmetrical garden. As they waited, Nathaniel spied a brass and wooden microscope, a blue butterfly wing pinned below it. He'd read about the device in Franklin's almanac. He put his eye to it.

"Look at that!" Nathaniel thought it looked like a slate roof, with little blue tiles overlapping one another. Next to it on the roll-top desk was a well-thumbed pamphlet, *Opticks* by Isaac Newton. A mechanical device with metal arms and orbs indicating planetary positions was labeled with a tag that read *orrery*.

The boy, still silent, gaped at a row of jars atop of one of the cabinets. The glass vessels contained rats, frogs, snakes, and other small creatures; all of them suspended in a liquid-filled death. Nathaniel and the boy both dragged their eyes from the contents as Wythe entered.

"We must study nature to know who we are." Wythe said as he closed the door. "Now, Mr. Mirtle, I know why you are here… but what about this one?" He waggled a finger at the boy.

Nathaniel summed up the last few days.

Wythe rubbed at his clean-shaven jaw. "He has not said a word as to why he was following you?"

"His mouth is as tight as Dick's hatband."

Wythe chuckled at the old adage. "Well, son?" Wythe pulled over another chair and sat facing the boy. The boy's gaze shifted to Wythe's feet. Wythe's voice took on a firm tone. "It seems you are at risk of being labeled a spy. Given my time as a lawyer and Burgess, I am willing to hear your case. What say you?" The boy's chin began to quiver, but his lips clamped shut. Wythe sighed dramatically and added, "If you are unable to speak to the contrary, your silence shall be taken as consent. We will notify your parents, so we shall need a name if nothing else. The current punishment is death by hang—"

"Name's John, and I ain't got no folks n' I just got so hungry n' the man gave me food. Says he knows that a rider goes to Virginia. Then New York. But he promised me more to tell him what that man carries," the boy's pale face collapsed into tears as he pointed to Nathaniel. Through a mucus-filled nose, John sniffed, "Once I seen that document with all the names on it, I figure 'tis all about that."

Nathaniel groaned.

Wythe reached out and raised the boy's chin with a gentle hand. "Who gave you the money?"

"I'll be hung by you if I say nothin', and I dunno what that man'll to do me if I say somethin'." The boy shook his head, his lips sealed back together, and his shoulders shook with sobs.

Spy or not, Nathaniel slumped against the desk, overcome with pity for the boy. A hungry child; another casualty hit by the shrapnel of war. Wythe caught Nathaniel's eye over the boy's head and motioned him into the hallway.

On the other side of the closed door, Wythe whispered, "Given your expression, Mr. Mirtle, I can see we are of the same mind not to put the neck of a starving child into a noose. But we cannot simply let him go for he knows too much."

"He got into it a few nights ago," Nathaniel said, patting his satchel. As he began to say more, his stomach grumbled. Wythe looked toward the belly with raised eyebrows, but Nathaniel pointed toward the office and said, "I'm sure he is hungrier than me; he has refused food for three days. Could we feed the boy before we talk to him again?"

Wythe smiled, and clapped Nathaniel on the shoulder, "In the words of the French fabulist, Jean de La Fontaine, 'A hungry stomach cannot hear.' We shall fill you both to bursting."

* * *

Wythe had suggested they put John in the guest chamber upstairs, where Nathaniel would also stay that night, lest rumors were already rumbling about the two strangers the man saw at the edge of town.

Nathaniel realized the depth of his own hunger as he delivered a breakfast to John. Meats were piled underneath a warm Indian pudding made of eggs, cornmeal, and molasses. The cinnamon and nutmeg of the thick mixture mingled with the savory spices of the scrapple beside it. The tray had barely touched the table before John pounced upon it. At last, he eats, Nathaniel sighed.

Back downstairs in the dining room with Mr. and Mrs. Wythe, Nathaniel tried to keep some sense of decorum as the same breakfast dishes were offered to him by the servants. Their black faces contrasted with the bright green wallpaper as they bowed lightly and made to leave. Mrs. Wythe thanked them generously, but did not yet pick up her fork. Instead, she finished describing her morning visit to a neighbor.

"Mrs. Hays already had three children when her husband joined the Cause. Although the Virginia Commonwealth agreed to pay her twelve pounds for his service, she is still riddled with debts and has not been well." Townsfolk like Mrs. Wythe had stepped in to help, even though Mrs. Wythe had not yet fully recovered from her own illness. It had prevented Wythe from attending the formal signing in August.

At last she picked up her fork and said, "Do please begin, Mr. Mirtle."

Nathaniel bit into a small apricot first. It made his jaw ache. Then he tasted a spoonful of the savory pudding, letting it linger on his tongue. His whole being warmed. The last three days receded into memory, and he soon relaxed into the meal, grateful for talkative company.

Before their meal, Wythe had given Nathaniel a letter received from Franklin. Invisible ink messages were hidden within a few pages torn from another *Poor Richard's Almanack.* One page contained a chart labeled, *The Anatomy of Man's Body as Govern'd by the Twelve Constellations.* Upon it was Franklin's confirmation to sail north by the stars to New York. The other sheet contained the forecast and calendar for September. Knowing Wythe was to take him to Yorktown, Nathaniel felt confident in sharing Franklin's message with him.

"It seems Mr. Franklin will be attending peace talks with the British on Staten Island. He is to arrive September eleventh with Edward Rutledge and John Adams. I am to sail in and wait in the harbor near Sandy Point."

"He wrote to me of this, too. Your ship, the *Frontier*, arrived in Yorktown yesterday." Wythe took a drink of warm cider from his crystal goblet, and mopped his mouth with the linen. "She's under Captain Hugo Blythe from Boston—Franklin has assured me we will have no difficulty in finding him amid the dockhands or at the Custom House in Yorktown. From there, weather pending, the voyage up the coast should take about four to five days. Although, if the British are there…"

Nathaniel finished the thought, "I could be sailing the Declaration to within a hair's breadth of the lion's den."

"I believe you may face the lion itself," Mrs. Wythe said.

Nathaniel and Wythe gave her their full attention.

"Mrs. Hays shared with me a letter she received from her husband, with the third battalion in New York. His letter describes dozens of ships from Red Hook to Hell Gate. Ships beyond a soldier's desire to count, he said." Mrs. Wythe held her own heart with her palm. "Despite her own ill fortune, Mrs. Hays was nearly in fits over hearing of what her husband endures."

"Should we send you by land instead?" Wythe asked.

"We have not the time to alter Franklin's plans." Nathaniel pointed to the almanac pages. "He has told me to watch from the ship for his signal. A lantern. Three flashes and I am to continue to headquarters upon Manhattan. If it burns steady, a treaty has been reached. He begs that I use any means necessary to never surrender the document." Nathaniel swallowed back his thoughts about what 'any means' could portend.

"What about that young one up there?" Nathaniel pointed toward the guest room.

"He does not know your new plans. Why not send him back over land?"

"Give him false plans?" Nathaniel smiled. He'd be rid of the boy. His conscience relieved of any guilt. "I have a map from my route here. We can review it and find a good way to send him home."

They finished their breakfast, but Mrs. Wythe paled with each bite. She excused herself from Nathaniel, and Mr. Wythe helped his frail wife to her private chambers just off the dining room. When Wythe returned, closing the door gently behind him, he waved to Nathaniel.

"Come, Mr. Mirtle. Let us adjourn and attend to the document."

* * *

In Wythe's study, Nathaniel took the Declaration from his satchel. Wythe cleared the center table of everything but the inkstand. He pulled a pair of small round spectacles from his waistcoat and slipped them on. Leaning over the document, he read it carefully and then clapped his hands together.

"Ahh. There you are T.J." He smiled broadly, the lines around his damp eyes deepening.

"I beg your pardon, sir?" Nathaniel leaned in.

Wythe pointed to lines within the text. "That wording is from Euripides, the Greek playwright." He pointed to the statement *all men are created equal.* "And John Locke here." He pointed to the line *life, liberty, and the pursuit of happiness.* Then Wythe waved a hand over the whole parchment. "But together, all of it... well... It reads like T.J.!"

"Thomas Jefferson?" Nathaniel asked through a laugh.

"He was a gifted student." Wythe remained bent over the parchment. "I taught him about Locke who said we must uphold the very truth that man has rights to 'life, liberty and property.' You can see it here within the second section, the statement of beliefs, where he mentions inalienable rights." Wythe *tisk-tisked*. "Although it is sadly spelled incorrectly as 'unalienable.' And Mr. Jefferson has also changed the word 'property' to the 'pursuit of happiness.'"

"To some property is happiness," Nathaniel said, thinking about Peter.

"Not within our ideal." Wythe turned to face Nathaniel. "Consider this; were you happy when you ate on your journey to Williamsburg but young John did not? Or were you happier tonight when you ate after he had finally eaten?" Easily Nathaniel admitted to the latter.

"Happiness is not acquired, Mr. Mirtle. It is not taken but given. Spread. Cultivated. Mr. Jefferson uses the word happiness for he sees it is not a reward. It is a duty," Wythe emphasized the last word with his fist. "It is a debt of service. A promise to make life better, not just for oneself, but for everyone."

Was that perhaps what Peter had been doing? Had he been trying to improve the gun shop for all of them and not just his own gains? But still Nathaniel puzzled over the thought he'd had that last night in the woods with John.

"Everyone? I can see why a man like Richard Henry Lee wants independence—he has so much to lose. But will John benefit?"

"Yes, because of a few lines including this one." Wythe ran his finger along the words *deriving their just powers from the consent of the governed.* "Who grants power, according to this line?"

"The governed."

"Yes, and who gives the King his power?"

"We do."

"Not according to the King," Wythe said. Spite filled the last word and his face soured with disappointment. "The mad King George believes that *God* has granted him a divine right to rule. In his world, God rules the people. But what if the Greek philosopher Euripides was correct? What if *all* men are created equal?" Wythe paused, waiting for Nathaniel to fill in the answer.

"Then we can all choose our ruler," Nathaniel said, the concept being familiar. Even the Shawnee believed a ruler was to be chosen by the people; Kalawi would be their chief only if the tribe agreed. And even then, the tribe had equal voice in the most important decisions.

"And what does it mean if we can all choose our ruler?" Wythe asked. "We all have the ability to rule?"

"Perhaps not ability. But at the moment we are created, we do have the opportunity. Should have the opportunity. Think of young John again." Wythe waved an arm toward where the boy was hopefully now sleeping. "When he first graced the world, what did he have in comparison to King George III or Richard Henry Lee?"

"Both of those men had lineage, wealth, property. John was born with far less, I am sure," Nathaniel said, thinking of the orphan boy's ill-fitting coat, and grubby face and hands.

"You are looking externally. Look internally." Wythe tapped Nathaniel's chest and then his own forehead. "Internally we are born free. Free of thoughts and beliefs. Free of fear and prejudice. True, what, and who, surrounds us contributes to who we become… but with our first breath, we are all born free. To nurture that inalienable right to freedom, we must choose a ruler who will wisely strive to improve our collective surroundings. But men must choose the ruler. Not God. If John starves because of who rules, he must have the right to request a ruler who will help ensure there is food."

Nathaniel's earlier joy at the idea of being rid of John softened. Could that boy grow to become King? Perhaps not, but thinking of him having a voice so he didn't have to resort to crime for food set Nathaniel at ease.

"This idea that we must separate divine right from natural right, is also supported by this statement here," Wythe turned back to the document, and ran his finger along it, reading aloud. *"The separate and equal station to which the Laws of Nature and of Nature's God entitle them."*

"But that line mentions God," Nathaniel said, his confusion returning. "How can it say a leader is not divined by God, but then state that God entitles them? So now John has to rely on faith again?"

"No. It says the *Laws of Nature and of Nature's God entitles them,*" Wythe smiled wide. Nathaniel saw the same confidence Franklin had displayed when he already knew the answers, like they were both three steps ahead in a game of chess.

"Please just explain," Nathaniel begged.

Wythe patted his arm, and then retrieved the Isaac Newton pamphlet from the desk. He handed it to Nathaniel, and tapped the page. "When Newton discovered gravity, what happened?"

"An apple fell on his head."

"Yes!" Wythe snatched it up and deposited it back on the desk with a flourish. He tapped his own temple again. "And in that instant, Newton thought! He reasoned by applying what he learned to the earth. To man. To the stars. He discovered a mathematical equation that not only fully explained gravity and why our feet stick to the earth, but one that he could apply to the universe." Wythe spun the orrery on his desk, the little orbs rotating around each other. "Now, if God created the universe, it follows that he created that mathematical equation, yes?"

Nathaniel nodded, beginning to grasp Wythe's logic.

Wythe continued, pointing to the microscope. "God created the equation. Which means, the universe follows those natural mathematical laws, right down to the wings of that butterfly. And if we believe we are created in God's image then he created man with the reason to discover those laws; to build the microscope. Therefore, God created reason. And therefore…"

"Therefore…" Nathaniel's mind grabbed hold to the edges of his fluttering thoughts. "Therefore, if God created the natural world, and us… then we are all governed by the laws of both nature and reason, not by a King."

Wythe smiled and lightly punched Nathaniel in the arm.

"Yes! All of us. Me. You. Thomas Jefferson. Lee and little John. We are all equal under that natural law. God's law of nature and reason. Not God himself. It means when we lead, we lead those who are the same as us. We are both the governing and the governed. This document is not written on faith. It provides a reason, a logic, to help even John ascend from a suffering life to affect his safety and happiness."

A tap came at the door. When bid to enter, Wythe's personal slave, Benjamin, pushed his head through the door.

"Master Wythe, the shower you ordered is prepared."

Wythe nodded. The door closed. The air in the study hung heavy with Benjamin's presence. Nathaniel looked down on the document.

"When it says *All men are created equal,* does it mean him, too? I have seen more slaves in Virginia than I ever did in Pennsylvania. At Mr. Lee's especially. Does this," he pointed to the Declaration and then opened a hand toward the door, "speak to that establishment?" Nathaniel searched Wythe's face hoping the man's expression would match his wish.

George Wythe's shoulders slumped, and he shook his head. "The state of slavery in Virginia is one I desperately wish would end." He sank into a nearby chair and looked up at Nathaniel like a child defending himself after a well-deserved lecture. "Some, like Mr. Lee, see slavery purely as an economic issue. Like his tobacco and cotton, he sees men like Benjamin as a commodity to freely trade, and the King restricts that trade. There was a brief period in the Congress when we believed Mr. Lee and others were on the road to abolishment. However, as Mr. Lee ran about Philadelphia extolling its merits, the scoundrel also ran a slave trade business with his own ships—until his brother finally made him put a stop to it." Wythe's face flushed hot at the memory and he took in a deep breath. "We hoped, many of us did, that words from Mr. Jefferson's first draft would put an end to our discussions and the issue. He had included two very specific, but contradictory, statements, about the abolishment of slavery. It was agreed by the majority to remove both and leave it as 'all men.'"

"So, it speaks to Benjamin's freedom, but it does not free him," Nathaniel said.

"Compromise among flawed men can be both a great and a terrible thing."

"So consequently, *the Declaration* is flawed," Nathaniel sniffed at the document.

"Perhaps," Wythe stood again, and joined Nathaniel to look down at the parchment. "We have left our words open to interpretation, that is certain. I hope it will not be inherited by fools, and instead be viewed as a good start. This document, like many legal agreements, is a thoughtful foundation upon which we continue to build. Some like Lee are likely signing it because they want their lives to be the same. Some will sign it because they want something different. I believe we should sign it as a unanimous promise to be *better.*"

Wythe picked up the quill and dipped it in the inkwell, tapping it lightly upon the edge of the bottle. He held the pen over the parchment for a brief moment. At last he signed his name in the space over the others from Virginia, just above Richard Henry Lee's signature. "Age and reason before beauty, Mr. Lee," he chuckled.

He replaced the quill on the stand and stood back to admire the document. He turned to Nathaniel, his face glowing with hope, his eyes damp. "If this Declaration sparks even one more conversation like ours today, mark my words, son… It will be the match to the gunpowder of freedom that will blow open wide the world."

Nathaniel smiled in return but he was speechless. His mind was a flurry trying to reorganize all they had discussed.

Wythe blew on the paper, sealing his name into the parchment. Into history. "Come now." Wythe refolded the parchment, handed it to Nathaniel, and steered him out of the study. "You must use this out-of-doors shower of mine. Pish-posh on that bathing once a week nonsense. A bucket of cool water a day, and woosh! Clean body, and so a clean mind."

Nathaniel followed Wythe out the back door to a private area near the house. Downwind of Wythe's smell of lye soap, he was ever more aware of his own odor of horses, sweat, and Virginia roads.

"We shall talk some more, but get some rest after you bathe." Wythe showed him how to work the shower and left him to it.

Exhaustion coursed through Nathaniel's body like Tincture of Opium. His feet and limbs were heavy as he undressed. Then he stood under the bucket and pulled on the rope, letting the water wash him clean.

That night, after another meal, as John licked the remaining gravy from the rose-patterned china, Wythe called Nathaniel into the hallway. There, just outside the cracked door, the two men openly discussed their agreed upon false plan.

"I will head over land through Philadelphia to New York," Nathaniel said in a loud whisper. "It is best I go alone, but with the boy." He heard the floorboards creak in the bedroom on the other side of the door.

"I shall not lock you in tonight," Wythe replied clearly, "in case you need to use the necessary. Your horses are saddled and in the yard for an early departure." For good measure he added, "Remember to take the boy to the stockades when you ride through Philadelphia." A sharp intake of breath came from behind the door. The two men smiled to one another.

That night, as Nathaniel lay on his back and feigned a low rumbling snore, he heard John slip from the room. Nathaniel propped himself on his elbows and cocked his head. A downstairs door clicked open then shut. Soon he heard hooves upon the gravel.

Nathaniel dropped back on his pillow, as the galloping horse faded into the night. He stared at the ceiling, but despite the miles stretching between himself and the boy, Nathaniel still felt concern pressing him into the mattress.

"God speed, John," he whispered. "May whomever sent you believe your every word. For your sake as well as mine."

CHAPTER TWENTY-FOUR

KALAWI FELT THE EARTH shudder just before the full moon returned.

He had been dreaming, hopping from one foot to another with Kisekamuta around the fire, but just as he reached for her, she let out a thunderous, howling cry.

Kalawi sat up, panting, blinking in the low light. In the far corner of their family *wegiwi*, Nakomtha slept soundly on her own palette. Kalawi flopped back on the skins and closed his eyes, hoping to continue the dream, but the earth rumbled again. Westward.

This time he flung his legs from the bed, yanked on his moccasins, and pushed through the rug over the *wegiwi* door. A band of orange, the first hints of sunrise, graced the horizon behind him as he padded off through the thicket. Soon, the air around him filled with a fine dust. Leaves and feathers swirled past him, catching in his hair. Voices filtered to him. He slipped closer, behind a petrified stump, and peered around it.

A half a dozen men gathered where the old-growth forest met the meadow stretching out to the Marten farm. Three men hacked apart a fallen trunk. A few took coordinated aim at an ancient, standing but wavering, chestnut. Birds took to the skies over Kalawi, fleeing from doomed bows trembling under blows gouging at the creamy flesh.

Thump. Crack. Thump. Crack. Soon the chestnut began to tip.

"She falls!" a tall man shouted, and the men ran.

The tree's green bows swayed and pitched forward, like a stumbling giant, her splayed limbs grabbing hopelessly at unscathed trees. Crying out in an agonizing, crackling wail, the trunk crashed to the ground. Limbs thicker than a man's thigh snapped like twigs. Chestnuts shattered to dust. The sound rattled painfully in Kalawi's bones.

The tall man waved them back in, turning his face toward Kalawi. An angry scar curved away from the man's right eye. Kalawi sniffed the down-wind air; lye soap trying to mask a night of heavy drinking. Beyond the man, far across the meadow, a line of wagons rolled up to the gun shop.

Kalawi slipped like a shadow through the forest circling the perimeter of the farm. He crept up behind the house, and ducked beneath the old hemlock next to the front porch. Concealed behind draping evergreen limbs, he spied several men unloading three wagons near Peter.

"Bake kettles and a spit-jack for the new kitchen can go in the barn for now." Peter's face was knotted with efficiency. He reviewed stamps on each crate or a tag on a piece of equipment, and flipped pages stacked on his black leather portfolio. "Flint and iron go to the gun shop. Father, show them where to put everything."

Kalawi's eyes tracked to Joseph Marten at the gun shop door, hands stuffed deep in his pockets. When Peter urged his father again, Joseph reluctantly followed the men inside.

Two middle-aged men—one with a bald head as round as his belly, and the other as hairy as a wild boar—hefted grain bags to the house. As Jane Marten came out the door, they dropped two sacks in repetitive thuds to the porch floor. A cloud of fine dust swirled and stuck to her shoes.

"I shall be standing on them to cook." She waved the dust from her face and looked at the pile remaining on the wagon. "Please put some in the barn."

"You gotta ask 'im 'bout that." The oldest man wiped a rag over his shiny head and waved it toward Peter. "I'm just 'ere to build yer kitchen house."

"And when will the cooks arrive to help me?" Jane's fine English diction was even more precise in contrast to the man's choppy Pennsylvania Dutch.

"Ain't my concern, ma'am. Ask that Mister Dawes, the one with the scar on his face. We answer to him first." He stuffed the dirty rag in his pocket and walked away.

Jane placed both palms on the porch railing and surveyed the strangers clamoring over their land. Kalawi followed her gaze. Dawes plus six men at the trees. Four at the wagons. Eleven men added to their three blacksmiths—Barton, Harry, and John—Joseph and Peter, and all of them working up a fierce hunger.

Jane sighed and hoisted one of the sacks onto her hip. At the door, she glanced toward the tree. Kalawi moved his face into the light. Her breath caught. *I am here,* he sent out the thought.

She smiled, but her eyes darted to the men at the wagons. When the bag began to slip, Kalawi took a step forward, but Jane shook her head and repositioned the sack. "I'll be just fine," she said as if whispering to herself before going inside. Kalawi tucked behind the curtain of needles just as the men returned with two more sacks.

"Never been outta Philly 'fore," the hairy man said, pausing to look eastward. "You?"

"Naw, but I figure a job buildin' for the army is better than gettin' shot by a Tory." The bald man glanced over his shoulder toward the house door. "Hard t' tell who is and who ain't one of those."

The hairy man nodded as he scanned the far meadow. "So long as der ain't no damn Indians to fight out 'ere."

A shiver ran through Kalawi, though the scar on his arm burned hot. When the two men went back to the wagon, Kalawi slipped away, retracing his steps, his feet barely a whisper.

Determination resonated through every limb; his promise to Nathaniel to protect his parents, reaffirmed.

Just as Kalawi reached the petrified tree again, another of the large chestnuts fell to the earth. He paused to look back. Before the dust settled, the workers came again, taking their hatchets to the fallen trunk, and Nakomtha's words cut through his thoughts. *Forest and fields. Without them we have no game, food, or materials to trade.*

A small hare darted out from amid the debris. The men shouted after it. They dropped their axes to chase it. Stumbled blindly, trying to catch it.

"Get it, you bloody bastards," Dawes yelled. After only few more seconds, he cursed their folly, and pulled a pistol from his hip. A single shot rang out.

CHAPTER TWENTY-FIVE

"ARE YOU SAYING, YOU BELIEVE the conference at Staten Island will not end in peace?" Nathaniel asked. He rode alongside Wythe, their horses sloshing through a small creek near Yorktown, as Wythe told him of his work to establish a constitution for operating Virginia's new state government.

The journey from Williamsburg had been easy under a cooling breeze tinted with the musty smell of the approaching autumn. Wythe steered his horse up the embankment and waited for Nathaniel to join him on the rise.

"A treaty of peace could still mean separation. I am simply preparing for all outcomes." Wythe squinted at the port city like he was seeing Yorktown's future. "But if we do separate, and that port is no longer British, then we must quickly explain to the people what it is. Ignorance breeds fear, and fear breads mistrust. Unlike the King, we must be transparent in how we will govern. We must show them our hands."

Nathaniel looked down at his own hands grasping the reins. They were chapped, red and scarred, much as his father's had always been.

"I used to fear my father. He was always so serious, his hands bruised. One day he taught me about the beautiful long-rifles his hands created; not for war, but to help his neighbors secure food. He was not stern. He was devoted. I feared him no longer."

"A lovely summation of my point," Wythe winked at him. "You would make a fine lawyer, Mr. Mirtle."

"Me? A mere rider?"

"You must prepare for all outcomes. Life is too long to remain the same." Wythe leaned back in his saddle and nodded toward Nathaniel's buttocks, "And I do hate to see a fine mind shrivel while a rump widens on the back of a horse."

Nathaniel threw his head back and laughed for the first time in what seemed like weeks. And yet as they rode into town, he pondered what would come after he'd acquired all the signatures. His father could resume his artistry. He'd marry Susannah. And then what...

The thought left him as he tried to stay next to Wythe against an ever-thickening stream of shipmen and port workers dragging cargo toward the Custom House—a two-and-a-half story brick building at the corner of Read and Main Streets where taxes on goods were collected, and Blythe was not found.

They inched down to the York River, where deep, raspy voices shouted over crates and sacks, and gulls cried and swooped over fishing boats bringing in the morning's catch. Bayard snorted amid the briny smells and chaos as they reached the river's edge, where the masts of more than two dozen boats stuck up like reeds.

"That is my precious South Carolina Indigo. Come down!" A woman in deep blue petticoats shook a finger at a man who stood atop a crate on the docks, his arms akimbo. Like many of the dockhands, Nathaniel and Wythe stopped to watch the exchange.

The man waved her off as he surveyed the crowd from beneath a black cocked hat adorned with a peacock feather. He stood at ease in a formal, blue-gray jacket and breeches-expertly tailored. Gold epaulettes added breadth to his wide shoulders.

"You break my crate open, and I will break you, sir!" the woman tapped her umbrella handle upon his polished buckled shoes.

The man removed his hat and bowed. Dark, shaggy hair tumbled around a handsome, square face spilling over with mirth. "Would not be the first time a woman tried to break me, Mrs. Eliza Pinckney. But with you, I would be a better horse for it."

The crowd at his feet erupted with laughter and Nathaniel asked, "You don't suppose that is—"

"Captain Blythe, come down this instant!" the woman stomped a foot.

Wythe glanced at Nathaniel's satchel and then back to the man who had hopped off the crate and was moving in their direction. "Indeed."

"Mr. Wythe? Mr. Mirtle? At last you are here," the captain said as the two dismounted and shook his hand. His clipped, Massachusetts accent made the word *here* sound more like *hare*. He introduced himself and waved his hat back at Mrs. Pinckney.

"She makes the highest quality blue dye in the world—our biggest export, second only to rice. She may be older than me, but that Eliza still has more spice in her than all the Orient." Blythe stepped back a pace and sized up Bayard's haunches. "I am told that horse is coming."

"Yes, sir," Nathaniel said. "Bayard stays with me."

"We've a crane to get him into the *Frontier*. She's the two-masted schooner down the end of the pier." The captain thanked Wythe for the safe delivery of Nathaniel and strode off toward the boat after adding, "We leave in less than an hour, Mr. Mirtle."

"Well…" Nathaniel said, reluctant at leaving Wythe's wise council. He held out a hand and Wythe shook it with both his own. "I do hope I survive so we can meet again."

"Then let reason guide you safely home," Wythe clapped him on the shoulder.

"And you as well, Mr. Wythe."

* * *

Cock-a-doodle-doo. A rooster crowed to greet the coming dawn.

Sleep swirled around Nathaniel like warm water. His eyelids refused to open as he drew in the smell of biscuits and coffee. He envisioned his mother pulling rolls from the fire in the warm kitchen of their stone house.

Cock-a-doodle-doo.

"Mum?" Nathaniel opened one eye. He stared into the whiskery, thick face of an old salt of a man. Several other weather-beaten faces stared on from behind.

Through four missing front teeth, the man gruffed, "Mummy ain't 'ere this morning. But ol' George is."

Nathaniel bolted upright. His hammock, hung between the rafters of the ship, rocked, and pitched him to the floor. The sound riled the chickens nearby, which set off Bayard in the next pen, which in turn roused the rooster again.

The sailors all burst out laughing as they wandered away to their breakfast. George helped Nathaniel to his feet and whacked him on the back with a thick, scabby hand.

"That damn rooster gets t' all of us the first mornin' out," he chuckled as Nathaniel lurched under the motion of the boat. "Let's see if a bit o' breakfast will settle in that green stomach, or if it be chum like your supper last night."

The moment the *Frontier* had lurched away from the Yorktown docks, Nathaniel's stomach had sunk into his legs. By the time they sailed through the mouth of the Chesapeake into the Atlantic Ocean, his retching had increased to such a fervor he swore his very insides would soon lie upon the deck before him.

Now, willing to give his legs another go, Nathaniel followed the old boatswain. He swiftly cracked his head on a crossbeam. He cursed and put a heel of his hand to his forehead.

"That beam ain't never gonna move! Duck, lad." The man pushed down on Nathaniel's head and steered him to a table. Nathaniel took one bite of the baking-powder biscuit. Within seconds it was obvious which direction the biscuit preferred to go. He pushed himself away from the table.

"Head for the deck!" George yelled after him.

Above deck, his stomach again emptied, Nathaniel leaned his cheek against the cool wooden rails. He gazed up at the masts swaying and was again overcome with spasms. He fell to his knees and heaved. A moment later, someone pulled him to his feet.

"Aye, you have gone green, but you cannot cut and run from it." Captain Blythe dragged Nathaniel by his shoulder to the back of the boat. "Look to the horizon. It alone remains stationary. Masts do not."

Nathaniel focused on the distant line where water met sky.

The captain thumped him on the back. "Breathe, Mr. Mirtle. This is like dancing, but you are the woman. Let your hips sway with the ship. Good god, is your horse fairing this poorly?"

"Bayard seems fine. Surprisingly. He usually hates crossing water."

Nathaniel let the weight of his body match the rocking, focusing on the distant shore. Slowly the discomfort began to cease, and his back muscles softened. His vision cleared for the first time since Yorktown, and he examined the captain.

Hours in the sun and salty air had tanned Blythe's face to a golden color. White lines, marks of his humor, stretched out from inquisitive eyes the color of the sea. Nathaniel envied the captain's robust complexion, a good bit healthier than his own, he imagined.

"'Tis not surprising your horse hates water," the captain said, the laugh lines deepening. "You cursed him with that name."

"Bayard? It means red in color."

"Aye," Captain Blythe said, "but an ancient French legend tells of a horse named Bayard, ceded to Charlemagne. Charlemagne punished the horse for his exploits during war, and had him dragged into the river to drown with a large stone around his neck. The massive horse broke the stone with his hooves and escaped to the woods, fearful of water from then on."

"How does a sea captain know of such ancient stories?"

The captain knocked the heel of his boot against the deck. "Things are not always as they first appear. She's a floating library gathering knowledge at every port." He scrutinized Nathaniel's face, and then seemingly satisfied he winked, "That your curiosity has returned is a sign of health. Your appetite is sure to follow. Come, let us break our fast together."

In the captain's private chamber above the quarterdeck, windows ran along the port and starboard sides, flooding the modest space with sunlight. Blythe instructed Nathaniel to sit at the long table set for breakfast with biscuits, ham, and orange slices. As he took a seat, Nathaniel caught a glimpse of a cot tucked behind an embroidered silk screen. The bed was tightly made as if it had never been slept in, covered in a fine rose-colored quilt. Over the bunk hung the captain's cutlass, the leather belt wound in blood-red velvet.

The captain took a chair across from Nathaniel and poured them both coffee.

"We shall speak frankly, Mr. Mirtle. My instructions from Doctor Franklin state I am not to ask about why we are transporting you." His cup in hand, Blythe stretched his legs beneath the table. "My crew and I only know we are to be anchored in the harbor off Staten Island by the morning of the eleventh. You will tell us where we go from there."

Nathaniel agreed, grateful to not have to dance through an awkward conversation.

"This leaves us to talk about three things: the weather, the revolution, or me." Captain Blythe waved his cup toward the starboard windows. "It is clear sailing this morning, so now we are down to two."

"Perhaps both? I assume you are part of the Continental Navy—"

Blythe held up a palm. "Absolutely not. Few of us are. When Congress approved the development of a navy last October, we began with only four."

"Four what?" Nathaniel leaned back and drank his coffee, coughing through the first sip. It was so bitter, he worried it would melt through the cup.

"Try some sugar." Blythe broke a chunk of sugar off a solid cone and dropped it into Nathaniel's cup. "The navy began with four ships."

"Are you telling me the colonies are rebelling against the largest navy in the world with four ships?"

"Initially. Congress has several more now."

"But you fly the Grand Union flag." Nathaniel recalled seeing it flying over the foremast when they lowered Bayard into the hull. He took a sip of the brew, thankful the sugar had killed at least some of the bitterness.

"'Tis for show. Why would I want to join the navy?" Captain Blythe sniffed, his face filling with laughter. Seeing Nathaniel's dismay, the captain pointed toward the food. "Eat. I will explain."

Wary of the biscuits, Nathaniel tried the ham. Blythe picked up a biscuit for himself, took a bite, and then spoke around it. "Think of the boats in the American ports: Royal Navy ships, or British transport ships that were part of the Dutch West India Company. The rest are private trade or merchant ships." He used the remaining piece of his biscuit to emphasize his points. "For years, I have run many vessels—like this schooner and other Bermuda sloops—down to the West Indies. St. Eustatius had the best cloth for my family's textile business."

"Ah. Hence your knowledge of indigo, and your fine uniform," Nathaniel said. The captain nodded, and then Nathaniel asked about the two decks of cannons he'd seen after coming on board. "This isn't a merchant ship."

"Mr. Mirtle, there are three ways for a young country to build a navy."

Blythe ticked them off on his fingers. "Buy the ships. But the Congress and thirteen colonies are all printing their own currencies, so financing the war is total chaos. The second method is to build the ships, but that takes both money and time, a problem when the Royal Navy is already at your port."

"And the third?" Nathaniel asked after swallowing a piece of ham. Thankfully it seemed inclined to stay put.

"It is far faster and cheaper to convert ships that already exist," Captain Blythe smiled, one eyebrow raised with the same playful expression he'd shown Mrs. Pinckney. "Which is why they hire people like me, to… acquire them."

"You're a pirate!"

Captain Blythe winced, and waved the rest of his biscuit at Nathaniel. "Pirates lack the authorization. We are privateers. Congress issued me a letter of the marque giving me the right to take ships in wartime. Myself and the crew keep half of the bounty I deliver to them, and I get to continually upgrade our tools of the trade." He directed Nathaniel to look behind the door of his cabin.

Two ports had been cut into the side of the hull, the block hinged shut. Inside the cabin, two large black cannon waited to be stuffed through each port. The black barrels were draped in canvas, their wheels fixed with blocks.

"I had her outfitted with fourteen six-pounders. From a distance, with the ports shut, we look like a merchant trader."

"Ah. Things are not always as they first appear," Nathaniel said.

"Consequently, we had a good run of luck down near South Carolina."

"Which is how you know Mrs. Pinckney?"

"That and we did a little business together," Blythe winked. "Then came a letter from Mr. Franklin, and a tidy sum of money. A request for a special transport." Blythe spread out his palms toward Nathaniel.

"Congress chose you over a navy ship? Why?"

Blythe shrugged, but there was cockiness more than apology in it. "I deliver. In six weeks we added a dozen ships to Franklin's fleet." He tore off another piece of biscuit. "That, and I refused if it meant joining the navy."

Nathaniel raised an eyebrow.

Again, the captain shrugged. "I prefer to be commissioned by what I capture, not by a distant commander. I sail where I am needed but under my rules, and my crew is not loyal to the rebellion, but to me."

Nathaniel knew the last statement to be true. At Blythe's word, the midshipmen set the sails or scaled the rigging as swiftly as squirrels scampering up a tree, and smiling all the way. When the *Frontier* had pulled away from Yorktown, the entire crew cheered as one.

"You don't believe in this war over separation?" Nathaniel asked.

Blythe looked out the window toward the east, his face pensive. "As you said, the colonies have picked a fight against the largest navy on earth. The conflict is still a little uncertain to be picking a side, eh, Mr. Mirtle?"

Nathaniel's shoulders lost all their tension. "You are a kindred spirit, Captain Blythe."

"Then 'tis right for us to take our meals together. Nothing aids digestion on a boat like an engaging conversation. Might prevent the crew from wondering about you or what you transport, too." The captain's eyes fell briefly onto Nathaniel's satchel. He begged his leave to meet with his crew, and waved an arm at the table. "Eat. I shall show you our intended course on my map later. For now, I open my cabin to you. Enjoy it. The sea gives a non-sailor the luxury of time."

As the door swung shut, Nathaniel clung to Blythe's last word. *Time.* Hours and hours of it. Five or six days of it. It spread out before him as both a reprieve and yet a worry. Each day they sailed north, the calendar sailed toward Susannah's marriage. The hammers drove nails into an armory that would slowly break his father. Blythe's comments gave him an idea of how to keep his mind and hands busy.

That rest of the morning, Nathaniel revised the maps he'd loosely sketched during his ride to and from Williamsburg, drawing details he'd been unable to add given the company of John and the Wythes. The pen felt good in his hand again. Each line or curve reminded him of Sunday afternoons with his grandfather as a boy.

Back then, after church, his mother's soft-spoken father would take him up Topton Mountain in search of plant samples. Upon return, drawing instructions were softened by stories. As the seasons came and went, Nathaniel's illustrations improved, and the tales grew more dramatic until even the story of Joseph's wooing of Jane included a shoot-out at dawn with silver pistols.

"Lunch is served, Mr. Mirtle."

Blythe pushed his way into his cabin, followed by two men carrying trays laden with food and wine. Nathaniel, unaware the morning hours had evaporated, scrambled to clear his papers from the table. The captain stepped in to help and picked up the map Nathaniel had redrawn of the coastline at the Yorktown port.

"By God, well done, Mirtle. You even captured some old pilings near the bank my old map never had." Blythe examined Nathaniel anew. And so, after lunch, the captain unrolled a chart on the table.

"The middling colonies and Atlantic seaboard—a damned old map. Settlements and weather have altered what is there," Blythe pointed out the port side toward the coastline. "Could you mark changes you see upon it?"

Nathaniel agreed, and Blythe showed him how to use the scope, compass, and the calipers to measure and mark their distance along the course he'd outlined for them.

"Paper is in the top drawer of my desk in the corner, as are ink and nibs." Captain Blythe headed for the door. "I shall thank you with a glass of my finest claret tonight!"

That day, as the *Frontier* trekked north, Nathaniel split his time between the cabins and the deck as they sailed past inlets interspersed with meadows waving hello with long grasses. Cranes and herons swooped over coastal villages at Chincoteague, Fenwick's Island, and Rehoboth Bay. Small, distant oases formed across the white-capped waters, as the *Frontier* slipped past the uppermost region of Virginia and on to Maryland.

Over the wine that night, instead of reviewing the maps not yet complete, Nathaniel shared with Blythe a gift given to him by Mrs. Wythe. Before he'd left Williamsburg, she had pressed *Gulliver's Travels* into his hands. Nathaniel had attempted to refuse it, for such a fine book was worth nearly ten pounds, double the price of a pair of pistols.

"A man will never travel alone if he carries with him a book," she had insisted.

As Nathaniel read aloud, Blythe rocked back on the chair's hind legs, his own feet on the table. Roaring with laughter at the image of Gulliver tied down and forced to fight by a tiny emperor, he said, "This was written nearly fifty years ago? 'Tis a great satire for now."

"Pray we meet no Lilliputians on our voyage to New York."

As the night dragged on, and the claret bottle emptied, they stumbled into stories of their own. Nathaniel told harmless tales of life with the Shawnee and his boyhood in a gun shop. In return, Blythe regaled him with his own adventures in the Caribbean—tales of sweet foods and women Nathaniel longed to taste.

And so their days and nights were spent.

Nearing sunset one evening, after a late supper, Nathaniel charted the *Frontier's* location on a map in the waning light. A scant crew was on deck. A gust of wind tugged at the pages. He looked port side from whence it came. Backlit by the deep orange of sunset, Nathaniel saw quite clearly the yawning mouth of the Delaware Bay. Her waters rode to Philadelphia. Nathaniel's heart leapt with familiarity.

"Hello again, Susannah," he whispered. He wanted to dive from the decks. To swim across the miles. To find her on her front stoop waving hello, smelling of lemon and honeysuckle. And as the *Frontier* slipped northward, he made his vow again, "I will return to you."

As the sun shrank below the horizon like a candle dying out, a deep purple blanket of darkness obliterated the distant view. Nathaniel dragged himself away from the rails. He made his way below decks. The ship creaked and groaned with him. His feet heavy. His heart aching. He climbed into the swaying hammock.

With his satchel clutched on his chest beneath his arms, he stared at the beams overhead. The ship rocked him into oblivion. Into a still distant, and incredibly uncertain, future.

CHAPTER TWENTY-SIX

ARTHUR WAS AT LAST alone to reply to Susannah's letter he'd received three nights ago. He dipped the pen in the ink and waited for it to drip. Waiting…

He'd had no idea that 'going to war,' words that conveyed action, involved so much waiting. Since escaping from Brooklyn Heights, they had been camped in New York City reorganizing. Positions left vacant from the fallen officers brought Arthur his second promotion inside of a week. Though his move up to Captain involved mostly sitting down. That he once expected an army to always be in the heat of battle now seemed a silly, juvenile notion.

Yet tonight, he willed his legs and hands, aching from hours of penning correspondence while sitting in a hard chair, to give a few minutes more.

> *My sweet cousin Susannah,*
>
> *How these four little words can give me such wings. First, the word 'my.' I own so little in this world. Even the ink belongs to the Army. But the memory you shared in your last letter!*
>
> *You and I, eight or nine, exploring your garden… me discovering that frog that later made your mother fall into the lily pond! The laughter you enclosed 'tis mine alone.*

Arthur picked up Susannah's latest letter, reading it again to form a proper reply. Beneath it, a letter to include from Matthew Pemberley. Arthur had seen him yesterday, when the officers ate at the Queen's Head tavern. The man, who Arthur assumed from his regal bearing and unwavering expression was as cold as the Susquehanna in winter, had embraced him warmly. Arthur sniffed at him, searching for sign of drink, but Pemberley was sober. Sobered.

"That battle on Long Island poured humility over my naïve ideals." Pemberley stabbed at his food, his plate clamped between his elbows on the table. While on the ship to New York, they'd quickly learned it was the only way to keep your dinner plate from sliding to the floor. Arthur's mother would be mortified to know he now ate the same way.

"I confess I do not recognize the man I was when I left Philadelphia a month ago," Pemberley sighed between bites. "Do you?"

Arthur swallowed a bit of potato, trying not to choke on the guilt of sitting with Nathaniel's rival. He hoped they could go on eating in silence, but Pemberley kept unfolding, his voice filled with an aching quality.

"When we see death, a part of us dies too, doesn't it? Perhaps that is the only way for what remains within us to go on living." Pemberley's words sunk into Arthur, and Jonathan Thomson's face swam up. Hadn't each order Arthur had helped write this week been a memorial of sorts? For Jonathan, Jimmy, Peyton and everyone they'd lost for the Cause.

"Mr. Bowman, I must also confess I was not looking forward to marrying your cousin."

Arthur raised his head. Pemberley's brown eyes were pools of such sincerity, that they begged for Arthur to ask, "Why?"

"When I left for New York, I was relieved to no longer pretend she meant more to me than glory. But, now I count myself among the fortunate. I am alive. A future ahead of me. I am free to marry Ms. Bowman who is kind, gracious. It will be an honor."

Arthur easily wrote the next lines.

'Sweet.' Please forgive my enclosing a letter Mr. Pemberley asked me to send. He promises to write more. I trust you will reply to him in kind. Even when your mother fell into the pond, I saw you swiftly

reach for her hand. We are all in it up to our necks here and a sweet word or two can keep a man from drowning.

A warm breeze blew in through the window over Arthur's desk. He let it caress his cheek. He could hear a few soldiers in the alley below propositioning a woman. While those comforts were abundant in the city, he knew not everyone had embraced the Colonial Army like the woman outside now seemed want to do. A week ago, when the army marched into the city from the east, Tories streamed off the island via Kings Bridge to the north. Their empty homes had become temporary shelters for the fatigued Continental Army. By some bit of luck, Arthur had ended up with a room and a bed to himself. With no fleas.

'Cousin.' In an endless stream of places uncomfortable and distant, my thoughts often turn to home. My Berks County farm dotted with white sheep. But also your parlor. Home is my family. It is you. It is Nathaniel and Kalawi, and Topton Mountain, too.

Arthur glanced at his possibles bag. It contained the one letter he'd received from Kalawi. The words were few, the Shawnee always preferring to speak English even though he'd grown quite proficient at writing it. *Letter received. Return in one piece, so keep your head down. Will write when I hear from Nathaniel. Please promise to do same.* Then one line from their shared knight's oath. *And so on this journey we each our own way go.*

"So many oaths and agreements," Arthur whispered aloud. He looked over the paperwork on his desk; requests, regrets, and compromises. Are they ever truly fulfilled? He refilled his quill.

'Susannah.' I worry for you. You wrote to me of Nathaniel's promise, of what he asks of you. Like your father, I caution you. But I will also honor your request. If I should hear from him, you will be the first to know of it. I want happiness for you, as I do for him. Even for Pemberley. For us all, really.
Yours with fond remembrances,
- Arthur.

He sealed Pemberley's letter inside his own and dragged his aching legs off to bed alone. His last thought was of Nathaniel, and hoping his friend was indeed somewhere safe and sound.

CHAPTER TWENTY-SEVEN

NATHANIEL COULD BARELY SEE the quarterdeck from the fore-deck. Fog had crept across the water during the night, wrapping around them like a cottony pillowcase. The wind, barely a whisper. Nathaniel could hear the waves upon the hull, but when he peered over the rail it looked as if the *Frontier* floated through clouds. As he crossed the deck to join the captain for breakfast, he bid old George good morning. The man, normally cheerful, only nodded. The crew remained quiet at their task of pushing the ship forward into the nothingness.

At the door of the captain's cabin, Nathaniel stopped to watch a sprightly watch-keeper climb the rigging to the top-gallant cross-trees, the boy and his scope disappearing into a cloud as if into heaven.

Inside, Nathaniel greeted Blythe with a comment about the mist being as thick as his head. He dropped his satchel over the back of a chair, ruing the bottle of Jamaican rum the two had consumed the night before.

Blythe, clean-shaven and seemingly ill affected, finished buttoning his breeches as they met at the table. "We were three-sheets to the wind," he chuckled then nodded toward the windows. "The dead air came in just after midnight. We're stalled just above Cape May near Ludlow's Beach," Blythe tapped a barometer on the wall. "However, the pressure has dropped. A stiff wind will move the fog out shortly. We'll make Staten Island in a day."

They were a cup or two into their coffee when George interrupted. "Your presence is requested on deck, sir. A blot spotted though the haze."

Both Nathaniel and the captain stood.

"Please. Stay and eat," Blythe said as he returned to his cot for his coat. "It's probably a whale like we saw yesterday."

Nathaniel picked up a biscuit and rocked back in his chair as they went out the door. As he dunked the biscuit in his coffee, a few rays of sun appeared, streaming in low through the starboard cabin windows, the lazy shadow of the coffee pot moving fore and aft with the gentle motion of the ship. Just as Blythe said, the wind was blowing away the fog.

Nathaniel righted his chair and picked up the pot to refill his mug. As he made to place it back on the table, the sun broke through again. With his hand still around the handle, he watched the westward shadow of the pot move southward along the table. Out the window, the sun slipped across the panes toward the ship's nose. Are we turning eastward? he wondered.

Footsteps thumped across the quarterdeck over the cabin. Blythe shouted a muffled order. The crew moved again. More shouting. Then, silence. Nathaniel looked about the cabin, wondering what to do. His eyes fell on Blythe's cot. His cutlass was not hanging over the bed as it had been during the whole of their sail. Nathaniel snatched up his satchel and rushed to the deck.

Captain Blythe was on the quarterdeck, his eye to his scope. The young watch-keeper pointed into the fog. Thick. Then clear. Then it swallowed them up. Half the crew watched the captain. The rest searched the half-concealed waters. Only the sails dared to flutter.

Captain Blythe suddenly dropped the scope. "Beat to quarters!"

The crew scattered, bumping into Nathaniel as they scrambled to their posts.

"What is it?" Nathaniel asked.

The captain swept the northeastern horizon with his scope again. "A ship. An Indiaman. Just before the fog rolled over her again the sails turned..." He squinted. "Come out..." The wind gusted. The fog pulled apart like a cotton shirt tearing at the seams. "There she is!"

Nathaniel saw her unaided by a scope. A massive ship, she thrust down into the water, a gush of spray sweeping over the nose.

"She's turned southeast, coming around us on the leeward!" Blythe shouted to the chief mate. "Ten points to starboard!"

Rigging ran, the wind whistled through the ropes. Sails shifted under the crew's collective hands. The *Frontier* turned northeast.

Nathaniel grabbed the captain's arm. "You mean to take her, don't you?"

"Of course!" Blythe shrugged off Nathaniel's hand. Wildness had turned his blue eyes a brackish green. He waved the scope toward the opposing ship. "That British vessel is likely a thousand tons—three times the *Frontier.* She wanted to disappear in the fog. That means she's loaded with goods she doesn't want us to have." He leaned closer to Nathaniel. "Oh, but I do." He strode off toward the foredeck shouting to his crew, "Prepare to take her!"

Nathaniel tried to elbow his way through crewmen scattering from post-to-post. The hinges on the ports below squeaked open. Beneath his feet, the vibration of cannons rolled into position. Nathaniel hopped over sun-bleached rigging. The sheets filled with the rising wind. The large-timbered boom swung to starboard. Nathaniel ducked. It brushed the tips of his hair, and the beam jerked into place.

"Captain, no. Wait!" Nathaniel's cry was lost amid the chaos.

He pushed toward the foredeck. In his path, a throng of men shoved a cannon through a port. They rolled up crates of gunpowder and shot. He could see Blythe near the bowsprit, looking north again. Nathaniel followed his gaze. The three-masted Indiaman barreled through the water. Her sails moved to leeward, holding the wind. She was aiming straight for the *Frontier's* nose at an incredible speed. Nathaniel leaped over the cannon and reached the foredeck just as the captain shouted over the now raging wind.

"To starboard!"

They responded. The ship listed southeast. Nathaniel gripped the rail. The oncoming ship trimmed her sails. But the heavy merchant vessel lumbered through the turn. Water spilled over her bow and starboard side as she finally leaned into it. She slid slightly ahead and parallel to the *Frontier.*

Nathaniel read the name scrawled across her aft: *Montagu.* The Royal Navy's flag, the Red Ensign, flew from the bow. Captain Blythe had seen it too, and he smiled broadly.

"Chain shot!" he shouted.

The *Montagu* opened her deck of gun ports. Nathaniel quickly counted them. She had nearly twice the firepower of the *Frontier.*

"You cannot engage, Blythe!" Nathaniel shouted. The gale force winds and the cries of the crew both rallied for a fight. Nathaniel hollered once more, "You must back down, this is too important!"

The captain spun on him. "What the hell is so goddamn important, Mirtle?"

Nathaniel hesitated only briefly. He grabbed Blythe by the back of the neck and spoke into the captain's ear. "I am carrying the one and only copy of the Declaration of Independence with all but five original signatures of the Congress."

"Blistering blackguards!" Captain Blythe stepped back. His eyes on Nathaniel's satchel.

"Yes," Nathaniel said, patting the leather. On the wind, they could hear the captain on the *Montagu* shouting his own orders. Nathaniel begged, "Turn. Flee. They outgun you, but you can outrun them. If you lose and I am captured, the document is incomplete. They'll hang us all. And it will be your head through the noose first."

Blythe looked to the *Montagu,* but then shook his head. "Too late. I prefer to win. Besides… look," Blythe grabbed Nathaniel's sleeve and turned him toward the rail. "Watch her starboard guns as she completes the turn. They are leeward, but we have the wind gauge."

As if on cue, the full weight of the wind filled the *Montagu's* sails. She heeled to starboard, listing toward the *Frontier.* The *Montagu's* crew scrambled to close the gun ports as half the hull fell below the water line, trapped beneath the surface. She lost speed.

The *Frontier* slid in alongside her and without even a glance at Nathaniel, Blythe yelled, "Bring down the masts! Fire!"

Nathaniel braced himself as the *Frontier* rocked to starboard under the power of cannon fire. Cannon balls chained together whipped across the water, pulling up spray, and with a whistle, snap, and crack they ripped through the *Montagu's* rigging and masts like a splayed hand through a spider's web. *Fire!* Another volley flung out from the *Frontier* tearing through the *Montagu's* mizzen and crumpling the topsails. Men dropped into the water tangled in sails and rigging. Smoke swirled. The boats raced eastward through the crashing waves, sliding closer together, the *Montagu* nearly crippled.

Nathaniel loosened his grip.

But then the *Montagu* began to tilt. With her sails damaged and no longer holding the wind, she began to right. She heeled away, her gun ports rising, opening, until Nathaniel could see straight down a barrel.

"Bloody hell" Nathaniel whispered.

But Blythe shouted, "Fire at will!"

The *Frontier's* cannon all fired at once. Nathaniel covered his ears. Raging shot cracked into the *Montagu*. It splintered the British gun ports. The hull. The bowsprit. Nathaniel ducked under his arm as shards from the *Montagu* clattered down upon the *Frontier's* decks.

As Nathaniel peaked out from beneath his arm, the *Montagu's* main mast moaned. It tumbled like timber into the sea. The *Montagu* tossed side-to-side on the waves. Smoke billowed away in the wind. Groans echoed from her decks. Each time she tilted to starboard, the scuppers spilled red stripes of blood down the hull. Among the flotsam in the water, the Red Ensign flag floated atop the waves.

A white flag rose slowly over the decks of the *Montagu* on the remaining rigging.

"They struck their colors!" The crew of the *Frontier* cheered. Nathaniel puffed out the breath he was unaware he had been holding.

Captain Blythe turned to his crew, his voice deep with victory. "Fine work, men. She's yours. Prepare to board her." Then he at last turned to Nathaniel. "I prefer to win."

Nathaniel didn't know whether to laugh or to punch him between his smirking lips. "The New York harbor is full of British vessels, Captain Blythe. I certainly hope you are not inclined to take them all."

"Go check on Bayard, Mirtle. Then go to my cabin until I retrieve you personally." He glanced over at the British *Montagu* then back to Nathaniel's satchel. "We needn't have our new prisoners finding out about you."

* * *

"How many are in the harbor?" The captain burst into his chambers.

Nathaniel had waited nearly the whole of the morning. Through the cabin windows he watched sailors swing between the two ships. They brought across supplies, and sent back tools, intent on making her ship shape again. He unfolded from a chair and stretched his back.

"How many ships?" Blythe tossed his cutlass on his cot. He dropped an armful of papers on the table between them. "You said the British are in the New York harbor. How do you know?"

"Mrs. Wythe read it in a neighbor's letter. It just said dozens. Whether that's three or thirteen…" Nathaniel shrugged.

Captain Blythe put both hands on the table, his fingers tapping. "I assume that letter was sent a few weeks ago, yes?" When Nathaniel confirmed it, Blythe pointed to the satchel hung over the chair. "Mr. Mirtle, we must speak frankly about that. What is happening at Staten Island? And after that, where am I to take you?"

Nathaniel knew in his gut he could trust Blythe, and he had no compunction this rogue could fight his way to shore if need be. Nathaniel nodded and confided in him about his task, the peace treaty, and his next steps.

"Franklin will have a lantern. No flashes, means peace is achieved. Three flashes and I go on. We go on. The Americans are camped in the city. You're to deliver me right into the docks in Manhattan past the Royal Navy ships waiting in that harbor," Nathaniel looked out at the *Montagu's* blood-stained gun portholes, "however many there may be."

Captain Blythe drummed his fingers on the table, but then a knock came at the door. George entered with a bundle of fabric cradled in his arms.

"Well?" Blythe asked, "Will the *Montagu* sail tonight?"

"I got every available mate climbin' all over her, but the mainmast cracked right at the keel. We best leave a crew behind workin' on her."

"And the shipment? Was it all there?"

George broke into a toothless smile.

"Aye, Captain. Every last one." He dropped his bundle of cloth on the table, and returned to his work.

Blythe unfolded the pile on the table and stretched out the cloth. Red, white and blue. The *Mantagu's* Red Ensign flag, dry from hanging over the rail all day. He fingered the fabric, and then a smile tugged at the corner of his mouth. "If you can't lick 'em, join 'em. We'll fly her colors into the harbor." The Captain grew serious again. "And just for safe measure, we need to be carrying the shipment they were expecting with the *Montagu.*"

"Which is…?" Nathaniel asked.

"Two thousand muskets from Bermuda." He pulled a page from among the papers before him and pushed it across the table.

Nathaniel reviewed it. "We're going to deliver the Declaration to the Congressmen and arms to the British… at the same time? Exactly whom are we joining?"

The two men studied each other, neither one willing to provide an answer. Finally, Blythe lifted his chin. "A privateer is not beholden to what he carries."

Nathaniel smiled at the familiar words.

"I am not the one signing the document," Blythe added. "I'm not firing the muskets. In truth, I wish no one could."

"That's a fine idea, Captain," Nathaniel reviewed the order again. Two thousand muskets and another full day at sea. "I'd need some of your men, but we could do it. I can show them how to disable them. After all, I am the—"

"Son of a gunsmith." The white lines around the captain's eyes disappeared inside his rising cheeks. He came around the table and thumped Nathaniel on the shoulder as he called for the boatswain. "Tell me what you need."

CHAPTER TWENTY-EIGHT

GENERAL HOWE STABILIZED HIMSELF by leaning on the back of his chair as he tucked his shirt into his pants. The smell of cheap rose perfume and liquor lingered in his tent from the night before. Without the admiral nearby to monitor his brother's behavior, clearly the general mixed dalliances with duty.

"A peace conference on Staten Island?" Silas blew the offending smell from his nostrils. "General, I do not understand why you would call this meeting at the Billop's House."

"Nor do you understand Lord Germain's two new orders," the general managed to finish buttoning his trousers. "First, he wants to offer the colonists a chance to reconsider before we take Manhattan. A peace treaty." The general yawned and reached for his boots.

"But if your negotiations end our business—"

"They won't." The general tapped his own chest. "I am the one permitted by the King to act as a peace commissioner, but I'm not going. My brother is, and the admiral's olive branch is thin and hollow; his fleets are waiting to move up the East River to take Manhattan.

"Which brings us to Germain's second order. He believes if we divide the thirteen colonies, separating New England from the others, routing out the leaders through proof of treason, the colonists will return to being the submissive, loyal subjects the King prefers. Taking New York City is the first step toward that." The general pulled on his boots then leaned both elbows upon his knees, staring at the ground. "Germain has it in his head the colonies are not united as one. How is that possible when they're amassing an army and fighting a damn war?"

"He's right," Silas smiled. When Howe's head popped up, Silas called to the door of the tent, "Come in, John."

The boy shuffled in, head down. His blue coat wadded beneath his arm, his face dirtier than it had been when Silas paid him to begin.

"What the hell is this?" the general wrinkled his nose as the boy's odor further soured the tent's putrid air.

"Tell the general what you told me." Silas jingled the shillings in his pocket.

"A rider. He's got a document with writin' on it. A declaration of independence, I 'eard him say."

"*The* Declaration," Silas clarified. "The delegates had signed a single copy of the document in August, a unanimous contract to bind them together as one country. Apparently, signatures are still missing. Germain is right; the colonies are not legally united."

The words slowly lifted General Howe from the chair.

"We also know the rider comes to New York." Silas rolled the coins again and nodded to John.

"He said he'd be ridin' overland, through Philadelphia and Jersey." John stared up at Silas' pocket through long lashes. "I stood on t'other side of a door and 'eard it with me own ears I did. Straight from the mouth of that Mr. Mirtle, the man carryin' it."

Silas fished the small bag of coins from his pocket. Faster than lightening, the boy grabbed it and ran.

The general paced. "I have to appease Germain, but those names will help us know who we're after with absolute certainty, from signatures not spies." He stopped at the table and unrolled a map. He ran his finger along the overland route, indicating where he could place men in Mirtle's path. "We must stop that rider before he completes his task. Once the congressmen show they have united as one, that document might spur on the colonists."

"I believe Congress would consider it unwise to publish the names of confirmed traitors—"

"I can't risk it, Hastings. With that document incomplete and in my hands, the pace of war is mine to control and I couldn't stomach a war that escalates. Taking Manhattan will be nauseating enough." Howe rubbed his belly and groaned. His hangover was setting in.

Silas took it as his cue to leave, but on the way out, he turned back. "If I might suggest... perhaps let it be leaked to Washington that you intend to take Manhattan. He will move the army out, so you can move into the docks without much fuss."

The general nodded. "You do that, Hastings, and I'll give them a warning shot or two. Heaven forbid we burn down the damn city."

CHAPTER TWENTY-NINE

NATHANIEL DROPPED THE LAST rifle into the crate, and stuffed his hands under his armpits to warm them. The frigid fingers of an autumn already feeling like winter had billowed in the sails this morning.

He and a dozen crew members had worked through the night to remove the flintlock's inner springs from two thousand muskets. The men, having survived the battle together, relaxed into telling bawdy jokes and exaggerated tales. It made the time pass more swiftly, but Nathaniel had missed his breakfast with Blythe.

As old George hammered the last crate shut, he glanced at the rosy pink sunrise. "Captain is waitin' for ye on the foredeck, Mr. Mirtle."

Nathaniel thanked him and found Blythe at the bow looking north. "Muskets dismantled, Captain," he saluted. "How close are we to Staten Island?"

But the captain's lips, like his jacket, were buttoned up tight. The wind tugged at the hair on his collar. His jaw was rigid.

"What is it?"

"Pull out your scope," Blythe said.

Nathaniel did as told. Far ahead, two warships crossed from the Atlantic, the Union Jack flying out their sterns, into lower New York Bay. The frigates disappeared behind a long skiff of land, leaving the waters ahead vacant.

"How many have you seen?" Nathaniel asked.

"Just those two," Blythe swallowed, but then he looked up to their own flag. The British St. George's cross was illuminated by the rising sun. "Red sky before morning, sailors take warning," he whispered, his voice haunted. Nathaniel's neck prickled.

"Sandy Hook," the captain nodded toward the long stretch of land a mile ahead. "Once we get around it, we'll have a clear view from Raritan to Gravesend Bays."

Together they waited at the rails. George joined them, awaiting orders. The crew silently moved the ship north. Blythe looked through the scope— again and again—as the sun moved higher. Grew redder. At last, the ship swung around the tip and headed northwest. The waters opened wide.

"Blistering blackguards…" Blythe dropped the scope. Nathaniel gasped.

The sun hit the distant sky like a far-off raging inferno. It reflected off the bay. It shone off the wet wooden hulls of the fleet, coloring them a deep scarlet. It set fire to their Union Jack flags. Ships and masts stuck up like bundled sticks. The waters tossed between them like blood. Supply ships. Frigates. Warships carrying eighty or ninety-six guns. There were over three hundred ships. Or more.

"We sail into the flotilla of the Devil himself," George whispered. The *Frontier* seemed like a small toy boat among them.

"Is it the entire British Navy?" Nathaniel asked. Boats in greater numbers than he thought possible to exist covered the American waters as far as he could see. They stretched far into the Narrows, the strip of water between Staten Island and Long Island that led to Manhattan. He felt a coldness rocket through him, deeper and more biting than the blowing wind.

"Find us that Billop's house," Blythe at last said to Nathaniel, then to George, "We'll have to get closer. Essential crew only. Everyone else below decks now."

As the crew organized, and with Blythe at his elbow, Nathaniel scanned the land beyond the masts and ships. He found a solitary, gray, two-story stone house near the shore that resembled his own back in Berks County. From a distance, the tip of land around the home appeared to glow red from fall foliage alighted by the sun. He looked through his scope and cursed under his breath.

"Those are not leaves," Nathaniel said.

Blythe followed Nathaniel's instructions to find the house and focused his own scope. He expelled a low whistle. "Ten, twenty thousand?"

"At least. There are more on the boats, too."

Redcoats.

From one side of the island to the other and around the stone house, British soldiers moved in droves—cleaning weapons, eating, sleeping. Nearly a third of the ships were flatboats dotted with soldiers, their woolen coats glowing crimson. Nathaniel's worry for their own safety turned to genuine concern for Franklin.

"Into all this three Americans come to negotiate peace?"

"Pray it goes well," Blythe said. "For us all."

The *Frontier* inched closer, squatting among the British armada. Once anchored, only Nathaniel and Blythe remained above decks, huddled together at the bow. Waiting. Watching. Mid-morning, a small ferry under a white flag sailed east to the island from Perth Amboy. They raised their scopes.

Franklin stepped off the boat, and two other men Nathaniel did not recognize alighted from the little scow. At the house, they shook hands with Admiral Howe, recognizable in his formal blue officer's jacket and powdered wig. Before entering the home, Franklin paused and glanced out at the bay, lantern in hand.

I am here, Nathaniel sent out the thought. But then he looked to the cloudless sky. "How will I see a lantern at this hour?"

"Perhaps they'll make a day of it," Captain Blythe offered.

Minutes came and went. Hours passed. Eventually, Blythe suggested they take turns at the watch, letting Nathaniel rest first. Within what seemed to be only a few moments, the captain nudged a dozing Nathaniel.

"Someone emerges."

Nathaniel scrambled to the rail and brought his scope to his eye. Two goats wandered out the door.

"I assume they are not part of the negotiations," Blythe chuckled.

"They must keep the livestock in there."

"Wise given all the soldiers, but a wretched smell to be sure." Blythe leaned his arms against the rail and nodded at the door. "Which one are you hoping for, Mirtle?"

"I don't fancy either goat," Nathaniel smiled.

Blythe's tone turned somber. "You know what I mean. Peace or war?"

Nathaniel let the scope fall, but he kept his eyes on the house. He'd asked himself the same question a dozen times today. Peace was better for nearly everyone, he knew, especially with a navy like this at your port. But if peace came too soon, he'd lose the honor of securing Susannah. How much would they pay him for a document no longer needed? And how much was enough to never have to work in the gun shop again?

It was all too much to explain, so he said, "Peace. Of course. What about you?"

"Of course..." Blythe squinted at the door of the stone house, then glanced over his shoulder at his ship. Within the look, Nathaniel saw his own longing. A desire for adventure. For something more. But Blythe only shrugged and said, "But..."

"Yes, but..." Nathaniel whispered. The waves lapped against the hull. Neither man looked at the other. Finally, Nathaniel waved him from the rail, "I'll stand watch now. You rest."

As Blythe slept, his jacket collar clutched at his neck, the last rays of sunlight slipped down the front door of the Billop's house and pulled across the water. The windows of the stone house brightened with candlelight. The light flickered. It moved. The door opened.

"They come," Nathaniel nudged Blythe. The captain fumbled for his scope.

Carrying his own lantern, came Admiral Howe, his face in shadow. Then the others came, heads down to mind their step over the threshold. At last Franklin's silhouette filled the doorway. He held the lantern at his side, and in the last vestiges of twilight, he took a few steps toward the harbor.

Nathaniel used the ship's rail to steady his scope. Blythe, too, had his scope fixed.

Unblinking, Nathaniel asked aloud, "What fate have you four men dealt us?"

Franklin pulled a handkerchief from his pocket. He wiped his brow. The lantern light held steady. Then he shook out his kerchief.

Once. He blocked the light.

Twice.

A third time.

Nathaniel and the captain lowered their scopes.

Nathaniel's mouth went dry. He found himself surprised the answer given was not the one he'd wanted. He looked northward, to what lay ahead. Now that peace was but a dream. Now that they had to go on. He had to go on. Remember, he told himself, a rider is not beholden to that which he carries. He closed his scope with a snap and turned to the captain.

"That's it then."

"That's it then." Blythe met Nathaniel's gaze, but a shadow of sorrow passed over him. Then he blinked and the expression was gone. Captain Blythe smoothed his jacket, and smiled too broadly. "Into the lion's den we go."

CHAPTER THIRTY

"YOUR FATHER HAS RECEIVED such fine news," Alice Bowman glowed with pride. Her own.

Susannah shifted in her seat, unsettled by the sight of her mother at their morning meal. She buttered her toast and asked her father to explain.

The colonel gripped his napkin. "Congress is sending me as Envoy to Spain."

Susannah nearly dropped her knife. "When?"

"The *Santa Lolita* sails on the thirtieth of September. In two weeks," her father smiled, but then he stared at the crumbs on his plate. "Your mother has decided to come with me."

Susannah gasped. Her mother had never once left Philadelphia. She had pooh-poohed the very notion of travel, even when her father went to Virginia the year before on business. But now, Alice Bowman thrust out her chin.

"You will have been wed two days before we leave, so my job here is done," her mother trilled. "Wars are won by the ties that women weave, and so I must manage his social hours. I've always said a well-planned dinner will yield more gunpowder than any old diplomat."

Susannah fingered her toast, unwilling to watch her father bear this latest insult as her mother moved on to jotting down an endless list of to-dos the new appointment prompted.

"What does this mean for your hemp fields in Maryland, and the two cotton farms in Virginia?" Susannah asked, eager to turn the conversation back to something familiar from their morning talks. He'd often shared news about his land holdings, which lawyers he trusted, and the best soil conditions to grow hemp. Sometimes he'd even ask Susannah which imports and exports she thought might yield the best return. While seldom had Susannah felt she offered much, she had often seen him go away satisfied by simply having talked ideas through. So now, he answered her question with a broad smile.

"I was thinking the options were to—"

"Your father will settle his business dealings as he sees fit. And before I leave, I will arrange the household affairs so you shall not be bothered by such trivial things." Her mother tapped the list at her elbow as her father stared at his empty plate. "You can set up your own home with Mr. Pemberley after the war. For now, you will stay here and wait."

A buzzing returned to Susannah's ears.

Stay. Wait. While two more left. Even their last housemaid had resigned the week before to attend a brother who had returned from the battle on Long Island without his legs. Susannah wouldn't wish such fates on anyone, but at least the woman was needed.

Lydia entered the room, a bundle of letters in her hand. "Post has arrived."

She handed a small stack to Alice, and then gave two letters to Susannah. Susannah thanked her and examined the handwriting. Both were from Pemberley.

"That nice captain keeps writing you," Lydia winked as she began to clean up the dishes.

"Yes, without fail," Susannah said. Lately, the letters had increased, just as Arthur said they would.

"No others?" her father asked. When Susannah shook her head, he glanced over at his wife deep into her own mail, and then whispered, "Maybe soon."

Soon? The days were hurtling toward the end of the month. Susannah sat the new letters aside to address them after breakfast when she heard Lydia humming. She'd heard the happy sound before and so said, "You have heard from Joshua today.”

“I shall read it again after breakfast,” the German woman winked again as she exited with their dirty dishes, unable to hide a smile. The news today, must be good, Susannah smiled. Or at least not dire.

Each day Susannah had found a way to ask Lydia about Joshua. She'd purposely bump into her in the hall, or seek a cup of tea in the kitchen. When the news was not good, Lydia would hand over the letter for Susannah to read then turn away to hide her worry. Between Joshua's letters and Pemberley's more recent confessions about the truths of war, Susannah had discovered the pieces Arthur had been leaving out.

“It is just as well we set sail in three weeks,” Susannah's mother waved a wedding reply in the air. “I can scarcely comprehend the people of Philadelphia anymore. In my time, no one would have dared dream of sending regrets with a note claiming their ‘status is uncertain.’ We would have lied or omitted an explanation. Uncertain! Probably Tories escaping to Canada or back to England.” Alice Bowman nearly spit the words across the table.

“Alice, darling…,” her father said, “I hate to see you bothered—”

“Bothered! Why should I be bothered? Their failure to behave properly is not a reflection on me.” She excused herself from the table and gathered up her papers. “Although our guest list is dwindling, we have much to do.” On the way out the door she shouted, “Come along, Susannah.”

Susannah and her father sat in silence. Then they both pushed back from the table, and tucked in their chairs, grasping tight to the backs.

“Look at us,” her father began to chuckle. “Preparing to battle the onslaught of endless lists. It's what I get for marrying a German woman.”

Susannah burst out laughing and ducked into the crook of his good arm.

“With all her travel plans, your wedding will occupy her mind far less.” Colonel Bowman looked down at Susannah and his grin subsided. “However, I fear your expectations are not matched by your reality. Might it be wise to give up the dream?”

Susannah's chest constricted, and she fingered the buttons on his shirt. “Not yet, Father. I will consider it… but only when I must.” She pushed her chin higher. “And I will manage fine with you gone to Spain as well.”

“I know that to be true,” he squeezed her closer. “You are your mother's daughter, but you have a little of me in there, too, you know?”

Which part, she wanted to ask. Head? Hands? Heart? She had yet to use any of them to any great affect.

"Fear not, my pup," he patted her shoulder and then let her go. "I promise we shall return soon."

Soon. And more promises from another setting sail into the future. She felt her heart sinking.

All that long, long day her head spun over her father's words despite how much her mother kept her hands occupied. What are my expectations? Adventure and freedom. What is my reality? Correspondences and corsets.

At last alone that evening, she sat at her bureau. A blank page waiting. The pen aloft. Pemberley's latest letters open before her. His letters these last few weeks had grown in affection, and in the last he promised more. Love. To keep her safe and secure.

She was floored by the pull of his declaration. To return words of kindness, as Arthur suggested, would not be difficult. Not when affection and love was what she wanted. But still she hesitated. Could her expectations be met within the confines of safety? In being kept? Was agreeing to a secure marriage merely an acquiesce to necessity?

Love, to her, was more than necessity. It was the thrill that ran up her arm each time Nathaniel's thumb ran over her glove. It was her own desire she saw reflected in Nathaniel's green eyes. But does such a passionate connection wither without a word or two of reinforcement?

"What is preventing him from writing?" she whispered.

There was only one other person who might help her learn more. One who knew Nathaniel. Who knew Pemberley. Who truly knew her. Whom she trusted beyond all others. She dipped her pen in the ink and began to write:

My sweet cousin Arthur,

I am at a loss. My circumstances have changed. Please help me understand so I can make the right choice…

CHAPTER THIRTY-ONE

THE BRITISH HAD TAKEN New York.

Soon after the Howes had fired two warning shots into the city, news reached the *Frontier* that the Continental Army was fleeing up the island. As George and the crew awaited the signal that it was their turn to come into port, Nathaniel paced in Blythe's cabin.

"The three delegates I seek... what if I cannot catch up to them?"

"Aye." The captain sorted through a pile of clothing they had acquired from the Montagu. "Even more difficult because of your horse."

"Bayard? What's happened?" Nathaniel moved toward the door, but Blythe waved a woolen stocking at him.

"He is fine, but we've been nearly ten days at sea. He'll need to find his land legs again, as will you." He found the matching sock and set the pair aside. "Best not to ride him until morning. I will direct you to a tavern and stables I know in town—the Queen's Head. My friend Sam owns it, though if he's there, I imagine his new occupants won't be to your liking."

"I am to sleep among the British?" Nathaniel looked to the satchel hanging over a chair.

"No way around it," Blythe said. "Now take off your breeches."

"Beg your pardon?" Nathaniel took a step back.

"You must blend in." Blythe held up a pair of leather breeches at arm's length, sizing up Nathaniel through one eye. Satisfied, he tossed them across the table, along with other garments. "Even that filthy Holland shirt is too fine for a British soldier."

Nathaniel slipped into the costume Blythe created, wondering when he'd wear anything of his own choosing again.

"When you ride beyond the British lines, change into this coat mid-ride." Blythe rolled a long, green overcoat and put it into a haversack along with a few other items. "It's neutral enough, and it will keep you warmer as winter approaches. But this," Blythe held out a redcoat with a look of apology, "this is either going save or kill you. Wear it with caution."

Nathaniel hesitated, but then took the coat and shrugged into it. He caught his reflection in one of the windows.

"Arthur would shoot me on sight."

"Unless he heard that ratty Pennsylvania accent of yours," Blythe laughed, his own Boston accent making the word *yours* sound more like *yahs*.

"If I see any Brits, I'll just drop in a 'God save the King,'" Nathaniel mimicked his mother. His father's thick German dialect and Arthur's Irish tongue had won out over his mother's proper English, despite her occasional thump as it failed.

A knock came and George poked his head in the cabin, "We've been given the signal to dock with the other merchant ships."

"Weigh anchor," Blythe nodded. When George ducked out again, Blythe donned the blue coat of a British navy officer. "Per our agreement, I will keep the *Frontier* at the docks for one week and take you wherever you go next." He looked out the window toward the docks, then down at himself. "But do hurry."

Nathaniel agreed and reached for the extra sack of clothing. As he slung his own satchel over his shoulder, once again Blythe's gaze followed the bag.

"Mr. Mirtle, we have both avoided choosing a side in a war so unpredictable," Blythe thrust out a hand, "but please know, with absolute certainty, on your side I will always be."

Nathaniel grasped the captain's warm hand. "And I on yours. Perhaps I will one day find you running your family's fabric business in Boston again. No longer a pirate." Nathaniel nodded toward all the remaining booty heaped upon the table.

Captain Blythe laughed heartily and put his hands on his hips, the same stance from when Nathaniel had first seen him on the docks in Yorktown.

"Aye, but until then I'll be the finest dressed pirate there is! Come, let us watch the boats tug us to shore."

* * *

Nathaniel was fairly certain he was stumbling more than Bayard.

When he'd leapt onto the docks, land sickness welled in his gut. As he staggered and pitched, he heard the crew chuckling through the buzzing in his ears. All their laughter was soon sobered by their precarious situation; British captains, crew, and soldiers swarmed the docks.

As Blythe and George shook hands with the customs official, arranging to unload the faulty muskets, George winked a goodbye. Nathaniel tipped his head and headed into town, half leaning into Bayard.

After merely a few blocks, the activity of the docks receded. Night cloaked the narrow streets. Bayard clopped over cobblestones, but Nathaniel could barely see his own boots. The lamps had not been lit. He stopped and cocked his head to listen. Silence. For a major port city, he marveled, one the size of Philadelphia into which many British boats and soldiers had come that day, it felt... deserted. A tingling fear ran up his back.

He heard a scratching sound. A rat hugging the walls of a nearby building scurried into an alleyway and was swallowed up by blackness. The homes and businesses lining the street had shuttered their windows and doors. Even the door-knockers had been removed as if to indicate that interested visitors needn't bother.

The quiet was punctuated by off-key singing. A block away, two men tumbled out of a building. Light fell through the open door onto the redcoats swinging from their hands. They staggered in Nathaniel's direction. The door creaked shut, blotting out the light. Nathaniel tensed. The singing came closer, their shadows coming into focus. Bayard shied back and snorted at the smell coming downwind. Then the men turned up a side-street and the sound faded away.

Nathaniel exhaled. He calmed Bayard and hurried them ahead to the tavern.

Sam had not evacuated with the others, but the spindly innkeeper looked wearily at Nathaniel's redcoat. At Nathaniel's whisper of being sent by Captain Blythe, Sam's thin face broadened with a smile, "That ol' dog's still alive, eh?" Sam laughed and pointed toward a room off the main hallway. "Get some dinner before bed—one I'm sorry to say you'll have to share with two others. For now, follow the smell of baked bread. Happy to settle Bayard for ya."

The salty, yeasty smell pulled Nathaniel down the hall, but on the threshold to the public room, Nathaniel stiffened. Two dozen men in redcoats, seated at every table, turned his way. After a brief glance, they returned to their food.

I guess clothes, not the man, make the soldier, he thought.

He made his way to a table near one of the two fireplaces. Brighter than the darkened taverns of Philadelphia, the Queen's Head had built-in cupboards lined with clay dinnerware that made Nathaniel long for his kitchen back home. A section of wall next to the door was littered with broadsides, the printed notices nailed haphazardly over one another. Across from it, two men were consumed in a game of draughts: buttons and stones littered the table between them.

As Nathaniel took a seat, the dishes upon the table made it easy to avoid making eye-contact with the soldiers. Baked breads, meat pies, and assorted root vegetables were heaped on pewter platters and in blue china bowls from which the soldiers helped themselves. Nathaniel picked a half-shelled oyster from the nearest plate. He tipped it to his lips. The salty juice hit his tongue, and the meaty oyster slid down his throat. His shoulders dropped, and he gave in and ate with relish, loading his plate with a variety greater than the simple fare of the last ten days on the *Frontier*— fried trout, pork pie, apple pudding, and more.

Upon his last bite, Nathaniel wanted to give into the contentment, but his situation was precarious. Although most of the men were still bent to their plates, staying seated with them might invite questions. Yet crawling into bed with a soldier unsettled his bursting belly. Nathaniel slipped away from the table, and went to read the notices.

The first sheet was a torn newspaper ad calling for all citizens to contribute household brass and iron for bullets. Well, that explained the missing door knockers, he reasoned. He was surprised to find a broadside of the Declaration, like the extra copy still in his satchel. Sam supports the Cause, while redcoats dine on his food? Nathaniel smiled at the irony.

As he half-scanned the sheets tacked below it, the two draught-players behind him conversed over their game.

"You here 'till morning?" one asked in a thick cockney accent.

"Leavin' at midnight. My regiment's coverin' the road out McGowan's Pass where the rebels ran."

Nathaniel tuned his ears to their talk, in the hopes of discovering where Washington's army was.

"The rebels, and all them New Yorkers what fled with 'em, are nothing but a bunch a whiffle-whaffle fop-doodles," the second man chuckled. "I say we finish 'em off now, while we have 'em trapped up in Harlem."

Harlem.

The first man puffed, "Yeah, but we got no orders to do that. We are just supposed to wait here guarding our occupied houses. From who? Them what's left in the city is either grimy paupers or Tories rooting for us."

Nathaniel glanced out the windows into the emptiness. The colonies may have declared independence, he thought, but the British have moved in. Into their biggest city. Into their ports. Their streets. Their homes. Even the chairs at their tables. Tonight, he was one of them.

He had always considered himself English, like his mother, as equally as he had felt he was German. Or Shawnee. But, here… something about the redcoat just didn't fit, and not because it was a tad tight. These uniforms and the British Army occupying a major colonial city having run the Americans out… well, that didn't seem to fit with his idea of who he was either.

Confused, tired, his legs heavy, Nathaniel headed for the bedchamber. He was grateful to hear both the British bedmates already snoring. On the lumpy mattress, he stared at the beams overhead. He swayed as if still at sea.

Nathaniel pinched his eyes shut, and silently he prayed… Please let me slip through the lines tomorrow to find those three delegates in Harlem. And then my last one, McKean, back in Philadelphia. Then I can return home.

Home...

He hugged the satchel to his breast, and imagined riding up the road between the trees, smoke curling from the chimney. He could almost smell his mother's stew. Hear her singing in the old stone house. He saw his father waving warmly from the top step of the front porch. And to the east, at the edge of the forest, he saw Kalawi. Welcoming him home.

CHAPTER THIRTY-TWO

KALAWI STOOD ON THE threshold of the Marten household, smiling broadly and holding two small pheasants at arm's length. In a low voice he said, "They surprised me, but I recovered."

"So I see," Jane whispered, ushering him into the kitchen. She took just one of the birds. "You earned the other."

Kalawi hung the bird, along with his quiver of arrows, next to the back door. The last two weeks he'd been sneaking to the Marten farm before the sun, the clan, or Joseph or Peter had risen. The first morning he'd appeared, Jane tried to shoo him away. Two mornings later her face was at the window, and now a lantern signaled when she was awake and the house was not.

"Will you pour the tea? It's ready," Jane said, as she grabbed an old edition of the *Pennsylvania Gazette* from atop crates filled with potatoes. She spread the paper on the table, sitting to pluck the bird before a lone candle as he poured. For Kalawi, the brisk smell revived a favorite memory of Jane teaching him to read with the book between two teacups. He'd taken an instant liking to the inky liquid and the inked words.

He smiled at the memory and glanced out the window to take in the changes to the farm in the orange predawn light. His smile slipped away. A section of the cornfield, once fruitful, was now a sawdust-strewn pit, a hole dug in the earth made to mill lumber. Behind the gun shop, the new armory building was nearly complete, as were two housing barracks further off. A foundation for the kitchen had been formed of bricks made on site, and the wooden-framed molds were stacked next to a kiln.

"The workers are swift despite the rum they consume at night." Kalawi sat with Nathaniel's mother, handing her a cup. When Jane raised an eyebrow, Kalawi shrugged one shoulder. "When I can hear their carousing from my village I grow concerned."

"Me too," she said into her tea, before beginning to tug at the feathers. "But your clan should not fear them. They stay pretty close to the food, or go northwest into Kutztown."

A week ago, Kalawi had heard shouting from the Marten farm, accompanied by gunfire. He ran through the thicket and found the boar-like man, drunken eyes blotting out reason, staggering about the barn shooting at shadows. Dawes wrestled him to the ground, but before the man passed out, he swore about what he'd seen. *Savages.* Kalawi knew the term usually referred to people native to the continent, living wild upon it. It was as common as the Indians referring to the Americans as Big Knife for severing ties to the King. But that night, the man's word had a bite to it. As a result, the clan had recently agreed to no longer go into Kutztown.

"I come not only for us," Kalawi admitted to Jane, "but for you."

"Because I'm one woman among men?"

"One English woman." He took a sip of the tea, and blanched.

"Sorry. 'Tis terribly weak." Jane gestured to the tin on the counter clamped tight with a small lock. "Peter purchased tea blocks for me, on his last trip to Philadelphia. Things as they are, I don't know when we will get more," she looked to the stairs, up where Joseph and Peter still slept, "or if."

She yanked out the feathers with such fierceness, she nearly skinned the bird. Kalawi put down his cup and stilled her hands. Her skin beneath his was dry as unoiled leather. When she smiled, and he let go, he asked, "What's happened?"

"I overheard Dawes arguing with Peter after a letter came yesterday." Jane chewed on her lip, and glanced at the stairs again. She wiped her hands on her apron, and fetched a letter from Peter's black leather portfolio, giving it to Kalawi. "I went hunting this morning, too."

Kalawi opened it, concern rising in him with each word.

Mr. Peter Marten,

An attempt was made for peace at a treaty in Staten Island with the British. It failed. Congress also fears the devaluation of paper dollars. We will switch from Continental Currency to silver from this point forward.

A delay in payments as we adjust contracts cannot be avoided. Another month at least. Continue production on the Armory as planned. Send a full report of status Post Haste. Let me know what supplies are needed. No guarantees.

Yours in the Cause,

- S.H.

"Congress paid these men to get here, but now Peter is responsible for their wages?" Kalawi asked. "I guess this means no kitchen help?"

"Barton, one of the blacksmiths, has been trying to help me." With the bird plucked clean, Jane held it over a candle to burn out the small bits of quill.

"I know Peter is building his future and we must let him guide us, but—" The candle singed her thumb and she drew in a breath through her teeth. She sucked on the thumb, and nodded toward the barn, where the workers slept. "Being hungry now makes it hard for them to envision the future."

Kalawi measured the sacks of grain in the corner. Once head-high, the stack barely came to his chest. He tried not to imagine the day when the last bag emptied, and looked back to the letter in his hand. "Who is S.H.?"

Jane shook her head as she set about drawing out the bird's innards, a sorrowful sigh overcoming her. "Peter was never my most forthcoming child."

And now the other is even less so, Kalawi thought. Jane glanced at his face, which held the question they both still had, then she whispered the same words as the day before. "No, still no word from Nathaniel."

"It has been two months," Kalawi scowled. Then, for Jane, he said, "Perhaps tomorrow Nathaniel will come through that door instead of me."

She tried to return his smile, but the dark circles under her eyes were mirrored moons of his own. Kalawi had promised his friend he'd protect her, but he hadn't expected Nathaniel to be the one hurting her the most. What kind of journey could Nathaniel have undertaken that would keep him so silent for so long?

The bloody entrails of the bird splashed onto the newspaper. Beneath them was the headline: *July 10th, 1776. The full text of the Declaration of Independence.* Kalawi had yet to read a copy of this declaration for himself, and he realized, too late, he might have asked Jane for the copy.

A week ago, two clan members sent to trade at Fort Pitt had returned with a message: as the rumor foretold, Colonel Morgan of the Congressional Indian Commission had called for a treaty, a meeting with the heads of many nations—Shawnee, Wyandot, Cherokee, and the Iroquois nations—to discuss neutrality at Fort Pitt. Nakomtha would go, and perhaps knowing what Congress' document contained could be of help to her.

"What do you make of this Declaration?" He pointed to the newspaper.

Jane hesitated, her face warming red. "I believe it speaks for all men… as if we're asking for humanity, not just the King, to be better. But there is also a list of grievances against the sovereign." Her hands shook as she trussed the bird for the fire. "The things he has done to us all…"

Kalawi waited, uncertain if it was hurt or anger at her own chief that robbed her of her voice. She looked at Kalawi, holding the bird naked and limp in her hands. When she bit her lip, he dared to ask, in the quiet between them, "Do you disagree with your Congress?"

"We took an oath to agree with them." Peter's voice startled them both. Kalawi stood, but then he took a step back, amazed by the change in Nathaniel's brother.

Rigid on the last stair, Peter's youthful, strong face had grown hollow. His proud shoulders, seemed weighed down by weeks of worry. His once bright eyes were red-rimmed, hard. They flit over Kalawi, but he spoke to Jane.

"What is he doing here?"

Jane stood and lifted the featherless bird. "He came to share—"

"We don't need his help."

"I think you do." Kalawi pointed to the dwindling bags of grain in the corner, but Peter saw the letter still in Kalawi's extended hand. He flew across the room, knocking Jane back against the table. The candle tipped over. Blew out.

"Get out." Peter snatched the letter and pointed toward the door. "We are not your concern."

Kalawi stood strong. "Indeed, you are. I promised."

"Promised who? Nathaniel?" Peter barked a laugh. "If he wanted to help, he should have come home. Now go!" Peter grabbed Kalawi by the arm, trying to shove him toward the door.

"Let him go!" Joseph's booming voice filled the kitchen. When Peter held fast, Joseph crossed the few steps and grasped Peter's wrist. Despite the fatigue also etched across Joseph's face, Peter winced under his grip.

"Boys, please…" Jane put a palm to her heart, leaving an imprint of blood on her apron's bodice.

Before Peter let go, Kalawi felt him drive his thumb in deeper. Kalawi rubbed his arm, certain it would bruise. Peter yanked his own arm away from his father, threw the letter into his portfolio, and headed for the door.

"He best go home," Peter snapped over his shoulder. "Unless you want my men to find him here."

As he slammed the door, the pheasant Kalawi had hung there thumped to the floor.

It was Joseph who broke the silence between them, filling his barreled chest with air, letting it out with a moan as he took in the room. Seeing the plucked bird, a smile touched his mouth. His gaze stopped to rest on the bloodied newspaper, then rose to Kalawi's face.

"Not everyone sees you as we do."

Kalawi heard the familiar tenderness in Joseph's voice, recalling a day he had spent in the gun shop learning alongside Peter and Nathaniel. At the end of that day, Joseph had praised them equally. And Kalawi had filled the empty position of father with Joseph.

"I know." Kalawi nodded.

"And I know you come here every morning." Joseph walked across the kitchen and blew out the lantern in the window. Kalawi and Jane stared at each other, mouths aghast. "After twenty-three years, my dear, I know when you lie beside me and when your pillow is empty."

"Joseph!" Jane turned bright pink.

Kalawi could not hold back a smirk. Joseph winked at him, but then his face grew serious. He nodded eastward; the low horizon was tinted with dawn's early light.

"You best go, son."

Kalawi agreed, gathering the pheasant and his quiver, knowing his tribe would soon be attending to their morning tasks. He kissed Jane goodbye on her offered cheek. As he opened the door, Joseph winked. "See you tomorrow morning, Kalawi."

Kalawi returned the wink. He slipped out the door and retraced his steps around the farm's perimeter toward home, but when he stepped through the thicket, he found Hunawe wearing a path in the grass, his face tight with worry.

"What has happened?" Kalawi grabbed tight to the pheasant.

"It's Nakomtha. Come quickly."

CHAPTER THIRTY-THREE

A DISTANT BUGLE CALLED out the tune *Gone Away*. Astride his horse, Nathaniel had one arm pulled out of the stolen redcoat, his armpits soaked. Both he and Bayard raised their heads northward toward the sound.

Nathaniel had left the city before sunrise. He had been astride Bayard when he had reached the British regiments. The cockney soldier from the Queens Head was posted on the Bowery Road near McGowan's Pass, about two miles from the tip of Manhattan, at the northern edge of town. Thankfully, he dipped his head with recognition. Nathaniel returned the nod, and rode through, passing more than three dozen soldiers. He steadied his shaking hands as the road rolled into expansive, vacant farmland.

He'd relaxed into the saddle, relieved to be alone for the first time since leaving Stratford Hall. He had passed a cannon bogged down in the mud, the earth around the wheels drying in an unseasonably hot midday sun, when he'd stopped to take off the coat. Now, the bugle called again.

Why the sound for a fox hunt? he wondered. Distant gunfire came next.

Nathaniel tugged the garment back on, clicked Bayard forward, and cautiously moved them up Manhattan island's west side, toward Harlem. Into what, he wondered.

First, he came to a small stone farmhouse. Vacant. He rode out the northern plateau of the farmer's land, heading toward a flimsy shrub-lined fence that ran west-to-east, and into a long line of trees that snaked northward. He pulled out a map. Beyond the west-east fence was a valley, called the Hollow Way. North of that, a distant, gray hillside. Nathaniel put the map in his pack, and puzzled over the bugle he'd heard.

Now, it was silent. So silent. Only dust and insects rose up from the plateau, catching the midday sun. But then Bayard pulled up and back on the bit. He snorted. Puffed.

"What is it, Baya—"

"Huzzah!"

Suddenly dozens of British and Hessian soldiers spilled red and blue from earthwork trenches just beyond the fence line. Dozens became hundreds. Drums pounded. Men shouted. *March!* They poured northward over the ridge and down into the Hollow Way.

Nathaniel's heart was in his throat. He was several hundred yards behind the British line, well out of harm's way, but British troops numbering into the thousands were rising up and tumbling away from him, forming a wall in the valley of the Hollow Way. They knelt. They aimed up the hill. *Fire!* But then, down from the clear, blue sky, a cannonball whistled and blasted through the British front lines. It tore the redcoats apart like wind gusting through a pile of amber leaves.

Nathaniel cursed and fumbled for his scope, trying to steady Bayard. Popping it open, he searched the northernmost heights. The ground of the hillside moved. Men, covered in clothes the color of earth, numbered in the hundreds.

"Rebels!" he whispered.

The Continental Army faced the British regiments head on from the northern heights, pounding them with cannon and musket fire. Holding tight to the hilltop. Drawing the troops northward. Then suddenly the rebels split. A battalion of a few hundred swung eastward into the long line of trees. The whole valley rattled with cannoned gunfire.

The Declaration burned hot in the satchel, tucked under Nathaniel's redcoat. Dickinson's warning returned. *We cannot have the Declaration riding through a battlefield.* Nathaniel shoved the scope in his pack and stripped off the redcoat. He swung on the green greatcoat Blythe had given him, followed by his rifle. As he wadded the redcoat into the haversack, he scanned the valley for a place to hide. To wait.

"The fence," he said aloud. It was two hundred yards ahead, a barrier between himself and the back of the British line, still a safe distance from the fight. He kicked Bayard into a flat run. But fifty yards from the shrub-lined fences, the British drums beat a new signal. A new command was yelled.

Retreat! South!

The rebel brigade high on the hill must have broken the British resolve… and the line of British in the Hollow Way scattered. Men and horses turned toward the closest cover. South. Toward the same long, shrub-lined fence to which Nathaniel now rode. On the northern hillsides, and now from within the northeastern tree line, the rebels ran hot on British heels. Soon both American brigades would be in position to fire down upon the redcoats. And upon *him.*

"Good God, quick!" Nathaniel shouted to Bayard. "East to the trees."

They turned, racing parallel behind the fence just as British and Hessians spilled over the weak wooden barrier. A crashing, agonizing blue and red wave of soldiers. The Americans fired. Blasts crackled. *Crack.* Shattered fence posts. *Crack.* Splintered wood. *Ka-crack.* Nathaniel held fast to the satchel. He leaned flat over Bayard's neck. The greatcoat flew out long and flat behind him.

Musket balls whistled past Nathaniel's head. Solid shot pounded into the dirt beneath Bayard's racing hooves. Redcoats fell around them. Still, he pushed them eastward. Until, at last, they flew into the safety of the grove of shrubs and trees, beyond the fighting. He pulled Bayard to a halt, and spun him around to look back. Bayard frothed. Nathaniel's breath was ragged and shallow.

It was clear to see the rebels held a higher ground advantage. Their wicked hail of bullets rained down upon the fences and the men crouched behind it. Cannonballs fired into the mounds of earth, thrusting clumps twenty feet into the air. Dirt and debris rained over the soldiers. Mud mixed with blood. Gun smoke swirled. It covered the view. But the rattle and hum of the fighting echoed across the battleground like a buzz of swarming wasps.

"It's absolute chaos," Nathaniel whispered.

Out of the choking air of the battlefield, two redcoats broke away from the group. They ran into the trees just north of Nathaniel, but a cannon shot blasted into the earth between them. One of the men was propelled to his death, his remains blowing backward more than ten paces. His fellow soldier ran on without a look back. The lone man headed into the trees. Musket in hand.

No. Not a musket.

Nathaniel swiftly secured Bayard to a nearby tree, setting off on foot to follow the soldier. Smoke swirled into the woods, wrapping around trunks, dampening down the sounds of war in the field. Through the haze, Nathaniel caught glimpses of the redcoat ahead of him. A sleeve. A shoulder. Then, two hundred yards ahead, the soldier scrambled up a tree. The man scooted out on a large branch. He reached back for his weapon.

Nathaniel found the man's sight line. High and clear above the heads of the dusty brown Continental soldiers on the field… an American in a blue uniform—an officer—astride his mount, shouting orders.

Without thinking, Nathaniel grasped his rifle. Swiftly now, he thought. *Powder. Ball.*

The soldier in the tree positioned the rifle along his shoulder. Already loaded. *Tamp it down.*

The redcoat put his eye to the sight.

Kneel. Ready to fire. Nathaniel swung his rifle to his shoulder. He took aim toward the tree. *Ka-crack. Ka-crack.*

Their shots echoed together. The redcoat fell from the tree, but the American officer slumped forward in the saddle, and dropped from his horse into the throng of rebels on the field. Nathaniel cursed his lateness.

But wait… The sound of the two shots. Nathaniel's eyes snapped back toward the now empty tree branch. That tone, that pitch. The distance. It was over two hundred yards between the officer and the tree. Nathaniel, his limbs thrumming, ran to where the soldier had fallen.

He heard the man gasping for breath before he found him, sprawled on a pile of wilting grass and gnarled roots. Blood ran and bubbled from a hole where Nathaniel's bullet had shot through his ribs. Nathaniel dropped to his knees next to the soldier. Smoke wafted in, cocooning them inside a curtain.

The boy's face was pale. Youthful. Sixteen, maybe. Nathaniel shivered. His gaze traveled down the soldier's twisted legs. There, like another appendage, lay the rifle. A long, slightly flared octagonal barrel. Smooth oak, smudged with crimson fingerprints. Engraved with the familiar *J~M.* Joseph Marten's initials.

"Where…" Nathaniel reluctantly pulled his eyes from the weapon to meet those of the soldier. "Where did you get the rifle?"

The boy's green eyes filled with confusion. "They issued it to me."

"Who did?"

The boy coughed. Blood sputtered from his mouth. Nathaniel swallowed, but asked again.

"When I joined with the loyalists," the boy pushed out the words, his accent more New York. "Yesterday… they issued 'em to us snipers." The boy took a slow gurgling breath. "I thought there would be more…"

The soldier's eyes filled with sadness, and then blackened with fear. He reached a reddened hand up to grip Nathaniel's arm. Nathaniel placed his own hand over it, grasping the youthful fingers, feeling the stickiness with his own. He slipped an arm behind the boy's head. Holding him. For comfort? Apology? To keep him talking, to stop the inevitable.

"More what?"

"More time… I promised momma I had a long time to fight them traitors."

The boy cried out through a wave of pain, but he tried to lift his head, to look toward the field.

"I think I got one… Did… Did I?"

Nathaniel nodded. "Yes."

The boy began to smile, but before it fully reached his lips, his head sagged into Nathaniel's chest. His eyes remained open. Staring blankly at the field where the battle still raged.

Nathaniel rocked back on his haunches. The lost boy cradled in his arms.

"You got one," he whispered. With a soft hand, he closed the boy's eyes. Then he closed his own. "As did I."

* * *

Hours had passed.

Nathaniel stayed hidden among the trees, staring at the boy's lifeless body. Numb. Hearing nothing. Immobilized.

Long after silence fell over the Hollow Way, the sun began to slip down the trees. The lengthening shadows stirred Nathaniel to move. As he rose, Nathaniel could hear a shuffling rumble of troops marching toward him. With one last aching look at the boy, he picked up the soldier's rifle and his own, and made his way back down toward Bayard.

"Sorry, ol' boy." He patted Bayard's black mane, but as he untied the reins knotted around the tree, the sounds of boots on dirt drew closer. His heart thumped. He held Bayard's head to silence him.

The two waited as one with the trees. The smoke receded. Then, one-by-one, the soldiers came marching by. Brown trousers. Torn shirts. Broken faces. Rebels, every last one.

Nathaniel knew of only one thing to do.

He slipped from his hiding place, his horse trailing by a slack lead. He wore his own weariness as transparently as the sweat-stained greatcoat, and the satchel upon his hip, scarred with a streak of blood. His arms hung limply at his sides. Two rifles, empty of their shot, were slung over his shoulders. He stared only at his feet. And he marched. He marched among the survivors carrying the dead, among the soldiers, among the wounded, the weeping, and the worn.

Nathaniel marched up the heights and crossed over into American lines. One with them all.

CHAPTER THIRTY-FOUR

"CHECK IN AT THE third regiment tent. Last one at the far end of the camp near the Morris Mansion. They will announce you at headquarters."

Nathaniel and the ragged returning soldiers were met in the valley by several aides counting the dead and assisting survivors. Nathaniel nodded his thanks and forced himself to climb the last stretch of road onto the heights.

His legs ached with each step. His belly longed for the bit of pork and biscuit still in his satchel from a full breakfast, long ago but not forgotten, at the tavern. He turned behind to pull an equally weary Bayard over the ridge. When he faced northward again, Nathaniel gasped.

He scanned the field slowly from one end to the other. It stretched for miles. And miles. And miles. A dusty, mud-coated, worn, broken, battered and tattered sea of men. How many? Ten? Twenty thousand? More men than all the citizens of Philadelphia.

The Continental Army camp.

"What have we wrought?"

Reluctantly, he willed his legs to walk through it. Through all of them.

Men. Soldiers. Boys. Boys with bones visible through stretched skin and tattered clothing. More exposed bits of flesh than full articles of clothing. No uniforms of any discernible color. Boys lay among tents, horses, cannons, and worn-out supplies. Over the fields, under trees, and along the banks of a muddy creek. Each way Nathaniel turned. Each direction he moved. More men on trampled grasses, ground into a fine dust that flew around them. It coated the inside of his nose. It stung his eyes and collected upon his boots. Good boots. Boots that walked by hundreds of men without shoes. Without shoes and with soles of their feet bandaged, bleeding. Bare and raw. Raw from marching. Raw from the cold wind that had begun to blow. It tore through Nathaniel's woolen greatcoat at his healthy, warm flesh. The wind brought with it a stench. Feces. Urine. Death. Fear. It hung in the air. It oozed from the tents. Tents designed to hold three held six, seven, or eight men. Men huddled together. Huddled with the camp followers—ragged women clinging to husbands—safer here than alone at home. Here trailing the enlisted men. The army. Waiting interminably. Collectively. As if their warmth could be combined. Some lay alone, trying to forget in fitful sleep upon the bare ground. Covered by a blanket of despair. Broken wills.

These are their finest troops?

Soldiers so weak they could barely raise their eyes to him. Their watery coughing made his throat thick. Their wailing. Moaning. Quarantine. Nathaniel staggered on. The third regiment please, he asked. He moved on when they pointed. When they eyed his clothing. Or the bags upon the horse. Or the horse itself. He pulled Bayard beyond a group of men with shovels. They dug out and filled in a long row of graves. No coffins. Faces of the deceased uncovered, staring up at heaven. He bit back tears and anger.

This is how we treat our finest troops?

Nathaniel pushed onward through the sick. The wounded. The dying.

For more than an hour.

Night had fully descended by the time Nathaniel found the office of the third regiment, a big canvas structure. All around it, soldiers stretched upon the ground. A few gathered near a small fire. Like them, the tent was a crusty, muddy brown. Nathaniel was announced as 'a soldier seeking an audience with Dickinson.'

Inside, a handful of men worked under a weak lantern, their heads bent to ledgers and papers. The commander stepped forward and addressed Nathaniel.

"I am Lieutenant Colonel Kachlein."

Nathaniel tried to recall where he had heard the colonel's name, but his fatigued mind was useless. Nathaniel handed him a note to take to

Dickinson announcing his arrival.

"I will have a messenger take it to the Morris house." The colonel barked at a boney-shouldered aide bent over a table behind him. "See that this man is settled with us until HQ comes for him."

The aide made to come around the desk. He faltered, his face mostly in shadow. "Nathaniel?"

Nathaniel's heart leapt. That voice… An Irish lilt. The man stepped into the light revealing the familiar freckled face. Nathaniel swiftly crossed the tent. He clasped his friend in his arms, his own voice breaking.

"Arthur."

CHAPTER THIRTY-FIVE

"SUSANNAH AND I HAVE WORRIED." Arthur offered a chair at a desk in the corner, his broken tooth making his smile awkward, lopsided. "Where have you been?"

Nathaniel warmed at the mention of Susannah's name, but his head spun over the events of the day.

"First, explain to me what I saw today." Nathaniel said. "I walked through the army camp. Never did I imagine… How did things get so bad?"

"I don't know where to begin," Arthur shrugged bony shoulders that looked as if they could tear his shirt seams wide open. Nathaniel felt gluttonous over his earlier longing for his breakfast remnants. He reached into his bag, and handed the pork and biscuit to his friend.

Arthur licked his lips, but immediately left the tent with it. Nathaniel watched from the flap as his friend divided it into equal bites for more than a dozen men. They'd devoured the minuscule portions before Arthur returned with only a small piece of the biscuit in his hand.

Inside, Arthur sank into a chair, admired his morsel a moment before placing it on his tongue. Nathaniel was wrestling with what to say, when Arthur choked on the floury crumb. Nathaniel pulled out a flask of whisky Blythe had given him.

"This is just for you."

Arthur took a long drink and stared at the flask, as if waiting for the liquid to unlock memories he'd suppressed. Then the words poured out of him. A boat to New York. Incredibly seasick. Digging trenches. Marching.

"I never thought I would walk that much in my lifetime, let alone in a month." Arthur stared at his feet, at the hole in the heel of his left boot. "And then we went to Brooklyn."

As Arthur relayed the fateful news of their Berks County friends, Nathaniel felt the weight of all the loses. At all Arthur had endured. But while Nathaniel wiped at his own tears with the back of a muddied hand, Arthur remained dry-eyed. He stared at a nonexistent distant spot. His tone flat, almost sterile. Were it not for the Irish inflection and the hat on his desk—the cream-colored stitching now stained by blood and dirt—Nathaniel would have sworn a different man sat before him.

"Since then, the British know where we are weak. Somehow, they just know it." Arthur cast a sideways glance at the officers in the tent. His lowered voice grew hard. "As for our supplies, the quartermaster Moylan… everyone distrusts him even when he's sober. Our requests are sometimes less than half what they should be. And here, to men who are deprived like dogs, distrust is like typhoid. Compassion shifts. Most won't admit it… we're almost grateful when a body comes back from a battle; there is one less mouth to feed and sometime the clothes are better than our own. Then today, we lost Knowlton, a remarkable officer, skilled in intelligence. Knocked from his horse by a bloody sniper."

Nathaniel swallowed thickly, now knowing the name of the man killed by the boy he had shot.

Arthur took another drink. Nathaniel was again searching for words to express his remorse, when a sparkle returned to Arthur's eye and he said, "Despite that, today we came together like men, for a little while at least. Our morale needed that victory."

"Victory?" Nathaniel wondered if more than Arthur's tooth had been damaged. "It was horrifying. It was hours and hours of stupid chaos."

A protective mask dropped over Arthur's eyes as he pointed southward with a firm hand. "We did not retreat. Five thousand of our troops pushed their British asses all the way back behind their lines."

Nathaniel looked away, and Arthur dropped his arm, his voice softened. "You think I don't see the awful shape we're in? The only thing more constant than our retreating, are the desertions." The next words he spoke were quieter. Urgent. "But I'm staying. It's not about me."

"Why then? For them?"

"In part," Arthur nodded toward the entrance where rain had begun to speckle the tent canvas. "For something far bigger. The British Army was *our* army, too. They were supposed to be *our* protectors. Yet, the King sends them to punish us. Why? For questioning the laws he makes, or ignores, in order to reduce us. Mere subjects forced to submit to suffering, no longer safe even at home." Arthur shook his head. "No, we are the new guards for our security now."

Nathaniel studied his friend carefully. How could a man so withered that he looked like a boy in man's clothing provide a safe harbor? How were twenty thousand starving, untrained farmers and merchants going to defend thirteen colonies against a professional army?

He said as much to Arthur and added, "None of you have uniforms."

"The man within, not his clothing, makes the soldier, Nathaniel." Arthur sat a little taller, then leaned back in his chair, settled. "I still want glory, to feel pride… but a man gains neither in seeking a fight. However, he gains both by defending those who cannot defend themselves. And maybe my being here, my pen, can somehow unite us behind that Cause."

Nathaniel dropped his gaze to his lap. In spite of his friend's weakened physicality, Arthur now seemed the bigger man. Was he fulfilling a duty far greater than Nathaniel could hope to achieve by carrying one piece of paper?

After a moment, Arthur reached out a hand to Nathaniel's knee. "Why are you here?" When Nathaniel didn't answer, Arthur kicked Nathaniel's shoe. "You can't talk me into going home. Tell me how you've been helping so I have another reason to stay."

Nathaniel knew, without a doubt, the parchment he carried would be the inspiration Arthur needed. Seeing first-hand that the congressmen and all thirteen colonies were promising to unite as one would unite all those soldiers outside this tent, too. Still, Nathaniel hesitated to reveal his task.

"I… I am running a message for the Post."

"A flagrant lie," Arthur sniffed. "Bayard is outside, and Post riders change horses every ten miles or so. Come on," Arthur's impish smile returned at last, "our parents still believe it was Peter who got us drunk when we were only eleven. I never told a soul about us stealing the bottle from the larder."

"I'd forgotten about that. To be sure, Peter never forgot the lashing he received." Nathaniel found his laugh. Perhaps he could tell Arthur what he carried. As he took a breath to begin, a young officer rushed into the tent, choking off the thought.

Rain blew in with the man, as he held out a letter. "A message from General Washington."

Kachlein came from the opposite corner, and broke the wax on the missive. His shoulders sagged with each word he read. With an ashen face, he handed Arthur the letter. Before Kachlein strode out of the tent with the officers in tow, he said, "Wait here. I'll get the chaplain so we can tell the troops tonight. What a damn waste."

Arthur read the letter, swearing under his breath.

"What is it?" Nathaniel asked, relieved they were at last in the tent alone.

"A few days ago, General Washington sent a volunteer down to Long Island to assess the position of the British coming into New York. And this man volunteered to go."

"Who is he?" Nathaniel gestured to the paper. "What did he report?"

"Nathan Hale. Young. Unqualified. They captured him on his way back to our lines." Arthur folded up the letter, and ran a hand through his matted, red hair. "He has been hanged."

Nathaniel grew cold. Franklin's words came back to him: *Our signatures are absolute proof of our treason. And if the British find the Declaration first, they will prevent us from uniting the best way they know how. They will hang the signers, and those associated with carrying it...* Nathaniel instinctively grasped his satchel closer.

Arthur's gaze fell to the bag. "Nathaniel?"

Nathaniel took a step back. The canvas walls closed in. Already there were too many people who knew, and soon a few more at headquarters would, too. Nathaniel had to keep this contained. He had to protect Arthur.

"I have made promises."

"To do what?" Arthur glanced to Nathaniel's firearms leaning against the chair. "And with two rifles?"

"I found one on a British soldier. I..."

"Your family's selling to the British—"

"No. Perhaps… I don't know what Peter's done." Nathaniel ran a hand over the back of his aching neck. "I haven't been home in two months."

"Susannah says you haven't been in Philadelphia either. Does she—"

"She knows nothing." Nathaniel's tongue was tangled in omissions. "Please… I beg you not to ask anything more."

Shadows from the candlelight etched anger into Arthur's brow. "Nathaniel, if you cannot say you are with us, then what am I to assume?"

Before Nathaniel could respond, a soldier entered the tent.

"Mr. Mirtle, the general is ready to see you at headquarters."

Nathaniel bent to pick up the rifles. Arthur grabbed him by the arm.

"Mr. Mirtle? But you are not—"

"Stop!" Nathaniel shrugged him off. Arthur reeled back as if stricken, and Nathaniel's heart folded in on itself, the taste of deceiving his friend more bitter than Blythe's coffee. He whispered, "One day, I promise to explain. For now, Arthur, we each our own way go."

Nathaniel ducked out of the tent and unhitched Bayard. Arthur followed him outside, the message about Hale hanging from his hand. The cold wind and hard rain bit at them. Soaked them through. The ground around them turned to mud.

And Nathaniel turned away. He pulled Bayard through the camp, unable to look back. Unable to bear the disappointment that would certainly be darkening Arthur's face. Forward was the only way out. For himself. For Susannah and his own family. For Arthur. And all these men…

But as Arthur watched his friend walk away, a sense of betrayal was what he wore heavily upon him. He watched the distance between them increase with each step. And when Nathaniel was swallowed up in the darkness, Arthur crumpled the message in his tired fist. He tossed it in the mud and turned away feeling more alone in the fight than any man could among nineteen thousand soldiers.

CHAPTER THIRTY-SIX

PICKLES? NATHANIEL'S EYES WATERED. Sweet memories resurfaced of his mother pouring boiling brine over cucumbers each summer. Here, however, after the bitterness of the camps, the smell was offensive. Sour. An aide who greeted him confirmed the odor.

"General Washington's personal cook found dill and garlic in the garden. Follow me." The aide guided him down the hall, but spoke as if giving a tour. "Colonel Roger Morris, a British officer, vacated the mansion to return to London." Candles cast their shadows onto callow yellow walls and elegant archways trimmed bright white. Deep red carpets deadened their footfalls. "His American wife bid us entrance—had quite enough of his loyalist bigotry they say—then left for family in Canada. Finally, we have tolerable accommodations."

"Finally?" Nathaniel said. He peered into a parlor off the hall, where a handful of officers worked at writing desks near a roaring fire while sipping from china cups. He was about to add that the soldiers outside were not so fortunate, but as they reached the end of the hall, sounds of bickering spilled from an octagonal dining room.

The aide held Nathaniel at the threshold, "Wait until called, please."

A dozen or so men stood around a superior mahogany table, framed by hand-painted, floral walls preening peacock blue. A few men were ensconced in chairs duly bearing their overstuffed weight. One man, his back to the room, looked out a window. A wrinkled map was spread out on the table, surrounded by dinner plates pushed aside, meat still clinging to discarded bones. Nathaniel felt almost seasick again. He swallowed back the bile of inequity and forced himself to focus on what the men were saying.

"Howe will storm Harlem Heights again from the south." A stout man, his mouth too small for his jowly cheeks, traced a finger over a corner of the map, then turned to the man at his elbow, a Jack Sprat to his massive girth. "They'll come right through a ridge of trees west of us, Mr. Gerry!"

Despite the larger man's obvious agitation, Nathaniel sighed with some relief. At least Elbridge Gerry was in the room. One of the three congressmen Nathaniel was to meet at headquarters, Gerry's frame was as slight as his whitening hairline. Sharply dressed in a black suit as if in mourning, Gerry tugged on his already crisp lapels before approaching the map.

"General Greene, this m... map does not show a forest." Mr. Gerry had an accent like Blythe's, but his speech was marred by a stutter incongruent with his aristocratic bearing. "I think the army will c... come down from Canada and join General Howe at Kings Bridge to the n... north. We are now retreating into their c... clutches."

"We did not retreat today. We held fast and won the day," Greene thumped the table. Candied nuts rattled in their silver tray like gunfire.

"This notion that we won, it weighs heavily upon me." The soft voice came from the man at the window. He was Nathaniel's height, his hair also fair. He turned to address the room, a half-empty glass of Madeira in hand. "Over one hundred soldiers injured. Thirty men and two exemplary officers lost this day."

Nathaniel knew without a doubt this man was General George Washington. Earlier, Arthur had shared his impressions of Washington. The general engaged his advisors regarding military options, yet he was also slow to act. Too slow. It was costing them lives. Causing the desertions. Arthur suspected Washington knew it, was perhaps even humbled by it. Now, Nathaniel could see the weight of the war upon the man's broad, yet sagging, shoulders as he took a spartan sip of wine and addressed the men.

"Maps too old and missing major landmarks, so not effective. Men, cannon, and supplies lost during two retreats in less than a month. Winter on the way, and men nearing the end of enlistments. Not to mention the deserters… the typhoid."

"When you suffered from fever a c… couple weeks ago, General Greene," Gerry said, swiping at the air with a rigid hand, "an entire regiment deserted in one night. They left behind their c… cooking kettles, but took their m… muskets."

"And what of our armament requests, Mr. Morris?" Washington's morose tone indicated he anticipated bad news. He turned to face a gray-haired, kindly-faced man next to Gerry.

Nathaniel felt another wave of relief. Lewis Morris was the second of the three men he was to find. If Wolcott was also in the room, Nathaniel had only McKean's signature to acquire. It was September sixteenth. That left enough time to return to Philadelphia. To Susannah.

"Since Brooklyn, the orders seem to be half of what we requested," Morris flipped open a report, "and construction on the armories is behind due to issues with funding and supplies."

Nathaniel wondered if Peter was receiving what he was promised, or if the situation at home was becoming even more intolerable. He turned his attention back to Lewis Morris, whose hands shook a little as he turned the pages.

"Meanwhile, the British are receiving massive shipments of firearms— mostly muskets from Bermuda, but…" Morris pinched his lips. He looked to Gerry, who nodded for him to continue. "There are rumors some rifles built by colonial gunsmiths are being diverted to the British Army."

The two rifles weighed heavy upon Nathaniel's shoulder. "The rumor is true." He strode into the room, escaping the grasp of the aide, and set both firearms on the old map.

The men reared away from him, shouting. General Greene pounced on Nathaniel from behind, and grabbed both Nathaniel's arms, demanding, "Who the hell are you?"

"Mr. Mirtle!" Dickinson pushed through the crowd and urged Greene to let him go. As the men begged for an explanation, General Washington swiftly crossed the room, and grasped Nathaniel's hand with both his own.

"Mr. Mirtle, at last." His warm smile returned an air of calm to the men. "General Dickinson and I have been praying you would catch up to us." The general glanced at the two rifles on the table, then examined Nathaniel. He took in the mud. The wet. The blood. The weariness Nathaniel wore.

"You, too, carry a great weight."

Nathaniel grasped the satchel.

Seeing this, the general assured him of the group's trustworthiness, and to prove it announced, "Gentlemen, this man delivers to us the one and only copy of the unanimous Declaration that, once signed, will unite us before a candid world."

Only one sound, a sharp staccato, punctured the silence.

Click. Snap. Click. Snap.

* * *

"What do you mean, Wolcott is not here?" Nathaniel whispered to Dickinson as they moved toward seats at the table. The certainty he felt just a few moments ago tightened into panic.

"He left. He was ill. I'm expecting a letter from him tomorrow." As he apologized, a wiry man appeared at his elbow. "Mr. Mirtle, this is Mr. Hastings, my aide."

Nathaniel grasped the man's hand. It was moist and fragile inside his own. Something about the man's craven carriage was familiar, but just as Nathaniel thought his memory might retrieve why, Dickinson pointed him to a chair across the table.

"That seat between misters Gerry and Morris is empty. You'll find Mr. Morris quite engaging despite being the closest thing to a noble lord the colonies have."

"Rich beyond even my imagination," Mr. Hastings offered before scurrying to take his seat.

Within moments a heavily laden plate of roast chicken and vegetables was placed before Nathaniel.

He struggled to reconcile the miserable conditions he'd seen all day to the riches before him now. The food. The well-attired men. The hand-painted walls. China. Crystal. His stomach turned. He looked away, toward the windows, out toward the camps, and gasped. Rain-soaked faces of soldiers were pressed against the glass. Sunken. Shivering. Arthur among them, shaking his head with disgust. Nathaniel pinched his eyes closed. When he opened them, the panes were black. Empty. Nathaniel groaned.

"Do you not feel well?" Lewis Morris placed a gentle hand upon his arm.

"I believe I suffer from a conscience, Mr. Morris," Nathaniel said.

"As does my brother," the man sitting on the other side of Lewis Morris grumbled. "I'm Gouverneur Morris—Gouverneur as in a first name, not a title. Call me Guv." He gestured to Nathaniel's plate with a glass of Madeira. "What's wrong with your conscience?"

Nathaniel tried to hold his tongue, but when Guv pushed him sharply, the words tumbled out. "I simply feel empathy for the twenty thousand soldiers who starve a thousand feet from your over-abundant table."

The men fell silent. A few looked to their laps. Guv harrumphed.

"The conditions are appalling, but let us remember whose fortunes fund this fight," he said. "Take Lewis here. We both give Congress our time, but he also gives money. Yet, he has it in his head to sign your document, further risking his estate, Morrisania, east of here. All two thousand acres could be seized if the redcoats get proof of his treason."

"I appreciate that, but Doctor Franklin said the congressmen committed both lives and fortunes. Not their lives," Nathaniel motioned toward the camps and then back to men at the table, "and your fortunes."

Lewis Morris flushed, but Guv sniffed, "A strong opinion from a mere rider."

"Position should not limit voice." General Washington, who had taken his seat at the head of the table, raised a palm. "If freedom of speech is taken away, then dumb and silent we may all be led, like sheep to the slaughter."

Elbridge Gerry, who sat to Nathaniel's left, pushed the plate toward him. "S… starving yourself will not help our troops."

"But telling us about those, might." Dickinson, who sat across from Nathaniel and next to his aide, pointed to Nathaniel's rifles between them upon the table. "Mr. Hastings shall add it to the Morris and Gerry report he delivers to Philadelphia two days hence."

"Indeed." Mr. Hastings smiled. It lacked the warmth Nathaniel easily found in Dickinson.

"The Tiger Maple rifle is mine. The other I found upon a redcoat today." He pushed away the memories of the boy's final pleas, and said, "Before the boy died, he told me it was issued to him yesterday. By the British. Both weapons bear the same initials from my father's gun shop in Berks County—a gun shop converting to a Continental armory."

Again, Nathaniel heard that sound. *Click. Snap.* He could not discern from whence it came.

"Surely your family signed an oath?" Dickinson asked, leaning forward, his face scrunched with a genuine concern. When Nathaniel nodded, Dickinson turned to his aide, and all eyes turned with him. "Mr. Hastings, you have made many of our arrangements for supplies. Who do you suspect might be diverting weapons?"

In the pause, Nathaniel cursed himself for not asking Peter more about the arrangements he'd made with his contact in Congress. Consequently, he held tight to his fork, waiting and hoping Mr. Hastings words would absolve Peter and his father.

"The orders we submit go directly to our Quartermaster Moylan," Hastings said, his expression flat and unreadable, as he turned to Washington. "Perhaps with him this issue might begin and end."

Nathaniel loosened his grip as Washington swirled the Madeira in his glass and then nodded.

"If not at fault, Moylan has certainly overlooked details, and at a time when not one detail can afford to be overlooked. Poor transfer of supplies during the last two retreats. Ever dwindling supplies." Washington instructed Morris to include the removal of Moylan in the report, then turned to Mr. Hastings. "Though if this continues after he is gone, you and I will speak again. Those in our own ranks who have been selling the British weapons… their treason is a sickness far worse than typhoid."

Gerry added, "It is the d… duty of every citizen, though he may have but one day to live, to devote that day to the good of his c… country."

"But are we a country, Mr. Gerry?" Nathaniel asked. "The army is diminished and fading further. The Howes have taken hold of New York. And the colonies are not truly united until you sign the docu–"

"I can help remedy that," Lewis Morris said.

"As can I." Elbridge Gerry smiled. "Please, if you will… the Declaration."

"Here? Now?" Nathaniel looked at the dozen or so faces, not all of them familiar, and his hunger tumbled into apprehension. When Washington confirmed all the eyes in the room could be trusted, Nathaniel pushed his plate away, his food still untouched. As he unfolded the parchment, the men left their chairs and gathered around it together. They approached it with such solemnity, such reverence, Nathaniel wondered how many of them were seeing it for the first time.

An inkwell and pen were soon delivered, and with very little fuss, Elbridge Gerry affixed his signature. His was a graceful script, made smaller to fit in the space next to those of the other Massachusetts delegates.

As Lewis Morris stepped up to the document, Guv blocked his arm. "Lewis… Think of your wife. The family estate. Could you bear the consequences? Your vote was one thing, but your signature… it could damn it all to hell."

"In hell we will surely be if we remain under the yoke of a tyrant." Lewis Morris shook off his brother's hand. He turned to Elbridge Gerry, and held out a steady hand. "Damn the consequences. Give me the pen."

CHAPTER THIRTY-SEVEN

THE NEXT MORNING, SILAS' head pounded as he stormed down the hall away from the dining room and his own barely-touched breakfast. He'd slept poorly knowing the rider and the Declaration were ensconced in a room in the same damn mansion. Within reach. Yet untouchable. This morning, before Silas could sink his teeth into a biscuit, the rider revealed he'd been marking up Franklin's old maps. When Washington insisted upon a review, Dickinson demanded, "Please fetch my glasses from my desk in the parlor will you?"

Now, the generals were collaborating with that rider over his bloody maps of Virginia and New York, and no one had said a word about where Nathaniel Mirtle was to go next. Not Mirtle. *Marten.*

Silas pinched the bridge of his nose, and cursed himself for not seeing the similarity when he first glimpsed the rider at the State House. Last night, when Nathaniel revealed being from Berks County, it was quickly clear he was Peter's brother. Same handsome square jaw. Same height. Same arrogant green eyes. Although, Silas reasoned, Nathaniel was only five or six the last time he saw him.

And Peter... through all their correspondence and meetings, he'd never once mentioned what his brother was doing. Did he not know? Or maybe Peter was just like everyone else—carefully withholding information that might later prove useful. Perhaps Peter, stupidly, thought he could protect his own brother.

Silas reached the parlor, overcrowded with desks but empty. A fire crackled in the hearth. At Dickinson's desk, he cursed. All the paperwork had once again found its way into a state of utter disorganization.

"I turn my back for even an hour…"

As he sorted through it in search of Dickinson's spectacles, a courier knocked on the door frame and entered the room. He confirmed Silas' identity, handed him a letter, and swiftly fled.

The note was sealed with the now familiar black wax, marked with an "H." He knew what the contents referenced before he opened it. It was the Howes' first communication since Staten Island. Silas unfolded the letter and decoded the two brief lines written in cypher upon it.

We expect a goddamn explanation. Where is he?
Deliver either him, or you. Mrs. Murray's home, NYC.

Silas winced. Of course, the Howes would blame him. But was it possible the brothers were the reason the rider had not been captured? If the Howes were double crossing Clinton, why not him, too? Or were they getting sloppy now that they were properly ensconced in a mansion in New York?

…Deliver either him, or you.

Silas tore the cipher into pieces and threw the remnants at Dickinson's desk. The pieces fell onto notes, ledgers, unfinished letters—mindless work that mocked him every minute of every day. Silas gripped the desk to prevent himself from overturning it completely.

Breathe, he told himself. In two days, you take the supplies report to Philadelphia, a welcome break from having to act the dutiful secretary. But first, he needed to find out where Marten was to go next. How?

Silas snatched up the torn pieces of the Howes' missive. The light caught the edge of a small envelope sticking out from beneath the blotter. The letter, sealed with vermillion wax, had Dickinson's signature "D" stamped in the resin. In Dickinson's refined scrawl, the envelope was addressed with the words, *To Doctor Franklin, Esq.*

Silas raised an eyebrow, then tilted his head, listening for footsteps in the hallway outside the parlor. He lit a candle. With a little heat, and the careful flick of his nail, he opened the envelope. The wax seal still one piece.

Dickinson foolishly, or in his haste, had written in plain English. Perhaps he thought the contents vague enough not to warrant a cypher. Indeed, pieces of it were a puzzle to Silas.

Doctor Franklin,

I received your letter dated twelfth September. The Frontier is now in the New York harbor. Gerry and Morris acquired. Two left. I will give him verbal instructions for the next, and write you again when we have secured the last.

Yours,

– Brigadier General Dickinson.

Several times in the last month, Silas had read and written letters between Dickinson and Franklin. He'd seen no letter dated the twelfth, and never, not once, had there been communication about this rider. For all Dickinson's praise, his kind hand upon Silas' arm, in the end… no confidences, and hiding a piece of his life from him. Silas felt a sword reopening a festering wound. In the end, he was left out again. Still not enough.

Silas tried to focus on Dickinson's letter in his shaking hands.

Read, he told himself. Listen for footsteps. Read it again. *The Frontier is now in the New York harbor.* It made no sense. The frontier was still west of the Ohio, Silas reasoned.

Then he saw it.

Frontier. It was capitalized. A name. Perhaps a ship? If the rider had not come overland to New York, it would explain why the post road maps Marten was now showing Washington were only of New York and Virginia. He'd sailed to Staten Island, and somehow right into Manhattan. Silas fumed hotter than the snapping fire.

That stupid little urchin, John.

As much as Silas wanted to rip the boy asunder, whether John lied, or had been lied to, didn't matter a damn bit now. There was a ship named the *Frontier* in New York. Waiting. Or perhaps it would not. Before he left for Philadelphia, Silas promised himself to find a way to honor the Howes' request. *Deliver him…*

He reheated the wax on Dickinson's missive and sealed the envelope again. He returned it to the same spot under the blotter and found Dickinson's spectacles. As Silas made to leave the parlor, he paused and squeezed the candle's fiery wick tight between his fingers. An idea formed. And he snuffed out the light.

CHAPTER THIRTY-EIGHT

"MONETO." THE SNAKE. NAKOMTHA held out a hand to Kalawi, her face pale, her voice thin. "I simply did not see it coming through the bushes until it was upon me."

Kalawi held her palm, sweaty in his own, as Kisekamuta, the Rabbit Clan girl, reapplied a paste of wet herbs to Nakomtha's swollen knee, attending to two bright red puncture marks. A half dozen snakes had been killed these last two weeks—twice the number typically seen all summer—since the men came to the Marten farm.

"Thankfully, the other women picking berries with her were faster than the venom." Kisekamuta wrapped the leg in linen, but her brow was knotted with worry. "The fever is weak, but so is the leg."

Nakomtha smiled and turned to Wapishi, weakly whispering, "I cannot go."

The old man crouched on a stool at the foot of the bed, leaning against his fishing spear. Since the Green Corn Festival, it spent more time supporting his weight than it did supplying food for the clan. Now, he turned to Kalawi. "It must be you who leaves for Fort Pitt tomorrow."

"Me?" Kalawi's gut tightened. The British had already met with the Six Nations near Canada, plus the Ottawa and Chippewa at Detroit and Fort Niagara. Some of those nations were prepared to attack the settlers they have been told are to blame for their loss of land, and surely this meeting with the Americans would be to counter that outcome. "You want me to go speak against the northern tribes?"

"No." Nakomtha raised a shaking hand to her ear. "To listen."

Kalawi could only hear Arthur chuckling in his head. *Silence is a great and difficult task for our young Kalawi.*

"Should not an elder go?" Kalawi looked over at Wapishi—the old face puckered with a doubt that equaled his own. "You provide much wisdom."

Chuckling, Wapishi pulled at the sagging flesh on his own boney ribs. "I am nearer to providing a scant meal for the buzzards!"

In the bed, Nakomtha puffed out a laugh.

"Her humor returns." Wapishi smiled. "But the journey would take everything from her. Your time has come."

Kalawi should have been honored to represent them, but if he left, even for a few weeks, what of his promise to Nathaniel? He looked down at his own arms and sniffed. One carried an old scar. The other a tender bruise. Like the two pheasants, Kalawi knew he was not enough to sustain them all.

As if reading his mind, Nakomtha reached for his hand and whispered in English. "Not by another's will, but for a nobler goal…" She looked to Nathaniel's last and only letter, open upon a pile of furs next to her bed. "What are the next words?"

Kalawi nodded, the next line of the oath washing over him anew. "Protect the meek."

This was Wapishi. Children of the Wolf Clan. Joseph and Jane. Maybe even Peter who was weakened by the decisions of men with concerns greater than Berks County. Now, Nakomtha, too.

Kalawi rubbed at the bruise. Perhaps at Fort Pitt, he could discover a way to protect them all—reason and knowledge, not arms, could become his weapons. At last, he nodded, "I will go."

His mother squeezed his hand and closed her eyes to rest, but a few moments later the flap on the tent cracked opened and Olethi and Hunawe were welcomed in.

Their marriage had taken place just after the festival. Since then, Hunawe was his wife's shadow when he was not attending his own duties. One morning when Kalawi had teased him for carrying her share of wood for the fires, Hunawe had confessed that one loving glance from Olethi was worth a thousand splinters. His sincerity left Kalawi speechless and longing for a similar fate.

Now, the young couple stood shifting from foot-to-foot. Hunawe nudged his wife.

"There is something concerning you, Olethi?" Kalawi asked.

"It's about the corn from the storehouse at the edge of town." Olethi dropped her eyes to the ground. It was her duty to collect the ears to make cornmeal each morning, to ration the summer crop with care so it could carry the clan through winter. "Several dozen stalks hanging from the rafters last night… they were gone this morning."

"I was with her." Hunawe clasped his wife's wringing hands tenderly, patting them. "The rug over the storehouse door was pushed aside when we arrived."

"Did anyone else have reason to use more?" Kalawi asked. Theft was uncommon in their clan. Once, when a comb of Nakomtha's had gone missing and the clan was told, a young boy produced it. He'd used it to remove thistles from his family dog. This time, Kalawi feared such a simple explanation might not be forthcoming.

"No, they would have told me." Olethi shook her head. "Or asked."

"Moneto." Hunawe nodded toward Nakomtha's leg and then toward the Marten farm. "Do such devils from the west usually ask before they bite?"

Kalawi's thoughts flew to the dwindling pile of grain in Jane's kitchen. He was about to answer when another line of the boys' oath returned to him. *Step gently into the future.* He asked Hunawe to gather the clan in the council house.

"If no one comes forward, I will talk to Peter before I leave for Fort Pitt tomorrow." Kalawi rubbed the bruise once more. "I must seek the truth without accusing."

"Ahh…" came Nakomtha's strained voice from the bed. "Your task at Fort Pitt as well."

CHAPTER THIRTY-NINE

NATHANIEL RACED BAYARD DOWN Manhattan island. He had to. Although he'd learned much from Washington—the surveyor-turned-general—about cartography during his five days at headquarters, Nathanial been relieved when Dickinson at last received word from Oliver Wolcott.

"You must take the Declaration to him in Litchfield, Connecticut." Then Dickinson shared news that made Nathaniel's concerns grow as invasive as bindweed. The British were thought to have taken the King's Bridge, the northern exit off Manhattan island to the mainland. Nathaniel had to return south, to the *Frontier*, and then sail north. Dickinson allayed his worries, adding, "Fear not, my aide Mr. Hastings rode Bloomingdale Road, down through the city on his way to Philadelphia. He sent back word assuring me it is passable."

Now, riding south before dawn, Nathaniel counted out the days. It was now the twenty-first. Two days sailing. One or two days of hard riding to Litchfield. Four or five to Philadelphia where they hoped to find McKean. He'd ride Bayard right up to the altar to stop Susannah's wedding if it came down to it. If he hurried. He kicked Bayard into a full gallop toward the city.

The rancid smell found him first.

Smoke, but not just wood smoke. And the light over the city seemed wrong. Odd. Wasn't it too early for sunrise? A mile more and a he could see a line, a dark cloud, trailing eastward across the city from the west, near Whitehall Slip. He pushed south, racing into half-constructed northern neighbor-hoods, past Fresh Water Pond. It was there, the sounds reached him. Shouts. Screams. At Broad Way, he turned.

Bayard pulled back, straining against the bit. Nathaniel struggled to steady him, and reached up an arm to shield his own face. Flames snapped and cracked within a wall of fire rising up through the city from below Beaver Street. All around was chaos as an incomprehensibly few citizens and soldiers dashed to save homes and businesses with what little water they could find. Among them redcoats and Hessians tumbled from homes and businesses. Their arms were burdened with stolen goods. They shouted and looted, pushing men into the fires.

Overhead, red hot shingles, fanned by the flames, lifted from the roofs. Fiery embers lofted eastward. Homes to the east, dried by several days of hot sun, took on the flames like torches lit by the lamplighter.

Bayard tried to back away from the heat, but Nathaniel dug in his heels. "No! To the *Frontier!*"

Bayard bucked, but at last the horse ducked his head and ran forward. But with each passing home, each block, the cacophony only grew. Wood splintered and split, screaming and crying out as did the people trapped in their homes. Flames ran up exterior doors and walls, as layers of brick, wood and windows crashed down, extinguishing all sounds of life within. Glass shattered and rained upon cobblestones.

Bayard's desire for safety was strong. He dodged women tumbling through the streets, children, half-naked, forced from their beds, nightshirts smoldering. He leapt over debris as flames soared around them. Behind them. Nathaniel leaned low and together horse and rider became one.

Ahead of them a trail of red sparks shot skyward over Trinity Church from its spires. Though no bell rang. At last they rode south of the fires, and past the untouched Queen's Head to the Coffee Slip. At the dock, Nathaniel yanked Bayard to a halt. "Good God."

Black, brackish water sloshed around the *Frontier.* She smoldered, listed, the hull half-sunk. Atop the mast, charred remains of the Union Jack clung to the fiery pole. The dock was scattered with dozens of dismantled, now broken muskets. Crates were torn apart. Splintered. And among the wreck-age, lay the bodies. The crew. Their lifeless limbs reaching for firearms, and their floating, bloated, bodies face-down in the murky water. Sprawled over ripped rigging. Crumpled on the docks. And ol' George, too. Nathaniel's heart seized.

The old man hung limp over the rails, a musket clenched in his fist, his lifeless eyes staring out to sea.

"Help, please," a voice came from behind a broken crate tucked at the head of the dock. A face peeked out. Smudged. Bleeding. Rogue.

"Blythe!"

Relief flooded the captain's face as he limped out, favoring his right leg. Nathaniel moved toward him, but a shot burst into the crate near the captain's head. Blythe ducked. *Crack.* Wood shattered. Bayard reared back, but Nathaniel pushed him toward the captain. Another shot whistled past Nathaniel's ear. *Crack.* Nathaniel bent to hoist him up. This time fresh shot tore through the captain's shoulder as Nathaniel yanked him to the saddle.

"Blistering blackguards, get us the hell out of here," Blythe cursed through clenched teeth as he grasped Nathaniel's waist with his good arm. *Crack. Crack.* Nathaniel took one last look south and turned Bayard north again. Gunfire snipped at their heels.

Together, they rode back through the inferno. Through the smoke. Through fiery streets. Back to Harlem. Leaving behind a quarter of the city engulfed in flames. In ruins.

Along with Nathaniel's hopes.

* * *

Nathaniel clenched the satchel on his lap, his leg bouncing as he sat at the captain's bedside in an upstairs room back in the Morris Mansion. Dickinson and Washington had been aghast when he'd returned, carrying the captain who had slumped into unconsciousness as they rode through the army camps. Nathaniel had carried Blythe upstairs, and left the statesmen dithering about which way he was to ride. When. Or if at all.

A clock in the hall struck midnight, as Nathaniel waited with his battered friend. Blythe's face was bruised under disheveled hair cast about like flotsam on the pillow, shoulder and chest bound in stained cloth. Although Washington's physician promised a recovery, it had been many hours, and the captain had yet to wake. And not yet did Nathaniel have an answer about his own task. He ran a hand over his own soot-stained face, his thoughts jumbled.

"How is he?" Dickinson asked from the door. Nathaniel shrugged as Dickinson walked to the foot of the bed. "We've agreed you should go out the King's Bridge. We will send guards with you until you cross into Connecticut, and you will ride overland to Litchfield. It might add a week or more, but we have no choice."

Nathaniel groaned. He put the satchel on the bed, and walked over to the south-facing window. He could see Manhattan still smoldering, eleven miles away. He pondered what would have happened if he'd been on the *Frontier*. It could have been his body floating in the brackish water. What if the ship had been destroyed because someone was looking for him? He'd be no help to his father or Susannah if he did not survive, and now his task was going to take him over more land, through more redcoats, and for how many more days? What other option was there? Only one.

Return overland to Susannah before the end of the month. Even empty handed. The Declaration incomplete. Wasn't a declaration of love worth far more than a piece of parchment?

"I do have a choice," Nathaniel faced Dickinson. "I am not going."

"But Mr. Mirtle. *Mr. Marten.* How will we finish if you don't—"

"Back in August, you believed your rider should have unquestioning faith in the Cause. I have seen the scale of what we're up against. The army in tatters. And now what you're asking of me… I am… I do not have that faith. Even if I did, how can one man, one document, possibly make a difference against such a massive force?"

"Just last night you were helping. The maps…" Dickinson's shoulders fell. "What has changed?"

"I have changed."

"As have I," Blythe croaked from the bed.

"Blythe! Thank God," Nathaniel spun to the bed and sat on the edge, then he blinked. "But… what do you mean?"

Through parched lips, the question Nathaniel didn't want to answer lurched from the captain. "Tell me. The *Frontier?* My men? Did any of them—"

Nathaniel shook his head. "I'm sorry. You've lost them all."

Blythe closed his eyes, his jaw tightening as tears seeped between his lashes. After a moment, he turned and looked to Nathaniel and said, "The men were not mine to lose. They were ours. They were us. American. Just as New York was before the British took it." The captain's eyes, those tumbling seas of mischief, turned dark, tumultuous. "Hundreds of British warships in the harbor. Our poor army in the camps… And that fire… I am altered." The captain winced through a wave of pain and turned his head toward the window. "The war men face, it is not out there." Blythe placed a palm on his own chest and looked back to Nathaniel. "Our conflict is whether we live for ourselves or for something greater. I have been a fool not to see it."

"But you and I agreed. We are not beholden to what we carry. And it was too early to choose a side."

"We were too late. It began without us. If the British have taken New York, what is next? The capital of Philadelphia? Our ports? Our farms? Your family and home in Berks County?" Blythe patted the satchel, and added, "General Dickinson is right, you must go on. Only if we stand as one will it end."

The general smiled, but he remained silent. Apart.

"But I…" Nathaniel hung his head, swallowed. "You don't understand what I might lose."

"What if David had walked away for himself alone? Imagine what Goliath would have wrought. Eventually, a tyrant will crush everything, and everyone, you find dear. And in doing so, he will crush you." Blythe sighed, a deep sorrowful breath, an ocean of loss permeating it. "Sometimes we must relinquish what we want in order to protect the meek."

Nathaniel's head snapped up. Those three words. *Protect the meek.* They were like a distant horn sounding a call.

Though he hated the image of Susannah saying I do to another man, her parents would surely go forth with the wedding if he came home empty-handed. There would be no wedding at all if Philadelphia and Susannah fell under the British because the colonies were not united.

"Our convictions can be our worst foes," Blythe grasped Nathaniel's hand. "We must forsake them, not by another's will, but—"

"For a nobler goal," Nathaniel whispered another of the oath's lines.

Blythe smiled. "For all those who have given their lives for freedom already."

Nathaniel pictured George's lifeless face staring eastward across the waves. He remembered their Berks County friends—Jonathan, Jimmy, and Peyton—all gone. He imagined his own father grinding upon a rifle manufactured solely for fighting, not food. And there was Arthur, tired and hungry in his tent, penning missives for thousands of men willing to stand up, to risk everything when they had nothing at all.

Nathaniel now stood, too. He grasped the satchel, and turned to Dickinson, "And so on this journey, I will willingly go."

CHAPTER FORTY

SUSANNAH PINNED A CURL behind her temple. She was grateful the dressing maid had been called off to help with her mother. So seldom had she been left alone these last few weeks, and she welcomed the quiet, the solitude, like a long-lost friend. Needed it. Especially now.

Wind wavered through the tree outside her window. Shimmering sun splashed across the mirror and over an open letter on the bureau before her. Yesterday, it had arrived.

> *My dearest cousin, Susannah,*
>
> *I have receipt of your letter just this morning. The news of your father being sent as envoy to Spain by Congress is not a surprise. We need their assistance greatly, sooner than his expected departure at the end of the month. I have faith his easy manner will secure it.*
>
> *That your mother is to go with him is indeed a shock. She has never had your sense of adventure, but her desire to keep his in check (especially after hearing rumors regarding the women of the Spanish court) is hardly out of character.*

The clock on the mantle chimed. Susannah turned toward it, letting loose another lock of hair. A quarter to the hour. She let the curl be, and returned to Arthur's letter.

As for character... You have written to me faithfully over these last two months, as have I with you. And yet, in all that time no letters arrived from Nathaniel, save that one in August. I now know why. Tonight, he walked into camp.

Susannah's heart skipped, a chill washing over her, as she read those five words again. Hope filled her every fiber that the next words on the page would be different when she read them this time. That she wouldn't feel torn in half when they were not. She put a shaking hand to her heart and forced herself to read the next lines again. All the way through...

I will not state what he does, should I be wrong in my estimation, and because we are beginning to see our letters cracked open by the British Post. Instead I will convey only that he has changed, Susannah.

And when I pair what he did not say to me with his silence, I ask myself three questions. Does he act honorably to fulfill a promise of security for you? Does he ride for others and not himself? Is this a man worthy of my sweet cousin? May I be proven wrong, but to all these I must say no.

With profound admiration for you, I bear you heed my sincere advice. Go on without him. Become Pemberley's wife not out of duty or obligation, but with sound reason as your guide. It will ease my mind to know that when this war is through, a good and courageous man will be standing outside your door, having come home fully committed to our Cause, our country, and to you.
Yours,
- A.B.

Susannah avoided her own reflection, letting her gaze drift to the letters stacked upon her dressing table. On the left, nearly three dozen envelopes in Pemberley's hand, each sent more frequently than the last, his longing and endearment toward her increased by the weight of war.

In the middle, an equally strong stack from Arthur.

And on the right, just one. With words that never changed. Worn. Stained. Now tainted.

Susannah closed her eyes and held her breath. As she exhaled she looked into the mirror. Into the pleading eyes of the young girl who had been clinging to fading dreams.

"He is right, you know?" Susannah whispered. "We must go on."

She began to shake her head. Then, she nodded, wiping away a tear.

"We shall be just fine…"

She tried to smile, but the clock struck the hour. Her father's knock came at the door. Susannah blinked and the girl in the mirror was gone. Turning away, she locked the letters inside the bureau. She stood, and with one last breath, she smoothed the gold silk brocade over her white wedding petticoat.

And out she went.

CHAPTER FORTY-ONE

FALL HAD BRUSHED HER PAINT across the Appalachian Mountains of northwestern Connecticut.

Nathaniel had thankfully slipped over the King's Bridge without incident. The rumors of the presence of British forces had been unfounded, and his guards turned back after he crossed the Spuyten Duyvil Creek. Left alone to ride the ninety miles north to Litchfield, Connecticut, he made his way across the meandering Housatonic River, inviting the solitude of the Berkshires to settle down into his bones. Over that first full day, leggy birch trees, sprouts of white papyrus, became dense forests of towering pines.

On his first uphill climb out of the river valley, Nathaniel was warmed by the sound of Bayard's hooves shattering acorns into splinters. Memories returned of his father's German nutcracker, bright red and green, a crown tipped in gold. It graced the mantle all year until December when it was finally placed in his hands to snap open chestnuts.

"Perhaps we shall be done this business by Christmas, Bayard," Nathaniel said. Near the top of a rise, he dismounted to pull them beneath a dense canopy, which opened onto a rock outcropping with an unobstructed view. Nathaniel groaned. A ribbon of lazy hills spiraled northward, stretching into a hazy horizon, seemingly into forever. Each mountain further, greater, than the next. A cold wind whistled over the ridges. The daydream of an easy ride home evaporated.

Nathaniel only clasped his coat around his throat, over his resigned shoulders, and nudged Bayard back down the mountain.

A few days later, when the sky turned as black as he felt, the wind blew as cold as his broken promise. It was September twenty-eighth.

The hail clipping at him was as hard to bear as the images of Susannah. A gown. A vow. Another man. Nathaniel pulled Bayard beneath a limestone outcropping, succumbed to his own mourning, and rode out the storm. The cold rain mingled with his tears. The loss of her complete.

In the morning, he awoke to another yellow fall day. Another mountain. Another valley. And on and on. When he'd stop to let Bayard rest, he'd bend to the map of Connecticut Washington had given him, marking each babbling creek, and each stone wall wrapping around each gaping meadow. When he ate, silence and emptiness were his companions around the fire. Before sleep, he'd gaze out at the majesty of the purple mountains, using the miles, the days, to try let her go. Then one morning, he pulled himself over yet another high overlook.

This time, the view was as General Washington had perfectly described. Atop the next rise, a swath of land, a wide street dotted with homes, cut through the patches of blazing autumn trees. A church steeple sparkled in the center like a cone of sugar.

"Litchfield." Nathaniel sighed. Bayard whinnied low after he added, "At last."

Upon reaching main street, however, Nathaniel found only winter sparrows and fat squirrels rummaging in the front yards. Windows were shuttered. The town that was reported by Washington to have nearly twenty-five hundred people, was eerily quiet. When he found the Wolcott's two-story white-washed home, unpruned shrubs and trees were splayed over the front door and windows. He tied off Bayard, and pushed his way past the brambles. He knocked. Waited. Then knocked again. Concern crept up his spine.

Have I really come all this way to find Wolcott not at home? he wondered.

As he turned to walk back to Bayard, his feet crunching along the slate path littered with fallen leaves, he heard another sound. The crack of metal on metal. Then came a scent of smoke, with traces of a familiar sharp smell.

Molten lead, like Barton used to heat in the gun shop. It made his nose twitch. He turned toward the house, in the direction of the wind. Rising up behind the Wolcott's plain pitch roof, three faint trails of black smoke snaked skyward.

He inched along the side of the house, between holly bushes. *Bang. Clank.* He pressed his back to the clapboard siding and peered around the corner. Small fires were built in rock pits, a kettle hanging from a tripod over each one. Nearby, men, women, and children worked at long tables. A small boy pulled apart a stone mold. With a thud, a single lead ball fell onto the table. A broad-shouldered man tending a fire, removed a smoke-stained hat from his head to wipe his brow, his thatch of gray hair slicked against his neck. He had a long, regal nose with a high brow over laughing eyes in a cheerful face that perfectly fit Washington's description. Oliver Wolcott.

As Wolcott donned his hat again, Nathaniel stepped from his hiding spot.

The boy yelled and pointed, the group startled, a woman squealed, and Wolcott nearly tripped over the fire pit.

"Oh, no… please!" Nathaniel said, holding up his empty palms. "I am Mr. Nathaniel Mirtle. John Dickinson might have sent word—"

"Huzzah!" Wolcott raised his lanky arms high above his head as laugh lines spread out across his square face like ripples on a pond. He came quickly forward and grasped Nathaniel's hand firmly between both his own. "Praise be to God you have arrived! But oh… we had terrible storms." He grasped Nathaniel by the shoulders turning him from side-to-side. "You look to be in one piece. And our document?"

"If you can see past the mud and muck," Nathaniel said. The heaviness of his days of brooding was suddenly lighter before Wolcott's jubilant greeting. He patted the satchel. "We are both safe."

"Good show," Wolcott's smile faltered, but then returned. "Dickinson also said we can expect a missive from Franklin about your next stop—it should arrive in a matter of a day or two. Here, you can rest a spell."

Relief ran through Nathaniel knowing news of McKean's whereabouts was soon forthcoming, and that he might have a day or two of rest, but then he confessed, "When I arrived out front, I feared you were not here, Mr. Wolcott."

"Oh, do call me Oliver. The townsfolk have smartly agreed to keep street presence to a minimum. We've seen no British yet, but in August the imprisoned Governor of New Jersey, poor Doctor Franklin's son, was moved up here."

It was no secret in the colonies that despite Benjamin Franklin's decision to support the Cause, his son was a loyalist through and through. He was jailed in Litchfield for those loyalist ties, which would certainly be cause for the populace to be on guard, should the British decide to come help him out. Nathaniel said as much to Wolcott, just as a petite woman joined them, wiping ash from her hands. Oliver introduced her as Mrs. Wolcott.

"Call me Laura, please," she said, pumping his arm with the same two-handed grasp as her husband. Their intimate welcome wrapped around Nathaniel like a winter coat; he had not expected such warmth to be languishing within Connecticut's monotonous hills. Then, Nathaniel felt a tug on his pant leg. The small boy from the table, his brown bangs flopping in every direction, was introduced as Wolcott's youngest son, nine-year-old Frederick.

"Did you find his head?" Frederick asked.

"Whose?"

"King George!" the boy threw up his hands as if it seemed preposterous to think otherwise. "We been choppin' up his body, and even his horse." He stuffed his hands in his pockets and, crestfallen, he added, "but I should have liked to have seen his head."

Nathaniel stared open-mouthed. Wolcott burst out laughing, then said, "Not *the* King George! His statue. The soldiers in New York pulled it to the ground after they heard the Declaration read aloud in Bowling Green."

"Father had it dragged here." Frederick flipped a thumb toward the tables. There rested a metal hand several inches larger than Nathaniel's head. Beyond the table, in a pile as high as Nathaniel's shoulders, were other limbs and body parts. He appreciated the effort it must have taken to transport it over the Berkshires.

"We're making shot to beat back the King's army with his own hide," Frederick added, dancing a little jig.

"You don't happen to know anything about making musket balls, do you, Mr. Mirtle?" Oliver Wolcott asked.

"A bit." Nathaniel laughed. "I was apprenticed to my father. He is a gunsmith."

Oliver Wolcott nearly leapt with as much glee as his own son.

"I'm sure Nathaniel might want a bit of rest before you set him to work." Laura waved off her husband, and opened a hand toward the house. "Come. We've a room ready for you, and I shall fetch some hot soapy water."

"Careful," Frederick's face grew serious. "Come Sundays they scrub me so hard I think God can see himself in my shiny red cheeks."

CHAPTER FORTY-TWO

SILAS HASTINGS STARED INTO the flames. He sat alone in a private chamber in the State House, turning a small, folded sheet of paper in his hand.

Six days ago, the trip to Philadelphia seemed inconvenient. He'd felt forced into trying to deal with that rider before leaving Manhattan. It had taken only a few coins, a couple gallons of lamp oil, and simple instructions: destroy the *Frontier* and capture the rider alive or dead. It was simple enough. It should have been easy.

Simpletons, Silas thought. Clearly, he'd chosen the wrong eager redcoats.

News of the great New York City fire had reached Philadelphia shortly after Silas rode into town. Soon after that a letter came with the black seal. This time, Silas was relieved to see the words, *help us find whomever set the fire,* upon the page. The Howes had not yet discovered he was to blame for burning their newly occupied city, but still Silas shivered, wondering what would happen when and if they did. Only one document would solidify his worth to them. However, it was still en route. To somewhere. The Declaration and that infernal Marten had missed the boat.

Then, a couple days ago, just at the moment that Silas' plans for what to do next seemed flimsy, the options scant, Mr. Charles Thomson, the secretary of Congress, ran up to him, his long face seemingly dragged longer with worry.

"Mr. Hastings, I am in a pickle. I must leave on urgent business for Hancock, the President. The delegates have to vote anonymously on an issue and I cannot stay to tabulate the votes." Implicitly trusted by Congress because of his education and fealty to the Cause, Thomson was trusted to decide which minutes of their meetings and decisions were recorded in the Secret Journal. Now, the secretary begged, "Please tell me you can stay to count them in my stead?"

Silas was about to decline such a menial duty when Mr. Thomson added, "They vote to appoint an ambassador to King Louis XVI's court. France has given indication they might help the rebellion. Congress will choose an envoy who must sail within the month."

Silas, afraid to speak for appearing too eager, tilted his head in a small bow. Thomson grasped him by the shoulders, and said, "As Heraclitus said, a man's character is his fate. I trust you as I would trust myself."

Now, the vote having been given that morning, Silas stood alone by the fire fingering the last of the ballots cast. He unfolded the small piece of paper. He found upon it the same name that had been affixed to the overwhelming majority. *Mr. Thomas Jefferson.*

Silas agreed, they were right to elect Jefferson. The man's French was unequaled. His dress and his manners were refined and European in nature. That he had drafted the Declaration made him an impassioned liaison, to whom the French would certainly acquiesce.

"But alas it shall not be you, T.J.," Silas whispered as he bent toward the fire. Flames licked the corner of the last ballot and he let the paper fall. He watched until the embers consumed the ink, curled the linen, and it crumpled into ash with the others. "What one fire did not consume, another shall provide."

A few moments later Silas sat in the assembly hall, his nails digging into his palms to keep from smiling, as President Hancock announced the decision.

"Congress elects Doctor Benjamin Franklin as ambassador to France." A murmur of surprise rose from a few in the Congress, with Franklin's brows lifting the most. The doctor quickly recovered, nodding his thanks as Hancock added, "Doctor Franklin you will leave as soon as you are able to right your affairs, and before the end of October."

The delegates rose and moved to congratulate their elder statesman. What a gift, Silas thought, but as Jefferson approached Franklin, his being within earshot provided another.

"'Tis just as well you go to France, Doctor. I must return to Monticello as it has been a difficult year for Mrs. Jefferson." Then with a lowered voice Jefferson, who himself looked sick with exhaustion, added, "We must send letters to Dickinson—one for him and one enclosed for him to forward to our rider. They must be told of the change; it's just the two of them now."

Then the two men glanced toward Silas. He tried to keep his expression neutral as they approached.

"Mr. Hastings?" Franklin said, "May we have a private word?"

An earnest favor, they said. An Express delivery. Confidential. Urgent. One envelope. For Dickinson at headquarters. A few promises from Silas about safe delivery, and within the hour the letter was in his hands. By sun-up the next day, he was driving his borrowed horse northward with it in his pocket. As he crossed into Maryland on his way back to New York, riding a post road through the forest, Silas yanked it from his pocket.

He sneered at it and said, "Having resigned your post, Doctor Franklin, I find your mail to be undeliverable."

With his horse at a full gallop, he flung the missive into the air, riding on without a backward glance as it tumbled and fell upon a pile of dying leaves.

CHAPTER FORTY-THREE

SUSANNAH, ALONE AGAIN AT the mahogany dining table, broke the yolk on her fried egg. Before this week, she could recall only once or twice ever eating alone. The last few days, however, the American Chippendale chairs her mother had deemed more fashionable were her only company.

She diverted her attention away from their vacant backs to the newspaper. October first. The Pennsylvania Packet was a shared favorite with her father, and she took comfort in keeping up their routine of reading it. An ad announced delivery of rum, molasses, and dry goods arriving from Jamaica. They'd also printed a letter from London dated April seventh about Lord Howe setting sail from Britain to command the fleets amassing in New York.

"How is it news if it's five months old?" she asked her father's empty chair, longing for his bear-like frame to fill it again and to provide a reasonable answer. Then across the table, "What do you think, Matthew Pemberley?"

Pemberley.

She had to admit, Matthew had been a surprise. Whether he'd been affected by their letters or the war, he had been as tender in his wedding vows as in their wedding bed. She'd allowed herself to find more than mere comfort in those moments with him. She remembered her mother once advising a cousin: *a wife must learn to bear a husband's nightly affections.* But nothing about her wedding night experience with Pemberley was unbearable.

Thinking of it now, made her flush warmly, and a part of her welcomed his return. Perhaps creating new memories with him might prevent her from forever making comparisons to Nathaniel who once sat in that same chair.

Although neither he nor Matthew had ever really filled it, had they? *A war leaves no room for honeymoons,* Matthew said, genuine sorrow in his voice. They'd had just two days together, and then he, like everyone else, promised to write. With the exception of Lydia, who'd been instructed to remain, the rest of their staff had found reasons to leave, or been let go.

In the end, it was just the two women waving goodbye.

Now, Susannah poked the runny egg on the Canton porcelain plate, and asked it, "Would you like to hear about my lifeless days, or my restless nights?"

Solitude had made sleep evade her, so she'd taken to wandering nightly barefoot down hallowed halls lined with Bowman family portraits. She, one woman among mostly men. Just once had she visited the darkened ballroom where fabric-covered chandeliers were held dormant in their shrouds, and the mirrors reflected memories of Nathaniel. The parlor entertained only dust, her mother's absence giving her callers a reprieve.

Last night, Susannah's feet had brought her to her father's study, off the front foyer. She'd stood outside the imposing doors in her nightgown, staring at the cold, glass knobs. Her hands clasped at her chin. She had been eight the last time she'd gone into that room. She could still feel the sunlight streaming in the ceiling-to-floor windows that faced Walnut Street. She'd been climbing, spellbound by a volume out of reach in the wall-to-wall bookshelves, when she'd been brought down, her mother's fist around her ponytail. *Too much knowledge in a wife, in a marriage causes strife,* her mother chastised, shutting Susannah out. Last night, the memory sent her running back to bed.

Now, made smaller by the shame of the old admonishment, the deafening silence choked her. Her lungs felt tight. She dropped her spoon. It clanged against the china—a tolling bell. She grasped her napkin. Her plate. Her silverware. She walked out of the formal dining room, heading to the back stairs. With each step, her feet flit faster down the hall. She nearly tripped in her race down the two narrow flights. Tumbling into the warm, stone-floored kitchen, she plunked herself in a weathered chair across from Lydia.

The German woman stared at her—one eyebrow arched, her fork aloft over a chipped plate. Silence fell over the scarred pine table between them as Susannah arranged her plate and silverware. Lydia opened her mouth to protest, but Susannah squared her back and held the older woman's gaze.

After only a brief moment more, Lydia's eyebrows returned to the same plane. A corner of her mouth rose. She pointed her fork toward an open envelope on the table. "Shall we read Joshua's new letter together?"

Susannah sank back into the curve of the comfortable chair, and placed a forever grateful hand upon her pounding heart. "Thank you, Lydia. I would very much like that."

* * *

Susannah tucked her needle into the pin cushion on her bureau. Holding the woolen petticoat up to the autumn morning light, she admired her stitches. Good as new. Lydia's woolen shift from last season had grown threadbare along the hem. With winter on the way, Susannah had offered to mend it. When Lydia protested, Susannah had presented a trade.

"You want me to teach you how to make an apple pie?" Lydia waved a wooden spoon at her, but when Susannah had begged, Lydia relented. "Your mother will whip us both!"

Susannah vowed never to tell of the cooking lesson. Nor would she confess it was one of her own woolen shifts now providing the mending materials. Besides, it seemed a small gift for Lydia's warm company over the last several days. Their mealtimes, spent reading the newspapers or sharing letters as they came, and given meaning to her days.

As she folded the finished skirt over her arm and headed downstairs, she pondered over lines from Arthur's last letter.

> *We still have no official uniforms. To see us fight the redcoats we look ragged and dismal. Easy to beat. I am thankful Nakomtha showed me how to make needles and sew cloth. I am one of a few men who is able to use scraps left by others to mend my moccasins and clothing. Now, if only I could stitch my hungry belly shut as we move toward Fort Washington...*

What I wouldn't give to send you this pie we are to make, Susannah thought as she descended the stairs to the kitchen. It seemed unfair to have food so plentiful when she was doing so little for the Cause compared to Arthur.

"Did I hear the Post come this morning, Lydia?" Susannah asked, stepping into the room.

Apple peels were laid out in ribbons on the table. Pale slices, already turning brown, were piled deep inside a blue bowl. Lydia sat motionless, staring at a letter crumpled in her fist. Susannah cast aside the skirt and rushed to her.

"Lydia!" She smoothed away the gray hair from the older woman's watery eyes.

Lydia opened her mouth to speak. No air. No sound.

"What is it?" Susannah asked, her heart sinking into her stomach. The memory of Joshua's quivering chin swam up before her. Susannah tried to push it down. "Lydia… is it from Joshua?"

The jowly woman shook her head and whispered, "A ship."

"When was Joshua on a ship?" Susannah blinked.

Lydia's composure returned in a wave. She turned her imploring gaze to Susannah, putting the letter into her hands, and holding them tight between her own. "No, my dear, it was not Joshua. It was the *Santa Lolita*… Your parents…"

The warmth blew out of room. Susannah felt herself floating apart, distant. She saw her trembling hands unfold the letter. She tried to read through the hail of words. Lydia's somber voice thrumming in her ringing ears.

"A terrible storm. A few days after sailing from Philadelphia… Off the coast of the Carolinas… No survivors."

A chill ran up Susannah's legs. She shook. Listed. She folded into Lydia's consoling arms, and together they rocked in a weeping embrace. Their teardrops splashed onto the cold, stone floor.

In the end, it was just the two of them.

CHAPTER FORTY-FOUR

NATHANIEL, ALONE, BURNED A CANDLE low at a desk in his room. Pen in hand, he poured worry into work, updating maps of New York and Connecticut using notes from his journals made along the way to Litchfield.

His first night at the Wolcott's, a bed to himself for the first time since the Wythe's house a month earlier, he'd slept soundly. Two days later, still no letter had arrived from Franklin, and as two days turned into a week, and more fall-burnt leaves collected around the base of the trees, sleep began to evade him.

He'd spent his days, at the Wolcott's urging, helping to make musket balls and fashioning for them a multiple-shot mold. Everyone had cheered as six balls dropped into the bucket at once; their production was greatly improved. But for Nathaniel, with each clang the monotony of the gun shop returned like a dull toothache.

Each night he suggested to Oliver they sign the Declaration, in case morning finally brought word. However, unlike Richard Henry Lee who could not attach his signature fast enough, Oliver always waved his hand and said, "Later. Before you leave it will be done."

Now, just after a clock in the hall struck midnight, as he tried to sketch away his concerns, the floorboards creaked in the hall outside Nathaniel's room. A gentle knock came at the door.

"Come in."

"I saw your light beneath the door." Oliver stepped in wearing a nightshift and cap. "I was having a bit of trouble sleeping."

"Me, too." Nathaniel turned in his chair, as Oliver leaned against the bed next to the desk. "It's been too many days, my being here. I'm half tempted to roam the countryside in search of McKean myself."

"You are right to be concerned," Oliver rubbed his face while yawning, "but in my experience, Congress is more like the tortoise than the hare. Especially now as we cobble together both a government and a military—delays in the action are inevitable. I'm certain Doctor Franklin will agree that we are wise to have you wait here. Finishing your task is more important than how swiftly it is done."

"His words almost exactly," Nathaniel admitted. The statesman's smile made it easy to then share his envy of Wolcott's situation. "In between what is required of you, you can return home. It seems only by completing my task away from home, can I return to it." As Oliver contemplated his words behind a furrowed brow, Nathaniel ran a hand over his map of Connecticut, the lands of which felt further away from Topton Mountain with each passing day.

"What's all this?" Oliver leaned toward the maps.

"Just a hobby… or it was." Nathaniel explained Washington's request to redraw the lands as he saw them changed, as he traced a finger along his new sketch of the Housatonic. "My grandfather taught me that while mountains tend to stay the same, weather changes the world. Seasons of leaves obscure passageways. Rain and water sculpt the rivers and roads. Game trails also change as a result." He pointed to two spots southwest of Litchfield. "Some of your post roads were washed away here and here."

"It would surely be nice to have a copy of this." Wolcott examined the map closely, and then searched Nathaniel with equal scrutiny. "Look at your face, Mr. Mirtle."

"Do I have ink on it?" Nathaniel wiped at his cheek with the back of a hand.

"No," Oliver smiled, his voice a whisper in the sleeping house. "When you make musket balls, you look like a grieving widow. Just now, you looked like a blushing bride," he chuckled.

Nathaniel wanted to laugh with him, but the last word swiftly brought to mind an image of Susannah. Nathaniel shook her from his head, and turned away.

"It is just a means to pass the time." He made to clean up his work and gestured out his upstairs window toward the backyard. "I should probably put things away and turn in. We are to melt down the King's legs tomorrow."

"Mmm, yes." Oliver nodded, but his brow was furrowed as he headed for the door. A hand on the knob, he turned back. "Nathaniel, bring the Declaration down with you in the morning, will you? And that map, too."

"Sure," Nathaniel agreed. Oliver said his goodnights, closing the door with a soft click.

Come tomorrow, the document would finally be signed, Nathaniel sighed. It would leave just Thomas McKean for him to find, and then he'd be done with all this. He traced his finger along the map of the colonies toward home. Then what?

* * *

In the backyard, Nathaniel set his map onto a separate table where Oliver arranged a few items—tools, paper, charcoal, wax, and a small inkwell. A few of the townsfolk had arrived to begin the day, and they and Frederick were already stoking fires and melting iron at their normal stations.

"Are we not working with everyone else?"

Oliver shook his head then pointed to Nathaniel's satchel. "May I have the Declaration?" Nathaniel obliged, and without ceremony, Oliver signed it and handed it back. "There, it is done."

As Nathaniel tucked the document away, wanting to ask what had motivated Oliver to at last sign it, a man from the yard brought them a small sheet of flattened metal.

"What's this?" Nathaniel asked.

"Copper. A bit of bronze and maybe lead in there perhaps. I'm sorry it's not as pure as necessary." Oliver said as he pushed a book across the table. *The Practickle Art of Engraving and Printmaking.* "Laura helped me find the booklet this morning. We are going to figure out how to make a copy of your map." His face filled with boyish excitement as he held out an apron to Nathaniel. "Roll up your sleeves, Nathaniel. Before Franklin writes, you and I are going to learn all we can."

For the whole of the morning, Oliver and Nathaniel pored over the instruction manual. As the day passed, they ran test plates. He botched drawings. Spoiled pages. Nathaniel could feel the memory of etching the rifles in the gun shop in his fingers. However, as he drew his map in reverse upon the wax-covered copper plate, something else in him stirred. With each crosshatch made to mark the Housatonic, he could taste the cool waters again. With each push and chase to define a high mountain ridge, he could almost feel the sun on his face. It was as if he rode the very map his hands made. It was as if his Grandfather and he were hiking and sketching together once more.

A few more days, and many failed attempts later, Nathaniel and Wolcott bent over the latest copy by the light of an oil lamp, the sun leaving a violet veil over the backyard. Upon the new map, lines lay where Nathaniel had intended. Ink rested evenly from one side of the print to the other. It was one of a handful of fine copies.

"Your map, your work is exquisite, Nathaniel." Wolcott put an arm around Nathaniel's shoulders and squeezed, and then perched both his hands upon his waist. "What a great help this will be as I come and go through my colony. Honestly."

"Are we being honest?" Nathaniel looked at Oliver, ink smeared on the man's kind face. "What was it, after all this time, that made you sign the Declaration? And why were you not in Philadelphia in August, or now? I thought you were ill."

Oliver's arms fell and he looked over his neighbors and family cleaning up for the night. "When were you last home, Nathaniel?"

"End of July." Down to his bones, Nathaniel felt the homesickness of nearly three months away.

"I have spent just three weeks here in the last six months in support of this Cause. In a fortnight, I leave again for an untold time." Oliver ran his finger over the map of his colony, the lamplight deepening the lines of fatigue etched on his face. "The illness that brought me home... it was my heart. I missed my wife. My life. I thought by staying here, I could protect my family from what was out there. Although I firmly believe in the words upon the Declaration, signing it felt like a death warrant." Oliver stared at Nathaniel's satchel containing the document. "But then, a few nights ago, you reminded me why I must sign it."

"Me?" Nathaniel couldn't recall having said anything noteworthy.

"You indicated that the only way to remain at home, is to leave. How true." Oliver looked over to where his wife was bundling a fatigued Frederick in her arms to cart him up to bed, and his face grew wistful, humble. "The only way my son, Frederick, can pursue a life of happiness, is for me to give up mine.

"My signature is an act of faith in a better future, a belief that I am one of many required to unite us. Embracing who I am and what I can personally do to secure our freedom… well, that is my task in this life. Knowing my role, accepting it, it gives me freedom, too." Oliver tapped the new map of Connecticut and smiled. Before he turned to take himself off to bed, he left Nathaniel standing in the yard with one last thought, "Figuring out your purpose and how you will contribute to us all… Therein lies the answer to what home means. Therein lies the answer to becoming something other than a gunsmith."

CHAPTER FORTY-FIVE

IT HAD TAKEN MORE than half of the ride to Fort Pitt, the hot October sun on his back turning the tree-covered western Pennsylvania hillsides a fiery orange, before Kalawi realized his anger was misplaced.

When no clan member had admitted to taking the corn, Kalawi, visited the Marten's home. No surprise, Peter adamantly refused to take Kalawi's concerns to the workers, and his final retort, despite Joseph and Jane's presence, was only, "Perhaps the corn is retribution for your dependence on us. For wheat. For firearms. For scraps of metal."

The comment had itched under Kalawi's skin like an infected insect bite for over one hundred miles, when at last he admitted his ire masked a grave worry. When he'd exited the Marten's house, a familiar lye and liquor stench lingered on the doorstep. Kalawi had left Berks County with the sour-smelling proof that Dawes had overheard every scrap of their discussion.

"Please let the treaty be swift," Kalawi prayed to the Great Spirit, but as he came over the last rise to peer down on Fort Pitt, the notion blew away with the autumn wind.

The star-shaped garrison stood sentry at the mouth of the Ohio, where dozens of longboats unloaded goods onto carts and packhorses. With a footprint greater than his Shawnee town and the Marten's farm combined, the Fort at the confluence of the Allegheny and Monongahela rivers buzzed with more souls than a hive of a thousand bees.

Nakomtha had told Kalawi to, "find your Shawnee brethren on the northwestern banks of the Ohio, opposite the fort, until the treaty begins." But she had not mentioned the tightly drawn, white faces he had to pass down in the valley first. Soldiers at the bridges leading into the fort grit their teeth and gripped their muskets as he rode by. After Kalawi passed a hunched woman tending the garden outside the fort walls, he felt a stone clip him in the back.

"They'll hang ye up like dogs if ye go in fightin'!" she muttered, staring at the ground.

He forced himself not to confront her. And not to run for home.

When he finally reached the opposite bank of the Ohio, the camps of a multitude of nations—Munsee, Mohican, the Iroquois Six Nations, and more—stretched from the banks and scattered deep into the forested mountains. Men, women, and children, their fire pits filled with the ash of several days, and their long-houses and *wegiwi* constructed for a stay longer than one night, made Kalawi see the error in the old woman's words and fears; nations on the war path would not bring housing or their families.

Yet, Kalawi's uneasiness remained as he rode past nations and tribes different from his own, their faces and language distinct from his. When he dismounted to walk through the thickening camps, women and children, and warriors and chiefs, as wary as the white woman, stood silent until he passed.

Almost an hour later, Kalawi found nearly a hundred Shawnee camped in a grove of Eastern Hemlocks. Children darted between sachems, grandmothers, and parents, giggling with new-found family from other clans. Finally, Kalawi breathed deeply, people who speak and look like me. Instantly, he chastised himself; to neutralize ignorant assumptions over differences was exactly why he was here. It was why they were all here.

Consequently, with humility, he approached a group of Shawnee men gathered around a fire. Among them, a woman near his own age spoke as she added sticks to the smoldering flames beneath a kettle of porridge.

"You have to speak first at the treaty." Her voice was strong. She crouched on lean legs, like a grasshopper ready to spring, a single braid down her back. "The Delawares call Colonel Morgan by the name Tamenend, after the great ancestor. Morgan fathered a son with your sister. So, it must be you."

She pointed one of her twigs at a man six inches taller than Kalawi, who stood with his arms, thick like tree trunks, knotted across his chest. The man tipped his half-shaven head beginning to disagree, and she waved the twig northward.

"The Mingos, the ones who follow Pluggy, even though he is a Mohawk, are causing us sorrow. Each time they scalp for the British, the Americans send the militia to our land to find them—a militia that cannot distinguish one Indian from another. You have to help Morgan see us differently, Hokoleskwa."

Hokoleskwa! Kalawi reexamined the man, known to the whites as Cornstalk. It was well-known by Kalawi and his clan that two years ago Hokoleskwa and his sister, Nonhelema, had been drawn into the Battle of Point Pleasant against the Virginians of Lord Dunmore. From the Shawnee's Mekocke peace-keeping sect, like Kalawi, they'd been saddened by the bloody massacre. Nonhelema had converted to Christianity. Hokoleswka had since negotiated for peace with his friend, Colonel Morgan.

Nakomtha had urged Kalawi to find this chief upon arrival, so he stepped forward.

"Chief Hokoleskwa? I am Wetakke of the Wolf Clan upon Saucony Creek. Nakomtha calls me Kalawi."

Hokoleskwa's stern face broke into a wide grin and he came around the fire to grasp Kalawi's shoulders.

"The boy who became the talker!" Hokoleskwa looked over Kalawi's shoulder and frowned. "But where–"

"A snakebite, but she is recovering." Kalawi suddenly felt inadequate. "It is just me."

Hokoleskwa gave him a wink. "No voice, even a singular one, is insignificant, Wolf Kalawi."

"Come sit." The invitation came from an old Delaware Indian man sitting cross-legged at the fire, his dark face as pruned as a peeled apple dried in the sun. He waved an arm toward the young woman, who dropped her gaze when Kalawi caught her giving him a thorough examination. "Sit next to Turtle Welakamsi–"

"I prefer Kamsi." Her voice was less strident toward the old man as she moved over to make room.

"Her full name means good water, though even she knows she can leave a bad taste in men's mouths." The old man smiled, exposing a row of yellow teeth, two missing. Those around the fire laughed, as he added, "Sit next to her so she can give you orders, too."

"I will not tease you in return." Kamsi's eyes crinkled into a smile that added a surprising charm to her serious face. "But only because I have been taught to respect my elders, Chief Netawatwees."

Half seated, Kalawi gasped, and stood again. "Chief Netawatwees!" He bowed, stunned to realize the head sachem of the Delawares—the Lenni Lanape—had traveled to Fort Pitt. Many eastern Indians considered the Lenape tribe the grandfather of their nations, and Netawatwees, known as "the skilled advisor," was the oldest living Lenape. He was, by many accounts, a few months shy of one hundred.

"Sit, sit." The old man said, waving at him. "Tell us how this White Family war is affecting your remote clan. What do you come here to learn from Colonel Morgan?"

Kalawi opened his mouth to speak, but the image of Nakomtha tapping her ear returned. Instead he looked over the Indian camps stretching more than half a mile down to the river banks, then to the massive fort across the Ohio that had once belonged to the British. The King's gardens were now producing food for the stone-throwing colonists.

"Why have the treaty here?" Kalawi asked.

"Because the future of this place relies on an answer to the Indian question," Kamsi said, offering him a bowl of the pumpkin and berry porridge.

"The Indian question?" Kalawi asked as he put aside his rifle to enjoy the warm breakfast. "Whether we remain neutral or fight for a side?"

"No." Kamsi pointed to his moccasins. "Whether you will fight for the dirt beneath your feet. Eight years ago, the Treaty of Fort Stanwix drew a north-south line between Indian and British territory. It divided the land down through Fort Pitt. That dissolved when the Americans declared independence."

"It didn't revert back to Indian territory?"

Netawatwees shook his head. "The Americans want the land—"

"Which Americans?" Kamsi flipped her long braid over her shoulder. Kalawi tried to focus on her words, and not the way the tip of her hair brushed her tailbone. "The land this far west, past the Alleghenies, has not yet been surveyed, so the Americans don't know if it's Pennsylvanian or Virginian? Both want it. It is a fertile bowl of densely-forested mountains and connected waterways. It is the main artery to the west, already used to transport trade goods, food, firearms, and negro slaves into Illinois country."

"The whole valley is now open for the taking," Hokoleskwa added.

Kamsi clicked her tongue. "And when a man is taught that a pearl holds more value than the meat of the oyster, he will wipe out an entire colony to claim it."

Her ability to sum up the issue in one thoughtful phrase was like that of Nakomtha, but this woman did so with her dark eyes blazing with such fire it left Kalawi's tongue tangled. He was thankful when Hokoleskwa spoke.

"This valley is part of the sacred hunting grounds of our all nations."

"Originally, it was twenty-five million acres. It's shrinking with each treaty." Kamsi said. "Before Stanwix they signed the Treaty of Logstown in 1752. There were others before that. Each time they deplete the land or run off the game, they must move the boundaries west to take more. When our people fight back and lose, our lands are taken in treaties written to confuse us."

"There are more than ten thousand of us," Hokoleskwa said. "The Americans are already fighting armies up in the northeast. Up there, Chief Crow of the Cherokee has already taken up the British war belt, refusing to attend these talks. I promise you, the Americans, they do not want a fight on the western frontier, too."

Kalawi, especially after having lost a father he barely knew, did not want war either. And yet, Wapishi had taught him that sometimes lives lost in battle granted long-term advantages, like the land the Wolf Clan occupied in Berks County.

"What if we do not lose?" Kalawi asked.

"You will eventually, because of that," Kamsi said, pointing to his rifle.

The fire between them popped and snapped. "Wars are no longer about who is strongest, but who has the most. We have no foreign trade as the British or Americans do. Our guns and gunpowder and knives, and even the hatchets some warring tribes use to scalp the white men, it all comes from the Big Knives. You've grown accustomed to being dependent."

Kalawi's breath came in shallow, and not just because she reinforced Peter's words. She spoke so passionately. The women of his tribe were always a part of discussions, but no Shawnee girl his age had ever been this forceful, this knowledgeable, about their history, their issues.

"How do you know so much?" Kalawi asked Kamsi, then took up a mouthful of porridge.

"How do you know so little?"

Kalawi froze, mid-chew. No one but Arthur or Nathaniel had ever challenged him with such intensity. His ears buzzed, and Kalawi admitted this woman could cause him great difficulty in being able to hear everything clearly at the treaty. He swallowed, and groaned. When a rose-colored apology rose on her cheeks, he merely smiled.

"Not much of a talker after all, is he?" Netawatwees whispered. Hokoleskwa laughed heartily, but Kamsi waved her spoon at them and brought them back to the subject of the peace talks.

"So, as I was asking you, Hokoleskwa. You will step up first to petition Morgan for the land, yes?" Kamsi's eyes were afire again. "To ensure it stays as it always has been. Ours."

"But it cannot be owned." Kalawi scraped at the last of his porridge, determined not to be the one lectured. "You forget the land was a gift, Kamsi. It belongs to our creator."

"I have not forgotten." Her blistering eyes changed like the wind, suddenly filling with the sadness of an abandoned orphan. She avoided Kalawi's gaze and stared into the searing fire. "But *she* is not here."

* * *

Before retiring for the night, Kalawi sat alone by the fire talking with Hokoleskwa. After much talk of war, land, and changes they'd both seen,

Hokoleskwa's gaze darted to the small tent where Kamsi slept alone.

"She walks with a shield," the warrior had said. Hokoleskwa's eyes softened as he told Kalawi about how Kamsi's own father had been killed during the Point Pleasant uprising. As her eldest cousin, Hokoleskwa had become her guardian. "No mother. No other siblings. She would never admit how hard it was, but it sparked an infectious passion for our future. You and I speak about being Shawnee, but she breathes it. This is why she was chosen to watch over the Mekocke pawaka, our sacred bundle. She does so with the same fervor as her father before her."

So that was her fuel, Kalawi realized. While the pawaka was a feeling, a vision, everyone carried for the tribe, there was also a physical bundle—relics and treasures handed down—that only a Turtle Clan member could carry. It was an incredible honor, with immense responsibilities. No wonder Kamsi saw it as her right to carry peace and fight for Shawnee independence. It was also her inheritance. Kalawi's opinion of her warmed along with his feet by the nighttime fire.

* * *

The next morning, Kalawi paddled the canoe across to Fort Pitt. Ahead of him in the canoe, Kamsi's back was straight, her hair brushed out full and long, and decorated with ribbons and feathers. She was a colorful bird of peace. In front of her, Netawatwees sat proud, jaw raised, his shoulders encased in a black bear fur.

The left side of Kalawi's own face was painted in vermillion, his eagle feather and red deer headdress affixed atop his head. He gripped the paddle as he steered the canoe, awed into silence again not just by the woman ahead of him, but by the surrounding sight.

He was one of five Shawnee in this canoe. One canoe among nearly twenty boats carrying a total of one hundred Shawnee. Twenty of them plowing against the current in a massive flotilla of over one hundred and twenty boats crossing the Ohio to Fort Pitt.

In all, they were nearly six hundred and fifty Indians from a multitude of nations. Each dressed in their most respectful adornments. Each feeling the hope of peace pounding in their hearts. Each feeling the eerie tension stringing the boats together.

Kalawi was consumed by a singular thought, as he imagined each person was. The coming days would either unite them or tear them asunder.

Then suddenly, cannons from high over the fort fired. Just once. It was a lone round, signaling friendship. In reply, echoing off the mountains, ricocheting throughout the valley, en masse the women and men of the flotilla emptied their muskets and rifles into the water. It was a thunderous rumble that Kalawi knew, down to his bones, he would never forget. When the smoke pulled away, they saw Colonel Morgan atop the garrison walls, waving them in, welcoming them to the first American-Indian treaty.

CHAPTER FORTY-SIX

"THE DAMNED INDIANS ARE the least of my problems," General Howe said, looking over the tally of their profits.

After leaving Philadelphia to rejoin Dickinson, Silas had first stopped at British headquarters in New York. He'd been surprised to find a quarter of the city still smoldering, a blackened ruin of charcoal sticks and spires. Meeting with the Howe brothers, Silas strove to avoid discussing who'd set the disastrous fire, instead showing them the favorable balance sheets for their business, and telling of the Indians gathering at Fort Pitt.

"The Cherokee have accepted my war belt. One flip of my hand and Chief Crow will have them heating things up on the Ohio frontier." General Howe handed the report to his brother.

The admiral scanned it, nodded his approval. He dropped it next to what appeared to be a battle plan on the table between them, and said, "The rebels can't fight on two fronts. They would surrender faster than Mrs. Murray."

Within hours of landing in New York, the Howes had been invited to a meal and Madeira by the city's well-to-do Mrs. Murray. Afterward, they'd moved their headquarters into her mansion. So now, instead of a drafty tent, the two were ensconced in matching wingback chairs near the woman's roaring fire.

"But if the rebels surrender, it would end our growing business." Silas pointed to the battle plan. "Would that end it, too?"

"Clinton's new plan." The admiral pursed his lips at the document. "He wants to trap the Americans in Harlem by coming down the King's Bridge from the north. He said if we do not end this 'tweedledum business,' he has threatened to return to London."

"And?" Silas asked.

The general got up to prod the fire with an iron poker. "I'm loath to admit it, but that little bugger Clinton is right; our hesitancy looks like we are failing the Crown. Occupying Manhattan isn't enough. Our desire to grow a supply business cannot ruin our reputation in London. At some point, we might have to go back." The general stabbed at a log, embers rising from the punctured holes. With the tool still in his hand, he moved away to a map pinned over a garish red wallpaper.

"It seems I'm forced to trap the damn rebels in Harlem." He glanced in Silas' direction, his face hot, and not from the fire. "Especially given that you can't deliver one simple document to me."

Silas didn't flinch. He only smiled, and said, "The document is more accessible than ever. Forget Harlem."

The admiral began to laugh but it died on his lips as Silas explained.

"Washington has ordered most of the troops to evacuate Harlem Heights. Hold back at Throg's Neck, and give the Continental Army time to escape toward White Plains."

"Escape! Why in the hell—"

"The Americans have left a garrison of over two thousand on Manhattan at Fort Washington," Silas said.

Howe's eyes narrowed, but as evidenced by his blank face and slack jaw, he'd not heard such news conveyed by his own spies. Silas spoke firmly as he strode toward the map. "Divide your troops. The fort is indefensible. If you move an advance from three sides, it is weakest here," he pointed to the southern wall. "Move the rest of your army to New Rochelle just below White Plains." Silas traced one finger up New York and ran his other hand down from Connecticut. "I will ensure our rider comes down to the same point."

The general rose an eyebrow and spoke to his brother. "Ensure it, he says, as if he knows where—"

"He's in Litchfield," Silas said, going on to explain what he'd learned the

258 ★ KAREN A. CHASE

last few weeks—from Franklin's new appointment, to the true identity of the rider.

"France wants in! The bloody traitors," the admiral scoffed. "And this rider's real name?"

"Nathaniel Marten," Silas said, "As in Peter Mart—"

"The one building the armory in Berks County?" General Howe turned toward Silas, his eyes narrowing.

"They are brothers." Silas confirmed. "I have no proof Peter knows what his brother carries."

"Wasn't this the armory that you insisted we include? The one that always seems to be behind schedule?" The general took another step toward Silas. Silas took a step back when the general asked, "And didn't you once mention being friends with this Peter as boys?"

"Is Peter the problem, or are you?" the admiral rose from his chair.

Silas fumbled for words, struggling to comprehend how he'd suddenly fallen from favor. The popping fire filled the silence until he pointed to the balance sheets next to Clinton's plans. "The numbers… they are proof of my fidelity to you." But even Silas could hear it. His voice was too high.

The admiral picked up the sheet, his mouth downturned. "These come from you, too, don't they?"

"And now you want me to divide our troops," the general said, his grip tightening on the poker.

Silas' heart was pounding faster by the second. "I… I…"

A knock interrupted them, and an aide swept into the room announcing an urgent message from Lord Percy.

"I'm not done with you yet," the general wagged a finger at Silas. He tucked the poker under his arm and tore open the letter from the officer. The words wiped the anger from the general's face, replacing it with a look Silas' could not discern. General Howe turned on the messenger. "Can you swear to the accuracy of this?"

"Yes, sir," the aide twittered. "I was there."

The aide was dismissed and the General handed over the message to his brother. The admiral read the missive and then handed it to Silas, saying, "I guess your proof arrived just in time."

As he read the words, Silas felt air rush back to his chest.

William Demont, a Continental Army adjutant for Colonel Magaw at Fort Washington, had snuck into Lord Percy's camp two nights ago. He'd divulged how many troops were in the fort. Over two thousand. He provided plans to indicate where it was weakest. The south. Hardly a fortress, he'd said. No barracks. No magazine for the ammunition. It was mere earthworks open to the sky filled with tents. And seriously undermanned.

Silas handed back the letter, his confidence returning. He tucked a hand in his waistcoat pocket, finding comfort in the engraving of the watch beneath his fingers as he asked, "Well, will you divide your troops?"

The brothers held a silent exchange, and then the general nodded. The admiral picked up Clinton's latest plan and tossed it in the fire.

"I'm going to miss that fat prig," the general said as he turned back to the map. "Though to be sure, I will not take the Fort until new Hessians arrive. I need to add their numbers—seven or eight thousand of them—before the army divides." General Howe pointed to the door. "Go find that rider, Mr. Hastings. When I get to White Plains with the rest of my men, he better be waiting."

"He will, sir," Silas said. He backed from the room, promising to handle it himself.

After the door closed, General Howe turned back to the map. "He better handle it," he said, stabbing the end of the blackened poker into the map. Into Berks County. "Or by God, I will."

CHAPTER FORTY-SEVEN

FORT WASHINGTON WAS QUIET before the dawn. Arthur, huddled alone in a pile of hay, was wrapped in a blanket, waiting for the Post rider. He'd crawled off to the haystack to read Susannah's last letter in private, and to respond to her missive while the company of two thousand soldiers snored off their drink.

A few weeks ago, Lieutenant-Colonel Kachlein had asked Arthur to stay behind with a garrison at Fort Washington, to be part of a special unit holding the rebel's last position on Manhattan with Colonel Magaw. He'd been honored, but then he'd hung his head in shame because he'd only felt relief. Relief at watching the rest of the army march away, taking with them the sick, the injured, and the dying. Perhaps they'd at last be able to win with a healthy battalion.

Now, however, Arthur wondered if the troops who had left for White Plains might be the lucky ones. Watching his breath blow into the cold, November blackness, Arthur had the sinking feeling he was waiting for his life to come to an end. That foreboding feeling had been reinforced when a double allotment of rum had been issued by Colonel Magaw tonight. Extra rum meant soon they might fight. Soon, some would die. All the men knew it. All the men drank to blot out that feeling of uncertainty. All except one.

Arthur looked toward the tent where Colonel Magaw slept.

Undisturbed.

A few nights ago, Magaw had celebrated with too much rum after winning a small skirmish. When a scout brought in news that the minor engagement had been a test, and that General Howe had designs on taking the fort, backed by thousands of redcoats preparing to engage, Magaw waved him away.

"I could defend the fort through constant siege through December."

"But General Washington is not convinced the fort is defensible," Arthur had suggested.

"That's why I am here and he is not, Bowman." Magaw had raised his glass, unaware his own adjutant, Demont, was sneering at his boss' arrogance. "Now go get a drink and leave me to mine."

Arthur had decided that if a bayonet was going to run him through, there was more honor in facing death sober. He knew his uncle would have concurred. Now, Arthur clutched Susannah's latest letter in his cold fingers, awash in disbelief that Colonel and Alice Bowman were gone. He remembered his aunt always fussing over his unruly, red hair before a ball, and the colonel's big, one-armed bear hugs after a long absence.

"I am so sorry, Susannah," Arthur whispered aloud, grateful for the soft spot to muffle his mourning. He could almost feel Susannah's sadness seep from the ink, staining his icy fingers. In what state had the colonel left his affairs for her, he wondered. "I wish I were there to help you wade through this."

From his jacket, he pulled the letter the Post rider would retrieve in the morning to take to Susannah. Arthur questioned the words he'd written. What was he offering but condolences? Encouragement. Love. Hopefully he'd not enclosed his fears about when he'd be able to write to her again. Or if.

Just like Nathaniel.

"She's not only married, you know. Now she's alone," he shook Susannah's letter at a distant shadow he imagined was his old friend. "You were supposed to protect the meek and secure a fair maiden. She was both. Stupid oaths."

Even the one Arthur had taken might now cost him his life. What good was an Oath of Allegiance if it meant taking orders from a fool like

Magaw? In the darkness, Arthur could hear a distant bell ringing. Tolling. He shivered, and pulled his collar up around his neck.

How many redcoats would descend upon them? Two thousand? Four? Maybe more. While here he lay. Waiting for the Post rider. Waiting for the end to begin.

CHAPTER FORTY-EIGHT

SUSANNAH WISHED THE REVEREND'S sermon intoned the same feeling she had about the church bells rung before it. She'd been going mad at home, pacing the empty halls, when she heard the bell's joyful dings echo with hope, and the deep dongs cry out with warmth. She'd run to attend the nighttime service at the nearby First Presbyterian, her first service since her parent's memorial.

"Nothing is causal or accidental with God."

Reverend Ewing's first words rocked Susannah against the pew, the rest of his sermon drowned out. Now, alone in the family pew, the congregation and their nods of pity long gone, she wondered... is it possible my savior has assigned me strife? Or am I so broken nothing is resonating correctly?

She scooted from the pew, resolved to seek out the pastor. When she knocked on his office door, where he usually lingered to meet aggrieved parishioners, she was bid to enter.

"Reverend?" she called, stepping from the candlelit hall into a darkened room.

"Close the door and come look, my dear," his voice, even and gentle, came from the same direction as a stiff breeze.

Susannah pulled her shawl tight around her neck and groped her way around his desk. When her eyes finally adjusted, she found him bent over a telescope poked out a window's open sash, moon beams casting a wave of light across his back.

"Reverend, you will catch your death."

"From fresh air?" he said, his eye remaining at the scope, though a finger moved back and forth across a rather prominent chin. "A scientist in Vienna is right now trying to prove that oxygen is emitted by the trees. If he is right, then your statement is false. Besides, the moon… she beckons me. Come see." He popped up, moonbeams shining on his boyish face, smiling and flushed with vigor, although he was a man nearing fifty. When he saw her solemnity, he stood to his full height, his small mouth down-turning with worry. "You don't want to look at the moon?"

"I do, but…" she sighed, her breath puffing like a ghost in the cool air between them. "What you said tonight… Did God intentionally take my parents?"

"Not exactly my words." He leaned against the open sill, examining her, a sympathetic smile rising. "Nor should anyone so arrogantly assume to know God's intentions. However, if you're asking if it's possible, then yes."

"But if…" She sorted through a thousand questions, yet not one could she grasp hold of to ask.

"Mrs. Pemberley, do you know how I've come to have this telescope?"

"You borrowed if from the Philosophical Society?"

The reverend had long been a learned member of the group of "Useful Knowledge" with Benjamin Franklin as its president. Ewing had been part of a team who had measured the trajectory of Venus when Susannah had been a small girl. Back then, her mother had sniffed at how science and theology mixed like oil and water, although Susannah rather liked the idea of him searching for a scientific solution to how God created the world.

Now Ewing patted the telescope and said, "Yes, but I want to use it because of a bird. I was a young boy when I saw a wren flying with great agitation from fence to road. Fence to road. I investigated and found a quite extraordinarily large snake on the ground below it. The snake was poised to attack, and its movements had so entranced the bird, it had lost the power to fly away." He patted the windowsill, making room for her.

"What did you do?" Susannah sat next to him, already warmed despite the breeze on her back. Many family milestones, including her own baptism and wedding, had been celebrated with Ewing in attendance. He was to her like a well-traveled uncle with thoughtful stories always at the ready.

"I tossed a stone and when the snake slithered away, the bird was so happy it performed for me a sort of winged dance." His face was wistful as he stared into the darkness as if seeing it again, that finger back at his chin like a bow across a violin.

"It is a lovely story, Reverend Ewing, but it still doesn't answer my question."

"Oh, but it does." His knowing smile spread over his whole face. "Perhaps what you perceive to be absence and loss, is actually God's way of removing obstructions that have kept you from finding your own wings. Your purpose."

Her whole being tingled at the notion of feeling as free as the bird, but doubt, like rushing water through a well-worn fissure, poured in.

"But I... I don't have a purpose."

"Ah, well," he nodded to the telescope, "then perhaps you should look in there."

Reluctantly, she stood and then bent to the scope, one eye winked shut. One wide open. Her gloved hand flew to her mouth, as she gasped. She'd never seen the moon so clearly. So well-defined. What's more, its surface—the highs and lows, the bright and cloudy undulations—appeared to her like a youthful, expectant face.

"You see the woman in the moon, don't you?" he asked. She nodded, feeling like a schoolgirl herself. As she took another long look he said, "That bird helped me realize our greatest gift—the power of observation. A power that can be multiplied if we have the right tools. In my modest opinion, three tools are all a person needs: books, a habit of close thinking, and a mentor. Find those and your purpose will rush over you."

Susannah pulled away from the beautiful image in the scope. She gazed down at her hands, hidden behind gloves. *To be a genteel wife and mother your hands must remain soft,* her mother often scolded.

"And what could I do with these? Women of my position... Aren't we trained to stay silent, merely slaves in fine clothing staying behind to bear the children?"

"Surely that's not all you are capable of?"

"Honestly, my accomplishments thus far are a knack for needlepoint, and spinning wool to yarn."

The reverend popped up from the sill, the impish grin returning. He darted to the door with a follow-me wave over his shoulder. Susannah had to run to keep up to him, petticoats in hand, as he led her through the church and down a winding flight of stairs to the basement. At a pair of double doors, he knocked once, then twice in succession, then once again. Then a bolt slid open on the other side, and the doors flung open.

Inside the candle-lit, stone-walled room, more than a dozen happy female faces spun toward them, chins nodding hello before returning to their tasks. Hands twisted rolags of wool into skeins of yarn. Saxony wheels whirred out a gentle, unified whisper.

A woman, perhaps ten years older than Susannah, waved from a far corner where she was carding wool. Half a dozen straw baskets of flossy fleece were gathered around her legs like a flock of lambs, and setting aside her paddles, she moved through the tight quarters toward the doors.

"The women tuck in their children to dream," Ewing said, "then secretly meet here, every night."

Many of the women began humming, their sound like a collection of bees. A pregnant woman at a small cantilever loom near the door pushed a shuttle containing a spool of the homespun woolen thread between tightly pulled strings.

"And the fabric they make?" Susannah asked.

"For shirts. For our men fighting the war." The carding woman said, greeting the reverend warmly, her face flushed like a fine peach beneath an elegant bun, and her dress as plain as the woolen fabric they made.

"Mrs. Esther De Berdt Reed," the reverend said, "this is Mrs. Susannah Pemberley, a new spinner."

Susannah shook the woman's hand, feeling the woman's calluses even through her own glove.

"I was sorry to have missed your glorious wedding," Mrs. Reed spoke softly, "but God has been pleased to afflict me with a feeble, disordered body." Then, without a hint of frailty she waved an arm about the room and said, "The Congress easily funds rum that weakens loins, but not shirts to strengthen backs. Consequently, as our husbands' duties must expand, so, say I, shall ours."

As Mrs. Reed turned to the group, clucking for them to make room in their already cramped quarters for Susannah's wheel to come, the reverend leaned toward Susannah and whispered, "A fine-feathered mentor for a bird learning to fly."

CHAPTER FORTY-NINE

WINTER WAS ON ITS WAY, painting a frost on the last of the yellow leaves. Nathaniel's heavy breath fogged the windowpane in his bedroom as he searched the distant hills in the early morning light. Horse hooves had woken him, echoing in the crisp air, and he'd flown to the window.

As he gripped the sash, at last, between the trees, came a Post rider.

Quickly he dressed, jumping into chilly breeches, but just as he tucked in his shirt, Oliver brought the letter to his door. When the statesman entered, the now familiar sounds and smells of breakfast being made entered with him. Nathaniel swallowed and begged him to open the envelope. It was addressed to *Mr. Wolcott Esq. & Mr. Mirtle.*

Oliver tore it open, as Nathaniel began to write out his cypher code in order to translate the message, but Oliver stopped him. "'Tis in plain English."

Worry dropped down in Nathaniel's gut like a lump of cold porridge. "Is it from Franklin?"

Oliver shook his head and handed over the note, written upon Dickinson's personal stationery.

Congress elected Mr. Franklin as envoy to France.
He sails 27 October.
Mr. Jefferson indisposed in Virginia.

Brigadier General Dickinson main contact now.
Mr. Mirtle should head south to Philadelphia,
first checking in at Colonial Army headquarters,
at White Plains, New York.

"Dickinson doesn't uphold the secrecy of our cypher?"

Oliver reread the note, but then he turned pale. "We've another concern. A letter came from Congress two days ago. You remember?"

Nathaniel nodded. Both of them had run into the yard hopeful it was from Franklin, but it had only been new requests for Wolcott.

"The runner said, although irrelevant to me until now, he could not guarantee my reply would be delivered post haste because of redcoats camped at New Rochelle, New York."

"Where? Show me." Nathaniel rolled open a map of New York—a new copy he'd made the week before.

"Headquarters is here," Wolcott marked White Plains with one finger and ran another south. "Fifteen or so miles south is New Rochelle. If you retrace the route you took to Litchfield, you'll come in south of White Plains—"

"Right into the hands of the British." The images of the dead soldier on Harlem Heights came flooding back to Nathaniel. His legs grew weak. "Is there another way?"

"The Heights of Northcastle." Wolcott tapped a spot to the northeast of White Plains. "Travel due west from Litchfield, crossing out of Connecticut into upper New York, and ride down through the mountains. Although cold this late in October, 'tis better than the heat of a battlefield."

By lunchtime, Bayard was saddled, Nathaniel's packs laden with extra blankets and food to carry him a few days. Nathaniel stood among the Wolcott family who had insisted on walking him to the front yard to say their goodbyes. Laura Wolcott stepped up with a small bundle.

"A delivery for Philadelphia. Address is on it," she said. As he took the package, she held his hands with her own. They were rough, red, and chapped from her daily work, but the warmth of her touch was all he felt. "I shall miss your company at our table. God speed, Nathaniel Mirtle."

As he turned away, after reading that the package was addressed to a church on First Street, Frederick tugged on his pant leg, and asked, "Will you look for his head?"

"I promise," Nathaniel chuckled as he stuffed the package deep into his pack, then ruffled the boy's bed-disheveled hair further. "And if found, I will bring it here myself. We shall sell tickets for all to see him."

"We shall be rich then!" Fredrick clapped his hands together as he jumped up and down around his parents, the Wolcott family a portrait of hospitality, kindness, and an unfailing faith in the future.

Oh, but you already are, Nathaniel thought.

"You have helped us immensely," Oliver Wolcott stepped forward and pumped Nathaniel's hand just as he had when he arrived. "More than two thousand musket balls, and truly good ones. I have recorded what you have done in my journal, but have not included your name. Among us here, however, you shall well be remembered not as the gunsmith or rider, but as the mapmaker." Oliver's smile grew morose, and he stepped forward and grasped Nathaniel fully with both his arms. "I will miss you as a father does a son."

Nathaniel, floored by the sudden sentiment, choked on his goodbye. When he recovered, he returned the embrace and said, "Perhaps we shall meet here again. My task complete. You at last at home to stay."

He pulled away, climbing into the saddle, surprised by the disenchantment of riding away alone. Yet, with a click of his tongue, he nudged Bayard forward. Several times he turned back to wave. Oliver's one arm was draped around his wife's shoulder as Frederick jumped up and down—all their hands raised high. At the street's end, Nathaniel began his decent into the Shepaug River Valley, and the road obscured their smiling faces.

Nathaniel turned westward. Into the quiet, into the oncoming winter, and into whatever might await him in White Plains.

* * *

The silence lasted but a few days. Just south of Newcastle, cannon fire ricocheted off the mountains like distant thunder. The crackling morning air trembled with the treble of an ongoing cannonade that made the satchel burn by Nathaniel's side, like a hand that signals getting close to a fire. Yet, he had to keep moving, had to find Dickinson.

The canopy of blue sky, far in the distance, filled with a plume of smoke as he zig-zagged over the mountains. However, as he picked his way south and west, fear rose in him with each step, each minute, each hour, until at a crest he felt forced to stop. The sounds of a full-blown battle rising from the valley below immobilized him, and continued to blast and bellow the whole of the rest of the day. Then, just as the day began to slip away, the rumbling ceased.

The odd curiosity of the sound, however terrifying, and now removed, made Nathaniel's heart thrum. The silence broke open too many possibilities of what real horrors lay ahead. He inched along, walking Bayard by a tight lead, looking ahead for anything that might be coming toward him, anything not a tree. After a hundred steps, his nerves fraying, he saw an overlook ahead. He tied Bayard off and crept toward the overlook, staying low.

Clouds hung and swirled in the valley below. He sniffed the air. Sulfur. Not clouds. Gun smoke.

Laying himself out long he put his scope to his eye, trying to steady his shaking arms on the ground, peering southward through the breaks in the haze. Nausea overwhelmed him.

Red. Blue. Gray. Bodies. They covered the ground. Hung over shattered fences. Stretched between stone walls, blown to pieces. Half-buried in the cratered hillside. Hundreds and hundreds of men. Lifeless. Their blood—the blood of Englishmen and rebels combined—pooled together, drained into rivers, emptied into the Bronx.

"Arthur?" The name flew from his lips as he swung his scope from face to face. Limb to limb.

Nathaniel's legs itched to run down the hillside, to join the dozens of soldiers picking through the wreckage, retrieving the dead. He had to stop himself from galloping to the field and turning over every last man until he was sure Arthur was not among them. "Please, please don't be down there."

No matter how awful their last parting was, Nathaniel could not have wished, nor imagined, this fate for anyone. Especially someone as hopeful as Arthur, because what was down there was hopeless. The carnage of a battle-field such as this—more than six hundred soldiers dead or wounded, and the vultures already swirling overhead—is what men should be made to witness before they ever cast a vote to go to war.

As smoke rose from behind burning, broken redoubts, Nathaniel swept his scope over the whole of the valley and into the camps. When he'd last seen the Colonial Army, there had been nearly twenty thousand men. Below now, a fraction lingered. A tenth, if that, perhaps. Had the army divided? Or were they so depleted?

Nathaniel lowered the scope, and leaned on his clasped fists, wondering what to do. If either Arthur or Dickinson were below, with the redcoats now camped at the far end of Chatterton's Hill, within a cannon's shot of the Continental Army encampment, it would be foolish to descend with the Declaration at his hip.

Returning to Congress was the wisest option, his only option. He looked westward, to New Jersey, mapping an overland route to Philadelphia in his head. Although tumbling gray clouds grumbled of another impending storm, he tossed his fears to the wind already tugging at his hair, and made a promise to himself. To the men below. And to Arthur.

"One more signature. I will unite us. I will finish this task… even if it kills me."

CHAPTER FIFTY

ON THE FIRST DAY of the talks, Kalawi's pride for his people burned as bright as the ceremonial fire lit by Netawatwees. Together, with Morgan and nearly three hundred American officers and commissioners, the Indian nations gathered to open the conference. It began with several minutes of silence, then with a dance, and the sharing of a peace pipe.

As Kamsi passed it to Kalawi, their fingers brushed, and he nearly dropped the pipe. She sniffed at his clumsiness. Hokoleskwa raised an eyebrow. Kalawi clasped his hands in his lap to keep them from shaking.

Hokoleskwa indeed spoke first at the treaty, and for several days. He relayed information about the Indian desire for neutrality, having met with many chiefs throughout the colonies. Just as he seemed to be making headway, many days into the treaty, Morgan read a letter he'd received. Pluggy's gang was killing again, threatening to bring down the Tomahawk if their lands were not left untouched. Colonel Morgan shook his head.

The crowd grew sullen, but Kamsi, Kalawi noticed—for he seemed to notice everything about her—scowled and crossed her arms waiting to hear Morgan's response.

Although a small man, the crown of his thinning hair barely brushing Kalawi's shoulders, Congress had put Morgan in charge of Indian affairs for the middling colonies. His appointment was because his knowledge of Indians was immense, and he also had a flawless grasp of several Indian languages.

"Blame for such atrocities must be directed rightfully," Morgan spoke in Shawnee to Hokoleskwa, then translated for others. "It should be aimed at the few, the criminals, and not cast upon the whole of a people or nation."

Kalawi's grip on his own fist lessened as an audible sigh of relief rose in waves from the Indians in attendance. Kamsi dropped her arms and carefully studied Morgan with pursed lips, as if reassessing her own assumptions. When she glanced toward Kalawi, he raised an eyebrow. She lifted her chin and looked away, her arms crossing again.

Is she intrigued or irritated by me, Kalawi wondered, or is it wariness? He imagined Kamsi had found very few men able to keep up with her intensity.

And yet, that night as he paddled them back to camp, just as he had each evening, Kalawi witnessed her kindness. Netawatwees slept in the canoe, the days growing longer for him. Kamsi cradled his head in her lap, tucking the furs around him, and per usual it was she who settled Grandfather in his tent after ensuring he'd eaten enough.

Now, with the rest of the clan long asleep, Kalawi brooded alone at the smoldering fire, staring into the dying embers. It was October thirty-first, seven days into the conference, and three days before the full moon. What had they accomplished?

Morgan's response after reading the letter about Pluggy's war had brought relief to the Indians, but Kalawi had also noticed the American officers in the room were not so quick to recover. Their eyes remained narrow with skepticism.

Arthur's words from last summer returned. *They believe you run wild and cannot manage your own people.*

How can we ask anyone to see us peaceably, Kalawi now wondered, when collectively we are not? He stared long into the fire, dozing in his disappointment, dreaming of an uncertain future. Suddenly he felt hands on him, shaking him.

"Kamsi?" Her face hovered over him. Kalawi whispered, "Am I dreaming?"

"Please... come help him." Kamsi's cheeks were damp, her face strained, her voice so insistent that Kalawi was quickly on his feet. He followed her into the small tent next to her own. "I heard him moaning. I thought he was sick, but…"

The old Delaware grandfather's withered frame was curled like a small bird in a nest of furs. He was gasping, the pale eyes fading. Kalawi took the ancient man's life-worn hand in his own youthful palm. Kamsi sat opposite, trying to restrain her sadness behind a hopeful smile.

"I want to help you, Netawatwees." Kalawi could feel the man's pulse weakening. "But…"

"…but I am ninety-nine." The corner of Netawatwees' wrinkled mouth rose slightly, and the man closed his eyes for a moment. When they fluttered opened, he whispered through parched lips, the words escaping slowly, but surely. "I am ready. I have seen much. Sadness. Illness. War. New white men arriving… Dutch. French. German. English. What great joys, too… The animals. The seasons. Games. Women." He breathed deeply, turning his face toward the sky, his eyes fogging over with a century of memories. "I was a young boy when our sachem made peace with William Penn beneath the Shackamaxon Tree."

Kalawi had heard the story before. It was because of that agreement his own Wolf Clan was granted land in Berks County, and because of it he had found Arthur and Nathaniel. His own joys were tied to the history of this man. Kalawi could feel his own heart tearing just as clearly as he could hear Kamsi sniffling.

"What may we do for you?" Kalawi squeezed the man's hand, asking a traditional question for the dying. It was a way for those left behind to build upon Netawatwees' life.

Kamsi nodded, and came closer, to the other side of the bed. "Yes, how may we honor you?"

Even in his last, weak moments, the old man reached for Kamsi's hand. She kissed his fingers, her tears falling unchecked.

"Peace is not granted, my children," Netawatwees whispered. His shaking hands joined Kalawi's and Kamsi's fingers together beneath his own, across his failing heart. "It is made by each generation… and for all those yet to come."

* * *

The next morning, Netawatwees was buried at the tip of the confluence of the rivers, Kalawi helping to lower his body into a shallow grave beneath the tree of peace. The meetings with Morgan ceased for a time, and word of Netawatwees' death spread like a sorrowful wildfire throughout the colonies.

Over several days, Kalawi felt pride for his people warm within him again. Leaders from outlying nations dropped their Tomahawks, their warring ways, and came streaming into camp, shouldering their condolences for their shared grandfather. Even the Cherokee sent fourteen members, including their grand sachem, the warrior, Chief Crow.

Chief Crow, his height and build as impressive and thick as that of Hokoleskwa, presented a string of white wampum to Netawatwees' grandchildren, and then, to everyone's surprise, the formidable man fell to his knees at the grave.

"The cause of your grief, Great Grandfather, it shall be done away." He sprinkled seeds upon the man's mounded grave, promising to return the war belt he'd exchanged with the British. "A new hope is planted that you may rest in peace beneath the feet of your grandchildren."

That night, Kalawi stood with his Shawnee brethren beneath the full moon, the many nations gathered for a memorial, Colonel Morgan and the commissioners among them. At Kalawi's elbow, close enough to feel the warmth of her, stood a sniffling Kamsi.

As was the custom, the Indians began their mourning in silence for a full thirty minutes. Then, as if being pulled from the people by one great spirit, the voices of more than six hundred Indians rose in song together. Their long, low melody rippled over the waters. It climbed the mountainsides. It touched the sky. It echoed back down into the valley. It howled. It howled long and strong like the familiar cry of a great white wolf.

The sound choked Kalawi. His own cheeks wet and ruddy, he closed his eyes, unable to sing. He wanted to be strong. He was failing. But then he felt a hand slip into his own. He looked down to find Kamsi's fingers intertwined with his own, and when he lifted his gaze, the dark pools in her eyes had softened. From proud, to compassionate. From cold, to loving. She squeezed his palm, and nodded an agreement to be his.

When he smiled, she sang out strong the song of peace for them both.

And so it was, with her by his side, and Hokoleskwa smiling his tearful approval, Kalawi once again found his voice.

* * *

The next day, with the collective thoughts of the newly humbled chiefs and elders gathered at Fort Pitt, Kalawi and Kamsi helped draft a message, in English, for Hokoleskwa to deliver. A promise for their grandfather; an equitable appeal for Colonel Morgan to present to John Hancock and the members of Congress.

> *You have taken our inter-tribal hunting grounds from us. This is what sits heavy on our hearts and on the hearts of all nations, and it is impossible to work as we ought to do whilst we are thus oppressed.*

If their land rights were recognized, and titles transferred with a joint share in the proceeds, their many nations promised neutrality. They would not raise arms on the frontier. They would not accept war wampum belts from the British. They would stay out of the White Family's war.

And in return, they hoped the wise men of Congress would agree to something more. Something they knew the colonists also cherished.

A Declaration.

For political sovereignty. Freedom of religion. An international code of human liberties. A granting of natural rights. A system of justice.

Kalawi's pen scratched these pleas across the parchment, and with each word, he hoped he inscribed a fair and independent future for all their nations. For in the end, he realized, what the Indians and the Americans, the Savages and the Big Knives, himself, Arthur, and Nathaniel were all desirous of, was quite self-evident.

They all wanted a mutual human right to life, liberty, and the pursuit of happiness.

CHAPTER FIFTY-ONE

SUSANNAH SPUN WOOL ONTO her wheel, preferring her sore hands to the ache she'd felt when she first joined the bee. Since then, Congress had passed a moratorium on slaughtering sheep, so the wool had doubled. Twice weekly now they worked through the night, and Susannah had come without fail, without complaint.

Today, a newcomer, Mrs. Elliot, had joined them. Barely twenty, her hair in a jumble of fraying knots pinned up in haste, she yanked at the wool, her paddles smacking together. She rubbed at her bleary eyes, as she said, "I've one child at home and my belly showing again."

"It is difficult while Colonel Reed is away, too," Mrs. Reed said, gently coaxing her wool threads into alignment, her paddles whooshing to a three-count rhythm. Susannah was about to agree to the sentiment when Mrs. Reed added, "It's difficult, with only myself, to manage our four children all under the age of five."

Susannah ceased her spinning, and she and Mrs. Elliot both stared open-mouthed.

"But then I get a letter from the colonel," Mrs. Reed's paddles fell limp in her lap as she gazed toward heaven. "I'm reminded that while I get to kiss our children's faces, he faces death morning and night." She began her waltzing, paddling pace again. "I want him to return home knowing I've maintained a peace he does not have now."

A serenity replaced Mrs. Elliot's scowl, as her rhythm slowed to evenly match Mrs. Reed's, as she nodded, "Right ye are. No sense sitting at home dithering like a niddy-noddy."

Susannah returned to her spool, grateful to not also carry the burden of mouths beyond hers and Lydia's, and for the rest of the night she imagined that her threads were weaving a woolen protectorate for Pemberley, for Arthur, and all those with them.

As the candles neared their end, signaling the coming dawn, Susannah put away her wool, and pondered her morning ahead. She'd received a request to meet with her father's lawyers. The estate had been settled and the will was to be read. Her mother's parting words bubbled up. *You needn't be bothered by such trivial things.* In light of the circumstances that had surfaced, who would be giving her orders now? Susannah wondered.

She ran a hand across another full spool. Mrs. Reed glanced over, the rosy cheeks rising high, and said, "You have contributed such fine threads since you have joined us, Mrs. Pemberley."

Susannah steadied herself on the bobbin. *Contributed?* She never thought anyone would ever attribute that word to her. It bolstered her like a back brace.

"'Tis a warm feeling to find patriotism come from your own hands, isn't it?" Mrs. Reed patted Susannah's hand warmly, then to the group she said, "Come, ladies, we shall have our communal breakfast together before we return to our domestic duties."

From satchels and bags, the women set out food on a table near the loom, unveiling whatever they could spare to share. Susannah delighted in setting out her latest cooking accomplishment from her time with Lydia: a rhubarb custard pie, the top crust woven criss-cross like a basket.

"My word, Mrs. Pemberley, you have outdone us all," Mrs. Elliot said.

Susannah opened her mouth to comment, but the young woman was looking down upon her own meager bowl of corn grits, and grasping at her plain frock fraying at the sleeves. Susannah suddenly felt overdone. Her pie was as fancy as her petticoats. And neither was necessary.

"It is not how much we have, but the spirit in which we share it," Susannah squeezed the woman's hand. Mrs. Reed gave her a wink from across the table as the women set about filling their plates.

"Such a fine meal," said one of the younger girls, licking gravy from her lips as they sat clustered close together, the meal near an end. "'Tis a shame we've no Madeira to round it out."

"It never did sit right with me," Mrs. Reed laughed, and then she leaned in to whisper to the group. "At parties, I have sometimes carried a full glass all night to save myself from an overbearing hostess."

As the women rolled with laughter, Susannah realized with a start how wrong her mother's impression had been. Mrs. Reed's glass had not been constantly refilled, but rather likely never emptied. Come to think of it, her mother's statement that the reverend was bearing the war poorly was not evidenced in his joyful and vibrant nature either. The absence of her parents, Susannah realized, was, like Ewing's telescope, a different lens that enabled her to see her own world more clearly.

When Susannah returned her attention back to the conversation, the women had moved on to discussing their tightening quarters in the church basement. It was true their wheels were nearly touching each other, and each night yarn baskets tumbled in an attempt to move this way or that.

"We shall be spinning on top of each other if new ladies join us," Mrs. Elliot said.

"We could make more shirts, and blankets if we had bigger looms, too," another said, then she pointed to the ceiling, "but if we move into the church our spinning's not what the reverend has in mind for 'Sunday Service.'"

As the women laughed again, Mrs. Reed grew quiet and then took a deep breath. "The beginning of November, you shall have space for one more."

When the women turned to her, she placed a gentle hand on her belly.

"Again?" Susannah asked, then instantly she covered her mouth.

Mrs. Reed laughed and squeezed Susannah's arm, saying, "It was a surprise to us, too. Colonel Reed was home in September for merely a few days. Still, the child comes. We've family in Burlington who will take us in to provide me some help. You will go on without me until I can return."

"But..." The words caught in Susannah's throat. Like everyone else in her life, Mrs. Reed was going away now, too? "Who will guide us?"

"The reverend, I suppose..." Mrs. Elliot said.

Susannah was about to agree when Mrs. Reed scoffed at the notion. "Reverend Ewing is a father to our Cause, but do not give into the idea that you are subordinates. Judith of the Bible did not shrink from zeal. Nor the women of Rome, who cast off their weakness to dig trenches with feeble hands." Although her voice was genteel, her words were filled with an enviable strength. She held up her palms to the group. "I have grown calluses against my King, but they are also in support of gracious queens and sovereigns—like Elizabeth and Catherine—who built empires of freedom before him, and did so with grace. With fairness. If Joan of Arc, the Maid of Orleans, can drive the British from the kingdom of France, then by the Grace of God we few women can weave the King out. And our fabric will be the chainmail of hope our soldiers wear into battle."

In the hush, Susannah shivered. Her pulse quickened. She'd never heard a woman give such a speech. Her mother and her acquaintances always spoke in snapping snippets of reproach. But this? This was a rallying cry!

It carried Susannah from their breakfast and into the streets. It stayed strong within her as she strode past half-empty market stalls, past boarded-up Tory homes, and down avenues covered in manure and mildewing leaves. It lifted her as she climbed the worn steps to her father's lawyer's office.

But over the next hour, it was drained from her a word at a time, beginning with, "I Colonel Bowman being of sound mind do hereby bequeath…"

* * *

Her world was spinning too fast. Or was it too slow? Susannah leaned upon the door frame at the entrance to the kitchen. Lydia took one look at her, put a fist to her hip, and shook the wooden spoon with the other, saying, "What did those lawyers do to you?"

Susannah put a hand up to her hair. It was damp. Had it been raining? She could not recall the walk home from the lawyer's office. Not one step. To be sure, her thoughts were tangled up over what was written in the envelope in her hand.

"Not the lawyers," Susannah whispered. "Him."

"Who *him?*" Lydia steered her to a chair, the table dusted with flour.

"My father." Susannah sank into the chair, her hand grasping the table for support. Her heart felt as if it would burst from her chest. She tried to still it, leaving a white handprint on her bodice. "All those times we had breakfast together…He told me about his imports. His exports. His farms… He wasn't just passing the time. He was passing a torch."

"I do not understand," Lydia begged, tapping the envelope. "What did he do?"

Susannah took out the copy of the will, and as she read the first paragraph, she saw on Lydia's face a repeat of what were surely her own expressions in front of the lawyers.

"It says, 'Should my wife meet her death with or before me, the entirety of my estate not otherwise disposed of as outlined below, shall be bequeathed to my daughter, Susannah Bowman Pemberley. She shall receive and manage all my goods, chattels, land holdings, and monies. For the term of her natural life, she may profit from it, using any and each as she sees fit without suffering the legalities of coverture.'"

Lydia fell into the opposite chair with a thump. The spoon rattled to the table. She stammered, "He does all this? I … I feel as if I hardly knew him."

Susannah nodded. The lawyers, although flabbergasted by Colonel Bowman's request before he set sail, had yielded and written specific language to ensure his wishes would be met. And kept. She would have much to learn if she was to run the estate, they said, but her father had been a kind man so they would help when she asked. To be clear, they said, it was not Matthew Pemberley, not the colonel's own brother, or Arthur or some distant male relative from her mother's side who would manage it. It was to be her.

"Lydia, there is more." Susannah held out the document. "Read the fourth paragraph."

Lydia wiped her hands on her apron before taking the sheet. "Oh, my word…" She read and re-read the lines and then handed it back, the page fluttering in her shaking hand. "Read it, Susannah… and tell my heart if my eyes see correctly."

Susannah read it aloud, her voice growing in a strength equal to the pride she felt for her father.

"He writes, 'In the spirit of my support for our Declaration of Independence, I grant that any and all indentured servants and slaves shall hereby upon my death receive their freedom. That all outstanding debts still believed owed by them, shall from this day forward be considered paid in full.'" Susannah reached out and took Lydia's hand. "He's left you a considerable sum, plus a yearly stipend if you choose to stay on with me. However, the choice... it is yours. You are a free woman."

"While my Joshua fights for our freedom," Lydia lifted her damp eyes up to heaven and then to the box on a shelf where she kept her son's letters, "we have been granted it."

And with that, Lydia, the stoic German woman, crumpled. Her sobs were enough to break the damn of emotion Susannah had managed to hold onto thus far. She wiped away tears from both their cheeks, with a flour-dusted palm. Although, when Lydia's shoulders began to shake, Susannah soon realized it was not from tears. The woman was chuckling. When Lydia dissolved into giddiness, Susannah could not suppress it either. The two women laughed and hugged and laughed until it ran out. Until they sat together in stunned silence.

Susannah looked around the kitchen. It was Lydia's if she stayed. But it was also hers. From the deep blue bowls, to the scarred table. The abundant garden out back, every room of her hallowed halls. Every farm. Every tuft of hemp and cotton. There was so much. She would have to cease joining the women of the bee, she quickly reasoned. With having to learn and manage so much, how could she be both there and here? The weight of responsibility pulled her down. Tears returned.

"With all this fine news, what is this?" Lydia waved a firm hand, but her voice was soft, sing-songy.

"What if..." Susannah looked down at her worn hands. Blistered. Pink. Inflamed. From gardening, cooking, spinning, and carding, and from merely a few weeks of work. "What if what is expected of me is more than I am?"

"Could it be," Lydia raised Susannah's chin, "your father saw something in you that you have not yet seen?"

Susannah's could hear her father saying, *You are your mother's daughter, but you have a little of me in there, too.* The thought calmed her, and for the first time she considered the possibility of a different life.

Not one dictated. Not dependent. A life chosen.

"'Fear not, my pup,' he'd often told me," Susannah said, a smile breaking through.

"There you go!" Lydia dusted off her hands and stuffed the papers back in the envelope. "Shall I get us some more flour—some that is not on your face—and you can help me make raisin turnovers?"

Susannah stared at her dearest friend, her only sense of family now, and asked, "Does this mean you're not going to leave?"

"Leave?" Lydia puffed and held out an apron. "To where? Joshua and you are my home."

Susannah sighed with relief, her smile broadening.

Finally, someone had decided to stay.

As Lydia hummed around the kitchen, gathering ingredients, Susannah tied her own apron strings and picked up the recipe. If she wasn't certain who she was, like a recipe altered for a new season, could she create the woman she wanted to be? Mrs. Reed's measured words returned about not shrinking from zeal, and she wondered if she could add a little bit of Judith or Joan of Arc to herself.

"I could barely crack an egg a few weeks ago. If I can cook now, I can learn everything else. Right, Lydia?"

"Of course," Lydia said, picking up her spoon. She waved it as she went to scoop more flour from the larder. "You just need the right tools, and the space to think."

The recipe slipped from Susannah's hand and fell to the floor. She gripped the table to prevent herself from being thrown backward by the force of the ideas surging through her. She could see it all… her future stitching together.

A way to help Arthur. To support Pemberley. To weave fabric. To make uniforms for all those fighting far from home. To use her home for something far more than herself. To expand the bee. Her purpose was right here. Within these walls. Within what were now her farms.

It was behind two doors.

"Lydia, you are a genius!"

Susannah ran from the room with Lydia calling after her, "What did I say?"

Reverend Ewing's words were surging though Susannah as she took the stairs two at a time. *Three tools are all a person needs to find their purpose… Her purpose.* The mentor had without doubt been Mrs. Reed. The right tools were the women of the bee. And as for the space to think…

Susannah stood in the front hall staring at the wooden barrier that had too long hidden a world from her. A world of books. Of close thinking. She grasped the glass knobs on the doors of the study. And with a twist and a shove, Susannah pushed them wide and walked into the light.

CHAPTER FIFTY-TWO

THE DARKNESS SURROUNDED ARTHUR as he gripped the edge of the small rowboat with his bloodied and bruised hand. Oars rose and fell through the black waves, knocking against the boat. A percussion of ruin rippling over the water. He closed his one eye not already swollen shut, fully blotting out the waxing moon, and pulled his hat down tight on his throbbing head.

What good had waiting at Fort Washington done? There had been three thousand rebels. Outmatched by eight thousand redcoats. Four thousand Hessians. Anger at Magaw's ignorance rose in Arthur's throat with each brackish swell.

"Write it down," Colonel Magaw had rapped the table next to Arthur's hand after the British had sent a man to the fort under a flag of truce, asking for them to surrender. Arthur had been forced to write the words, "We shall defend it to the last extremity."

The volley of cannon and musket fire flung at them in retaliation for such arrogance still rang in Arthur's ears. The southern and eastern defenses fell before noon. By mid-afternoon the British flag was flying over the fort and that jackass Magaw had surrendered. The rebels were marched from the fort. The Hessians, hell bent on beating them to death, descended upon the men.

Fueled by defeat, Arthur had thrown all his frustration into a man twice his own weight. His knuckles split open as they glanced off the man's chin.

The German lurched backward two paces, shook off the punch, and laid into Arthur.

Now, as the rowboat jostled in the waves, Arthur checked his own jaw. He'd fought Nathaniel and Kalawi on many an occasion, but never had he been hammered like that. He thought his own will would break with his bones. Thankfully, several officers had intervened before he'd shattered. In the end, it was remarkable only thirty men had died.

And the rest of them?

Arthur turned to look behind, beyond his own small rowboat. Across Wallabout Bay, boats stretched far into the darkness. On them, over twenty-nine hundred men. Redcoats faced forward in every boat, cold to their captors. Arthur searched ahead, wondering where they were being taken when a putrid smell wrapped around his face like a urine-soaked woolen blanket. The man in front of Arthur retched into the murky water, the vomit adding to the unbearable stench. Arthur pinched his nose and squinted through his one good eye, straining to see ahead.

A silhouette appeared. Outlined by the moonlight, it grew as they rowed nearer. A ship. A monstrous ship. The muddy waters of Wallabout Bay sucked at her hull. She was stripped of her masts and rigging. Ports sealed shut. A few holes smaller than a hand, barred with iron, had been cut at random. A deep groaning sound seeped from the holes.

Arthur's little rowboat was the first to nudge against the curve of the hull.

"The *Jersey* awaits," the redcoat muttered. A rope ladder was held out and Arthur was shoved forward. "Prisoners, board!"

It took hours for them all to ascend. They went up in waves. Prison guards took down Arthur's name. Rank. A Hessian dragged him to starboard by his collar. Huddled on deck, once again waiting, the cold November wind cut through his torn shirt. He clamped his jaw to keep his teeth from chattering. He prayed for a way to get out of the cold.

Moments later, he heard metal grinding, grates lifting from the deck.

He was herded among the masses, like a sheep on his farm back home in Berks County, corralled toward the opening. They jostled and bumped shoulders. Feet moving inches at a time. At the edge, he looked down into the blackness. The smell of shit and filth overwhelmed him. He swallowed, gagged, but cried out as the butt of a musket was jammed into his back. He stepped onto the ladder. His legs shook. Nearly buckled. But another man's feet were one rung above his head. He was forced to climb down. He dropped into a cluster of men at the base of the ladder. They wept. Moaned. Shivered. Unsure where to go, he tried to see through the pitch blackness. And failed.

And then the grinding sound once more. The metal grate dropped over the hold with a deafening clang. A finality.

Arthur looked up through the opening. The moon, waning and three-quarters full, glistened beyond the crosses of metal. It floated free in a starry sky. It broke him.

Arthur hung his head and begged for death to take him swiftly.

CHAPTER FIFTY-THREE

THE GLASS OF WHISKY SAILED across the tent and smashed against the pole next to Silas' shoulder.

"Long Island. Staten Island. White Plains. I wait." General Howe could have lit the entire British Army camp on fire with his rage. "We all wait for you to deliver one man. I look like a damned fool."

Silas wiped the splatter from his cheek, brushed away bits of glass from his sleeve, and swallowing his growing distaste for William Howe, chose instead to coddle the man's ego.

"But your reputation grew after your victory in Brooklyn; I hear the King granted you Knighthood of the Order of Bath."

"Pfft. The one time I followed Clinton's plans." Howe reached for another glass, but his bluster had somewhat blown away. He filled it with whiskey then placed the decanter in a box at his feet.

"And you just took Chatterton's Hill," Silas said. "I dare say White Plains was another success."

Howe pulled the tipped glass away from his lips.

"Success?" He wiped liquor from his chin with his sleeve and pointed to the open ledgers on his desk. "Over two hundred of my men are dead. Then the Americans sat within a cannon's shot for days while I waited for your precious Mr. Marten to come striding into camp. My brother pushed the Royal Navy around and around like toy boats in bath water."

Silas tried to quell his own fury at how that rider had managed to skirt around White Plains. He had sent explicit instructions on Dickinson's stationery. Why wouldn't Wolcott and that twit have followed his directions?

"To add insult to injury," Howe was roiling louder, "it rained so bloody hard, the Americans retreated all the way up into the Heights of Northcastle, just as Clinton said they would. So, he's returned to London to sulk, while you… You give me nothing."

"I handed you three thousand soldiers at Fort Washington," Silas kept his voice calm, trying to appease the general. "Stay, enjoy the luxuries of New York. I know you prefer not to fight in winter, so I will go after the—"

"No." The general snapped his ledger shut.

Silas flinched. He hated that word. It had a finality that slammed the door on dialogue, on possibilities. It was a single word used by small minds and small men. Like his father.

"I am leaving." General Howe stacked papers and journals from his desk and dropped them in the box with his whisky, as noises filtered in from the camp. Shouting. Hammering. "And with the army."

"To where?"

"I have instructed General Cornwallis to take Fort Lee before the weather changes. He will achieve it; Cornwallis is far better than Clinton at following my orders." Howe shook a book at Silas. "That's something you might also learn."

Silas jammed his hands in his pockets to stop himself from punching the general across his smug face. If the Howes finished the war now, business would be at an end. There wasn't enough yet. He had to have more.

"Dickinson is sending me to Philadelphia again," Silas said. "When I return, how will I know where to find you?"

"If Fort Lee doesn't fall, I will advance on New Jersey next, and Philadelphia before the end of December, then I shall take the winter off from fighting."

Silas tried not to smile. Unwittingly, Howe had transferred power back to his hands. Silas only had to leak a few words to Washington about Howe's plans to take Fort Lee, and the troops would move out before the British arrived. He could help the Americans stay just one step ahead, and it would keep Howe up in New York. It would give Silas time to stash more of the silver, to find and capture Nathaniel Marten, and…

"As for that rider carrying the Declaration," Howe said as he snapped his writing desk shut, "I have given orders to root him out from another end." Before Silas could ask, Howe crumpled up a piece of paper in his fist and tossed it into a pile of garbage. "The brother."

"Peter Marten? I doubt he knows anything, and I told you I could—"

"I want results not directives, Mr. Hastings. When I storm into Philadelphia in December, either you or my men will hand me an incomplete Declaration *and* a very dead Nathaniel Marten. However," Howe leaned both hands on the desk, fixing that hawkish gaze on Silas, "if anyone presents either of them before you do, I will send you to rot in a prison ship in Wallabout Bay. Are we clear, Mr. Hastings?"

Silas stared at the shattered glass next to his feet wishing it were Nathaniel Marten's skull. "Crystal."

CHAPTER FIFTY-FOUR

KALAWI AND KAMSI LEFT Fort Pitt as husband and wife, and after Hokoleskwa extracted an additional promise from Kalawi. "Reunite with us in the Scioto River Valley, along with the rest of your Wolf Clan, after the coming of the first snow." He gave them a warm goodbye after presenting Kalawi with a bundle and message for Nakomtha, a gift for sanctioning their marriage.

Now, as Kalawi and his bride crossed Pennsylvania, he realized he had traveled blindly to Fort Pitt. He saw the land anew as they explored their way home. And each other. He discovered the various layers of strata within Kamsi, and she within him. Layers upon layers like the rock formations they passed as they wandered through stories of who they were before. He saw anew the gentle curves of the Allegheny River upon each bank, and felt the softness of each bed of ferns on which he lost himself in her. He languished within each rise, each fall of the valleys and mountains they rode together. The night sky was deep like the blackness of her hair, its length curtained around them as they whispered and moved together. The trip back to Saucony Creek was an easy journey of discovery, over too quickly.

As they reached the western meadow leading to the Marten farm, though he hoped Nathaniel had at last returned, concern tapped at Kalawi. He had left Peter in a foul temper, one he hoped hadn't worsened. Kalawi glanced at Kamsi, riding tall, her long legs wrapped around her horse as they had around him just a few hours before. She trusted him now, he felt certain, but Kamsi had not had his years to build trust for the Martens.

Behind Kamsi, strapped tight to her saddle, was the Mekocke sacred bundle, the Shawnee *pawaka*, rolled into the furs of noble animals. While Nakomtha would be honored to see it, that his wife was carrying it would be a surprise. His stomach churned. He hoped it would be a happy one.

Kamsi eyed him without turning her head. "Your mother and white friends are not expecting me, I imagine."

"I did not say anything," Kalawi said, shaking his head, marveling at how her mind-reading had come so easily. He reached out a hand to hers. "If they love me, they will love the woman who chose me."

"As if you had no say in my being here," she winked.

Kalawi was about to retort when a pistol shot rang out. It came from the Marten farm. Their horses startled to a stop. Kamsi dropped his hand. A man's voice blasted curses. Then a second man shouted. Followed by a woman's scream. *Jane.*

"Stay here!" Kalawi kicked his horse into a dead run, though he had no way of knowing what he rode into, and then he heard Kamsi's horse pounding behind him. Two Indians darting from the woods would surly divert every bolt of anger their way. He halted his horse, dropped to the ground, and tied it to a nearby tree. Kamsi followed suit.

"You can come but…" he put a finger to her lips. She nodded and they were off on foot, following a stone wall at the edge of the forest. Nearer the Marten's yard, they crouched, and peered over the wall.

The hired workers were clustered nearer the gun shop. Opposite them, Jane held tight to Joseph. Harry and John, the two blacksmiths, knelt on the ground, and writhing between them, clutching his leg, was the other blacksmith, Barton. Over him stood Dawes. Red faced. Panting. Pistol in hand.

Dawes turned on his heel and hoisted himself onto his horse, to which another horse was tethered. Hung over the second saddle, bound and gagged, his limp head sagging, was Peter.

When Dawes rode north from the yard, Kalawi wanted to run after Peter, but in the vacuous air left behind by Dawes' anger, the remaining workers argued heatedly over whether to stay. Joseph squirreled Jane into the house, and Barton was carried to the blacksmiths' shared barracks.

Two of the hired workers loaded up a wagon and fled.

And Nathaniel was nowhere in sight.

* * *

Kalawi and Kamsi remained hidden behind the rock wall until after dusk, long after the yard cleared and the lights went out in the newly completed barracks beyond the gun shop. Even in the low light, Kalawi could see the kitchen house was now built and shingled. Near the armory, a new water mill slowly rotated over a newly created pond. In the pens where the sheep and hogs always wandered, considerably fewer remained. When the winter crows began to fill the silence, a lantern was lit in the Marten's kitchen window.

Kalawi smiled, and slipped over the wall.

"Come," he said, reaching back for Kamsi's hand.

When Jane opened the door to him, her red-rimmed eyes dropped new tears. She bundled Kalawi into her arms.

"I thought I'd lost all three of you."

"She's hung the light each morning. Each night, too." Joseph also warmly welcomed him, but both Martens faltered when they saw Kamsi lingering at the door. Upon the introduction of Kamsi as his wife, they regained their welcoming faces, swift to welcome her inside. They settled at the table and Kalawi begged an explanation. Jane hesitated, but when Kamsi patted her wringing hands, graciousness gave way to grief.

"The arguments with Peter had been escalating." Jane dabbed at her cheeks with a handkerchief. "Over payments mostly. And then today…"

"A rider brought a letter to Dawes. Within seconds he'd turned on Peter." Joseph turned his rueful face away to add kindling to the fading fire in the hearth. "Loaded him, groaning, onto that horse, waving that pistol at the rest of us."

"So, Peter's still alive," Kalawi confirmed. "But why shoot Barton?"

"He'd tried to talk sense into Dawes," Joseph said, adding a split log to the fire. It popped and cracked. "A man with a finger on a trigger is deaf to reason."

"Where could he have taken him?" Jane asked, picking at her kerchief. "And why?"

Kalawi surely didn't have an answer, but he could see that grasping for an explanation about Peter was not their only pressing concern. The grain sacks had depleted to but a few, the wooden crates of potatoes nearly empty save a dozen or so with rooted eyes. Jane and Joseph's woolen sweaters that usually covered their heavier winter weight, hung loose on them. With both Nathaniel and Peter gone, who would help them manage the men who were left?

Kalawi cursed his own absence. He'd been needed by his clan at Fort Pitt, but he'd made a promise to protect the Martens. He realized now, too late, that meant Peter, too. He'd failed them. In the hopes of soothing them all, Kalawi reached for the tin of tea on the counter.

Before he could open it, Jane shook her head. "That is gone, too."

CHAPTER FIFTY-FIVE

ARTHUR WAS WEAK, AND YET surprised he was alive. He trudged around the deck of the *Jersey* among the men, counting out the days he'd been aboard.

Each morning, they were ordered from the blackness of the hull, blinking and shrinking once the bright sun had risen to walk in circles upon the deck. Today it was later than yesterday.

Each day, they were given rations, and it was by those rations he knew the days of the week. Monday was oatmeal, one pint. Wednesdays included two ounces of suet. A half a pint of peas on Sunday, same on Thursday.

Each night, before being pushed into the hull, he glanced once more at the moon. Last night it was waning again. Three-quarters full.

It had been nearly a month, he reasoned.

Among the camps, Arthur had thought the lack of victuals in the army would kill him. On the *Jersey*, it was the rations that might kill him the quickest. Especially the dozen brown peas floating in water cooked in the ship's copper. After two days of violent retching, Arthur had learned where that water came from; it was pulled from inside the lower hold of the hull where the sediment of the ship's exhausting life had collected. Now, he took his chances eating the rations raw.

On the days the copper was not in use, the prisoners were sometimes granted small fires on bricks. On those days, there was something of the humane among the men. Together, they pooled their rations and their spirits; their imposed misery their glue. When a man prepares his own food, Arthur had learned, it elevates him above the scavengers and animals.

Now, as they once again circled the top-deck under a drenching, wintery rain, a British guard yelled at a man too near the rails. He whipped him back with a cat-o-nine tails. As the man cried in agony, Arthur bristled. The redcoats not only dished out physical and verbal abuses at random, and with an indescribable vengeance, they seemed to delight in sharing too loudly their stories of life outside the ship, thereby adding salt to the wound of incarceration. To Arthur's amazement, it was better when the Hessians were on guard. Their apathy didn't add another lashing to the already brutal conditions.

"How can they be so vicious?" Arthur whispered to a withered man walking next to him. Icy wet drops bit at their remaining flesh. "There are rules for how you treat prisoners of war."

"Ay, but you're a traitor, you is." The man kept his head bent to his shuffling, raw feet. "We rebels is treasonous so the King ain't bound by the codes of war."

Arthur shook his head. Doesn't that make the treatment all the worse? he wondered. This is what the British do to their own wayward sons? Barely keeping them alive and not caring if they survived. Many did not.

This morning, like each morning, Arthur helped bring up the dead from the dank hold. Some barely clothed. Some sewn up into bags by their shipmates using sheets or torn shirts. Five. Ten. Twenty. Typhoid. Dysentery. Starvation. Small pox. There were times he was glad his own wounds had not festered. There were days he looked upon the dead, laid out on the wooden deck, with pity. There were moments he felt only envy.

"And they wonder why we rebel," Arthur whispered to his frail walking companion.

"You there!" A guard dragged Arthur and the weak man toward the ship's rail. Arthur panicked, as he was ordered over the edge. Had they been heard talking? He waited for the whip, but the man pointed to the rails.

"Climb down."

As Arthur scrambled down the rope ladder, the frail man below and the redcoat above, for a moment he wondered if he weren't being released, but then he saw what awaited him. The morning's dead were heaped in a boat.

"Row."

The two of them were forced to row the skiff to the nearby shore, and directed to a shed containing handbarrows and shovels. At the point of a bayonet, they each dragged a corpse from the small craft. Arthur heaved and pulled at a naked body, the man's face covered with only a torn shirt, and hefted it into a handbarrow. Arthur's own weakened arms shook. His legs wobbled as he rolled it down the beach.

But then the wind came across the land.

The fresh fragrance of terra firma coursed through his tired soul. His lungs rejoiced. He pushed his cart onward, breathing deeply, eyes half-seeing. He pictured the rolling fields around Topton Mountain, by now dusted with the first snows of winter. In his mind, the cold, brackish waves became the clean, babbling brook of Saucony Creek. His mouth longed for even a sip of that familiar spring water of home.

"Halt!"

Arthur yanked back on the wheelbarrow. The body slid from it, falling with a sickening thud upon the sand.

"Dig!"

Arthur slid the shovel into the soft sand. *Woosh chunk. Woosh chunk.*

"Stop and put 'em in."

But the hole was barely deep enough for his own moccasins. Arthur made to object as the butt of a musket dug into his ribs. He fell to his knees.

His hands grasping the sand, Arthur could see them now. Limbs. Boots. Rotting arms. They jutted from the sandy soil like broken, blackened reeds. The shallow, careless graves lined the beach and dozens stretched into hundreds down the long, desolate, and winding shore.

"Put him in now!"

Arthur scrambled to his feet. He tried not to think about how many men lay beneath the sand, as he laid down the unknown soldier. With a blessing said beneath his breath, he pitched sand back over the grave.

"Enough."

...but he'd barely covered the man's torso.

Four more times Arthur repeated the process. Four more men. Four more shallow graves. Four more prayers. When he and the other man at last returned their tools to the shed, the withered rebel grabbed his arm, his eyes wild and red. "If I go, promise me you'll cover my face. Cover it so I never has to look upon this forsaken world again."

The man sobbed openly as they rowed away from shore. Tears slid down Arthur's own sunken cheeks, as they lurched back toward the *Jersey*. Back toward the misery. The land slipping further away. His freedom shrinking with each wave.

CHAPTER FIFTY-SIX

NATHANIEL WAS UNSURE WHERE to go. At last in Philadelphia, as the sunrise kissed the tops of buildings, he looked down avenues once familiar, that now felt foreign. Even in these wee hours, boulevards that would have been bustling were barren. Trash and manure had gathered in unkempt gutters. Garden beds were tangled and withered and not just by the change of season. Shuttered businesses, once bursting with imports, were like all the rest: holding their breath, waiting for the war to end.

He wanted to run to the State House to find McKean, but the business day had not yet begun. Without orders to be here, he did not want to chance being seen except by the statesman himself, or whomever might know of his whereabouts. The greater part of him wanted to run to Susannah.

How would that meeting begin? he wondered. So, how was your wedding without me? He shook his head and longed for a sanctuary.

Sanctuary.

The word reminded him of his delivery from Laura Wolcott, and he pulled the package from his satchel. She'd written the address and also the word *buttons*. That a church needed buttons seemed odd, nonetheless he turned Bayard toward the First Presbyterian. Within seconds of his arrival, barely having foot through the door, he was turned away. A kindly-faced reverend stepped with him into the street, pointing him to a different address.

Nathaniel knew the way. Knew the house.

And so now, with his heart in his throat and Bayard tied to the post on Walnut Street, he stood before the three-story Georgian home, also altered. The honeysuckle was a jumble of wintery sticks, and curtains once pulled open behind pristine glass were now drawn closed, obscured by filthy panes.

Nathaniel ran his thumb across the package, as he once had her glove, the memory moving him toward the door, up the stairs, his mind flailing at what to say. His fist hovered and he made to knock, but the door flew open.

"Nathaniel... Thank God." Her hands were clasped together near her heart, tears running unabashedly down her cheeks as she ushered him into the foyer. Inside, Susannah wiped away her tears with the hem of the apron tied over her dress. "I heard the horse. When I peeked through the curtains and saw Bayard... you—a friendly face—standing on my stoop, well I just..."

As her voice trailed off, he heard it echo off the dusty marble floors. The stale smell of vacancy poured from the darkened parlor.

"When I had not heard from you, I..." She fiddled with her apron but looked him over. "You seem to be in one piece."

"Pretty much." And you look exactly the same, he wanted to say. Same dimpled smile. Same blue gown. Same blue eyes—though not quite. Before he could determine what had changed, she nodded to the package in his hands.

"Is that for me?" she asked, tucking a stray hair into her chignon with her left hand, the simple gold band upon her finger catching the light. As he gave her the package, their fingertips brushed. It sent a familiar, indelible fire up his arm.

"Buttons..." Then he heard a thump from upstairs. He looked toward the ceiling. "Are your parents here?"

"No... They... No." Her face clouded over. She shook her head and gathered up her skirts. "Just come with me. Then we'll talk."

He followed her up the sweeping staircase, down the hallway past proud portraits, pausing with her outside the ballroom doors, a humming coming from within. When she opened them, and walked in, Nathaniel took a step back.

Along the mirrored wall where dining tables had once been set with place cards, girls now bent combing fibers of flax. Across the expansive dance floor where he had once watched Susannah swirl in the arms of the gentry, she now moved among two dozen women spinning wheels. Where the musicians on that last July night had pulled their bows across the strings of violins, a woman pushed the wooden shuttle between loom strings. Where Susannah had once bowed to the officers near the fireplace, she now reached up to place the package of buttons on the mantle near a line of women affixing them to shirts and skirts. The vast place had been transformed from a gilded room that served to impress, to a space pressed into service for over thirty women.

"It's mostly for the army," Susannah said as she joined him at the doors again, and pointed to the women near the hearth. "We also heard about ladies traveling with the army being in tatters. There was no point in having so many dresses here if the camp followers barely each had one there. We make our dresses more serviceable, and off they go."

Nathaniel reexamined Susannah. Her gown was fraying at the wrists and collar, a rougher cloth than the soft blue implied, and her hair, hastily pinned up, was on the verge of tumbling down. She, too, was more serviceable, but her cheeks were flushed with an enthusiasm he'd often seen when telling her stories of elk hunts. It was a look that always made Alice Bowman check Susannah's forehead for fever.

"What does your mother think about all this?"

Her warmth fell and that same storm passed over her eyes. "Come with me."

Back downstairs, in her father's study, she sat behind the desk in her father's chair. Various papers were neatly stacked and pinned down with weights or volumes that had been bookmarked.

"After you left, I found myself alone," she began her tale as Nathaniel took a seat across from her. Soon, his heart broke in waves for her, for the loss of her parents, for the sinking hopelessness she'd felt at being abandoned.

"And even my husband…" she stumbled over the word, "Mr. Pemberley was unable to come home, and it forced me into realizing my problem wasn't society, or the war, or inheritance." She plucked a book from the desk and opened it to a dog-eared page. "The problem was me."

Her finger traced the short passage as she read.

"In 1645 when Governor Hopkins of Connecticut was worried that his wife was nearing infirmity, his friend John Winthrop Governor of

Massachusetts replied that her insanity was the result of reading books. A woman's mind was simply too frail to comprehend such matters and so she had lost her wits.'"

Susannah smacked the cover shut, and Nathaniel had to bite his lip to keep from smiling at her ire.

"'Tis not funny," Susannah said, pounding her finger on the cover of the book. "Here I was thinking I'd go mad from loneliness, but madness comes from idleness. From being ignorant."

She tossed the book aside and picked up her own story again, telling him about the reverend. The spinning bee at the church. Esther de Berdt Reed. The inheritance. Lydia.

"And after all that," she snapped her fingers, "it all became so clear."

"What did?"

"I could contribute. *Me.*" She shook her head as if still not quite believing it to be true. "But, how? The army and the State House have no place or positions for women. My only option was to contribute from home, but I had to choose to do so. From here."

She looked around the room at the dusty shelves, and he with her. The wood and book bindings were smudged with her fingerprints, and the chair, he realized, was no longer her father's.

"Once the spark ignited, I moved the spinning bee here. Here was safer. Bigger. I bought new looms. And if the King wants to restrict with whom I can trade my cotton or flax, then next year my own American crops will be the fibers we weave."

"And after your husband returns?"

Susannah did not shrink from the challenge, but leaned in.

"He will return to a flourishing life. A flourishing wife. Besides, the men of Congress and the army are lacking funding, clothing, uniforms, and so much more. You men cannot keep us out," she pointed a finger at Nathaniel, "or you cannot fully be in."

Nathaniel was stunned by the force of her strength. Even her once delicate and finely manicured nails were shortened for work, and so the hands of a woman had developed where a girl's had once been. And now with a ring. Nathaniel realized with a start, it was only in his absence, and after her marriage to Pemberley that she had grown. Nathaniel had not in any way, to use her word, 'contributed' to this woman across from him now. Melancholy washed over him.

"Now, you answer my questions. Are you fully in, Nathaniel?" Susannah tried to hold his gaze. "Tell me where you have been? What do you know of the war? I've been so worried… I've not heard from Arthur in a few weeks, nor Mr. Pemberley for that matter."

Her brow was creased over hopeful eyes that begged him to tell her everything. He wanted to confess, to apologize, but the words stuck in his throat. And now he could hear the bell of the State House beginning to ring. Tolling.

"Express deliveries," he said. *Ding. Ding.* "Confidential ones." *Dong. Dong.* "I… I best be going."

She studied him for only a moment more, then said, "Well, perhaps one day you will come visit me again."

Visit? he thought. I have never wanted to leave you. And yet he did. Again. This time it was her waving from the stairs where he had first seen her, and he moving forward, his heart breaking, knowing it was their last goodbye.

CHAPTER FIFTY-SEVEN

NATHANIEL HELD FAST TO his satchel, as he once again stood upon the threshold of the assembly room at the State House. Laughter roared from a small group of men nearby. Was one of them McKean? he wondered. If not, did any of them know Nathaniel even existed, or why?

A man in the middle, his fit frame towering almost a foot above the group, held them captive with a story, and although his mouth was downturned below a razor-straight nose, the laugh in his voice grew along with the thickness of his Irish lilt for the story's ending.

"I told this gentleman, although my eyesight was affected by the pox, so distorted were his ears by his convictions, he could not hear the yelping of the dogs at the Boston Tea Party. Then as if to prove my point, the man asked, in all seriousness, 'Which dogs at the Boston Flea Party?'"

The group erupted. As one man bent with guffaws, the dark-haired storyteller squinted at Nathaniel over the crowd. He excused himself from the group and strode up to Nathaniel, a hand outstretched.

"Mr. Mirtle? Matthew Thornton of New Hampshire."

Nathaniel searched for any recollection of having met the man. Thick and expressive eyebrows arched over heavy-lidded eyes, his carriage so open and pleasing, his accent so distinct, that Nathaniel could not imagine anyone forgetting him.

"Good heavens, it is right for you to be suspect. Dickinson asked me to find you." Thornton waved him out of the room. "Come with me."

They slipped into the small chamber beneath the rear stairwell, where Nathaniel had met with the three congressmen in August. Thornton pulled the door shut, taking two letters from his coat. He folded one open: a letter from another of New Hampshire's delegates, Josiah Bartlett. In the letter, Bartlett wrote to say he'd received word from Brigadier General Dickinson instructing Thornton to come to Philadelphia in search of the secret rider.

"Why you?" Nathaniel asked.

"Each colony was to choose the delegates they believe would keep the Declaration unanimous, and would fairly represent our constituents. I'm certain it comes as a surprise," Thornton shrugged, "but my colony has had the insane notion of electing me to Congress just this September. I am here to sign your document."

Nathaniel grasped the back of a chair. One last signer had now become two? If they were adding congressmen, when would this end? Could it go on interminably?

Another nagging doubt—about Dickinson having written him in Litchfield and now Bartlett—picked at Nathaniel, and he asked, "If you were elected in September, were you here when Doctor Franklin was?"

Thornton shook his head. "I took my seat November fourth. Franklin had sailed the week before, after Congress held a secret ballot to elect him, though I hear Dickinson's secretary helped with the voting. Oh, speaking of Mr. Hastings, he was here earlier and gave me this for you, should you arrive."

Matthew Thornton handed Nathaniel the other letter. Still sealed. When Nathaniel read the contents, his whole being elated.

"Good news?" Thornton asked.

"Very much."

The letter, on Dickinson's same stationery, same hand, same signature, not only described Matthew Thornton and the necessity of adding his signature, it told Nathaniel where to find McKean. A crudely drawn map was enclosed, though it was a place he knew well from long hunting excursions with his friends. Pennsylvania, along the Susquehanna River, due west of home, at Sturgeon's Falls in the Kittatinny Mountains. It was a three-day ride at most.

Nathaniel committed to fully trusting the information Dickinson's letter contained, and so he unfolded the Declaration.

Upon looking at the document, and the organization of the signatures by state, Thornton frowned. "There is no room for my signature."

Nathaniel leaned in to look and it was true. There was no space left between the signatures of Thornton's two fellow New Hampshire delegates, and those from Massachusetts.

"Perhaps there," Nathaniel offered and Thornton agreed, affixing his signature in the document's lower right corner.

"Now, when people ask me where the Declaration was signed, I can honestly answer," Thornton chuckled through his punchline, "at the bottom."

Nathaniel laughed with him, and in it was relief. Two signatures to gather had swiftly again become one. With this letter, he could now envision himself galloping toward the end.

"All joking aside, I was surprised it was Franklin and not Jefferson that Congress sent to France." Thornton returned the pen to the ink stand, and nodded to the document. "Jefferson drafted that, plus he's far more suitable to the French than a drunken printer in a coonskin cap. Although, I suppose what with Jefferson's wife ill…"

"Yes. I suppose Congress must have thought it best." Nathaniel stretched out a hand in thanks to Thornton, adding, "Although I should be on my way before they find reason to add other delegates."

"Seldom is politics about reason, Mr. Mirtle." Matthew Thornton smiled as they shook hands and stepped from the room. As Nathaniel headed down the hall and out the State House door, the man who had his ear pressed to the door, once again, was this time not far behind. And this time, not alone.

CHAPTER FIFTY-EIGHT

"WE WILL NOT GO until Peter or Nathaniel return." Kalawi chopped a firm hand at the air, then rubbed at his own forehead. The tension inside the council house as the clan debated whether to stay or go, was making Kalawi's head pound.

Nakomtha had been waiting at the thicket when Kalawi and Kamsi had returned. She'd heard the gunshot, too, and she'd run to embrace her son with relief. Her leg and her worry healed, she'd turned to welcome Kamsi as if she'd always been a part of their clan. Over the next few days, Kamsi's stories of Netawatwees and Fort Pitt endeared her to the clan, even to Kisekamuta. However, as the weeks had ticked by, and Kalawi refused to discuss leaving for the Scioto River, the women of his family had turned as cold as the weather.

Now, as Kalawi took his hand from his brow, he looked to Kamsi. Her mouth was pinched shut, her back stiff like the winter wind.

"You secured your future at Fort Pitt," Nakomtha nodded to his wife, "but what of everyone else's?"

"We have others to consider," Hunawe said, putting his hand on Olethi's belly. She was just beginning to show new life growing within.

"What of our past?" Kalawi said, "Nathaniel is of the Wolf Clan, and by extension, so are Jane and Joseph. Are we to abandon them?"

"They have abandoned us." Hunawe's voice was sharp. "First they took the corn, and now the fish."

Kalawi's heart sank. While he'd been at Fort Pitt, the workers had installed a mill, which had taken the power, the life, from Saucony Creek. In August, he and Wapishi had waded through a burgeoning creek, thigh-high. Now, despite autumn rains, the waters ran thin, barely high enough to cover his ankles. *Like the sturgeon, we need water,* he remembered Nakomtha telling him. Kalawi felt torn, bound by two obligations, promises, and he said as much.

Only Wapishi's head tipped with sympathy in Kalawi's direction. "It is noble to try reconcile your needs with the promise to protect your neighbors. A wise man embraces interdependence."

"Interdependence should be with our own people," Kamsi finally spoke. "What of your promise to my cousin?"

"Do you think Hokoleskwa's life will be changed or harmed if we do not join them until Spring?" Kalawi pointed westward, then cut at the air. No. *"Mata.* He does not need us."

"I suspect your anger is not toward your wife." Nakomtha handed him Nathaniel's letter. The one—the only one—he'd sent five months ago.

Kalawi crumpled the letter in his hand, hating that she was right. Hating Nathaniel. How could he send no word? How could his friend grow so thoughtless?

"You assume he has changed." Nakomtha put a hand on his knee. "But it is you who has."

"Me?"

"You saw much in Fort Pitt, as you have told us. When a man travels far from where he is born, he gains the ability, and the burden, of choosing what home means. That will always be more difficult for you."

Kalawi looked toward Topton Mountain where it all began. "Because I have two."

"Mata, nikoti." Hunawe held up one finger.

Kamsi crossed her arms, strengthened by Hunawe's conviction. "Home is with our Shawnee brethren on the Scioto where there is water, land, and more importantly, Shawnee. I will not yield to you, even though I hear your concerns."

"And I have heard you, Kamsi." Kalawi locked eyes with his wife.

"A good chief does not issue commandments, but I cannot yield to you. We are divided."

The clan sat in awkward silence, the two brooding at one another.

"I thought it might come to this." Wapishi tossed an oblong leather ball filled with deer hair on the ground between them all. *"Pahsahëman."*

A murmur circled through the council house. A ball game.

Kalawi and Kamsi stared at the nine-inch ball, then at each other. The game was often used for fun, and up to a hundred could play in fields nearly a mile long. Usually, the men played against the women, but sometimes the game was used within clans to settle disputes. Unlike friendly European ball games, Kalawi knew it was serious. He'd once seen a man crippled for life from a blow to the back.

"Pick your teams, begin your pre-game fast, and prepare you war paint." Wapishi selected two men to make the goal posts. "You play tomorrow morning."

* * *

Kalawi faced Kamsi in the center of the gaming field, their shadows stretched out long to the west. Behind each, their teammates began to fall in line. A handful of men stood behind Kalawi, the women behind his wife. As Hunawe walked up to the center line, Kalawi heard the man's stomach rumble.

"Are you weak already, Wolf Hunawe?" Kalawi raised a mirthful brow, his own face half-streaked with vermillion.

"I am stronger than you." Hunawe, his forehead and eyes covered in a horizontal band of charcoal, looked over at the men, then back at Kalawi. He turned and fell in line behind Kamsi. "Because I will fight to be Shawnee, Kalawi *Marten.*"

Kamsi cleared a chuckle from her throat, as Nakomtha came to the center line, the ball in hand. "Kamsi, your team is aiming for the two poles near the cornfield. Kalawi, the two poles near the creek. Remember the rules. Men can only use feet. Women can carry the ball, but the women can physically be picked up by the men. Given the division in whether the clan stays or goes," Nakomtha nodded to Hunawe, "you will play as a woman today."

"Or perhaps like a girl," Kalawi growled at Hunawe, but he narrowed his eyes at Kamsi.

She held his stare and crouched into a solid stance. "All the best players are."

Nakomtha held up the ball. A great cheer rose up from the clan on the sidelines. She also waved a handful of twigs. "There are twelve sticks, so twelve goals to earn. The game is won by the team that captures the most."

The rest of the clan lined the field, many placing last-minute wagers, betting everything from blankets to the labor of their own husbands. Nakomtha whispered to Kalawi, "I have placed my bet on your wife."

She threw the ball high and ran from the field. It came down on Kalawi's side but Kamsi sprung high, knocking Kalawi across the shoulder, as the ball went skittering to the side. Without a thought, Kalawi took off after it, Hunawe on his heels. With the ball at his feet, Kalawi's teammates joined them in a tight scrimmage, swarming together like wasps, their war cries blending with the yelps and insults of the spectators.

Inside the tangle of players, Kamsi and Hunawe pushed in, squeezing Kalawi between them, their feet clipping at his calves and ankles, leaving blistering bites. Hunawe slammed his hip into one of the men, knocking him to the ground, where he fell between Kalawi's feet. The ball popped up and a woman caught it in her arms. As she turned to run downfield, a man picked her up and flung her to the ground. The oblong ball bounced away unevenly, and the players circled back around.

On and on they moved together, the sun sweeping overhead. One moment they ran toward the two trees, the next pushing closer to the creek, the crowd jeering. By the time their shadows pulled beneath the play- ers' feet and stretched eastward, Kalawi's team had five points. Kamsi and Hunawe's five. Three of Kalawi's teammates had been sidelined with injuries. Two women had been hobbled. Jammed in the fighting mob, fatigue and hunger jerked through Kalawi's limbs. One leg was bleeding, but righteous- ness still ran in his blood.

Then, near the creek, Hunawe's leg locked with his. Suddenly, the ball sprung high in the air. Kalawi could see it coming down outside the cluster, nearer Hunawe, who was bending to retrieve it. Kalawi slowed. He spun. He kicked his leg wide. He felt his foot connect with the ball. The leather flew straight. Sure. Between the boulders. But as his leg swung through the kick, his heel cracked across the back of Hunawe's head. The man crumpled to the ground.

A hush fell over the field. Kalawi stood over his friend panting. Hunawe didn't move. Olethi ran onto the field and dropped by her husband, her *no, no, no,* ringing in Kalawi's ears.

After agonizing seconds more, at last came a small moan. Hunawe stirred. He blinked, winced, and reached a hand toward his wife.

Kalawi sighed with relief and he turned to the crowd, ready to revel in his winning goal. But the late evening sun glowed red, alighting two silhouettes huddled together at the thicket. Jane and Joseph.

Kalawi's heart dropped into his gut and he ran out to meet them.

"We came because…" Jane nodded toward the field, trying to smile at the clan watching their exchange, "although Joseph and I know, and love, the sounds of your ball games…"

"The workers," Joseph's brow was pinched with worry, "fear of the hatchet has consumed them. They believe you are on the war path." Kalawi opened his mouth to protest but Joseph shook his head. "We've overheard them. They're readying their rifles. Before sunrise tomorrow, while you still sleep, they plan to come in shooting."

"Half a dozen men, against fifty?" Kalawi sniffed, but then he turned and looked over his clan, the setting sun illuminating their worried faces. Hunawe, one of several injured men, was cradled on Olethi's pregnant belly. Kisekamuta stood with Wapishi, the old man leaning ever-heavier upon his fishing spear. Nakomtha and Kamsi were hand-in-hand, a dozen children gathered at their feet. At last, he truly saw his people.

To remain Shawnee, to become strong, they could not stay. Kalawi felt like the land upon Saucony Creek: cleaved in two. He turned back, looking imploringly to Joseph, the only father he had ever known.

"But I promised Nathaniel—"

"No, my son," Joseph shook his head, his chin wavering. "All promises are good and valid, until the conditions change. They have. You cannot stay for him. Or for us."

"We are not asking this of you, Kalawi." Jane took his hand, her tears falling unchecked. She ran a finger gently along the faded scar on his forearm. And then, the woman who had taught him English, the very language that had helped him declare independence for his own people, spoke the words he could not. "It is time we say goodbye."

CHAPTER FIFTY-NINE

DEEP IN THE BOWELS of the boat, Arthur was forced to find a different spot to sleep. While he'd been on shore burying the dead, a new group of prisoners had arrived—greater in number than the dead removed. Some healthy, some already ill or wounded, the men dropped in like newly fallen leaves mixing with those decaying beneath a tree. Arthur crawled into a space near two infirm men laid out on stretchers.

Nearer a small opening, he pulled his knees to his chest as the winter wind whistled through the bars, stinging his exposed flesh. It was nearing the middle of December, he guessed, unreasonably still counting the days as if he had a schedule to keep.

"How long before I give in to eternity?" he whispered, expecting no response.

Many men spoke to themselves at night. Soothing themselves. Steeling themselves for another day. Each man trying to reconcile their desire to support the Cause while stagnating toward death. If Nathaniel had thought Arthur's joining the army was futile before, his viewpoint would have solid evidence now.

Arthur replayed their last conversation, as he had dozens of times since Harlem, still wondering what it was Nathaniel had refused to share with him, still sorrowful to think that his friend might be working against them. And if Nathaniel rode for another cause, had Arthur shared too much with him?

Was he stuck in here because of what his friend had done out there?

Boots thumped across the deck over Arthur's head. Arthur cursed as if it were his friend who walked above him. Free. Dust fell between the planks, and onto Arthur's head. One of the infirm nearby sputtered, attempting to protect his face with a frail arm. Arthur crawled over and brushed dirt from the man's hand and chest, moonlight from the hole falling in a patchwork upon a tattered sleeve.

"You will be okay," Arthur said, knowing there was a lie in it and cursing their conditions under his breath. "I'd trade a sister for an ale, as I'm sure would you."

"Arthur?" The man pulled his arm away from his face.

"Who are you?" Arthur squinted, moved closer.

Coughing, the man turned his face into the light. The shock of dark hair was plastered against a feverish brow. Cracked lips pulled against a strained, square jaw, but the blue eyes were the same as they always had been. Brilliant yet reserved.

"Arthur, you must find him." Peter Marten reached out a shaking, scarred hand. "You must find Nathaniel before they do."

CHAPTER SIXTY

THE KITTATINNY MOUNTAINS ROSE up on either side of Nathaniel, their bulk as gray as the cold morning sky. Ice spread out from the banks of the Susquehanna River like thin layers of glass, steam rising from a center strip not yet frozen. The frigid waters cut a slice through the mountains leading up to Sturgeon's Falls.

Nathaniel relaxed into the familiar ride through what was once their boyhood hunting grounds. A few miles ahead at a thick shelter of trees beneath a series of rocky cliffs, he knew an east-west game trail cut across his path, perpendicular to the riverbank—a crossroads for an abundance of elk, deer, squirrels, fox and rabbit. The boys had deemed it the most perfect hunting grounds in all of Pennsylvania.

"Bayard, did I ever tell you the tale of King Arthur?" Nathaniel whispered, happy to let his mind wander through memories of excursions deep into these forests, and relieved to know his journey was nearly over. Bayard chomped at the bit. "No? Well, there was this boy..."

Low, dense clouds darkened and soon enough the snow came. Light at first, then heavy, it piled over the trail like a white woolen blanket. Nathaniel marveled at how such snowfalls muffled the world, calmed and quieted it, and how even the flit of a winter sparrow's wings was often more distinct in the crisp air. Bayard's hooves crunched upon crusty snow between leafless trees as Nathaniel went on with his story.

A mile from the crossroads, Bayard yanked his head back. He stamped. Snorted. Steam shot from his nostrils in bursts as he cantered on the trail.

"What is it?" Nathaniel grasped tight to the reins.

Swiftly, he scanned the trees. He struggled to hear beyond the deafening snow. Beyond their small trail. Beyond the thumping in his chest. He searched the rocky ridge of the mountains above, turning Bayard round, and round again. Should they go back or through? But the mountains seemed to close in on him.

Pa-pow. The bark of a nearby tree splintered as musket fire echoed through the valley.

Everything in Nathaniel surged forward and he kicked Bayard into a run toward Sturgeon's Falls. Another shot ripped into the trail behind them. Then another. As they maneuvered the path, it ripped into trunks and limbs. It blew through snowy shrubs. It threw flakes up from the path. Nathaniel heard the whistle and rip of a musket ball pass through the flaps of his great coat trailing out behind him. The barrage rattled on. He pushed Bayard on. But ahead, a massive oak was down across their path.

Gunfire from the ridge above followed him toward the felled tree. How many men? Three? Four? He couldn't count. He couldn't stop. The trunk was too big to go over, but beneath it, the path dipped down. Nathaniel prayed there'd be enough room. Blood pounded in his ears. He hunched and hugged the saddle. Under they went as musket fire rained down upon the brittle bark. He felt the gnarly trunk tear a hole through his sleeve. Narrowly they passed. As they rode from beneath it, and pushed on, the hail of gunfire suddenly ceased.

Men shouted. Men hollered. Then the gunfire doubled. Not just musket fire. *Ka-crack. Ka-crack.* Rifle fire. Nathaniel pushed on. He could see the intersection of the game trails ahead. He had to reach it. Had to turn east. Into the mountains. Away from the fire.

"Yah!" He kicked Bayard. The trail straightened out. Horse and rider flattened out.

Pa-pow. Nathaniel felt heat sear along his shoulder blades. He tried to grip the reins as Bayard ran on heedlessly.

His chest constricted and heaved as the gunfire suddenly died away. A warmth ran down his back. His hands turned cold. His legs lost their grasp.

Under the slack lead, Bayard stamped to a stop. Spun. Nathaniel's ears hummed. He gasped for air: a windy, wet gasp. Steam rushed from his hot mouth as he pulled open the lapel of his coat. Wavering, he looked down.

Bright red spread across his white shirt and seeped through his fingers.

The trees turned inward on him. He heard footsteps pounding toward him. Voices all around him. He lurched to one side and reached for the reins, but his hands flailed at the cold air. The path tilted upward. He slid sideways, and dropped from the saddle. Thick, forceful arms clamped around him. Pinning him.

Nathaniel twisted, trying to break free but pain convulsed through him. He cried out. Snow swirled. His head whirled. And the white, wintery world around Nathaniel went completely black.

★

PART III
grievances

*The mind once enlightened
cannot again become dark.*

– Thomas Paine

CHAPTER SIXTY-ONE

ARTHUR CLEAVED TO PETER as he lay dying.

Peter's once strong shoulders now cut through the moth-eaten blanket rumpled over his withered frame. Arthur stayed in the hull, feeding Peter the meager broth from his own rations, but he did not improve. Peter's open sores had given the ship's filth a new place to fester. As his body struggled toward darkness, in bits and pieces, over hours and days, the story came to light.

"I made such a mistake." Gone was Peter's arrogance. Instead he confessed, "Agreeing to the armory was the beginning of the end."

The men, led by scar-faced Dawes, had been determined to beat something out of him, he said. And clearly, they had. Beneath the blanket lay a man equally broken inside and out.

"And then… the night before they sent me here, when Dawes assumed I was unconscious," Peter stared at a distant spot, "I heard it all."

Their shipments of firearms had been split, a portion going to the British. Dawes, working for the British, had hired half the men who'd come to the Marten farm to build the armory. The man with whom Peter had signed the oath, was working for both sides, for the Howes.

For the first time, Arthur felt sad for Peter, who had been so consumed by his own greed, he had not paused to question why the deal was so great.

"But it was not me they were after." Peter turned his head, catching

Arthur's pitiful expression. Peter strained to speak the truth, "It was Nathaniel they wanted."

Arthur bristled. Why did it always come back to Nathaniel? At least, perhaps, he was to finally hear what Nathaniel had done. At last, the truth, and from Peter of all people.

"All this time. All those miles. He's been riding for the Cause." Peter took a deep, shuddering breath. "He carries a single copy of the Declaration. Gathering signatures. Riding for us all…"

The words washed over Arthur like waves against a broken hull. Every word of his conversation in Harlem with Nathaniel was redefined, rearranged. Nathaniel's loyalty was not less than but greater than his own. His friend was not riding free, but had been riding for freedom, for independence, and Arthur had cast him out. He groaned with shame, and when Peter reached out a shaking palm for Arthur's hand, he took it.

"Nathaniel is not done, he still rides," Peter whispered. "Find Nathaniel before that man finds him."

"What man? Dawes?"

"Silas… he's still hunting him…" Peter said, his voice cracking, fading.

Arthur was about to ask who Silas was when Peter shivered, his body arching. Death was coming for him.

"You must ask them to forgive me, Arthur," Peter begged, his weak fingers suddenly gripping Arthur's hand. "My parents. Nathaniel. You… Please forgive me."

Arthur was trying to be strong for them both, but grief tightened in his throat. He took gentle hold of Peter, cradling him close as if he were his own brother. As if he were Nathaniel.

"Of course, I do, Peter. I forgive you. We all will."

Peter finally smiled, moonlight shining on his resigned face. His confession over, he shuddered a long, low, tired breath.

And Arthur cleaved to Peter as he died.

CHAPTER SIXTY-TWO

SILHOUETTES MOVED ABOUT IN the low light. Nathaniel blinked, but the blurred shapes refused to come into view. His vision was clouded by hazy memories of pushing Bayard through a barrage of gunfire. Unable to hold on. Arms catching him. Caught by who?

"Where am I?" Nathaniel was unsure if he spoke the words aloud.

A rhythmic humming enveloped him. It rumbled deep in his chest. He turned his head toward the sound and fell back out of consciousness. When he awoke again, the figures and their shadows jostled about under a low flickering firelight.

"Where am I?" This time he was certain the words fell from his lips.

A hand reached toward his head and he recoiled. Pain ripped through his shoulder. Again, came the humming. It eased his worry. He knew that song. Nathaniel turned toward her.

"Nakomtha?"

"*Ho*, Nathaniel." Hello.

Nathaniel felt her palm, tender on his cheek, but a groove between her brows remained deep. She whispered over her shoulder for someone to fetch Kalawi, as Nathaniel's eyes began to find their focus. The hair around her temples had grown grayer in the last months. The downturned grooves around her mouth were more severe than he recalled. Yet she found a smile for him.

"It is good to see your eyes open with life."

"How did…" Nathaniel's voice was scratchy, his tongue thick. He swallowed and tried again to speak. "How did I get here?"

"I found you."

Kalawi was in the doorway, the cold winter sun setting behind him. He remained rigid in the open door, his shoulders made broader by the furs draped over them, until Nakomtha told him to come in and sit down. *"Lamatahpee."*

From the bed of furs that cocooned Nathaniel, he longed to reach for his friend, but Kalawi yanked the flap shut and sat at a distance. The firelight shot across Kalawi's face, revealing a tumbling mix of emotions. It was the same look Nathaniel's mother had given him once when he had been gone too long on a hunt: joy at his returning, but a strong desire to whip him for his lack of concern for others.

Nathaniel, puzzled, only asked, "It was you at Sturgeon's Falls?"

Kalawi nodded sharply, cutting the air with his chin. At Nakomtha's prodding, he explained.

"We had been here one day when we heard men come to the mountain, stomping louder than a heard of elk. Five men. Four of them Redcoats. At first, we thought they'd come for us, but they tucked into the rocks, looking south, waiting. I slid that way to find their prey. A few hundred yards later I heard it: you reciting the story of King Arthur." Kalawi's eyes filled with warmth, but then he blinked and they hardened again. "They moved in. We moved in. Now four redcoats lay dead on the hillside. One small man got away. I sent scouts but…" Kalawi looked to Nathaniel's chest.

"But not before the redcoats got you," Nakomtha said, as she smoothed on a strong-smelling, but not unpleasant poultice of dried yarrow, hops, and lavender. "The ball went in your left shoulder and out your chest just below the collarbone." She covered the salve in wet willow leaves and bark, and the pain eased.

"Niyaawe." Thank you, Nathaniel said to her, and then turned to his friend. "It was you who caught me as I fell from Bayard? You who saved me?"

"Perhaps I should not have." Kalawi spoke so coldly, Nathaniel felt plunged into an icy river.

Nakomtha threw Kalawi a dark look, and to Nathaniel said, "You need a few more days."

"A few more? How long have I been here?"

"More than a week."

"But I had only one left…"

Panic suddenly replaced the pain in Nathaniel's chest. The satchel. He remembered adjusting it across his chest before he'd been shot, but where had it been after his fall? Nathaniel struggled to rise, to ask about it, but a spasm ripped through him. As Nakomtha pushed him back on the bed, Kalawi pointed to a stack of blankets near the doorway.

"What you seek is over there."

On top of his washed and neatly folded clothes, Nathaniel's satchel rested. When he turned to thank Kalawi for saving it, fury smoldered in his friend's eyes. Kalawi held tightly to the furs wrapped around his shoulders, the veins rigid across his hands. He turned on his heel and shoved his way out the door.

"What has happened?" Nathaniel asked Nakomtha.

"The morning light paints a brighter picture of the same sky. We will talk then." She picked up a bowl, stirring the contents with a tight fist, then she held out the spoon. "For now, eat."

CHAPTER SIXTY-THREE

ARTHUR STOOD AT ATTENTION on the deck of the *Jersey*, icy wind smacking his sunken cheeks.

Twice in the last week he had been sent to that blasted sandy shore with the dead, and this morning, the blisters inside his fists now burned from having buried a friend. With each scoop of sand he'd been forced to shovel over Peter's shallow grave, Arthur's soul recommitted to finding this man Silas. Somehow.

And somehow, miraculously, the escape route was waiting for him when he returned to the prison ship. All he had to do was volunteer, and submit to a simple examination.

Signs of sickness? None.

Skills? Read and write.

Previous rank? Captain.

He'd passed. Now, Arthur stood, hat in hand next to twelve others, on the port side of the *Jersey,* as one stern redcoat paced before the pitiful, ragged line of men, setting out the terms. "If you disavow this rebellion, and declare peaceable obedience, General Howe will graciously provide amnesty for your treason."

The truth, Arthur had learned, was that Howe lacked the patience to wait for more soldiers to come from overseas. Pardoning rebel prisoners, whose broken spirits and flagging army had reinvigorated their loyalty to the Crown, would bolster not only Howe's troops, but his reputation as a benevolent leader.

Even so, as the British officer reached Arthur, demanding he look at him, blood pounded in Arthur's ears.

"Do you, Arthur Bowman, join the ranks of the British Army and swear unending loyalty to King George III and the Crown?"

It was a damnable way off a damnable ship. Could he do this?

He *had* to.

Arthur looked over the rest of the inmates gathered at starboard side. Hundreds and hundreds of them in tattered and torn rags, their faces marked with disgust. Marked by the impending, miserable death that would reward their loyalty. He gathered from them a new strength and looked into the face of the enemy redcoat before him.

"I swear it. I swear loyalty to *him*."

With shaking hands, Arthur signed a new oath. With weakened legs, he took the rope ladder down to the waiting boat. One of thirteen defectors. Traitors once again. As the rowboat shoved away from the *Jersey*, Arthur gripped the edges of the small craft. Spit and piss rained upon their heads from the men left aboard, but tucked beneath the brim of his hat, Arthur drew the fresh air of freedom deep into his lungs. He closed his eyes and held tight to his loyalty. His fidelity. Not to the Crown, but to all the prisoners he left behind.

To all the soldiers still fighting for the Cause. To the Declaration. And most of all, to Nathaniel.

CHAPTER SIXTY-FOUR

ALTHOUGH NATHANIEL FELT STRONGER from the herbs and the medicinal broths Nakomtha had fed him every other hour, as the morning sun shone through the cracks in the longhouse, he felt heartsick. Across from him, Kalawi and Nakomtha waited for an answer with stony faces.

The Declaration was spread open across Nathaniel's lap.

"Is this what you think of us?" Kalawi pointed to a line of text. It was the last of the twenty-seven grievances about the King's actions, reasons for separating from the Crown.

> *He has excited domestic insurrections amongst us, and has endeavored to bring on the inhabitants of our frontiers, the merciless Indian Savages, whose known rule of warfare, is an undistinguished destruction of all ages, sexes and conditions.*

Nathaniel was mystified. He'd yet to fully read the document, and, like Kalawi, he now had questions. Jefferson had drafted this? Congress had approved this? Why had all the Indian nations—Shawnee, Delaware, Cherokee and Iroquois—been described as one? How could intelligent men, demanding fair representation, represent their American neighbors so unfairly, and in the same document? It was like the rain refusing to believe the rivers were wet.

"Is this your *pawaka?*" Kalawi asked.

Nathaniel could not blame him for feeling betrayed. The clan had rallied to save him from certain death, after months of silence, and all the while he'd been carrying a document that damned them all.

"Delivering it was just a job. I was paid to—"

"And who pays you?" Kalawi cracked the back of his hand across the document. The parchment crackled. "These white men who call us merciless?"

Nakomtha's hands were in her lap, clasped tight, and when Nathaniel merely nodded, they rose to her face as if to wipe away her disappointment.

"You carried this sacred bundle, while I negotiated for peace." Kalawi stood, knocking over his stool. The firelight made his hot face redder as he told Nathaniel about the treaty at Fort Pitt. "How can our plea bring peace to the colonies while all of you are beholden to this *messawmi?*"

You.

For the first time since he was nine, Nathaniel felt shut out from the Shawnee. A man apart. Kalawi sniffed at him and made to leave, but Nakomtha grabbed his wrist. She pointed for him to sit, and righted the toppled stool. Kalawi turned back, but he remained standing, arms folded.

"Your body works for them," Nakomtha said to Nathaniel, "but what of your spirit?"

Her words reminded Nathaniel of what George Wythe had told him: people will assume you are not with them unless you show them your hand.

"It is conflicted," he began, "especially after all I've seen."

As Nathaniel told them of his encounters from Virginia to Connecticut, of Captain Blythe and the battle in Harlem Heights, Kalawi's shoulders softened. Nakomtha raised a mother's worried hand to her mouth when he told them about shooting the boy from the tree. It stayed there as he described what Arthur had been enduring in the camps.

"When I see the British Army marching forcefully across this land, I can see why the Americans want to defend it, to separate," Nathaniel said, tapping the document. "It is tyranny, but…"

Nathaniel realized he had begun to believe men like Franklin, Wythe, and Wolcott who saw this document as a prescription for the colonies. Now, however, as he looked into the expectant faces of his second mother and brother—his Wolf Clan family who shared food as willingly as their counsel—he wondered if the document was a disease. The grievances would fester if poured into the open wounds of an already fearful populace. Could the words like "merciless" and "destruction" create an epidemic just as fatal to all the Indian nations as the small pox had already proven to be?

Nathaniel refolded the document and tossed it aside. "After the war, if they fully believe in this, it is possible America will become that which she has fought against."

"Then why not stay out of it as we have promised?" Kalawi asked, as he sat down again. "Why align yourself with either side, if you believe both could be wrong?"

Nathaniel's shoulders relaxed under his friend's compassionate tone. He told them of Arthur's uncle arranging their commissions, and his first meeting with Franklin.

"What were my options? I was going to have to carry a rifle at my shoulder, or carry the Declaration in a satchel across it. Help my father, or become him. Sign an oath against my mother, or swear allegiance to the one we made as boys. What would you have done?"

Kalawi chewed on the question for only a moment. "I would not have chosen differently."

The two men looked into the souls of each other. Connected. Boys again. At last Nathaniel felt the warmth in Kalawi's smile.

"Perhaps what you have brought us is not their *messawmi?*" Nakomtha nodded as a thought settled into her. "Perhaps that is ours."

"Ours?" Kalawi and Nathaniel said in unison.

"A *pawaka* and *messawmi* are woven together. What Nathaniel carries, helps us confirm our decision to fly, to move toward peace." She waved an aging hand through the air like a bird. Nathaniel watched the familiar gesture she gave each fall when it was time to leave Saucony Creek, and then he grew cold with understanding.

"You were leaving when you found me. This time, not just for the winter."

"Ah-huh," Kalawi nodded, his deep brown eyes filled with sadness. "The men building the armory... They saw us only one way, just as that document suggests." He explained, as best he could, the situation with the workers, and Peter's being taken away. "Even though they would be alone, your mother and father insisted we go."

Concern for his parents ricocheted through Nathaniel. Nakomtha saw his concern and said, "As soon as you are well, it will be time for you to return home."

"Just as our home is with our Mekocke Shawnee brethren," Kalawi said, "With Hokoleskwa."

"Your wife's cousin," Nakomtha said, a teasing eyebrow raised.

"Wife?" Nathaniel chuckled. "You left that part out of your Fort Pitt story."

As Kalawi told him of Kamsi, Nathaniel could see more than the light of love and joy in his friend's eyes. The passion for his people that had been an ember in July, now roared as strong as the fire in the longhouse. An aged wisdom filled Kalawi's words, and he was clearly determined now to lead, not to follow.

"With her by my side, we now move to where we can remain Shawnee," Kalawi finished.

Nathaniel slumped back against the furs, envying his friend's sense of belonging, and wanting more than ever to maintain his connection to him. "Where is this place, so that I may one day find you?"

"In the Scioto River Valley."

"Toward the skies of our Great Grandfather, *Takwaaki*," Nakomtha added.

Nathaniel smiled upon hearing the spirit's name. He remembered Nakomtha's stories about the grandfathers who watched over their four seasons. *Takwaaki* appeared from mid-October to mid-January, bringing sleep to the earth and a sense of calm to his children. It was no wonder they longed to move toward him now.

Nathaniel listened to the crackling fire, wishing he could go with them, but the invitation was not extended, and he was needed at home. A home, that come spring, would be much changed without their return to Saucony Creek.

"It does not mean the Wolf Clan will not remain with you," Kalawi said. He put a palm to his own chest, as did Nakomtha.

Nathaniel nodded and placed a hand over his own heart, but it ached at the thought of having to say goodbye.

CHAPTER SIXTY-FIVE

ARTHUR HAD SPENT WEEKS trapped in a different hell, his hat and his loyalty tucked inside a redcoat. He'd been assigned to one British unit after another, swallowing his meals surrounded by low-level redcoats. Sleeping, and not sleeping, next to them. Pretending to be a dutiful member of the British Army in the hopes of learning something, anything, about Nathaniel and the Declaration. He was dutiful to his own disgust, until he was rewarded with enough trust to be tasked with delivering a message to the Howes at the Murray Mansion.

As he rode into New York City, the smell nearly eclipsed the stench in the bowels of the *Jersey*. Arthur retched, and wiped his mouth on his sleeve, squinting through the darkness. The streets leading to the Queen's Head, where he'd dined with Pemberley in August, were filled with months and months of trash and excrement, both horse and human. In the quarter where the fire had raged, refugees had moved into the ashes, living beneath canvas torn from sunken sailboats. A little girl, with soot-stained, sunken cheeks, sat among the charred remains of her childhood, starving, shivering. Impoverished women begged at Arthur's knee until he turned west, riding away from ruin toward riches. In this part of the city, bright British flags flew from balconies of homes that grew in grandeur with each avenue. While withered home-owners pulled onions from winter gardens, the redcoats cheerfully danced and drank on their porches.

Arthur's heart broke. Was this America's future? A populace where a small percentage of the elite devoured and squandered wealth, while taking it from the rest who lived in a squalor more detestable than the pig pens back home? This was not a country of the people, by the people. Certainly, it was not a country for the people.

Arthur dragged himself into the Murray's house, an opulent mansion that he'd heard suffered from divided loyalties. The family's iron furnace still produced musket and cannon balls for the Colonial Army, while the family mansion supplied the British with fine imported goods and gaudy soirees for their generals. He wondered how divided it truly was—how thick the tension, how rife with spies.

The front hall, glittering with a dozen candles, was empty, but he found Howe by the sound filtering out a nearby door. When Arthur entered, he found raucous men circling gaming tables, littering the whole of a gilded ballroom. At the nearest table, a man with a puffy, ruddy complexion bellowed, "You're a cheat."

"I won fair and square, General Howe."

"You did not, you artless boor!" The general, who faced the door, was half out of his seat. He threw his cards at his fellow whist player then tossed a handful of silver coins onto the table. "Deal again. This time, it would be wise for you to lose to your superior officer." As he sat and rocked back into his chair, his blazing gaze turned on Arthur. "What the hell do you want?"

"A… A message for you, sir." Arthur held it out. As Howe tore it open, Arthur kept his eyes to the floor, trying to be invisible, and desperately trying not to lunge at the arrogant prig before him.

"Washington bought the damn story!" Howe began laughing, his distended belly bouncing. He tossed the letter at the man who had won the last hand. "What of that? We started the rumor that we were moving into Philadelphia so Congress has moved out. To Baltimore. Meanwhile, half the Continental troops are going home or coming to their senses." He laughed harder, his face turning purple.

The other man laughed with him and said, "You were right, sir, there was no need to move the Hessians out of Trenton."

"I am done for the winter. Let the Germans stay in Jersey. Deal the damned cards," Howe instructed the man then he waved a backhand at

Arthur. "Get out of here."

Gladly, thought Arthur. Howe was clearly squandering time and money at the gaming table, relishing in a fidelity he had no desire to earn, and without concern for the citizens he affected. Arthur made to storm out the front door, but an officer stopped him.

"Messengers go out the back. Don't let me catch you using the front door again."

Arthur did as told, and as he walked through the yard, he glanced back over his shoulder to fling a curse at the house. He stopped with a hand on the back gate. A servant had come from the house to hang a pair of breeches out to dry.

What's this? Laundry, after midnight?

Arthur ducked behind a holly bush, and through a hole in the shrub, he watched the man glance over his shoulder before turning to put a note in the pocket of the breeches. When the servant slipped back in the house, Arthur waited a moment or two, then ran to read the note.

The Jersey Bratwurst is undefended.

He smiled. It was a mansion divided indeed. Howe had a spy in his midst, and soon another would be coming to retrieve the note. That spy might have knowledge that could lead Arthur to Nathaniel. A way in, and hopefully a way out.

He replaced the note, ducked into the shadows, and waited, his heart pounding. Within the hour the man arrived, slipping through the gate next to the holly. His back to Arthur, he looked this way and that, and he limped across the yard. As the spy returned to the gate, the note in hand, light from the mansion's windows shone on the angelic face.

Arthur's mind flashed back to Brooklyn, to extending a hand to help a man into a boat escaping eastward. To Philadelphia, to long visits under the same roof with the kind, indentured boy. Arthur stepped into the light.

At first started by the redcoat, the man took one look at Arthur's freckled face, and smiled broadly.

Arthur smiled, too. "Joshua."

CHAPTER SIXTY-SIX

THE WOLF CLAN WAITED a few more days to ensure Nathaniel was stronger before preparing to leave, sending out two more scouts to check the roads and bring back news from Philadelphia.

During that time, Nathaniel came to know Kamsi. She sometimes changed his poultice, sharing stories of her life in the Scioto Valley, her passion infectious. As the Shawnee began to dismantle the camp, Nathaniel found her bundling Wapishi's items before her gathering her own. Nathaniel congratulated Kalawi for having fully achieved one aspect of their oath. He had indeed secured a fair maiden.

Now, as Nathaniel tied food bundles to his saddle using his strongest arm, the biting winter cold making his wound ache, Kalawi stood on the other side of Bayard, tightening the straps. Kalawi chatted on about the Green Corn festival, making Nathaniel sorry he'd missed it. The tale was interrupted when the two scouts rode back into camp.

The lead man dropped to the ground. "The trails were devoid of redcoats between the camp, Saucony Creek, and Philadelphia." He was out of breath from a swift ride back to camp, and spoke between bursts of steaming breath. "Still no sign of that scrawny man who shot you either, Nathaniel. However, we are not the only group on the move. Your Congress has left Philadelphia."

Nathaniel gripped the saddle. "To where? Why?"

"We know not where, but the British are rumored to be advancing on the city. Meanwhile the Colonial Army, like your Congress, is fleeing like rats on a sinking ship." The messenger handed Nathaniel a broadside, a desperate call for soldiers. "Thousands of their enlistments are up this month."

As the scout ran off to help the others pack, Nathaniel realized with a start, that if he'd taken Colonel Bowman's offer, his enlistment would be ending. If he'd survived six months of battles like the ones he'd seen.

Now, if the British occupied Philadelphia as they had New York, and there were fewer American soldiers to defend it... he shuddered for what that meant for Susannah and her spinning bee.

"You cannot go to Philadelphia." Kalawi eyed Nathaniel as he tightened the saddle. "She is not your greatest concern."

Nathaniel nodded as he finished tying his packs. The Declaration was in his satchel again, missing only the last signature, tapping on his conscious. However, after his talk with Kalawi and Nakomtha, what little loyalty he had for the job of carrying it was falling with the temperature. If the workers on his farm were causing as much trouble as indicated, his parents needed him most of all. The document could wait.

"Home is a good decision," Kalawi nodded. "You will arrive a day or two before Christmas."

"I did not say anything," Nathaniel laughed.

"Your whole face is like a book," Kalawi smirked as he tied extra furs to Bayard's pack, but then his mouth grew serious. He ceased his work, the rope in his fist. He studied Nathaniel's face as thoroughly as he had the first time the Wolf had introduced them in the forest. "I will miss reading the rest of your story, Wolf Nathaniel."

Nathaniel placed his hand upon Kalawi's.

"I will miss hearing your voice tell your tales, too, Wolf Wetakke." Nathaniel said. Then, to hear his friend's laughter once more he added, "I truly hope for Kamsi's sake, Hokoleskwa does not prefer a quiet camp."

Kalawi's head fell back and his throaty laugh rang out like the playful bark of the wolf. Nathaniel tucked it away in his memory.

A few hours later, with the midday sun shrouded by darkening, cold clouds, Nathaniel and Nakomtha embraced. Even Bayard nudged her shoulder as if he, too, knew it was time to say goodbye. She stepped back and held Nathaniel at arm's length.

"When I first saw you as a boy, I looked down upon you. *Kokweenefa.*" Stranger. She ran a hand across his cheek, and Nathaniel swallowed his sadness when she said, "But now… we see eye-to-eye, Wolf Nathaniel Marten."

Nathaniel felt the warmth of her touch linger on his skin as she returned to her own horse. Next to her Kalawi sat astride his own, his hands gripping the reins, trying to keep his chin strong. Next to him was Kamsi. Then Waphishi. Olethi and Hunawe. Kisekamuta. Behind and all around them the entire clan—some on horseback, some on foot—lined up between the trees.

Nearly ten years ago Nathaniel had faced them like this when he and Arthur first followed Kalawi into camp. To the boy he'd been then, they indeed had seemed foreign. Now, their familiar, kind faces were like his own. Smiling and striped with tears.

Nathaniel placed a hand on his heart and gathered his voice for one final phrase. "*Wela ket nee ko ge.*" We are one.

A slight nod from Kalawi, and then, they turned to go. One-by-one. Westward. Hooves thudded on hollow ground. Moccasins padded across a trail of frozen leaves. One last time, Kalawi and Nakomtha turned to look behind. Hands waving high over their heads, the forest folded around them, and they became one with the trees. Their sounds and figures faded away.

And Nathaniel stood alone. Grieving.

CHAPTER SIXTY-SEVEN

SILAS WAITED IN THE small room beneath the stairs at the State House, ruing December. It was a month of deaths. His mother's. His brother's. His father had waited until January to die, as if to make December more unbearable.

Now the month was stalling profits in his business, too. Over two thousand rebel troops had returned home after their enlistments ended on December first, most of them eager to go due to the lack of victuals. Before the bloody tracks from their shoeless feet might be covered in snow, another three thousand would expire by the end of the month. New enlistments were abysmal. This week also brought another missive from the Howes.

> *Dawes was useless. Peter revealed nothing.*
> *We are finished fighting for the winter.*
> *Merry Christmas.*

General Howe's insistence on fighting in the English manner, taking the winter off as if granting himself a well-deserved holiday, meant silver from the King's coffers would cease for a season. Yet, within those few lines, Silas had been given a possible gift. An opportunity for alliance.

The knock came at last. When the man stepped into the small room and closed the door, Silas wasted no time.

"Mr. Dawes, it seems you and I, are both seeking the same two things," Silas said, offering the man a head taller than himself a chair. "Silver and Nathaniel Marten."

Dawes declined the seat and said, "What makes you think I care about either?"

"I know during your time building the armory, Peter Marten has paid you less than a Continental—"

"How do you—"

"Because I was the one not paying Peter Marten."

Dawes sniffed, but remained silent.

"I also know you're not in good standing with the Howes. They have written to me, about your efforts with Peter being... what was the word... useless."

Dawes' eyes narrowed, but Silas knew tough men like Dawes were like horses: the best way to ride with them was to break them first. He looked Dawes up and down and said, "You're a pauper, and a failure with weak alliances." When Dawes cursed at him and made for the door, Silas added, "However, I still have all the silver that Peter never received—some of which might be yours."

Dawes turned from the door. "I am listening, but get on with it. The State House is no place for a man without loyalties," he scratched at the scar running down his cheek, looking Silas over, "as you can imagine."

Silas threw a purse on the table, the coins clanging inside.

"Half now because I need you to be where I cannot," Silas said. He then explained his last encounter with Nathaniel Marten. "I saw my own shot hit Marten in the back, his satchel in his lap, as his horse rode on." Musket fire had been coming from somewhere else, from the opposite side of the mountain. "I did not see him fall, and a band of Indians forced me to flee before I could capture the Declaration."

Silas did not mention that when the hired redcoat standing next to him was shot through the head, Silas had run. Nor did he share how when he saw those ruthless Indians scrambling up the hill toward him, rifles and tomahawks in hand, he'd pissed himself. He still had no recollection of how he'd managed to outfox them.

He did tell Dawes, "If Nathaniel Marten is dead, the satchel lies in the mountains, and I will go in search of it. If it's not there, the barbarians have it, and Congress will have to start over with a new document."

"And if he's alive?"

"If he is at all the sentimental fool his father is, he will return home to lick his wounds. Deliver him to me—alive or dead with that Declaration—and your coins double."

"Back to Berks County then…" Dawes picked up the purse, measuring the weight of it in his hand. "The Howes have told me to return to New York by Christmas, for some other business they have, so what if your boy isn't there?"

"Take what you want," Silas shrugged. "If the Howes aren't fighting this winter, they won't miss an armory that has barely begun."

CHAPTER SIXTY-EIGHT

NATHANIEL TURNED TOWARD HOME and minutes later, the first snowflake spiraled from the sky. It looped down, landing upon Bayard's red neck. Soon the flakes fell in ones and twos. Then by the dozens. Hours later, the fat flakes came, obscuring where earth and sky divided.

Nathaniel lost track of the days, and his shoulder screamed from the motion and cold. One night, the wind gusted with shards of ice and hail, forcing him to drag Bayard beneath tarps and furs lashed to an old stone wall. Holding the flaps closed with one hand, ice bit at his fingers like wasps.

The next morning, he emerged to a dingy day crackling with a deathly cold. He picked eastward the whole of another long day, Bayard's legs plunging deep into drifts until they came over another snowy ridge.

"Look," he whispered. Bayard raised his head as if hopeful himself.

In the last vestiges of twilight, sagged low under the weight of the snow and nearly sweeping the ground, was the unmistakable sight of the massive oak at the edge of Bieber's farm. Nearby, the light flickered inside the familiar Lutheran Church. Relief warmed Nathaniel.

As he picked his way toward the church, from within the stone walls, a sound fell over him. Singing.

Good master and good mistress,
While you're sitting by the fire,

Pray think of us poor children
Who are wandering in the mire.
Love and joy come to you,
And to you your wassail too;
And God bless you and
send you a Happy New Year

It was the familiar carol his mother used to sing between Christmas Eve and New Year's. He'd missed Christmas, but if it were near New Year's, his parents would likely be cracking chestnuts by the fire on such a night. He turned Bayard toward home, joy tingling in his limbs.

Soon, he reached the long drive curving upward between the white oaks. Beyond the barren, gray trees, the Marten fields, last summer alive with sheep and corn, now slept beneath a fresh blanket of white. Ahead, the familiar pitched roofline of the two-story stone house came into view. Smoke curled upward. His heart warmed and his mouth watered at imagining what his mother might be cooking in the hearth. Then he crested the hill.

The smoke came not from the chimney, but beyond the house, from three heaps of smashed bricks and wood, smoldering remnants of buildings he did not recognize. At the barn, the corral gates were ripped from the fences, and in the pens carcasses of sheep and hogs lay carelessly stripped of their meat. Freezing. Rotting. A disoriented ewe wandered and bleated among the carnage. Nathaniel looked to the house and his heart lurched.

A curtain waved out a second story shattered window. The front door hung awkwardly from its hinges. Adrenaline coursed through him.

He dropped from Bayard's back, readied his rifle, and ran on light, swift feet toward the house. On the walkway, he leapt over a frozen puddle of milk next to a broken urn. The porch floor creaked under his feet. His breath drew too ragged. His pulse raced too loud. Barrel first, he stepped into the house.

Their dinner table and chairs were overturned, and his feet crunched over broken earthenware, cracking like rifle fire in the eerie quiet. Nathaniel moved about the house, room-by-room, downstairs and up, his heart pounding around every darkened corner, until he reached the last room, the bedroom he and Peter had shared. The dresser had been emptied of its contents. Only a growing wind tugged at the drapes through the broken window, the rod half-torn from the wall.

"Where are they?" he whispered.

Then he heard it. A thud. A groan. The gun shop. He ran between house and yard, tripping over broken pieces of a wagon, iron, and tools. When he eased open the door, praying for it not to creak as it so often did, the moaning came again. Rifle at his shoulder, he leapt into the open room.

"Please, no more. I… don't know where he is."

"Father!" Nathaniel ran to him. Bound to a chair, blood oozed from Joseph's temple. His right hand hung limp in his lap, the fingers bent and bloody. On the floor, staring vacantly through a pool of blood, lay the wooden nutcracker. The lever broken.

Nathaniel untied the ropes and Joseph Marten slumped forward. Nathaniel caught him and eased him onto the worktable, his father whimpering. Nathaniel pressed his kerchief over the gash on his father's head, begging, "What happened?"

His father's eyes blinked open. His mouth quivered. "The workers… they were already on edge… primed. Dawes returned. He rallied them, and she—"

"Where is Mother?"

"She ran… trees."

"To the forest? Behind the house?"

His father barely nodded, "Go."

As Nathaniel flew from the shop, his mind raced ahead of him. She would have come out the back of the house. Past the old well. He found her scurrying tracks, fresh snow falling into the small indentations left by her feet. A few steps later, two larger sets of tracks joined hers.

"No!"

Nathaniel sprinted deeper into the woods, slipping through drifts of white, white soon speckled with tiny holes rimmed in red. A scrap of pale yellow fabric fluttered from a branch near a bolder, thrust up from the earth and scarred with a streak of blood. A handprint. Hers.

"Mother?" Nathaniel followed the tracks behind the rock.

Only snow drifted over the ground where she lay. Only her skirts lifted in the wind. Nathaniel sank to his knees and slipped an arm behind her head.

"Please… I am here now." He tugged her bloodied bodice back together. He brushed at wisps of her tangled, graying hair, to which stiff snowflakes clung. He brushed at her cheeks, waiting for her green, hopeful eyes to look upon him once more. "Do not forsake us, Mother…"

His appeals were in vain. He could only cradle her as she had once cradled him. He rocked with her, trying to blot out the image of how he found her, the evidence of her final moments. Jane Marten had died alone, reaching westward. Toward home.

CHAPTER SIXTY-NINE

THE YEAR OF THREE SEVENS was well under way as Arthur reached into the hollow tree, retrieving two new letters from Joshua.

After they'd met in the backyard at Howe's headquarters, Joshua had eagerly confessed to infiltrating the Hessians. He'd put to good use the German Lydia had taught him, admitting that his own plain, boyish face seemed forgettable enough to strangers. The chaos of the war, and so many rebels having been pardoned by the Howes, further complicated the ability for anyone to distinguish a loyalist from a rebel.

Now, this particular tree stump had become a regular dead-drop between them. Through it they had funneled information to help Washington and the rebels win Trenton and Princeton while Howe wasn't looking toward Jersey.

Today, there was a letter with false information for Howe, plus a letter for Arthur. Joshua included news from a scout sent to the Marten farm just before Christmas. The gun shop was expanding into an armory. Yet, as he always did, Joshua offered an apology for offering no solid news about Nathaniel. Arthur cursed. It was as if both Nathaniel and the document had simply disappeared.

He pocketed the letter and rode off to New York and the Murray Mansion with Joshua's false missive. When he arrived, he found Howe bouncing his half-dressed mistress, Mrs. Loring, on his knee.

Nicknamed "Billy Howe's Cleopatra," Mrs. Loring's reputation was so well-known even the New Jersey Congressman, Francis Hopkinson, had penned a poem about her:

Sir William, he, snug as a flea,
Lay all the time a-snoring;
Nor dreamed of harm, as he lay warm
In bed with Mrs. Loring.

She had traded favors so her husband could become the Commissioner of Prisoners, in charge of the *Jersey* and other prison ships. Arthur swallowed the bile he felt toward that vile woman and the general. The drinking, jeering officers and soldiers in the ridiculous ballroom were not only adopting the general's entitled behavior, they were oblivious to those suffering beyond their four walls. Rumor had it even New York loyalists were fleeing to join the rebellion because of the debauchery.

Arthur tossed the letter on the general's desk and made to leave, just as another man blustered through the door. The newcomer, plainly dressed in a dark frock, was too sober, too cocksure, to partake in Howe's orgy. Curiosity coursed through Arthur and he stepped amid a group of redcoats near the door. When the general gave the blustering visitor his attention, the man's confidence dwindled to that of a shaking rodent.

"General, something has come up," the man squeaked.

"You mean, something else." The general laughed, too drunk to be embarrassed by his own erection.

"General, the Congress… They've had a change of heart."

The words flooded into Arthur's fatigued frame.

"You've nerve coming here…" Howe swiped at the air with a bottle of Claret, spilling it across the little man's hand, adding with a slur, "But now that you are, tell me, has Congress decided to come lick my boots?"

The newcomer wiped himself clean with a handkerchief, folding the linen into a perfect square and pocketing it, before he said, "The delegates have agreed to print and distribute copies of the Declaration of Independence with all their names typeset upon it."

Arthur bit down to keep from gasping.

"Off, woman." The general shoved Mrs. Loring from his lap and adjusted the bulge in his trousers as he stood. "Why would they do such a stupid thing?"

"After you ran them out of Philadelphia, when you threatened to invade the city, they fled to Baltimore. This printing of their names would offset rumors that the congressmen are running. It would show the colonists they are unified. It would increase morale already on the upswing after two pitiful defeats at Trenton and Princeton. Though there is one signature missing."

"It's as good as finished if they distribute the damned names!" Howe's face darkened, sobered. He threw the bottle of Claret through a nearby window. It shattered and the northeast wind whistled in.

Arthur clamped his lips tight, trying not to shout huzzah. He knew that Congress' decision would do more than improve morale. It would rally the troops. Soldiers will blindly follow cowardly leaders for only so long.

The mousy man continued. "To match the original exactly, Congress has called for the signed parchment of the Declaration to be delivered to Baltimore, to Goddard's print shop."

"Where is that rider?" Howe leaned forward, as did Arthur.

"An anonymous letter was delivered to Congress a few days ago. It seems at home is where we'll find Nathaniel Marten."

Arthur gasped.

The informant spun his black gaze toward the door, but Arthur stood stock-still amid the group of inferior redcoats, and the man turned back to Howe who was making his position clear.

"Marten must not reach Baltimore!" The general reached for a new bottle of Claret. "The last thing I need this winter is a bunch of inspired, war-hungry traitors. The fun has just begun and I am not going back to Britain. Or my dreadful wife."

"Two days hence, I take missives south for my employer. To Congress," the wiry man said. "I must keep up the ruse with him that I am still supporting the Cause, but I will delay and ride to the Marten home. Send Dawes to meet me in Berks County in three days' time. Marten will be gone before the month's end."

The general agreed and the informant headed out the door. Within seconds, General Howe's trousers indicated his thoughts were returning to Betsy Loring.

Unnoticed, Arthur slipped from the room and sprinted to his horse, determined to arrive in Pennsylvania well ahead of the general's minions, and with his mind set to root out who this spineless man was who festered within the bowels of Congress.

With the redcoat still upon his back, Arthur rode from the city. When he reached the wilds of Pennsylvania, to the familiar lands of Berks County now covered in a blanket of snow, he kept the jacket on, but took out his leather hat and yanked it down tight. Patriotism pounded warmly within him. Galloping toward home, toward Nathaniel, he was once again a rejuvenated rebel.

CHAPTER SEVENTY

NATHANIEL SWUNG THE AXE HIGH, as the sun fell low behind him. His breath blew in puffs with each thrust, his muscles screaming as he brought the blade down hard.

The first day after returning home, he'd tried to swing that axe high over his head, but his shoulder had failed. He'd crumpled to the ground, his hands in the snow, pain raking through him. The winter wind laughed at his tears. Tears that fell unchecked, just as they did when he and his father had stood beside her grave.

He had been the one. The one to plunge the shovel into the frozen ground. To dig the grave with her blood still beneath his nails. Him. Not them. They'd left her to die, just as they'd left his father a mangled, broken man. Joseph's silence by day, a hollow silence that made Nathaniel feel more alone in his own home than he had in the hills of Connecticut, was not enough to mask the mournful cries he heard through the bedroom wall each night.

All these days later, Nathaniel's tears were roiling into fury. With each crack down through the wood, he envisioned the metal blade cutting out months of images that still came unbidden.

Tethered to the young spy John in Virginia. *Crack*. New York teaming with redcoats, and the hills of Harlem moaning with miles of ragged, starving soldiers fighting a losing Cause. *Crack*. Arthur's accusations. *Crack*. His

Wolf Clan now gone, leaving only the brown grasses jutting up through snow as flimsy reminders they ever lived upon land next to the fractured Saucony Creek. *Crack.*

He slammed the blade down through the wood. The log at last broke. A section separated and spun into the cold earth and thumped into a nearby drift. In the plume of snow, his mother's ravaged face seemed to swirl up before him. His shoulders collapsed under the deep, raw ache that swelled up within him.

Nathaniel knew where the fault for that sorrow lay. That damn document. It was supposed to provide one thing, but it invoked another. It was irony on parchment, and he had buried it—shoved it deep in his dresser, along with the scope, the remaining silver, and even Washington's precious maps.

It wasn't enough. It needed to be destroyed, never to be found. So he wouldn't be found.

Before he bent to pick up another log, Nathaniel looked eastward, the axe hanging by his side. He searched the darkening winter horizon, as if it held all he had lost. He was lost.

But a shadow in the distance moved.

The last light of sunset reflected off a figure moving toward him. Nathaniel strained for a clearer view. What was it? In and out of the trees it moved. An elk? No.

A horse. A man. A redcoat.

Nathaniel's heart pounded out a warning. He flung down the axe. He ran to the house. To his father he shouted, "Someone comes."

Nathaniel readied his rifle as Joseph headed out the back door, an imprint of the last encounter stamped across his fearful face.

Back in the yard, Nathaniel climbed the old oak, tearing frozen bark from the trunk. He stretched out long on a strong limb, and aimed his rifle at the lone rider. Six hundred yards. His shoulders drew up tight as the figure flew across the land. Five hundred yards. Nathaniel kept his gaze focused on his target, his weapon steady in his hands. The last time he had fired it for a reason beyond hunger, the enemy had fallen.

He had been only a boy.

But that was war. Three hundred yards.

This was survival.

Nathaniel steadied his finger on the trigger and trained his sight on the invader's chest. Two hundred yards. He eased back his finger. Not the chest, he thought, the head. He raised the barrel. And then he saw it.

A hat. A brown brim stitched with dirty, yellow thread. It flopped over a smiling freckled face.

Nathaniel grew cold, then surged with energy. He uncocked his rifle, scrambled down the tree, and dropped to the ground as the horse skidded into the yard.

"Arthur!"

Horse and rider spun. Arthur drew a pistol from his side. He aimed the gun. As the horse steadied, and Arthur's gaze focused, his eyes fell to the rifle hanging from Nathaniel's hand. Arthur lowered his arm. The two men locked eyes with one another. Both breathing heavy. Hearts weary.

It took but a moment more, and Arthur slipped from the horse. He crossed the few feet to take Nathaniel in his arms. "Please, please forgive me."

CHAPTER SEVENTY-ONE

"THANKFULLY, THOSE MEN DIDN'T find my liquor." Joseph poured whiskey into three cups from a bottle he'd retrieved from the gun shop.

Next to a crackling fire in the old stone house, Nathaniel and Arthur stood at the table with Joseph to drink a toast. Arthur's redcoat lay on the pile of logs next to the hearth, as if the next thing to burn.

"To Jane, to Peter," Joseph's voice wavered. One gulp and he turned to the window, staring at nighttime's purple haze, his shoulders shaking.

"And to the Wolf Clan," Arthur whispered, his eyes still red from learning they were gone without his being able to say goodbye. He drained his cup, and went to stand by the fire, stoking it with an iron poker, as if rooting around in the embers for his lost friends, for Jane.

"To them all," Nathaniel said. He drank, but the whiskey tasted bitter. Discarding the cup on the table, he gripped the back of a chair trying to reconcile his brotherly impressions of Peter, with the truth of him as Arthur had shared. Peter had been building an inheritance to sustain them all, and he'd died thinking of everyone else in the bowels of that stinking ship. Because of me, Nathaniel realized. Then another thought registered.

"Arthur, if you found Peter in the ship, that means you were—"

"A prisoner, too. Captured when Fort Washington fell." Arthur stared into the flames, shivering. "After being beaten to a puddle by the Hessians, mercenaries hired by the King."

"How did you escape?"

"The British provided only two ways off that ship. Peter took one." Arthur used the end of the poker to pick up the redcoat.

Nathaniel gasped. "I assumed you found it, stole it maybe…"

Arthur shook his head and tossed the coat aside.

Nathaniel thought back to when he'd worn a British uniform into New York to save himself, but Arthur… he examined his friend anew. Arthur, who had wanted nothing but glory for himself, for the Cause, for his country, had chosen to become a loyalist to save everyone else.

Arthur turned away from Nathaniel's look of admiration, and said, "Nothing I've done these last few weeks feels noble." Arthur knelt to add more logs to the fire, explaining his joining a spy network in the hopes of finding Nathaniel, just as he'd promised Peter. "Then one night I heard that Congress had received an anonymous letter telling them of your whereabouts, here in Berks County."

Nathaniel's mind raced through the long list of everyone he'd met. "Who knew I was here?"

The growing fire and the flickering candles on the table threw their shadows around the room, adding to the mystery, until Joseph turned from the window.

"I did." Nathaniel's father flexed the fingers of his healthy left hand. "Dawes assumed just because guns shoot right-handed all gunsmiths must be, too."

Nathaniel, silenced, questioned his ability to read anyone correctly as Joseph slipped from the room. A moment later, his father returned holding the parchment, the maps, and the purse of silver.

"These last weeks you were so sullen. Who could blame you after…" Joseph swallowed and set the items on the table. "But your anger… when you were out hunting one morning I went through your room, your satchel, as any good parent would do. A couple of days later, in the *Pennsylvania Journal,* I read about Congress moving to Baltimore. I thought they might want this." Joseph unfolded the Declaration, and then folded his arms. "I heard you curse it and slam it into the dresser this evening. Would you like to tell me how this came to be in our home?"

"Good heavens," Arthur said, joining them at the table. He ran a finger along the signatures, reverence in his touch. Nathaniel realized his friend was looking upon the document for the first time, but then Arthur was jolted by urgency.

"Howe and his spies know about this. About you." Arthur implored Nathaniel to leave no later than the morning, explaining Congress' desire to distribute the copies, regardless of McKean's missing signature. "They can't find him, so you must take this to Goddard's print shop in Baltimore. It can't stay here."

"But first," Joseph asked again, his voice softer, "*why* is it here, Son?"

Nathaniel leaned heavily upon the back of the chair. Seeing the document after all he'd learned from Arthur, all the three men had shared, Nathaniel no longer wanted to throw it in the fire. To destroy the document, he realized, would not unburden him of what he really carried.

"It is here because of you, Father."

"Me?"

Nathaniel nodded. He pulled out the chair and sank into it.

"The gun shop... Peter was making changes you hated and I hated them for you. Most of all I hated what they meant for me. The idea of becoming you... a gunsmith... that path wasn't for me. I didn't know what I wanted." He glanced at Arthur, whose frown was as deep as Joseph's. "Except for Susannah."

Nathaniel looked down to his hands. Hands blistered and raw from trying to repair damage caused by himself. Hands that had been unable to help anyone but himself.

"Pemberley was gallant in his own right, your uncle said. Could I prove to be as worthy of her, the colonel had asked." Nathaniel laughed at the idea of it now. "I did exactly what you had warned Peter of, Father. I accepted short-term gains at a long-term cost greater than we were willing to pay. I took money for delivery of a document I couldn't even be bothered to read. I took it to avoid shooting anyone... which I did anyway. In the end, Susannah married the right man. I'm not worthy at all."

The fire snapped and cracked in the silence. Nathaniel could look at neither man. The sound of his father's deep, shuddering sigh filled the room. It echoed in Nathaniel's heart, and he closed his eyes.

"Son, look at me," Joseph whispered. Nathaniel did as told, but tears, not anger, were what he found in his father's eyes. "All we've lost, is not because of you. Or Peter. Or because of that document."

Joseph swept an arm eastward, toward the armory buildings now in ruins, toward his wife's grave.

"'Twas an Englishman working for the Howes who confessed it during his beating of me. He turned the men here—men already ignorant, already wary—into a lynch mob. It was the Germans, my own country-men, who were brutalizing men like Arthur. All these men are working for a King who refuses to bring his children into the light." Joseph rubbed a hand across the back of his neck, as Nathaniel often did. "His horrendous actions are the truths I hold to be self-evident. And I... I want no more of this darkness."

"You have read Thomas Paine's *Common Sense*," Arthur said, his eyes filled with admiration.

Joseph, his voice growing strong, quoted a passage from memory, "'The cause of America is, in a great measure, the cause of all mankind.'"

"And Paine's *American Crisis*, too... I remember his words," Arthur said. "'The harder the conflict, the more glorious the triumph. What we obtain too cheap we esteem too lightly: it is dearness only that gives every thing its value.'"

The two men smiled at one another, but then Joseph turned to Nathaniel. "I can see by your confused face, you have read neither pam-phlet."

His father retrieved Jane's family cookbook, the binding bulging with letters stuffed between recipes, one of her few possessions left untouched in the destruction. Joseph took two booklets from within and held them aloft.

"*Common Sense*. When it came to me in spring last year, I tucked it in a drawer instead of my conscience. Until they took Peter."

"*American Crisis*." Arthur looked upon the other leaflet with fondness. "When it was read to the Continental Army in December, the men wept. Three days later they won Trenton."

Joseph set the pamphlets on the table next to the Declaration.

"My son, it is time to do what you should have done months ago."

Nathaniel's father replaced the dying candle in the pewter holder on the table. The new wick burned brighter, steady. "The only person more ignorant than a man who cannot read, is one who can and chooses not to."

Joseph waved Arthur upstairs to bed. "Come. In a man's life, the greatest decisions he makes, he must make alone." And before his father ascended, he kissed Nathaniel's head and whispered his consent. "You are free to walk your own path, my son, but the time to choose it is now."

CHAPTER SEVENTY-TWO

ALONE, THE CANDLE CASTING shadows about the somber room, darkness descended beyond the window, Nathaniel reached for the first pamphlet, reading aloud the first line.

"*Common Sense; addressed to the Inhabitants of America.*"

Paine's words wrapped around him. This land, this colony, this country had been his home since birth, and if America was born of Great Britain, how could she 'harm her children so brutally,' Paine asked him.

Nathaniel's chest tightened, his loss for his mother magnified by Paine's comparison, for Jane Marten had seen more value in books than brute, in protection over punishment. Absorbed, he read on, drinking in the words like water, then reaching for the other pamphlet, still thirsty for more.

While *Common Sense* shone with ideology, *American Crisis* was ablaze by the gravity of war the author had seen first-hand, corroborating all Arthur had shared about Brooklyn, and reiterating all Nathaniel had witnessed on Harlem Heights and White Plains.

Still Nathaniel wondered, how could the actions of one man, one uncertain rider, have any impact against so large a foe? And for that, Paine provided an answer:

Your conduct is an invitation to the enemy,
yet not one in a thousand of you has heart enough to join him.

Howe is as much deceived by you
as the American cause is injured by you.

Paine's words pulled away the blanket of blindness from Nathaniel. If every man had followed Nathaniel's disengaged and apathetic example, darkness would have descended long ago. Thousands had not. Many he knew had not. Arthur. His father. The Shawnee. Susannah. Lydia and Joshua. Captain Blythe. His mother and Peter and all those already gone. Jawara and all those not yet free. And fifty-six men.

Not only for himself, but in honor of them all, Nathaniel, agreeing it was long overdue, reached for the one document that had been there for the reading all along. The Declaration of Independence.

Within that first paragraph, within the Preamble, Nathaniel's very reason for reading was succinctly set down.

When in the Course of human events, it becomes necessary
for one people to dissolve the political bands
which have connected them with another,
and to assume among the powers of the earth,
the separate and equal station to which
the Laws of Nature and of Nature's God entitle them,
a decent respect to the opinions of mankind
requires that they should declare the causes
which impel them to the separation.

"Reason," Nathaniel whispered, remembering his conversation with Wythe.

Back then Nathaniel had believed that patriotism was a feeling, but what if it was a tangible Cause he could come to know, to understand? Could he, with reason as his guide, as the second paragraph began, "hold these truths to be self-evident?"

Nathaniel opened wide his mind, allowing in this new statement of beliefs.

We hold these truths to be self-evident,
that all men are created equal

that they are endowed by their Creator
with certain unalienable Rights
that among these are Life, Liberty and the pursuit of Happiness.
That to secure these rights,
Governments are instituted among Men,
deriving their just powers from the consent of the governed.

Nathaniel recalled the smudgy face of little John, the orphan, the urchin, the spy. The governed. If his government, his King, had reduced him to starvation, destitute as he was in spirit compared to Arthur or in wealth compared to Richard Henry Lee, so must John have an equal voice to affect change.

That whenever any Form of Government
becomes destructive of these ends,
it is the Right of the People
to alter or to abolish it,
and to institute new Government,
laying its foundation on such principles
and organizing its powers in such form,
as to them shall seem most likely
to effect their Safety and Happiness.

But, the words within that long second paragraph also allayed Nathaniel's rising concerns—concerns that they were being hasty, rash, foolhardy.

Prudence, indeed, will dictate
that Governments long established
should not be changed for light and transient causes;
and accordingly all experience hath shewn,
that mankind are more disposed to suffer, while evils are sufferable,
than to right themselves
by abolishing the forms to which they are accustomed.

Nathaniel drew in a long breath. Hadn't he believed Peter's demands in the gun shop to be neither light, nor transient? His father had stayed and suffered because the life of a gunsmith was all he knew. For Nathaniel, he had historically had a poor view of his brother and his role in the gun shop, so Peter's ascendancy provided further justification for Nathaniel's leaving, just as the colonists had with the King.

But when a long train of abuses and usurpations,
pursuing invariably the same Object
evinces a design to reduce them under absolute Despotism,
it is their right, it is their duty,
to throw off such Government,
and to provide new Guards for their future security.

"Provide new Guards."

Hadn't Arthur used those very words when they'd reunited in the Harlem army camp? Nathaniel could still see the withered faces of all those soldiers, their wives sometimes beside them, each man and woman barely clothed, each standing up for everyone else. While throughout the colonies, on farms, on battlefields, in Boston, in New York, and on those prison ships, punished by the dismissive hand of their sovereign, they were falling down by the thousands.

Crack. A log in the hearth popped.

Again, Nathaniel's mother's absence filled the room. If she had fallen after months of hopeful waiting, how many mothers had?

How many still would?

Such has been the patient sufferance of these Colonies;
and such is now the necessity which constrains them to alter
their former Systems of Government.
The history of the present King of Great Britain
is a history of repeated injuries and usurpations,
all having in direct object the establishment
of an absolute Tyranny over these States.
To prove this, let Facts be submitted to a candid world.

Below that, in all, twenty-seven grievances were presented, many of which referred to legislation altered or ignored, but nearly all began with "He." He has refused. He has forbidden. He has obstructed. He has plundered. He has constrained.

With each fact, Nathaniel gripped the table, first in anger, and then out of staggering surprise. Nathaniel, and those he loved, had personally felt the blow of eight of the grievances.

Numbers eleven, fourteen, and twenty-three. Standing armies in peace time. Quartering troops among us. Waging war against us.

He recalled, after British ships sailed into Boston, despite the army never having left after the French and Indian war, his father reading in the paper the words "red-coated devils." Back then, Nathaniel, but eight or nine, had been plagued with nightmares. Just this September, he'd seen his own terrors realized from the bow of the *Frontier*.

Ships, four hundred.

Redcoats, too many to count.

Howe's minions, quartered in Manhattan, and even here at his own home. Nearly half his life, he now realized, the King's men had inhabited their shores. Not inhabited. Occupied.

Number twenty-four. Plundered our seas, burnt our towns, destroyed our lives. The smell of smoke, the heat of flames racing through New York, came rushing back to Nathaniel, his heart breaking once more over the loss of George and Captain Blythe's crew. Those who might have survived no doubt taken prisoner. Like Arthur.

His friend had been cruelly captured and put on that ship because of number twenty-five, hiring foreign mercenaries. Hessians paid to bring death. Destruction. The only way for the traitors like Arthur to survive, was to sign yourself over to the King, grievance number twenty-six: Constrained to bear arms against their own country. Against their own brethren. Constrained like trade had been, which was number sixteen.

Both Susannah and Captain Blythe had been forced to step in to weave, and to acquire, what the colonies' once open ports had been shut to. Fabrics, gunpowder, ships, and so much more.

As for the last grievance, twenty-seven, which Kalawi had railed against. Although Nathaniel still glowered at Jefferson's wording—the assumption that all Indian nations behaved as one—Nathaniel now pointed a new finger of blame.

The King could have chosen to be humble and gracious toward a people who had lived on this land first. The King could have chosen to protect his colonial subjects, through inclusion and education, when he left them to live among those original inhabitants. Instead he chose to divide, to stoke fear, to incite some Indian nations into fighting the White Family's war. He did not unify. He tore asunder.

In the face of such facts, Nathaniel could see it was only right, despite numerous attempts by the Congress for redress, vain appeals marked only by repeated injuries, the King be labeled a tyrant. King George III was, as the document stated, 'unfit to be the ruler of a free people.'

"How can I be free, if I am under the yoke of ignorance?" Nathaniel whispered and shook his head. "I cannot. We cannot."

Despite the east wind blowing hard against his home, the candle now but a low flicker, and the embers in the hearth faintly glowing, Nathaniel was warmed. The fog of uncertainty had lifted from him.

He agreed with the final words. He gave his consent. He declared a new oath.

That these United Colonies are, and of Right
ought to be Free and Independent States;
That they are Absolved from
all Allegiance to the British Crown...

And for the support of this Declaration,
with a firm reliance on the protection of divine Providence,
we mutually pledge to each other
our Lives, our Fortunes and our sacred Honor.

He ran a fingertip over the signatures of the fifty-five men, several of whom he had met. Were they men defined by their pasts, or personal motives? Some, perhaps. Were they affected by their present? Without doubt, but they were also simply men, the governed, who had committed to a better life for more than just themselves.

And each of them was waiting for him to take the document to Baltimore. Needing him to find Thomas McKean.

Asking for him to finish his task.

Nathaniel refolded the parchment and stared at the words written upon it in his own hand. *'Original Declaration of Independence dated 4 July, 1776.'* Back then, he had not been ready to carry such a sacred bundle.

Now, he understood why the conditions had to change.

It was as Dickinson had said about the statue of David. Although the boy looks back, beyond the burden carried over his shoulder, a man chooses to step forward. It is only by the act of choosing independence, for himself, and for those unable, that a man can truly set himself free.

A calm settled into his bones—a deep feeling of both sureness and relief that comes with finding a way out of the darkness.

A caw of a crow interrupted his reverence and Nathaniel raised his eyes to the window. A lone black bird swooped across their farm. The crow spun, floating upward with abandon. He kept watch until, with a single sweep of its wings, the bird turned toward the rising sun, and flew beyond Topton Mountain.

CHAPTER SEVENTY-THREE

WHEN THE SUN BROKE THROUGH the torn bedroom curtains, Arthur stumbled from his rumpled bed. Nathaniel's bed, opposite his, was made. Arthur stretched, thankful his friend had let him languish in the first solid sleep in what felt like years.

How much easier it is to dream among those you love, he thought, as he shuffled downstairs in stockinged feet.

"Did you get much sleep, Nathaniel?"

Arthur stood alone in the empty kitchen, scratching his head, the rays of late morning sun refracting through the whiskey bottle next to their cups on the table. Outside, it glinted off the snowy fields, sparkling like shattered glass, the air clear, quiet, save for one distant crow. Arthur looked back to the room. To the table.

Wax was puddled in the pewter candleholder, a small sheet of paper pinned beneath it. Arthur picked it up, and read the words. The first quote he knew from Paine:

> *"The period is now arrived, in which either they*
> *or we must change our sentiments, or one or both must fall."*

And then a declaration…

Move my father to a safe place. Let Congress know I am carrying our Declaration of Independence. Find McKean, one among a list of men I've enclosed whom you can trust. Bring him to meet me at Goddard Printing in Baltimore.

Wela ket nee ko ge.
E pluribus unum.
We are one.
- Nathaniel.

Arthur lifted his eyes to the ceiling, clenching the note to his chest. And then with a small huzzah, he ran to get them ready, his fist waving the letter high in the air.

CHAPTER SEVENTY-FOUR

"HELLO?" A BELL TINKLED over Nathaniel's head, as he ducked into the print shop, having ridden up the colonies, arriving in Baltimore without incident, and now grateful to find a morning fire warming the stone room.

The pristine space, quiet save a tick-tock of a clock on the mantle, was filled with two lumbering wooden machines, a long worktable beneath a window overlooking a small stone courtyard, and sheets of paper waiting on a shelf next to a series of metal racks. In the far corner, a narrow stairwell rose to rooms above. Nathaniel called up them.

"Mr. Goddard?" He startled when, at his feet, a charcoal cat mewed, thumping a fat head against his shin. "Hello, you."

The bell jangled at the door, and the cat scurried to greet a young woman, kicking the door closed with her heel, who struggled under the weight of a large bucket of water. Nathaniel rushed to help, grasping the pail, the cat sidewinding between them, nearly tripping them.

"Thank you, sir. Just put it near the fire." The woman righted a pair of glasses tumbling from her auburn hair. "Might I be of some help?"

"I am here to meet Goddard, the printer. Do you know where he is?"

She wiped a palm on her canvas apron and stretched out her hand.

"I am Mary Katharine Goddard. And you are?"

"But you are a wo—"

"A woman? Yes, for quite some time."

Nathaniel failed to take her hand, and she dropped her own and laughed—a forgiving, sweet laugh. She put on her glasses and examined the whole of Nathaniel, taking in the gentleman's clothes he'd chosen to wear.

"What is it you require on this cold day, sir?"

"I… You, er …," He pulled the Declaration from his satchel, showing her his words written on the parchment. "I believe you volunteered to print copies of this."

"Nathaniel Mirtle at last! I was told you would come." A smile spread over the whole of her almond-shaped face and she rushed to clear a space on the long table. "Will you please unfold it?" She showed him her open palms, stained with the permanent tattoo of her work. "I'd hate to get it inky."

Nathaniel obliged and as she read it, her fingers opened and closed as if the desire to touch were sometimes out of her control. She was older than him to be sure, but her delight made it hard to tell by how much, her tongue working the corner of her mouth before asking, "How many have had the fortune of seeing this?"

"Fifty-six for certain. A few more."

"Soon the whole of the colonies." She popped up, sweeping past him, and returning with another apron in hand. "Shall we get started?"

"We?"

"So long as the document stays, so do you. I have to follow the original to replicate it exactly, and I was told your being here should be hush-hush." She waggled the apron at him, and he took it from her. "Also, my pressman is ill, and my best type composer joined the Cause last week. It must be you."

As Nathaniel donned the apron, Mary Katharine sorted through the drawers of a nearby case, bringing over two trays of metal letters, and shooing away the purring cat.

"To your bed, Benjamin."

"Benjamin?" Nathaniel tied on the apron as the feline climbed into a basket of linens beneath the presses. "As in Franklin?"

"It seemed to suit him. You know he was a printer?"

"The cat?" Nathaniel smirked. She laughed, but when her hand settled upon her curving hip, he answered. "Yes, he mentioned it when I met him last July."

"I hope we've done well sending him to France," she said, but then she picked a metal letter from the tray, twisting it to the light falling through the window. "We will use this font for our copies. Caslon. An English font. I ordered it right before trade restrictions prevented me from getting more."

"Number sixteen."

"Pardon?" She lowered the letter.

"A grievance against the King," he nodded to the parchment, "'number sixteen is cutting off our trade with all parts of the world.'"

"A fine memory! It will come in handy here, Mr. Mirtle." She handed him a composing stick and showed him how to set the letters and spacers between words. "Put each letter in backwards, just a few words at a time. When flipped onto the printed sheet, your words will read correctly. I will start on the first paragraph, you set the type for the second?"

"Easy enough," Nathaniel said.

Not quite. The letters were so tiny, and for every one line of type he assembled, she was completing three or four. Additionally, Mary Katharine's soft humming, the first feminine sound he'd heard in months, only made his mind wander too far.

"So, Mrs. Goddard how long—"

"Miss Goddard."

He dropped a letter, cursing his meaty, betraying fingers. "How long have you had the print shop?"

"Hmm…" She looked up to the ceiling as she correctly added letters to the stick. "Two years now. Since seventy-five, the same year I became Postmaster for Baltimore."

Nathaniel ceased his work and stared at her anew.

"It does not take a man to organize the mail." She reached for another letter, giving him a sideways glance. "I was already writing and publishing both the *Maryland Journal* and the *Baltimore Advertiser*, so why not know the post routes, too?"

Nathaniel finished a row of letters and set them into the wooden galley on the table, all the while trying to imagine this slight Mary Katharine riding the post roads as he had.

"Before that I ran a shop in Philadelphia with my mother," she pushed her glasses higher with the edge of one finger, but her voice grew morose, "until she died seven years ago."

368 ★ KAREN A. CHASE

"I am sorry," Nathaniel said as he built the word *life*. "My mum is gone, too. Too sudden… too young. My brother also."

"The war?"

When he only nodded, keeping his chin down, bent to the work, her voice softened more. "When our loved ones go, grief sets up house in us; it moves out a bit over time, but our home never feels quite the same, does it?"

He shook his head, but nagging at him was that word again. *Home.* Nathaniel cast aside his thoughts over where that would eventually be, and asked, "What was she like, your mother?"

"She could balance a ledger, quote Shakespeare, taught me Latin and French, and cursed like no other woman. Phenomenal, really." Mary Katharine laughed, a tonic for the somber mood, like cool rain on a hot day. Nathaniel realized he'd missed two words in his line of type. He took it apart and reset it, as Mary Katharine continued.

"She was fierce, often saying printers would be the ones to advance the world. She was right. In sixty-four when the King failed to veto an arbitrary tax to track each sheet of paper—the Stamp Act—printers fought it."

Nathaniel leaned forward, scanning the document, and pointing to a line with the composing stick.

"Number seventeen. Imposing taxes without consent." That now made nine grievances experienced by himself and those he knew. How many more before this all ended? he wondered. "Did you protest with the printers—"

"You're damn right I did! We rallied together!" She snapped a letter into place. "That we won, and the legislation was repealed, was the beginning of the end for that tyrant of a King."

"Fierce, hmm?" Nathaniel smiled, but when she made to defend herself, he added, with warmth, "Though as Paine said, 'Tis the business of little minds to shrink.'"

A flush grew on her high cheeks. "You are kind."

He lowered his gaze to his work, and admitted, "But not always selfless. Too long I waited to read Paine's pamphlets. By his words, I am changed."

Mary Katharine smiled, her eyes keeping to her work, as she said, "For the better, it seems."

Soon, a late-afternoon meal was set out by the housekeeper. Nearer the fire, talk meandered from traveling the colonies to the status of the war.

Benjamin sat in a third chair, relishing in the morsels passed his way as easily as Nathaniel enjoyed their conversation. It was effortless. Yet, quite enlivening.

However, long after they returned to their work, when the clock over the fireplace chimed a late evening hour, and the candles flickered low, his thoughts ran dry with fatigue. His feet and back, used to a saddle rather than standing, ached. Nathaniel looked over their work and groaned.

"We're barely half through?"

"A good start. A document that size can take two or three days with two people. But 'tis enough for one day. The special paper Congress ordered is not yet delivered anyway." She held out a hand for his apron, and hung them together. Benjamin hopped from his basket and stretched out long as if he had done all the work. Mary Katharine bent to pet him, but her hazel eyes were on Nathaniel. "You are a fine partner, Mr. Mirtle, especially after traveling to get here, too."

Had he imagined it? Was there was tenderness in her look? Perhaps, but she stood, and with steady hands, smoothed her skirts. "Come, I will show you to your room upstairs."

That night, alone in a clean bed, the Declaration in his satchel by his side, Nathaniel's dreams were filled with the repetitive task of sorting and stacking letter after letter, word after word, row after row, next to an intriguing, unmarried woman who smelled of both lavender and ink.

CHAPTER SEVENTY-FIVE

"A NEW BAG OF MAIL, Reverend Kendall."

The young man groaned as he dropped the hefty, canvas sack next to the mountain of mail already at Reverend Kendall's feet. Nodding his thanks, the reverend opened the new bag, and pulled out a stack of letters.

Dead letters.

The small department within the Continental Post had grown since the war began, and Reverend Kendall was grateful for it. His humped shoulders beneath his stark white hair were no longer fit to carry the weight of a congregation. Moving the offices from Philadelphia to Baltimore, to stay ahead of the British, had been arduous enough for him while still trying to redirect all the lost mail.

The reverend, just one of fourteen retired clergy sitting at the long table slicing open the missives, reached for his knife, a gift of his predecessor who had explained to him the reverence behind the profession.

"We are old, poor, and unworldly men, clergymen not of this world and close to the next. Our lifelong vow to seek the truth permits us to read what has gone astray."

It was still unfathomable to Kendall that over three thousand people would post a letter or package with an insufficient address, and yet that was how many they had sifted through in just this year. Though to be fair, some came to him in a condition such as the one he now held. Weather-beaten from somehow being lost or discarded en route, rain and filth had wiped away any trace of the intended recipient from the outer envelope.

Reverend Kendall, the same feeling of cat-like curiosity that tingled in him with each letter, sliced open the envelope and pulled out two letters. So often he was left dissatisfied, finding a lack of names or reference to locations thereby requiring him to send the letter to the trash bin. Though on one frightful occasion, he opened a box and found within it a scalp. Unable to determine the body of origin, it ended up in the same bin.

Now, however, he was pleased to find the two enclosed letters, though lightly soiled, were quite legible. The first, though without an addressee, was simply a collection of letters and numbers—a cypher, he reasoned. Without the code, it was a useless bit of information. The other, dated *26 September*, written in the same hand, was in English.

Reverend Kendall read aloud in a low whisper, "Brigadier General Dickinson. It is with regret I must inform you, you are the sole member of our secret Carrying Committee…"

As the reverend read on, a chill ran through him.

The fate of our Declaration of Independence and the future of our states uniting rests in your hands. Send letters to our rider, including the one enclosed, using the below cypher. Trust no one. (Not even Silas Hastings, who I hope proves my suspicions wrong by delivering this to you.)

Below the cypher, there was a scrawled signature Kendall squinted to read.

Yours in the Cause,
- Benjamin Franklin, Esq.

"Heaven help us." Kendall looked to the date again. "Months ago!"

Words from Kendall's late predecessor, spoken only last July just after the Declaration had been read aloud on the steps of the State House, came roaring back. Standing together in the throng of citizens, after hearing how the King had plundered, deprived, and refused his subjects, the old reverend had grabbed Kendall's hand, squeezing earnestly, exacting a promise.

"If you believe the contents of a dead letter will in any way jeopardize this Cause, you run it to the men of Congress. Run, as if your soul depends upon it, and deliver us from the evil sufferance of such tyranny."

Reverend Kendall shoved away from the table, the two letters in his fist, his old bones creaking as he grasped his walking stick.

CHAPTER SEVENTY-SIX

"WE PRINT TODAY," MARY KATHARINE said, slicing open a brown-paper wrapped package as Nathaniel joined her in the print shop for breakfast. At her request, Congress had paid for two hundred cotton and linen sheets, cut to sixteen by twenty one. The bookshelf contained another stack of lesser-grade paper cut to the same size.

"Those cheap sheets are for test samples to compare to the original," she said.

As she had predicted, they had worked for two more days setting type. Two more days of sharing stories and meals, her company as warm and welcoming as the smell of her fresh coffee he now sipped. Benjamin was still snoring in his basket, moved nearer to the fire, away from the ink.

Setting aside his cup, Nathaniel pulled the Declaration from his satchel, a new illustration of Maryland slipping out with it. The last two nights his sleep had been so fraught, he'd poured his restlessness into drawing what he'd seen on his ride from Berks County.

"How lovely," Mary Katharine leaned over the table between Nathaniel and the map. "Such exquisite detail. Equal to William Faden, but with finer shading."

"William who?"

"The royal geographer and publisher to the King. Who drew this?"

"I did."

She popped up, knocking into him. He grasped her arm to steady her, a warmth spreading up through his hand. She gripped the table, but squinted at him.

"But you are…"

"The son of a gunsmith? Yes, I was." He explained his grandfather's journals, his time with Oliver Wolcott, and the work he'd been doing for Washington. As he ran a finger along his latest map, his thoughts spilled from him without effort. "When I draw what my eyes have seen, my hands retrace each curve of the Susquehanna, each valley and forest, as if I still move across the land itself."

"Why, Mr. Mirtle, you are an artist." Mary Katharine whispered, but when he tried to protest she insisted, "You speak of your work like a painter describes a woman."

Nathaniel was riveted to the floor. His mother's description upon meeting his father resounded in his head, and he burst out laughing. Mary Katharine took a step back, but he waved away her worry, "Fear not, Miss Goddard. It is just that I swore I did not want to become my father, and you have, with one sentence, proven I have done exactly that."

"Well," Mary Katharine smiled, but as she turned to fetch their aprons, he heard her say, "Your father must be quite something."

The whole of the morning they printed test samples, her taking up the dirty job of inking the plates, and Nathaniel, his hands kept clean, taking each one to the table for her to compare to Jefferson's text on the original Declaration. Several times they bumped into one another coming around the press from opposite directions. Each time, an awkward silence fell between them, until one of them moved on to complete their task.

After lunch, with more than two-dozen tests complete and two paper-cuts on Nathaniel's thumb, Mary Katharine pronounced them ready to print the fine copies.

Nathaniel turned the original upside down on the clean table to protect the text, and on they went, silently working, the clock over the fire ticking on, and the printed pages added to the drying racks. First by daylight. Then by candlelight. Until, nearing midnight, the two-hundredth copy lay next to the upside-down original.

Mary Katharine examined the last document, her inky hands curled backward into fists upon her hips. The examination complete, she whispered, "A fine job."

"And now a woman's name is upon it, too." He pointed to the bottom of the sheet, and the words she'd typeset: *Printed by Mary Katharine Goddard.* "Perhaps they should not have limited it to all *men* are created equal."

"Not at all." She shook her head, a strand of auburn hair falling loose. "It is good grammar to use the masculine pronoun. We don't say 'womankind.' This defines our humanity, not our society, and frankly, this is a beautiful, thoughtful way to begin again on our own. Don't you agree?"

She looked to him imploringly, an eyebrow raised, waiting for his confirmation.

How much George Wythe would be smitten by this well-reasoned, passionate woman, Nathaniel thought, but then he admitted… oh, how much I am. He had shared more with this woman, and knew more about her, than any other before her.

"I… I suppose we have to leave, to be on our own, before we can define who we are," Nathaniel said, trying to cast aside his desire for her, but the truth of it was, he was lost in her. "Before we can define what we want."

Under his scrutiny, she brushed a hand across her chin, leaving an inky streak beneath her lip. He reached up to wipe it away with his thumb. She did not back away. She did not look away.

"After all your months alone, Mr. Mirtle… Nathaniel," she paused but a moment, "what is it you want?"

Nathaniel could take no more. He closed the space between them, and lowered his mouth to hers, his arms around her, she tasting of candied oranges, her leaning into the length of him, he leaning into her against the table, and her reaching back to brace them, their kiss deepening.

Abruptly she pulled out of his embrace, spun toward to the table, and gasped, "Oh, hell."

Her small inky handprint was sinking into the back of the original parchment.

She grasped a nearby rag, trying to blot the ink, but a stain in the shape of her petite fingers had been set. Her mark forever on the document.

Forever in him, too.

Nathaniel stilled her hand. "Mary Katharine."

When she turned toward him, the hunger of her expression mirrored his own.

"If you would permit me..." Nathaniel hesitated, hoping he'd correctly read her signals, holding her small hand in both his own, praying it was so. "I think what I want, after all these months, all these miles, is to sleep with you instead of that Declaration."

A mere nod, and Mary Katharine blew out the candles, leading the way upstairs.

CHAPTER SEVENTY-SEVEN

CONGRESS WAS ABOUT TO begin another day. Arthur pushed into Baltimore, having safely ensconced Joseph, and the one remaining sheep, with his own Bowman family in Berks County. Now, his horse slipped through dank streets, corroborating a reputation the city, merely a quarter the size of Philadelphia, had for being unkempt. Upon seeing that the harbor town's energy turned to the construction of a dozen warships for the Cause, Arthur forgave them their trespasses.

At Henry Fite's house at the west end of Market Street, the temporary assembly hall for the delegates, Arthur scraped mud from his shoes and slipped into the long conference hall. As the heavy door clicked shut behind him, he scrutinized faces, hoping to root out the spy he'd seen at Howe's headquarters. Not one of the faces was familiar, not even the man in uniform who was addressing the assembly.

"President Hancock, I have failed in a promise I made to this Congress, sir." The officer's hands, thick like those of a farmer, fidgeted with the brim of his hat.

Arthur, hoping the man would soon get to his point, reviewed the list Nathaniel had left for him. Jefferson. Dickinson. Lee. Wythe. Wolcott. Morris. Gerry. Thornton. And most of all McKean. Arthur might have recognized Jefferson if he'd been in attendance, but he'd have to ask about the others. Perhaps after the officer, who was visibly shaking, had gotten to his point.

"I must resign my post, for reasons beyond my Quaker sensibilities…"

"Pray do tell about this supposed offense, Brigadier General Dickinson," Hancock prodded.

"We have not only lost our copy of the Declaration carrying our signatures, I have lost the rider with it," Dickinson said, hanging his head, but Arthur gasped and rushed forward.

"No, we've not!" The words flew from Arthur's lips. "I know where he is."

Dickinson, hat in hand and amid mumbles of consternation from the assembly, rushed to Arthur and grasped him by the shoulders, begging, "Who are you? Tell me our Mr. Mirtle is still with us."

"I am Captain Arthur Bowman, sir." Happy to once again adopt the rank he'd never wanted to give up. "And yes, he is very much with us."

"Do t… tell us what has h… happened," a man introducing himself as Elbridge Gerry urged, his hands ringing with worry. Arthur shared much of what Nathaniel had told him, from the trouble at White Plains, to the trap set near Sturgeon's Falls.

"But who…" Dickinson turned pale, his fingers picking at the hat brim again. "I've been scrambling to find him ever since Franklin left in early October. Since then, I've not received a word from Nathaniel."

A tall, kindly-faced man came forward. "Oliver Wolcott at your service, Captain Bowman. Your friend was with me and my family, for most of October. I wrote to you after he left us, General Dickinson."

"And I wrote you as well, after signing the document with Mr. Mirtle in November, in Philadelphia." Another man introduced himself as Matthew Thornton, giving a slight bow. His Irish lilt thick with concern, he added, "My fellow congressman, Mr. Bartlett, even received a letter containing instructions from you, General."

"As did I and Nathaniel," said Wolcott. "Instructions hand-written on your stationery."

Dickinson frantically shook his head. "I neither wrote nor received such letters."

"If you did not," Arthur said, examining the small group of men, all of whom Nathaniel had listed as trustworthy. "Who did?"

"The only other person with access to my stationery, was my Aide-de-camp," Dickinson sighed, "Silas Hastings."

"Silas...?" A cold rage ran up Arthur's spine, his promise to Peter revived. The man Arthur had seen at headquarters with General Howe was Mr. Hastings. Could it be the two men were one and the same? Through gritted, accusing teeth, Arthur asked, "Where is he?"

"I sent him to Philadelphia with letters for my law practice and for Mrs. Dickinson." Dickinson said, but he shook his head. "He's been a loyal servant—faithfully managing my communications. I kept our Secret Carrying Committee to myself. How could it have been Mr. Hastings? If so, we must have some proof that he was diverting my messages—"

The door to the hall flew open and banged against the wall. An elderly man, near to collapse, grasped the frame, his white hair wind-blown about his head, the hem of his cleric robes stained from hobbling through muddy streets.

"Pray tell me Dickinson is here!" Reverend Kendall from the Continental Post's dead letter office held up two letters. "The fate of the Cause has not been in his hands."

CHAPTER SEVENTY-EIGHT

NATHANIEL HAD FUMBLED AT FIRST. Mary Katharine helped him to unwrap the unimaginable layers of skirts and petticoats and buttons and ties. Not wanting to rush, but wanting to memorize her, like the lines upon his etched maps, he'd unveiled her with care, and when he finally made to reach for her, she instead reached for him, adding his clothes to the mountain of fabric beneath them.

When she pulled his shirt over his head, his scar revealed, she winced. She ran her finger delicately across the raised skin of his shoulder, her healing touch smoothing away the anger behind the wound, her lips replacing the memory of pain with a lingering pleasure. Soon, cocooned inside the heavy winter draperies of her bed, they explored together, folding and unfolding until drifting to sleep, wound together.

Now, a soft knocking interrupted Nathaniel's slumber. He awoke to find traces of inky fingerprints across his arms and chest —a trail marking her exploration. She was curled into him, matching his own side-sleeping curve. He ran his hand down the dip in her waist and up over her hip. She rolled back into him, awakening his longing. Again.

Another knock, this time more insistent, the housekeeper's voice peeping from the other side of the door.

"Begging your pardon, Miss Goddard. Two men are waiting downstairs."

"Mmmm. Okay," Mary Katharine purred, turning her cheek toward him.

"Good morning, Nathaniel. It seems the day awaits." She reached back for a kiss, then stretched out a hand to open the bed drapes.

"Whoever they are can wait," Nathaniel attempted to pull her back inside, but she slipped from his grasp.

"We must get up," she said, wriggling into her shift.

"I am."

"What if they are riders from Congress?" She threw his breeches across his chest. "Two hundred copies can't wait because you are unable to stand."

He relented, pulling himself from her warm bed. He dressed along with her, the task taking longer than necessary as they struggled to keep their hands to themselves. When they descended the stairs together, the first to step into the room, Mary Katharine said a bright, "Good morning."

"Good morning, Miss Goddard," came a voice familiar to Nathaniel. Pulling his rumpled hair into a ponytail, he tumbled into the shop. With an all-knowing grin across his face, Arthur added, "Not much sleep, Nathaniel?"

Mary Katharine looked between them, "You know one another?"

But Nathaniel's heart was pounding as he stared at the other man waiting just inside the door, a solid wooden box the size of an apple crate in his hands. A warm relief swept through Nathaniel to see the man's face after so many months. After so much silence.

"Why John Dickinson... At last."

* * *

"Silas Hastings' little business was making quite a bundle." Nathaniel handed Mary Katharine a ledger.

They had gathered round the fire with Dickinson and Arthur to examine the contents found inside a locked trunk Silas had kept among Dickinson's papers. The papers spread out on a table between them, Benjamin was happily curled inside the empty box.

"And all the while plotting to capture you and the Declaration," Mary Katharine said, the concern in her voice palpable, sweet.

"Under my nose, all this time," Dickinson refolded the few messages Silas had foolishly saved from the Howes, and ran a hand over his eyes. "And there I was promising to keep his trunk safe each time we moved or I sent him off on errands."

"And with all that currency in it," Arthur nodded to the piles of Continentals counted and stacked between them. "Money meant for an armory. Money that belongs to your family, Nathaniel."

Nathaniel could hardly look at it. The bills were tainted with the stain of all they'd lost. All who suffered.

"It belongs to the Cause. Our soldiers need shoes," he said, nodding to Dickinson.

"That's not all of it. Look." Mary Katharine held up the ledger for them and pointed to a long column. "More than half the payments were made to him in silver, but there is no record of it being spent."

"Maybe we can search for him and in so doing find the silver," Nathaniel offered. "After I get McKean's signature, of course."

"What did you say?" Mary Katharine's mouth fell open. When Nathaniel repeated his statement, she dropped the ledger and ran to her printed copies, stacked and now dry on the table. She ran a finger down the list of names on her copy and then the original Declaration.

"No, no, no…Damnit!" Her hands flew to her cheeks. She waved off Dickinson's objection to her cursing, and growled at Nathaniel. "You said fifty-six men had seen this!"

"Fifty-five delegates. And me." Nathaniel went to her. "But not Thomas McKean."

She thumped Nathaniel with the back of her hand, and sighed, "My greatest accomplishment, ruined by one man."

"I was told Congress wanted to print it, even without his signature, and assumed you knew. Plus, I was a bit distracted." He wanted to console her and kiss her at the same time, were it not for the others in the room. That desire aside, a nagging thought picked at him, and he looked to the original parchment.

Even with two hundred copies bearing the names, the world about to be shown their Declaration of Independence was unanimous, he knew it was not. His task was not finished.

"The truth is, I do still have one more." He smiled at the feeling of pride in wanting to complete it, but then it slipped from his face. "Although I worry about how. I have no idea where McKean is."

"I could not find him," said Arthur.

"I know not where he is," Dickinson also shrugged.

"Oh," Mary Katharine said, her bright smile returning, "I do."

Nathaniel lost all words.

Taking a key from her pocket, she unlocked her desk drawer, and with her voice warbling with emotion, she handed Nathaniel a letter, explaining, "McKean's wife and I are dear, old friends. Sharing far more than any man knows. You will find him in a log house, on the eastern side of the Susquehanna, just south of where the river is joined by the Octorura Creek. Cecil County, Maryland. About sixty miles from here."

The letter shook in Nathaniel's hand. At last…One man. One rider. One signature.

"My greatest accomplishment," Nathaniel bundled Mary Katharine fully into his arms, Arthur winking at him over her shoulder, "saved by one fine woman."

Dickinson, too, smiled, but then he waved a hand at the papers on the table. "I hate to break up such joy, but there is still the business of Mr. Hastings. He's likely on his way here to capture you, even though he and the Howes might wrongly assume we would never release the names of the men on that document."

A spark of an idea hit Nathaniel. "Arthur, do you still have that redcoat?"

Arthur nodded to the satchel at his feet. "In case I needed to cross enemy lines to get here. Why?"

"Can you wear it one last time?" Nathaniel picked up one of the discarded test copies of the Declaration, and handed General Dickinson a pen. "It is time the Howes learn, without question, who stands united for the Cause. And who does not."

* * *

Within the hour, Nathaniel stood at Mary Katharine's door, satchel in hand, Arthur and Dickinson already gone.

"So," he said.

"So…"

"Might I return? Make an honest woman out of you?"

"Oh, Nathaniel, I have not been that in years," she smiled, tugging his hand, and growing serious. "Thank you, but... even though it means losing you, no."

"But I..."

She remained strong, asking him to look around her shop.

"I have struggled to build this life, a respected business; coverture will not take it from me. Besides, you have a talent—those maps, the way you see the land as if you were a bird—that requires you to fly, to ride, not to stay." She put a hand to her heart. "Though fear not, part of you will stay."

Nathaniel nodded, knowing she was right, knowing he would be just as miserable working with her in print shop as he was in the gun shop.

"Besides, I am far too old for you. You need a woman willing to bear both your wanderlust and a pile of children."

"Then I shall ride from you carrying much more than the Declaration." He touched his own heart then reached for her, gathering her close, his nose buried in her rich auburn hair—taking in her inky, lavender smell once more. "These fond days with you will carry me home."

Yet, as Nathaniel headed north alone, he pondered that word once more. *Home.* Where on earth would he ever truly feel at home again?

CHAPTER SEVENTY-NINE

"GET OFF ME," SILAS HASTINGS tried to yank his arm free as two men dragged him into the ballroom at Murray Mansion, through a cluster of redcoats and officers gathered near the door.

General Howe sat stone-faced behind a desk covered in papers. His mistress was surprisingly absent, but the decanter of liquor was, per usual, well within reach.

Two horrific storms irritatingly delayed Silas while he delivered Dickinson's useless messages to Philadelphia. When he at last arrived at the Marten home, instead of finding Nathaniel, two of Howe's men had shoved him inside the black carriage. Silas had tried to fight his way out of their grasp, but was easily overpowered by the lumbering men.

"You fool." Silas now spit the last word at the general as the two men let him go, shoving him toward the desk. He skidded to a halt, tugged his coat tails into place. "You called me off at the precise moment this was to be resolved."

"I received some rather enlightening news while you were away, Mr. Hastings."

"Which was?"

"It came from an interesting source. Can you guess who?"

Silas shrugged. This question and answer game was a waste of his time.

"Perhaps I should have said sources. Plural." General Howe picked up a document from next to the decanter and unfolded it. Cotton and linen. Twenty-one by sixteen. "Fifty-five men to be exact."

Silas gasped and swallowed back a tinny taste of fear.

"Copies like this are spreading out from Baltimore as we speak." Howe's face inflamed as he punched out each of his next words as if a full sentence. "An insufferable. Morale-boosting. Plague!"

The window panes behind Howe shook. In the silence that followed, Silas could hear his watch ticking, the seconds amplified by the blood thrumming in his ears.

"I… I can explain–"

"No point. This also arrived." Howe picked up letter. "From your dear friend, Brigadier-General Dickinson."

Silas grew cold. He grasped tight to the watch in his pocket, his heart beating double time.

"You were too meticulous. Too careless. In private ledgers kept in your trunk, they found proof you were selling arms to the Americans…" Howe crumpled the letter in his fist, "and to me."

The floor beneath Silas' feet began to tilt, and he wondered aloud, "But, how… how did he know? Why would he look?"

"Does it matter?" The general flung the letter on the desk and waved a hand at the broadside. "With that damned document and all those men inspiring the colonists, I am actually going to have to fight this bloody war now."

"What are we to do?" Silas asked, his voice too high.

"We? There is nothing for *you* to do. I on the other hand…" Howe poured himself another drink, but left it untouched. "I cannot hang you for being a spy when I was the one who hired you. That would make me look cruel. Although our little venture is clearly over."

Silas backed away from the desk. He looked about the room. Men either looked to the floor, or looked upon him with sour disgust. Or hatred. One freckled-faced boy, standing tall among the redcoats, was smiling.

Silas turned to rush the door, but two soldiers quickly descended and confined his arms. Restricted his chest. A chest already tight. Silas fought the weakness rising in his legs. He squirmed, and strained and yelled at Howe, "We were making money! All you had to do was keep fighting, and it would pile up around us!"

"That reminds me," Howe said as he came around the desk, his demeanor calm but black. "Somewhere you've stashed a pile of silver. Which means, at the very least, I judge you to be a thief who owes me."

Howe's eyes trailed down to Silas' pocket.

"No, not... Anything but..."

Howe snatched it from him. He held it up by the chain. The delicate, beloved casing spun—a scene of a mother and son cast forever in gold.

Silas' heart broke as he watched it swing, watched his life unwind.

"Please, you can have it all. The silver lies beneath my father's grave. Saint Mary's Catholic Church in Philadelphia." His eyes stayed on the watch. Too dear. Too precious. "Please, it was the one thing that was mine."

Howe turned away, and moved toward the window. *Click.*

"You won't be needing to know the time." He clasped the watch and nodded southward just beyond the tip of Manhattan. *Snap.* "Your ship awaits."

As they hauled Silas from the room, his pleading screams echoed down the hall and into the streets.

The smiling, freckle-faced boy in the redcoat, didn't hear any of it. He was already riding south, pushing his horse toward Saint Mary's.

CHAPTER EIGHTY

NATHANIEL RODE ACROSS A ROLLING, snowy field in Cecil County, Maryland late in the day, furs pulled tight around him. The meadow curled into the northward curve of the Susquehanna River. Waters that swiftly flowed in spring were now blanketed in a solid sheet of ice. Ahead, the last orange rays shimmered across the logs of a small home nestled into a crook of the Octoraro Creek. With a silent prayer that McKean would be there, Nathaniel gave a click-click of his tongue and dropped Bayard down the hillside toward the cabin.

As he skirted the edge of the field, the figure of a man trudged through the snow toward him. As they grew closer, Nathaniel could see the man wore a weathered Monmouth knitted cap, pulled down tight to his brow. Two young turkeys swung from a rope over the man's thin shoulder. Nathaniel forced himself to loosen his grip on the satchel, and slide from the saddle.

"Good evening, sir," Nathaniel dipped his head.

"'Evening." The man's dark eyes avoided Nathaniel's, staying stuck to the ground between their boots. He ran a gloved hand across a hawk-like nose, red from the cold. "Where are you headed, traveler?"

"I'm in search of a gentleman, a... a friend." Nathaniel turned his eyes toward the cabin. "Is he—"

"No one is there now."

"Please, sir, do you know where he is?"

Smoke curled lazily from the stone chimney, rising grey and golden up into the evening sky. The man chewed on his lower lip, and switched the rope with the two jakes to his other shoulder, mumbling, "He left. A few hours ago."

Nathaniel groaned. Where was he to go if McKean had already left? A cold wind gusted, cutting through the furs, making it clear it was far too cold to stand out of doors chatting much longer. Then an idea came to Nathaniel, and he said, "I come having just visited his wife's dear friend, a Miss Goddard of Baltimore."

The man's head snapped up and Nathaniel, warmed by the man's now friendlier expression, took a chance. "Pray tell, do you know the whereabouts of this Mr. McKean?"

"Indeed." The man before him held the two turkeys at arm's length. "He is out hunting."

It took Nathaniel a moment, but then he tipped his head back and laughed. "At last. It is you!" He grabbed McKean warmly by both shoulders, shaking with relief. "I am Nathaniel Mirtle… well, Marten really. I have been carrying—"

"The Declaration. Yes, I know." McKean shrugged out of Nathaniel's embrace, harrumphed, and strode swiftly toward the cabin, shouting over his shoulder. "It's about time you found me. Come inside before we both freeze."

Nathaniel gathered up Bayard and ran to catch up with the fast-moving McKean.

Inside the single-room cabin, Thomas McKean and Nathaniel were warmly welcomed by his wife, Sarah. Her face was as red as her husband's, but her glow was clearly from a pregnancy several months along. Five of McKean's children, all under twelve, clustered around Nathaniel's legs the instant he came through the door.

A girl introduced to him as Anne held up four fingers, "I am this many." She then began to climb Nathaniel, while asking, "Did you bring us the turkeys?"

Nathaniel gave the document to McKean and obliged Anne's affection, lifting the lamb of a girl into his arms.

"Your father secured the turkeys, but I delivered the Declaration of Independence."

She looped her cherub arms around Nathaniel's neck as her father unfolded the document on the table. Next to the parchment, a modest bowl of peeled potatoes and turnips had been awaiting the turkeys now resting upon an old newspaper.

"We have been hunted by the enemy like foxes," McKean said as he plucked a single feather from one of the birds. He began to clean and trim the end of it.

"Four moves in eight months," Sarah said. The shelves in the kitchen held fewer plates than number of people in the room, and a small crate of books was piled near a rumpled bed of quilts in the corner. When Sarah looked at the document, it was with the same tenderness she then showed the little girl in Nathaniel's arms. "Do you remember my reading this to you, Anne?"

The little girl nodded, her tiny fingers flipping Nathaniel's ponytail. "Last summer. Just after mommy died and you came to stay as our new mother."

"Yes, my little pet, just after that." Sarah patted a hand to her heart.

McKean winked at his new wife, the gruff man defrosting in the bosom of his family. Nathaniel's heart warmed for him, and for Sarah—a remarkable woman who had taken on the task of rearing so many, and during a time of war.

"Why is this document so important?" McKean asked his oldest boy, while showing him how to attach a nib to the end of the turkey feather. "What one word in this document is for all of you, Joseph?"

Nathaniel smiled at the name, imagining his own father Joseph nearing puberty like the boy who now leaned across the table and searched the text.

"To provide new Guards for their future security."

"Future is the word!" Anne bounced in Nathaniel his arms, her flossy hair dancing around rosy cheeks.

"Right you are," McKean chuckled. He turned to his eldest daughter, a pensive girl, no older than ten, lingering at his elbow. "And why is that one word so important, Elizabeth?"

She spoke without hesitation, but her voice was rousing, not rote.

"If we allow those who govern us to hold us back, to keep us stuck in the past, we permit them to limit our future."

"Indeed," McKean said, slipping an arm around her. "In order to unite behind that promise, with a firm reliance on one another to uphold that spirit, all thirteen colonies have agreed to sign it." He dipped his newly fashioned quill in the ink and tested it on a corner of the newspaper.

"I cannot write yet," Anne whispered to Nathaniel, but then she jiggled with a new idea. "Maybe you can sign it for me, Papa?"

"For you, yes. For each and every one of us." He surveyed each of his children, and then winked again at his pregnant wife. "And for those yet to come."

And so it was, in the silence of a humble, one-room cabin, surrounded by a burgeoning, blending family, that Thomas McKean finally put his pen to the document. The nib scratched across the parchment.

Nathaniel swallowed back the emotions tugging in his throat. The Declaration of Independence of these thirteen united states. Colonies no more. Unanimous at last.

CHAPTER EIGHTY-ONE

NATHANIEL RODE NORTHEAST ACROSS Pennsylvania. An early, warm spring brought forth the crocuses, pale green grass shoots reaching up to wave from among brown fields now awakening from winter. Bayard tugged on the bit and shook out his mane. Nathaniel patted his neck, grateful for his loyal companionship.

"I am sure you are ready to find a meadow you can call your own, too, Bayard."

Nathaniel had waited at McKean's until Arthur, as they agreed, sent word that Silas was no longer a threat. Nor the British. The Howes had removed to New York, leaving Philadelphia untouched, safe from imminent danger. Congress had voted to return to the State House by March fourth. Nathaniel was expected to meet them there. Arthur, too.

He had stayed and hunted with McKean, read and played with the children, and for the first time in many months, felt like part of a family again.

Now, as Nathaniel looked up from his meandering thoughts, he pulled Bayard to a stop. From this small hill of clover beginning to bloom white, the Schuylkill River curving below, he could see Gray's Landing beckoning.

It was where he'd waited with Arthur and Peter last summer. Where he had begun his journey, his task, eight long months ago. Eight months ago, before he'd ridden across fields, farms, and battlefields, and navigated oceans, mountains, and streams. Across seven colonies and through enough goodbyes to last him a lifetime.

Beyond the river, the sun cast a welcoming glow over the church spires and the State House tower. The city stretched up out of the valley, as if it were heaven itself.

"Philadelphia." Nathaniel's heart thumped with excitement, as he pulled his leather satchel between himself and the saddle. "Come, Bayard. Let's carry it in. Hya!"

With a playful nudge of Nathaniel's heels, Bayard leapt forward. They raced down the hill toward the ferry, Bayard's hooves thumping strong and sure across the land. Riding flat. Riding smooth. The black mane flying. Nathaniel leaned forward. Express rider and horse becoming one.

One, for a last, long, and glorious run. Heart rejoicing. Free.

CHAPTER EIGHTY-TWO

NATHANIEL STOOD ON THE THRESHOLD of the assembly room at the State House, the hall in chaos. Men, boxes, and papers were shuffling about the room in a disordered fashion. He entered without invitation and approached two men at a table.

One man leaned over the table, his broad back to the door, facing a seated Secretary Thomson.

The secretary flipped through a stack of papers before him, then scratched at his own head, saying, "How are we to give soldiers land three years hence when we cannot locate funding for three hundred blankets today?"

Thomson reached back, dropping some of the papers behind him, on a table already piled chest-high with documents. When he swung back around, he acknowledged Nathaniel's presence with a raised eyebrow.

Nathaniel nodded to him. "I am Nathaniel Mirtle. I'm looking for—"

The man bent over the table spun around and stood to his full height. Over six feet. Quiet. Familiar. Reddish hair. Last seen by Nathaniel months ago in this very room. Nathaniel smiled warmly.

"Mr. Jefferson, you have returned."

"As have you, Mr. Mirtle."

The secretary immersed himself in opening new letters, as Nathaniel and Jefferson took a step or two away from the table. Jefferson looked Nathaniel over from head to toe.

"I'm happy to see you're in one piece."

"For the most part. A scar or two on the outside." He rubbed at his chest, then tilted his head in remembrance. "A few within, too."

With eyes that also see you differently now, Nathaniel thought. Jefferson was not merely a writer or a delegate, but merely a man. A man with great wisdom to be sure, but one confounded by circumstance, with his own flaws and faults like everyone else.

"Well," Jefferson pointed to the satchel, an eyebrow arched, "is it done?"

Nathaniel nodded. He opened the leather flap and took out the document. He ran his palm over the fine grain of the parchment, feeling it beneath his fingers, and reading the words he had written upon the back last summer. He had been only a boy. Now, the journey had etched the lessons of life within him.

"You were right, you know," Nathaniel said, looking up from his revere. "Last July… you were right when you said a man should be willing to risk everything for two things. Only back then I thought you were referring to the document and money. I know better now."

"For what then?" Jefferson asked, though by the smile on his face, Nathaniel could see he knew the answer.

"A man should risk all he has for two ideals." Nathaniel felt worthy at last to hold the delegate's intelligent gaze. "Love and freedom. One cannot exist without the other, and only together can they truly provide independence."

Jefferson nodded softly and Nathaniel held out the document. A sense of loss overwhelmed him as Jefferson reached for it. The Declaration of Independence left Nathaniel's fingers, returning to the hands of the man who had authored it. The circle complete.

Jefferson unfolded it, and reviewing the names along the bottom, smiled wistfully as if the journey had been just as long for him. He refolded the parchment and was about to speak when the secretary waved a letter at Jefferson.

"The brig *Lexington* has been captured by the British frigate *Pearl*. Howe wants a prisoner exchange."

The announcement brought several delegates to the table, as the secretary began to read aloud. Jefferson shook Nathaniel's hand.

"Thank you, Mr. Marten. We are most grateful. I will ensure your final silver payment is delivered to you in the next week. Just let us know to where." Jefferson turned and gave the document to the secretary with the instruction, "'Tis the original Declaration."

Secretary Thomson nodded. Mid-sentence, he grasped the folded parchment, reached back, and dropped it indiscriminately on one of the piles behind him.

Nathaniel's gaze stayed with the parchment as more delegates gathered around the table, pushing him outside the circle, their discussion billowing like storm clouds. Thomson began to search the stacks behind him for papers they required. Papers shuffled. Another stack was moved. And just like that, a mound of letters was dropped over the Declaration of Independence.

Now just one document among many. Obscured by the urgency, the ever-growing history, of war.

With one last look, Nathaniel walked away. He crossed the threshold into the quiet hall. Pausing just outside the assembly room door, he looked up at the carved face of the woman he'd seen so many months, and so many miles, ago. Although she still gazed down upon him with vacant eyes, her high brow, like his, was still afflicted with uncertainty.

CHAPTER EIGHTY-THREE

"WHAT A STERN FACE." Arthur was waiting with Bayard at the foot of the State House steps. "You should be cheering like I was at the ferry landing!"

As Nathaniel had come across the river to Philadelphia, true to his word, Arthur had been waiting waving his hat high overhead. Seeing his dear friend again had made Nathaniel feel buoyant, like the raft. Now, however, as he descended the steps, he felt weighed down.

"Oh, I think I understand." Arthur scratched at his cheek as the two began pulling their horses down the street, Nathaniel following along, happy to let someone else lead the way. "What to do now? Is that the trouble?"

Nathaniel shook his head. "General Washington has asked to meet to discuss a new department—a geographic division."

The message had come to Nathaniel while at McKean's. Wolcott had apparently forwarded a copy of his Connecticut map to the general, who had realized that without up-to-date surveys and American-made topographical maps, his operations would always have to rely on the cartography of the British.

"The problem isn't what to do. It's more a question of where," Nathaniel admitted. Jefferson's question about where to deliver his earnings was rattling around in him, and he wondered how he had traveled all this way to feel so lost once again. "Home isn't what it once was."

His father had written to confirm he felt the same. The memories of Berks County, and the family they had lost were too sharp. He was prepared to sell the land and follow Nathaniel wherever he wanted to go.

"And Madame printer?" Arthur asked as they crossed beyond Market Street and rounded a corner.

Nathaniel shook his head and explained their parting. "This isn't just about finding a place to live. It's more than that."

"Well, you're not as good a shot as me," Arthur said as he kicked a stone ahead of them. "Which means you're no good to me in the battalion they've given me to lead."

Nathaniel watched the stone bounce and roll down the cobblestones. He was pleased for Arthur's new appointment, but he worried for him, too. A Declaration had been signed, but a war still raged, and for how long? He prayed his friend could outlast it. Or at least outrun it.

"Maybe what you long for is some sort of… sanctuary," Arthur said, studying Nathaniel's face, as they pulled their horses to a stop. "A warm spot to rest where you might discover what you've been missing."

He nodded over Nathaniel's shoulder. Nathaniel turned to find they were in front of a familiar three-story Georgian home, at the corner of Fourth and Walnut streets. Sun shone upon the windows, snow-melt splashing from the eaves to the stones at his feet, the drapes inside pulled back to let in the warmth.

Nathaniel shivered. He had been so sure he was over her, but standing outside her home once again, he knew he was not. He turned away, searching his friend.

"I told you about everything that happened with Sus–"

"Yes, but I have not explained everything to you. Look."

Nathaniel raised his head to where Arthur pointed. In the shadows, behind the wavy glass of the tall windows, at her desk, reading a letter, was Susannah. Her honey hair was piled in the same tumbling chignon falling over the same porcelain skin. A melancholy smile rested on her face. She moved closer to the window, and the sun caught her fully. Her blue, faded frock had been replaced by a gown of another color. Black.

Nathaniel gasped.

"Pemberley was killed at Princeton in January. Valiant to the end."

Arthur gave the man's memory a moment's peace, then said, "He was kind to her, but she barely knew him. Unlike you."

Nathaniel wanted to run to the stairs, to burst through her door, but he felt pinned to the ground, guilt and doubt filling the shoes pinching his tired feet. His beginning would be at the expense of another man's ending. More important, now that the choice was entirely hers, he wondered, would she indeed choose him?

Then he heard a soft click. He looked up. Susannah stepped across the threshold onto the top step, exactly where he had first seen her. The midday sun added to the familiar warmth radiating from her face. The letters she'd been reading were crumpled in one hand, her trembling fist held tight over her heart as if trying to hold herself in. Then, she held her other hand out to him. "At last, Nathaniel. You have returned to me."

The words were everything Nathaniel needed to hear. To move forward.

He dropped the reins, and took the stairs. He swept her into his arms, the letters fluttering to their feet.

"Yes, Susannah." Nathaniel breathed her in deeply, his chest rising and falling in time with hers, spinning them together, round and round, time suspended inside their own sweet minuet. "At last, forevermore, I am home."

★

EPILOGUE
the signatures

*The Revolution was in the minds
and hearts of the people…*

*This radical change in the principles,
opinions, sentiments, and affections of the people
was the real American Revolution.*

– John Adams

Ohio
August 23, 1814

PACKS BUNDLED. *WEGIWA* SKINS STACKED. Women carrying children and goods. Wary men astride mounts, scanning the fields ahead.

The long line of Shawnee once again heading west beneath gathering clouds was a sour reminder of a day Kalawi would never forget, the ache of leaving his friends and Saucony Creek always simmering beneath his weathered skin, always hoping Nathaniel or Arthur might find him again.

Only once, many years ago, he happened to glance to a ridge overlooking their town on the Scioto River, and there a familiar figure appeared. His heart yearned, but when the wind blew, crying like a howling wolf, the rider turned away, and Kalawi's heart had burned again. As it did now, leaving the Scioto River Valley.

He sighed with the weight of it.

Kamsi pulled her horse alongside and reached for his hand. "Are we escaping from, or moving toward something better… Is that what you wonder?" Her voice was scratchy with age, her face painted with the lines of both a joyful yet worried life.

"I did not say anything." Yet, Kalawi took comfort in her knowing his thoughts. "Yes, I worry, for those of us still here."

He turned to look behind, counting heads. When his Wolf Clan had reached the Scioto Valley in seventy-seven, the small clan had been welcomed by nearly ten thousand strong. Colonel Morgan, as promised, had taken their peace treaty to Congress, but by the summer of three sevens, Morgan had been replaced. The new Indian Agent was blind to, or culpable in, death warrants being issued for the head sachems of several nations on the frontier. Chief Crow of the Cherokee was one of the first to fall. Now, the Shawnee numbered fewer than four thousand.

"I vowed, as we all did, upon the grave of Netawatwees that his grandchildren, and our grandchildren, would walk in peace over this land," Kalawi said to Kamsi. "Just as Cornstalk, your cousin Hokoleswka, had."

Hokoleswka, true to his word, had entered Fort Randolph in seventy-seven to negotiate peace, his own son joining him. But a fight outside the fort caused the soldiers inside to rage, and so with fear as their fuel, on the same November night Kamsi had cried out delivering their first child, her cousin and his son had been murdered. Mutilated.

Now, Kalawi looked back upon their two daughters trailing behind, their own children in tow. He shook his head, thick with years of sorrow.

"Look at us, we are many generations still struggling for a foothold."

Kamsi squeezed his hand, but the truth of it no one could deny.

Two years ago, the United States had declared war upon Britain. For new reasons. For some unresolved. And again over sacred lands. This new war, and three signs from the Great Spirit, was forcing the Shawnee to answer the same question: Which side will you choose?

In 1806, Tecumseh saw the eclipse of the sun as a sign to rally a dozen nations for a unified pan-Indian nation, replacing the peaceful voice of Hokoleskwa. But when *Waasha Monetoo* sent the comet, burning across a blackened sky, and the Americans pushed hard against the nations, Tecumseh was weakened toward war. It also rocked Nakomtha, whose ancient heart grew so weary, that when the third sign came, a massive earthquake felt throughout the south, she left them with a whispered warning: Tecumseh's rage will not let the fight go unanswered.

"And so once again the Shawnee are divided." Kalawi now rubbed the deep grove between his brow, inherited from his mother.

"Divided, yes. Even within families." Kamsi glanced behind her to Olethi, whose tears fell unchecked. Hunawe and her sons had left in 1811 with nearly half the tribe, joining a dozen other nations in support of Tecumseh near Detroit. In the Battle of Thames in Canada, Olethi had lost them all. They had lost Tecumseh, his death blowing away his vision that one day the nations would unite.

Now, the British were rumored to be taking the capital, now at Washington, and a Great Migration of settlers was moving west. West beyond the war. Toward freedom. Toward sacred Indian hunting grounds they hoped would bring them a peace the east could not provide. Forcing thousands of Shawnee to wind their way west again, across Mississippi territory, and toward a deep, burning desire to stay out of the White Family's war. To still remain Shawnee.

"It feels like we must begin again, and again. And again." Kamsi's voice cracked, her eyes brimming over with loss on leaving the only home she'd ever known.

"Will our trail of tears ever end?" Kalawi asked, the wind gusting hot and hard across his back. Will it be a matter of minutes or months before these new settlers lay claim to our new land?

And what happens when the land runs out?

This time, as he rode west, Kalawi no longer expected an answer.

Washington
August 24, 1814

"THERE IS NOT MUCH TIME!"

Senator Arthur Bowman gathered papers from his desk and yelled to his aide in the outer office. The sound of cannon fire rang in his ears, bringing back the taste of watermelon as it always did. It had been there as he'd guided men into battle through the remaining years of the revolution. It returned when he'd stood proud, thankful, at Yorktown, as they'd fired the cannons one last time, as Cornwallis surrendered.

"Do you have it?" Arthur called for his aide again.

When he'd been an aide himself, Arthur had barely had time to consider his life after the war. When the sun rose after the truce, he was grateful that among the many freedoms their independence had wrought, albeit hard-won, was the inalienable right to opportunity. For the second-born son of a sheep farmer to become a senator—to be both the governed, and the governing—was truly an American ideal. It enabled him to contribute to the Constitution, to which he also swore allegiance.

Now, however, the capital, his capital, would soon be the seat of two perfect storms. A hurricane—a thunderous torrential downpour of wind and lashing rain—was expected to hit Washington with a vengeance before the day's end. The second was blowing in hard from the northeast. Two days ago, the British had landed at Benedict, Maryland. An advance guard was expected to arrive in the city within hours. After all his years spent rebuilding the country and protecting their freedoms, once again Arthur found himself facing the same enemy.

They had to get out.

Arthur's aide came rushing into the room, his face white with fright. Arthur took the rolled parchment from the man's shaking hands.

"Are you certain it will be safe? You know where to take it, sir?"

"Not where, but to whom. And yes."

It had been nearly forty years since Arthur had last seen the document. The edges were slightly curled. A bit tattered. Yellowed. Weathered. Aged. But he, too, had been much younger then. Crow's feet had settled in around aging eyes now looking upon the document from behind a pair of much-needed spectacles.

To better protect the parchment from being crushed altogether, Arthur unrolled it and folded the sheet. The paper cracked. He winced, praying it would not crumble altogether. After all they had done to secure the fifty-six names upon it, he refused to see such a sacred document destroyed. He tucked it into his leather bag.

"What about everything else?" The aide frantically looked around the office and out the window at the national buildings, as if just two men could save it all.

Maybe they could, Arthur thought. They had once.

"What about the books in the library?" the aide cried, his hands rising to pale cheeks.

Arthur's heart ached to think the British would be so foolish as to burn a history that included their own. The first shipment of books in that library had been ordered from England. But he could not think of those now.

Some things could be replaced. Some were irreplaceable, and far too priceless.

He flung the strap of the satchel over his shoulder, and tugged on his hat.

"Gather your things and come find me." He embraced his aide warmly, and whispered instructions on where he would go. "I must do as I promised long ago."

Leesburg, Virginia
August 25, 1814

THE RANCID SMELL OF smoke inflamed Nathaniel's memories, and he winced. Those memories, though now coated with the patina of time, could still be so sharp.

From the threshold of his home, he looked eastward where, though Washington was forty miles away, flames leapt into the air. Hot. Blood red. Like the sun that he had seen rise over the Atlantic Ocean, over the Royal Navy, all those years ago. The sounds of the distant booms reverberated in him again, like cannon fire over a chaotic field of fallen soldiers in Harlem.

Nathaniel's shoulders, aged yet still strong, ached anew. They had fought so hard for independence all those years ago. Was freedom so fragile, he wondered, that it must constantly be defended? And with the same enemy? Must our children and grandchildren continue to battle against those who hold it so less dear?

"Grandpapa, what is it?"

Nathaniel looked down into the sleepy face of a worried little girl, not yet five, and grasped her hand. "Darkness has found us again, my dear, Anne."

Susannah joined them at the door, tugging at her bottom lip with strong fingers. Despite the whitening of her hair, the years had been as kind to her as she had been to Nathaniel.

Their love had blossomed amid a turbulent and trying, seven-year fight for independence, and when the British had come to Philadelphia, his heart had remembered Virginia. They fled to this cotton farm, her farm, before the children came, and after war receded they found a sweet freedom on the sweeping, open meadows. Bayard had run across these hills a few more years, his spirit riding the wind waving through the tall grasses.

For Nathaniel and Susannah, their family had grown along with her burgeoning textile business. Captain Blythe, as promised, had been on their side, delivering cottons and linens to markets far and wide, enabling them to live in comfort at home, yet free to ride the road. A surveyor's wife, Susannah had come with Nathaniel as he explored a map-maker's life. Maps that lead him to the Wolf Clan just once.

Nathaniel had stood on the ridge of the Scioto River valley, listening to the joyful sounds rising from the village below. It was like the lone cry of a wolf. He could not bring himself to encroach where he no longer belonged, on a people that had asked to be left alone, and who had suffered for it. Instead he'd turned toward his own life. Toward an expanding consciousness. To maps that helped Jefferson's men find their way to the Pacific. That helped define a country. His country.

"And yet, war has found us again." Nathaniel now looked out across the land, and grieved.

"We have weathered such storms before." Susannah slipped an arm around his waist, but then she raised a hand to her eyes, and squinted. "Look. Someone comes."

"Who is it, Grandpapa?"

As the wind tugged at Nathaniel's white hair, he looked toward the trees at the far edge of the field, the city behind it glowing with the rocket's red glare. Each flash reflected off the familiar figure flying toward them, horse hooves thumping strong and sure across the land, a leather satchel slung low across the rider's hip.

A profound feeling settled into Nathaniel.

"We made a promise," he whispered.

A new oath, sworn by two men, by two lifelong friends in 1777. To cherish not just the document, but to fight for what it stood for.

To never forget why. For whom. Or for what.

And now the time had come.

Riding hard and fast toward Nathaniel, his greatcoat flying out behind him, Arthur raced across the land, an ancient brown leather hat, well-worn with a hand-stitched brim, waving high overhead.

For freedom. For friendship. For their country.

Nathaniel let go, running out to join him, shouting on the wind. *Wela ket nee ko ge. E pluribus unum.* "We are one."

Together, they would once again be carrying independence.

★

READER INSIGHTS
and extras

THE DOCUMENT
THE DECLARATION OF INDEPENDENCE

WHEN STUDYING THE DECLARATION of Independence, it helps to break the document into sections. There are varying opinions as to whether there are four, five, or even six different sections. When broken into five, the sections are:

PART I – THE PREAMBLE
The set-up for what is considered one of most notable "Dear John" letters in history, Part I outlines the people who have collectively made "America," and explains why, generally and unanimously, "we should declare the causes which impel them to the separation."

PART II – THE STATEMENT OF BELIEFS
This section holds most of the phrases we commonly know and repeat. "We hold these truths to be self-evident." "All men are created equal." "Life, liberty and the pursuit of happiness." "Consent of the governed." It was an overarching collection of moral beliefs and standards, brought into one document, under which humanity—not just Americans—should strive to live.

PART III – THE GRIEVANCES
Outlining all the wrongs of King George III, this section was appro-

priately named "grievances," for it covered all the reasons why Americans grieved the death of our relationship with Britain. An additional piece was added, insisted upon by John Dickinson (the peaceful Quaker from Pennsylvania) called, "Vain Appeals." It stated how we had tried, in vain, to appeal to the King. Some consider the appeals to be a separate section, but it is often combined with Part III as it also spoke to the King's failure to make the relationship work.

PART IV – THE DECLARATION
"That these United Colonies are, and of right ought to be, free and independent states…" This section was the final and forceful statement of, and commitment to, not only separation of the colonies, but to uniting together as states.

PART V – THE SIGNATURES
The president of Congress and the delegates from all the united states, with the names of the delegates in the order of the colonies from south to north, with a few notable exceptions.

* * *

FULL TEXT OF THE DECLARATION OF INDEPENDENCE
(With the sections noted in parentheses and grievances numbered.)

The unanimous Declaration of the thirteen united States of America,

(PREAMBLE) When in the Course of human events, it becomes necessary for one people to dissolve the political bands which have connected them with another, and to assume among the powers of the earth, the separate and equal station to which the Laws of Nature and of Nature's God entitle them, a decent respect to the opinions of mankind requires that they should declare the causes which impel them to the separation.

(STATEMENT OF BELIEFS) We hold these truths to be self-evident, that all men are created equal that they are endowed by their Creator with certain unalienable Rights that among these are Life, Liberty and the pursuit of Happiness. That to secure these rights, Governments are instituted among Men, deriving their just powers from the consent of the governed. That whenever any Form of Government becomes destructive of these ends, it is the Right of the People to alter or to abolish it, and to institute new Government, laying its foundation on such principles and organizing its powers in such form, as to them shall seem most likely to effect their Safety and Happiness. Prudence, indeed, will dictate that Governments long established should not be changed for light and transient causes; and accordingly all experience hath shewn, that mankind are more disposed to suffer, while evils are sufferable, than to right themselves by abolishing the forms to which they are accustomed. But when a long train of abuses and usurpations, pursuing invariably the same Object evinces a design to reduce them under absolute Despotism, it is their right, it is their duty, to throw off such Government, and to provide new Guards for their future security.

Such has been the patient sufferance of these Colonies; and such is now the necessity which constrains them to alter their former Systems of Government. The history of the present King of Great Britain is a history of repeated injuries and usurpations, all having in direct object the establishment of an absolute Tyranny over these States. To prove this, let Facts be submitted to a candid world.

(GRIEVANCES)
1. He has refused his Assent to Laws, the most wholesome and necessary for the public good.
2. He has forbidden his Governors to pass Laws of immediate and pressing importance, unless suspended in their operation till his Assent should be obtained; and when so suspended, he has utterly neglected to attend to them.
3. He has refused to pass other Laws for the accommodation of large districts of people, unless those people would relinquish the right of Representation in the Legislature, a right inestimable to them and formidable to tyrants only.
4. He has called together legislative bodies at places unusual, uncomfortable,

and distant from the depository of their public Records, for the sole purpose of fatiguing them into compliance with his measures.

5. He has dissolved Representative Houses repeatedly, for opposing with manly firmness his invasions on the rights of the people.

6. He has refused for a long time, after such dissolutions, to cause others to be elected; whereby the Legislative powers, incapable of Annihilation, have returned to the People at large for their exercise; the State remaining in the mean time exposed to all the dangers of invasion from without, and convulsions within.

7. He has endeavoured to prevent the population of these States; for that purpose obstructing the Laws for Naturalization of Foreigners; refusing to pass others to encourage their migrations hither, and raising the conditions of new Appropriations of Lands.

8. He has obstructed the Administration of Justice, by refusing his Assent to Laws for establishing Judiciary powers.

9. He has made Judges dependent on his Will alone, for the tenure of their offices, and the amount and payment of their salaries.

10. He has erected a multitude of New Offices, and sent hither swarms of Officers to harrass our people, and eat out their substance.

11. He has kept among us, in times of peace, Standing Armies without the Consent of our legislatures.

12. He has affected to render the Military independent of and superior to the Civil power.

13. He has combined with others to subject us to a jurisdiction foreign to our constitution, and unacknowledged by our laws; giving his Assent to their Acts of pretended Legislation:

14. For Quartering large bodies of armed troops among us:

15. For protecting them, by a mock Trial, from punishment for any Murders which they should commit on the Inhabitants of these States:

16. For cutting off our Trade with all parts of the world:

17. For imposing Taxes on us without our Consent:

18. For depriving us in many cases, of the benefits of Trial by Jury:

19. For transporting us beyond Seas to be tried for pretended offences

20. For abolishing the free System of English Laws in a neighbouring Province, establishing therein an Arbitrary government, and enlarging its Boundaries so as to render it at once an example and fit instrument for

introducing the same absolute rule into these Colonies:

21. For taking away our Charters, abolishing our most valuable Laws, and altering fundamentally the Forms of our Governments:

22. For suspending our own Legislatures, and declaring themselves invested with power to legislate for us in all cases whatsoever.

23. He has abdicated Government here, by declaring us out of his Protection and waging War against us.

24. He has plundered our seas, ravaged our Coasts, burnt our towns, and destroyed the lives of our people.

25. He is at this time transporting large Armies of foreign Mercenaries to compleat the works of death, desolation and tyranny, already begun with circumstances of Cruelty & perfidy scarcely paralleled in the most barbarous ages, and totally unworthy the Head of a civilized nation.

26. He has constrained our fellow Citizens taken Captive on the high Seas to bear Arms against their Country, to become the executioners of their friends and Brethren, or to fall themselves by their Hands.

27. He has excited domestic insurrections amongst us, and has endeavoured to bring on the inhabitants of our frontiers, the merciless Indian Savages, whose known rule of warfare, is an undistinguished destruction of all ages, sexes and conditions.

In every stage of these Oppressions We have Petitioned for Redress in the most humble terms: Our repeated Petitions have been answered only by repeated injury. A Prince whose character is thus marked by every act which may define a Tyrant, is unfit to be the ruler of a free people.

Nor have We been wanting in attentions to our British brethren. We have warned them from time to time of attempts by their legislature to extend an unwarrantable jurisdiction over us. We have reminded them of the circumstances of our emigration and settlement here. We have appealed to their native justice and magnanimity, and we have conjured them by the ties of our common kindred to disavow these usurpations, which, would inevitably interrupt our connections and correspondence. They too have been deaf to the voice of justice and of consanguinity. We must, therefore, acquiesce in the necessity, which denounces our Separation, and hold them, as we hold the rest of mankind, Enemies in War, in Peace Friends.

(DECLARATION) We, therefore, the Representatives of the united States of America, in General Congress, Assembled, appealing to the Supreme Judge of the world for the rectitude of our intentions, do, in the Name, and by Authority of the good People of these Colonies, solemnly publish and declare, That these United Colonies are, and of Right ought to be Free and Independent States; that they are Absolved from all Allegiance to the British Crown, and that all political connection between them and the State of Great Britain, is and ought to be totally dissolved; and that as Free and Independent States, they have full Power to levy War, conclude Peace, contract Alliances, establish Commerce, and to do all other Acts and Things which Independent States may of right do. And for the support of this Declaration, with a firm reliance on the protection of divine Providence, we mutually pledge to each other our Lives, our Fortunes and our sacred Honor.

(SIGNATURES)

Centered, Massachusetts:
  John Hancock, President

Column 1
Georgia:
  Button Gwinnett
  Lyman Hall
  George Walton

Column 2
North Carolina:
  William Hooper
  Joseph Hewes
  John Penn
South Carolina:
  Edward Rutledge
  Thomas Heyward, Jr.
  Thomas Lynch, Jr.
  Arthur Middleton

Column 3
Maryland:
  Samuel Chase
  William Paca
  Thomas Stone
  Charles Carroll
   of Carrollton
Virginia:
  George Wythe

Richard Henry Lee
Thomas Jefferson
Benjamin Harrison
Thomas Nelson, Jr.
Francis Lightfoot Lee
Carter Braxton

Column 4
Pennsylvania:
  Robert Morris
  Benjamin Rush
  Benjamin Franklin
  John Morton
  George Clymer
  James Smith
  George Taylor
  James Wilson
  George Ross
Delaware:
  Caesar Rodney
  George Read
  Thomas McKean

Column 5
New York:
  William Floyd
  Philip Livingston
  Francis Lewis
  Lewis Morris

New Jersey:
  Richard Stockton
  John Witherspoon
  Francis Hopkinson
  John Hart
  Abraham Clark

Column 6
New Hampshire:
  Josiah Bartlett
  William Whipple
Massachusetts:
  Samuel Adams
  John Adams
  Robert Treat Paine
  Elbridge Gerry
Rhode Island:
  Stephen Hopkins
  William Ellery
Connecticut:
  Roger Sherman
  Samuel Huntington
  William Williams
  Oliver Wolcott
New Hampshire:
  Matthew Thornton

DISCUSSION POINTS
READER & BOOK CLUB QUESTIONS

1. All of the main fictional characters—Nathaniel, Arthur, Kalawi, Susannah, and Silas—are striving for independence in their own way, but so are the supporting characters (both real and fictional). Discuss how, if at all, a desire for independence might mean something different to each of us. Can one document support all of those different viewpoints?

2. As he is walking or riding away, Nathaniel often turns to look back upon family and friends. After he reunites with Arthur in the army camp, it is the first time he does not. What does this say about how Nathaniel was changing? Does looking back, as McKean indicates, prevent us from moving toward a more prosperous future? How is understanding history an asset?

3. Nathaniel often waits to be invited into discussions or rooms—an outsider on the threshold—such as at the Assembly room door, and on the veranda watching Susannah at the ball. He is asked to wait outside the door at General Washington's headquarters in Harlem, despite having marched in with the American troops. When do we, like Nathaniel, stand apart and what are the motives that might help or compel us to feel empowered to engage?

4. What makes a person a hero or heroine? Nathaniel is considered the protagonist of the story, however, it is Arthur who first joins the revolution. It is Kalawi who rises to protect the Martens and his own clan. Even Susannah rises to the challenge of supporting the war effort using her own means, skills, and home. Discuss if/how choices or contributions create heroes.

5. Nathaniel reluctantly agrees to carry the Declaration, yet he still does not support the war against the British. Are there circumstances in which you might act for a cause, and yet never fully believe in it?

6. Clothing changes are plentiful in the story. Nathaniel goes from frontiersman to gentleman to redcoat. Arthur adopts a British uniform. Kalawi wears his new ceremonial headdress at the treaty. Susannah casts off her fancy dresses. How do our personas and beliefs about ourselves change with what we wear? Or does what we wear change how we think of ourselves?

7. Nathaniel notes the disparity between the gentry/generals and the slaves, common folk, and soldiers. Yet, some generals at headquarters in Harlem support this as necessary. Discuss how this, and our view of income inequality today, compares with two lines within the Declaration. "All men are created equal," and "our lives, our fortunes, and our sacred honor."

8. Nathaniel doesn't fully read the Declaration for himself until after he has lost the Shawnee, the farm, and his mother. Would reading it earlier have helped him feel more invested in the Cause during his journey, or was it only after he suffered personal loss that he was able to understand the meaning behind the decision and document? At what point during the story, did you feel compelled to read the full text of the Declaration?

9. George Wythe and Mary Katharine Goddard both share the opinion that the document is "a beginning." How do you think the Declaration and the concepts of independence, freedom, and equality apply to our country over two centuries later? Which pieces of this document should we still uphold? Whether you're American by birth or not, how do you see your role in defending such ideals not just for fellow citizens, but for humanity?

AUTHOR'S NOTE
FACT vs. FICTION

WHENEVER I READ HISTORICAL fiction, I always wonder what is real. What changed? What was invented? What moved? I've always been appreciative of authors who attempted to set the record straight about their part in the writing. Most of the events in *Carrying Independence* surrounding the Revolution happened as they are depicted, to the best of my research, and of course filtered through the lens of my fictitious characters and their personal experiences. The battles, the Staten Island treaty, the Fort Pitt treaty, the death of Netawatwees, Esther Reed and the spinning bees, Goddard printing the copies, and even some of the lines from founding fathers... all true. Below are some notable exceptions. If there are other historical facts or details incorrectly referenced, it was not intentional.

First and foremost, was the Declaration of Independence carried to all the signers? Maybe. As many as six or seven men (with Elbridge Gerry being the wildcard) were not in Philadelphia on August second for the formal signing. I chose seven, and based on letters and records regarding the comings and goings of those congressmen, determined where it might have been carried.

As for hard evidence to either support or deny the possibility that it was "carried" to some of the founding fathers, I found none. On the website for the National Archives and Records Administration, the nation's current record keeper and holder of the Declaration of Independence, it says, "Once the Declaration was signed, the document probably accompanied the Continental Congress... After the signing ceremony on August 2, 1776, the Declaration was most likely filed in Philadelphia in the office of Charles Thomson, who served as the Secretary of the Continental Congress." I love explanations that include "probably" and "most likely." In the absence of facts, I inserted fiction, and you got the book.

So when was it signed? Quite often history books jump straight from the July dates approving separation into detailing the war with no further remarks about the Declaration. Some sources contradicted each other (and sometimes themselves) about where and when the final signings happened. All accounts indicated that Matthew Thornton signed it in Philadelphia. He was the biggest clue that all the signers weren't there on August second, because he wasn't voted in by New Hampshire until September, 1776. A few terrific books about the signers all seemed to support that the remaining six or seven names were affixed over many months, with the last signature being affixed between 1777 and as late as 1781. Mary Katharine's broadside copies, which were printed in January, 1777, do not list Thomas McKean's name—another clue that he had not signed it yet.

Was there a *Secret Journal*? Yes, it was a collection of minutes from Congress laughingly called the *Secret Journal*, with notes and voting records the delegates didn't want the King to see. My state's Library of Virginia has a bound copy. The excerpt included from August second, on page 82, about an importer receiving thirty thousand pounds and the Congress hiring a ship for said importer came right from the journal.

Was there a Carrying Committee? While that, too, was my invention, there was a Secret Committee of Correspondence to help Congress communicate with potential allies—both at home and abroad. If the Declaration was carried, and did not stay with Congress, it made sense to me that a committee would have been created. Certainly Benjamin Franklin, who did indeed inspect all those miles of post roads, would have been on it.

What is on the back of the Declaration? Sorry Nicholas Cage, there are only two things. Handwritten words on the back that read, "Original Declaration of Independence dated 4th July 1776." They were likely written by either Timothy Matlack, who was hired to inscribe the calligraphy on the front, or the secretary of the Congress, Charles Thomson. When the

Declaration stayed with the Congress, it was often rolled, and by being marked as such, it would be easy to spot amid other documents. However, when documents of this size were carried, it was better and safer to fold them. When my research turned up no proven fact about who put the writing on the back, I claimed it for Nathaniel. The second item on the back, bottom left corner, is a shadow of a small handprint of unknown origin—another tidbit I happily claimed for Mary Katharine Goddard.

Were the Howe brothers involved in a supply business? Their profiting from a supply company was my invention. However, the idea of creating a reason for the Howes' behavior came upon me when I read Barnett Schecter's book, *The Battle for New York*. He, among other historians, speculated as to why on earth two leaders tasked by the Crown with ending the war, would allow the rebels to slip by and retreat out of their grasp on multiple occasions. I, too, wondered why General and Admiral Howe delayed when they could have attacked the Colonial Army at Brooklyn, and throughout 1776, when the rebels were the weakest. The Howes' lack of initiative infuriated General Clinton each time they ignored his plans, and he did return to London in protest. Do I believe the Howes were really trying to drag out a war in order to profit from it? My head wants viable proof, but unfortunately the private papers of the Howe brothers were mysteriously and accidentally burned by descendants after the war. Accidentally? Curious.

I moved two historical dates. First, that of Nathan Hale's execution. Historically, Hale was hanged on the same day as the great New York fire, September 21, 1776. It is believed by some that he was executed after being suspected of being involved in the Manhattan fire, though there was no proof of it. (No proof as to who set the fire, either.) It is generally agreed that Hale was a youthful and inexperienced spy, and that he had no business volunteering for gathering information on Long Island. His youth and lack of experience were so much like Nathaniel's, that using word of his being hanged was the tension I needed between Nathaniel and Arthur in the camp at Harlem Heights.

Second, the *Jersey*, that claimed Peter's life and where Arthur was imprisoned, wasn't actually put into use as a prison ship until the year 1780. One of the most staggering statistics I learned about the Revolution was that while just over 4000 American soldiers died in land and sea battles combined, historians estimate between 11,500 and 18,000 men perished aboard prison ships. The *Jersey* alone claimed more than 8,000. Given its notorious and deadly interior, I wanted to use the ship to highlight what I thought was one of the worst atrocities of the Revolution and British-colonial history. It was convenient, in my mind, for the British to ignore the rules of war, and treat their own citizens as traitors, considering them lucky enough not to have been hanged. A noose might have been preferable to the suffering those men endured, in those stinking, rotting, despicable hulls, not to mention the egregious burials on the sandy shores of Brooklyn, ironically where the U.S. Navy yards are now.

As for how the novel ends… It is recorded that during the War of 1812, when the British were marching into Washington, the Declaration of Independence was taken to a "safe-house" in Leesburg, Virginia. I could not discover precisely where, or by whom, however that piece of history gave me a method by which to convey what I hope will be the takeaway for readers.

Gathering the last signature on that document was not the end, and honoring all the ideals it contains—by the people, of the people, and for the people—is not limited by time, citizenship, or geography. The Declaration was a beginning, and as Wythe states in the novel, it was the match to the gunpowder that blew open-wide the world. That document was the catalyst for more than fifty other such declarations.

For humanity, independence was, and is, a freedom often hard-won by ordinary individuals, like you and me, who are moved to contribute during extraordinary times.

But it isn't granted. It's chosen. It's cultivated.

By our pens, our voices, our actions.

And by each and every one of us.

– Karen

THE FONTS

The fonts used to design the print version of *Carrying Independence,* were specifically chosen to add to the reader's experience.

1776 INDEPENDENCE
Used in the chapter headers and on the cover, the font was created by Gilles Le Corre, an engraver from France. His lettering is based on historical research, and often relates to printers or styles from a time period.

P22 DECLARATION
The quill-pen font, used on the cover and section dividers, was created by independent design house, P22. Inspired by the original calligraphy of the parchment, it includes the signatures as part of the collection.

CASLON PRO
The original font was created by William Caslon in England in 1722, and revived by designer Carol Twombly and Adobe, an American company. Caslon is the main paragraph font for the novel, chosen because it was the font used by Mary Katharine Goddard for the 200 broadside copies of the Declaration of Independence she volunteered to print in 1777.

ACKNOWLEDGEMENTS

IN 2008, WHILE ON A TOUR through Berkeley Plantation—the home of Benjamin Harrison who signed the Declaration—I found inspiration. Moving through the rooms, the docent pointed to a copy of the document and said, "Though Harrison was there, not all the men were in the room on August second to sign the parchment. Some signed it later, we don't know where or when…" The central question to this story came in a flash. What if it were carried?

The late Pauline Maier, one of the premier historians on the Declaration, answered my most important concern. Was there any proof as to where the Declaration was kept during the war or how it was signed? The same day of my inquiry, her gracious reply included, "I don't know of any document collection to which I could send you to verify its whereabouts." If she'd answered differently, my pen would have stalled.

Once the project began, it took a decade to research, write, edit (and edit and edit), and publish this book. The support I received was astonishing. I know most acknowledgements leave the best to last, but those I love most, who gave the most of their time and hearts, should be read about first.

Ted Petrocci, my partner in life and adventure, was far more than a reader. We had deep conversations about character motivations, he drove all over the countryside relishing in our road trips, he visited countless museums with me, and he made the best coffee and eggplant parm. Most important, when others gave up on the book, and in a few horrifying moments when I was ready to, he was the one to say, "You've got this, now get back to writing."

The support of my family—Bruce, and Telva, and *especially* my parents—and their never questioning my desire to write this, was second only to what they gave me before I began. A love of travel, history, and reading that have culminated in the pages you now hold.

I blame some of these ten years on friend and author Laura Scott. When I told her of my idea for the novel just a few nights after visiting Berkeley, with great enthusiasm she said, "You have to write this. It's a perfect story, and *Carrying Independence* is the perfect title."

Fellow readers and writers, and dear friends, Katharine Herndon and Kris Spisak, helped me set goals, and gave my writing soul sustenance far beyond tacos, chocolate, and tea. Leslie Saunderlin, Bob and Brooke Rhodes, Ann Jewell, Steve Farber, Brenda Goad, Jennifer Hays, my book club—Karen and Kent Shipman, Karen and Mark Rankin, Becky and Derek Metzler—they have all been thoughtful sounding boards and wonderfully distracting friends sharing hours of bookish talks. Author and fellow Canadian, Kathleen Grissom, is best described as a fire-starter. Far out ahead of me, she has shown me how bright and warm the light of an author can be.

Beyond these mighty few, the number of people, places, and organizations contributing to the story and my development grew with each passing year. I attempted to keep a spreadsheet, but please forgive me if I've left anyone out. It's not because of a lack of gratitude. As many of my closest friends know, I see spreadsheets as an antagonist, and that devil is in cahoots with time's ability to erase a well-intentioned memory.

CRAFT TEAM

Editors and early readers not only helped shape the story, simply put, they were my teachers during this self-directed near-MFA. Dougie and Bob Scudder, Meredith Bass, Kathy Watkins, and Helen Sarrett not only read the early drafts, but returned it with incredibly detailed notes. The magical Leslie Saunderlin was nearly an editor—poring over the manuscript and deconstructing it with me chapter-by-chapter-by-character over numerous cups of coffee. The interior layout is now in your hands because of her, too. Dear friends, Brooke and Bob Rhodes, read and contributed, and their printing company BambooInk printed and shipped whatever I needed. Working with them also helped me sustain an income when, during my darkest days, the hope of publishing the novel was nearly extinguished at draft number nine.

The reason the book survived was in part because I didn't want to let down folks like Don Houtz, Suzannah Kearsley, Kelly Justice of Fountain Bookstore, Linda Steadman of Too Many Books, Leah Weiss, Beth Macy, A.B. Westrick, Kristen Weber, Sally Marshall, Bradley Harper, Jenna Dela Cruz, Kelly Fitzgerald, Stephanie Caruso, and Christina Reeser—friends, confidants, and author marketing gurus who encouraged me to keep writing. The book exists because of kind people like Paul Aaron and Lisa Hagan who helped me seek alternative publishing paths, and my local literary organization, James River Writers (JRW). JRW's members, October conferences, monthly socials, and writing shows helped me hone my craft, realize new opportunities, and ultimately build nuanced story arcs, settings, and characters. You've all helped me become a better writer.

As I galloped toward publication, I had three POST RIDERS at my side. They volunteered to receive the book early, read, proof, and share my publishing news wildly. Many thanks to Catrina Hall (The History Lover), Robert A. Makley, and Judy Lynn Turner. You would make Nathaniel and Paul Revere proud.

Early on, pages were professionally edited by the likes of Alan Rinzler, and most fortunately by Jane Rosenman. All of my editors gave me the reins in decision making, but she also gave me the tools to build a better horse. Moreover, with just fifty pages and an outline, she believed in me and the story. I learned so much from her editing and our conversations, that by the time it fell into the hands of Rebecca Gradinger and Jennifer Herrera, the story had real merit. It was exponentially deepened by their questions and wonderful input until it was further refined by the insightful Kris Spisak, and last but not least, by Lisa Bess Kramer. Your corrections and insights were as kind and freeing as the spirit of Bayard, which I think lives in you.

HISTORIC TEAM

I am not an academic historian, so some of my early readers were advisors on this near-dissertation in American Revolutionary history. William (Bill) Ochester personally guided me through the streets of Philadelphia, erasing the modern world to reveal the streets of 1776. Given that he's a first-rate Doctor Franklin reenactor, his insights and early readings made Ben's scenes ever so much more authentic. That tour was the most fun three hours of my research and not just because it culminated in a better understanding of the period or historic beers at City Tavern. It yielded a friendship.

John Millar advised on the chapters with Captain Blythe to ensure the boat, rigging, flag, and high-seas adventure scenes were ship-shape. Rick Britton, an extraordinary cartographer, historian, and so much more, offered resources about the history of mapmaking, and the passion for his craft spurred my idea to give Nathaniel a greater purpose. Bill Welsch, from my own American Revolution Round Table of Richmond group, read the manuscript and fact-checked many of my Revolutionary-era details. I dearly hope none of the genuine concern he carried about me or this book contributed to his back problems.

Aside from enumerable books by Revolutionary-era historians, several responded to my calls or emails, and most with great enthusiasm. Colin Calloway pulled books from his own shelf and mailed them to me to guide me through the passages on the Shawnee and Native American involvement. Gregory Shaft's work on the Colonel Morgan journals and the treaty at Fort Pitt was the missing piece to a complex puzzle that enabled me to keep and deepen Kalawi's part of the story. That understanding was helped along by Sherman Tiger of the Absentee Shawnee Tribe, and Laura Reddish of the Native American Language website, who stepped in to counsel me on names, terms, and language. Charlie Petrocci, known for tall fish-tales, gave me legitimate details on Indian fishing techniques.

The late John Nagy advised on spy-craft, and confirmed basic details about the Declaration being folded when carried. Cokie Roberts inspired the women's stories, and her input on newspaper sources helped me write a more authentic picture of our lesser-told stories about founding mothers and spinning bees supported by the women of Philadelphia. Some historians, like Edward Lengel, Woody Holton, Marc Leepson, and James Horn met with me over food (and more than a few tinctures), to help me see more clearly our founding figures, the sources, or the concepts of independence and colonial separation—they, too, became fast friends.

I truly believed the best way to build a book about an average citizen traveling through historical places in the colonies was to travel it myself. As a result, the historic places I visited and thus featured in the book were insurmountable in helping me see and feel the American Revolution first-hand. Stratford Hall (especially Judy Hynson), Colonial Williamsburg, Yorktown Customs House, the Old Stone House in Brooklyn, the Customs House in Staten Island, Morris-Jumel Mansion in Harlem, City Tavern (thank you Chef Staib), Fort Pitt Block House, the Litchfield Library, my neighborhood St. John's Historic District, and so many more stops along the way. Del Moore, now the retired Reference Librarian from the Colonial Williamsburg Rockefeller Library, patiently answered some of my earliest questions. George Suiter, the Gunsmith at Colonial Williamsburg, showed me rifle making and the inner workings of a gun shop. Jennifer Patton and her team at Fraunces Tavern in New York not only spent a morning with me in their offices; on her lunch hour, Jennifer walked me to parts of lower Manhattan relevant to 1776.

Places and organizations such as the U.S. Postal Museum, Monticello, Mount Vernon, and local and state historical societies contributed on matters great and small. My own Virginia Museum of History and Culture (Virginia Historical Society—especially Paige Newman, Katherine Watkins, and Elaine McFadden), the Library of Virginia, the Richmond Public Library (RPL), and Henrico Public Library—all helped me find sources and gave me quiet places to read and write. A particular hug to Patty Parks, formerly at RPL, who made this writer feel like an author from the beginning, as she does for so many.

Countless times on my journey, I stood before plaques installed by the Daughters of the American Revolution (DAR) or received help from a member ahead of my travels. I am a DAR by proof of lineage, a DAR by thankful association, and now I feel like a DAR in spirit through action, through publication.

Last, though not least, I am also truly thankful to all those in publishing—both great and small—who graciously or silently passed on the book. I am now independently (fittingly) published because of them, even though to say so is a falsehood. As evidenced by all the above, books are not built by an author alone. Independence, just as it was during the Revolution, is carried and shouldered by many.

E pluribus unum indeed.

– Karen

ABOUT THE AUTHOR

KAREN A. CHASE IS AN AWARD-WINNING author, designer, and photographer. Her first book, *Bonjour 40: A Paris Travel Log*, garnered seven independent publishing awards. *Carrying Independence* secured runner-up in the 2017 William Faulkner, William Wisdom Unpublished Novel Competition, and was a semi-finalist in the 2019 Screencraft Cinematic Book competition.

A long-standing member of James River Writers, the author is also a member of the National Society of the Daughters of the American Revolution, the Historical Novelist Society, the Women's Fiction Writers Association, and the American Revolutionary Round Table of Richmond.

Originally from Calgary, Alberta, Canada, throughout her childhood Karen traveled through the United States in an R.V. with her family. Those journeys instilled a lifelong love of history, travel, and learning. She has lived in the United States since 1990 when she enrolled as a foreign-exchange student, studying advertising art in San Antonio, Texas. She now resides with her partner, Ted, and a couple of scrappy cats, in Richmond, Virginia.

To travel with adventure with Karen, subscribe to her e-publication, *Chasing Histories*, featuring historical research, travel tips, and upcoming presentation and event details.

KarenAChase.com

@14mos by Margaret (mum) Chase

2018 by KimberlyFrost.com

To find out more about inviting Karen to book clubs, and for presentations to organizations (lineage, historic, or travel-related), please visit KarenAChase.com/talks.

Follow and engage on:
Facebook: KarenAChaseAuthor
Twitter, or Instagram: @KarenAChase

For books, research, and imagery related to the novel, visit the author's Pinterest page: @kachase_author

WATCH FOR...

Carrying Independence is the first novel
in The Founding-Documents Series.

Thanks in part to a visiting-scholar fellowship at the
American Antiquarian Society (through funding from the
Fellowships for Creative and Performing Artists and Writers),
the next book in the series is in development.

A Letter of Introduction focuses on the later years of the Revolution,
and the need for the newly found country to form the Constitution.

* * *

Decoys, a southern-based novel, set on fictitious
Gullwin Island in 1950s North Carolina,
is due to be released in 2020.

*"A beautifully written book that contains all the elements of good fiction—a
unique voice, a well-drawn setting, and a story question that keeps the entire book
barreling toward the end. I was hooked from the first haunting line."*
– Sheila Athens, Editor and Author of *The Truth About Love*

CPSIA information can be obtained
at www.ICGtesting.com
Printed in the USA
JSHW022127090919
1412JS00002B/14

9 781733 752800